The meadow behind them

All around her, hotshots ~~~~~~ ~~~~~~ ~~~~~~ ring to watch the fire approach. But ~~~~~~ ~~~~~~ fire met and surged even higher, a b~~~~~~ wall of orange. The flames reached a hundred feet. Two hundred. She had not seen anything like it. As entrancing and electrifying as it was, she hoped never to see it again. *Dear Jesus. Dear God in heaven. Help us!* She turned to run.

Many crew members were already tucked under shelters, working to seal the edges with knees and elbows and, Reyne was sure, mentally preparing themselves for the coming onslaught. They looked like Jiffy Pop bags exploding this way and that as they moved inside. Some of her team were not yet covered.

Reyne reached Janice, a trembling rookie from Tucson, and ripped the shelter from her hands to unfurl it. "You'll be okay!" Reyne shouted to her. Their hair flew madly about, and Reyne fought off the insane urge to laugh. "Remember your training! Seal the edges and ride it out!"

She turned from Janice as the rookie finally got under her shelter. Next to her was Larry, on her crew for the last three years. He looked at her in macabre resignation, gesturing toward a rip in his shelter. "No!" she shouted. "Remember what they told us! Grab the rip and tuck it under you! You'll be okay!"

The heat became noticeably worse. Reyne glanced over her shoulder. The fire was licking at her heels. With a last look around her team, packed tightly on the road—sometimes two or three in a row—she picked her spot next to two others and frantically shook out her shelter. She dove under it, tucking and praying madly.

Then the dragon came hunting.

Firestorm

LISA TAWN BERGREN

Firestorm

WATERBROOK
PRESS

FIRESTORM
PUBLISHED BY WATERBROOK PRESS
2375 Telstar Drive, Suite 160
Colorado Springs, Colorado 80920
A division of Random House, Inc.

Scriptures taken from the *Holy Bible, New International Version*®. NIV®. Copyright © 1973, 1978, 1984 by International Bible Society. Used by permission of Zondervan Publishing House. All rights reserved.

The characters and events in this book are fictional, and any resemblance to actual persons or events is coincidental.

ISBN 1-57856-466-2; formerly 0-88070-953-7

Library of Congress Cataloging-in-Publication Data
Bergren, Lisa Tawn.
    Firestorm / Lisa Tawn Bergren.—1st WaterBrook ed.
        p. cm. — (The full circle series ; 6)
    ISBN 1-57856-466-2
        1. Women fire fighters—Fiction. 2. Smokejumpers—Fiction. I. Title.

PS3552.E71938 F57 2001
813'.54—dc21

                                                                00-067313

Printed in the United States of America
2001—First WaterBrook Edition

10 9 8 7 6 5 4 3 2 1

To Ryan,
my brother and friend,
who has gone through
some of life's many firestorms
and come out on the other side
richer for the experience.

"Then they cried out to the LORD in their trouble,
and he brought them out of their distress.
He stilled the storm to a whisper;
the waves of the sea were hushed."

PSALM 107:28-29

ACKNOWLEDGMENTS

If you are interested in learning more about forest fires and the people who battle them, you must read the resource I found most informative in researching this book, *Fire Line: Summer Battles of the West,* by Michael Thoele (Fulcrum). It is incredibly well written and reads like fiction itself. I am indebted to Mr. Thoele for allowing me to retell several stories that appear in his book and, in addition, for reading through my manuscript to make sure I had my technical details straight. Any overlooked errors, however, are entirely my own.

I also gleaned helpful information from *Forest Fires,* by Margaret Fuller, and *Young Men and Fire,* by Norman MacLean.

PROLOGUE

*R*eyne Oldre was the first to pick it up. The sense of danger was subtle, intangible, but definitely there.

Two hundred feet in front of her, Stan Shaw, a long-trusted squad boss of the Lolo Hotshots, suddenly stopped digging. He sensed it too.

Reyne watched Stan lift his head as if to trace the wind—apparently to see if it had changed direction or speed—and looked beyond him to the last six chains he had dug. A "chain," a trench sixty-six feet in length and two feet in width, was required every hour of a groundpounding firefighter. Stan was a chain ahead. She smiled to herself. He was always ahead.

Reyne looked back at him, meeting his eyes, listening with him. Beyond the Snap Crackle Pop that made fighting fires a nightmarish Rice Krispies experience. Beyond the shimmering heat from the flames and the hardworking firefighters around her. Beyond the radio at her hip that crackled with frequent transmissions from the fire bosses in the fire camp far below them on Boise's county fairgrounds.

What had changed? The wind seemed to be coming from the same direction as before. But tiny hairs on the back of her neck stood on end, despite a layer of sweat and grime. She could not shake the sense of dread, the foreboding. It did not help that Stan, a seasoned firefighter, stood motionless, awaiting her direction. He obviously sensed the danger too. *God,* she called silently, *what are you trying to tell me?*

Reyne scanned the line of fire a hundred feet away. Her unease did not make sense. The fire, named Oxbow after the reservoir near where it had begun, was a mild one, slowly eating away at summer-dried Idaho grasses and scrubby pines, one hill after another. It had traipsed on that way for days, the flames rising no higher than two feet. Now the wind was slowly pushing it downhill toward them. It was their job to stop its descent into a small suburb outside of Boise.

"No problem," Reyne had said with bravado to the fire commander after receiving their assignment. "We'll kill it by noon." She was sure of her crew of hotshots, a solid team of twenty, five of them women. They had fought four fires together already and proven themselves. Even the rookies had quickly come up to speed, making sure they would not be assigned back to the crews who dug hiking trails or painted Forest Service picnic tables. They were tough, and no baby hill fire like this was going to stop them.

But now, as the morning persisted into afternoon, as the Lolo Hotshots finished lunch and began digging again, Reyne knew that something was afoot. She shook her head at Shaw after checking with the command center. They saw nothing different on the weather instruments. Reyne went back to digging and Stan did the same, still eying Oxbow like a dog not to be trusted.

They crested the next hill and spotted another crew a mile away, past a thicket of pines that fed off the seasonal valley runoff. The other group of hotshots had two bulldozers and a pump engine. They would meet them in the middle of that valley, Reyne decided. Show them what her hotshots were made of, even without the extra equipment. She powered into her own chain with renewed energy, swinging her Pulaski, a small ax-hoe, as if she meant to wear it out. Most crew bosses did not do much digging. Reyne felt it was important to show her team that she was working right beside them when she wasn't scouting ahead, talking with the fire boss, or checking out the line.

A helicopter flew overhead, dumping water beside the chains they'd dug to fortify the suburban defense. The choppers were an excellent asset on the line. They could turn around quickly, refill their giant buckets from nearby lakes, and enter places that were difficult for tankers to reach.

Reyne's radio crackled again, her name filling the airwaves.

"Crew Boss Oldre, come in," the division supervisor said.

"I'm here, Thomas."

"Good to hear your voice, Lolo. Just wanted you to be aware that the winds are picking up a bit. You better hustle on to a rendezvous point with the New Mexicans and come on home."

Reyne pulled out her own tiny, experimental anemometer and watched as the flaps whirred to life. The wind velocity *had* changed. She and Stan had been right.

Reyne eyed the distance to the ravine where the pines were and calculated how long it would take them to close it. "We'll be done in an hour, Thomas. I spotted the New Mexicans an hour ago. We're meeting 'em in the middle of this pretty little ravine." She glanced at her worn map. "Starburst, it's called. Over."

"Got it. FYI—in case something goes awry—according to our chopper pilot, there's a meadow just northwest of you. Say an eighth of a mile. Over."

"Thanks, Thomas. Maybe we'll have a little picnic dinner after we're through."

"You trying to make a date with me?"

Reyne smiled, picturing the weathered, grinning face and grizzled hair of Thomas Wagner. The older man, the first fire boss she had ever served under as a Forest Service rookie, relished giving her a hard time.

"That's right, Thomas. It'd be a private occasion. A simple, romantic affair with just me and my crew of twenty."

"Ah, well. I always say that more than two's a crowd."

"Don't feel too bad. You can buy me a Coke when we come in tonight."

"Promises, promises. Now quit flirting with the fire boss and get your hotshots back to those chains, girl. Over."

"Work, work, work," she groused, still smiling. "It's only July, and I already need a vacation. Oldre out."

Reyne slipped the radio into her belt loop and walked the line again, checking their progress. Stan shook his head as if in warning, lifting his face to the wind. Waves of smoke were blowing into their ranks now, separating digging member from digging member for seconds at a time. *It's nothing*, she told herself. *Thomas'd call us off if there was anything to be concerned about. We're almost there.*

They moved into the edge of the forested ravine called Starburst Gully. Reyne called her sawyers forward, carefully avoiding eye contact with Stan, knowing he thought they should leave. A team of three went to work with chain saws, cutting a swath of trees down before them. She set two groundpounders to work with fusees—small torches that lit the dried tinder behind them—creating a backfire to stop Oxbow from simply climbing trees and crossing their fire line.

Reyne occasionally thought she heard a dozer and surmised the

New Mexican team was near. Once they met, their lines would form an effective flank; Oxbow would be cut off, and hopefully their work would be done.

They drove deeper and deeper into Starburst Gully's forest. Fifty feet. A hundred. Suddenly Reyne lifted her head and listened. The bulldozers were just around the corner. She waved the sawyers to silence. But the wind…the wind had definitely changed again.

Stan ran to her side, his face a silent mask of apprehension. She pulled out her anemometer and took another quick reading, her eyes flying to Stan's. He'd known a second before she had. The wind had died for more than two minutes, then picked up speed as it changed direction, suddenly angling toward the gully instead of straight downhill.

Both feared the proverbial calm before the storm. It was the staple of a firefighter's war stories. "When the wind dies, get the heck out of Dodge," Thomas had said just the night before, regaling the troops with the story of a firestorm his own crew had survived.

"Crew Boss Oldre, Crew Boss Oldre," Thomas's voice urgently crackled, barely discernible over Oxbow's growing growl. She lifted the radio to her ear to hear him.

"Yeah, Fire Boss, we know. *We know.*"

"Reyne, the New Mexicans have to be right there. Get together and get out of that ravine."

"We've almost got this line tied in, Thomas!" She shouted to be heard over the fire. "Ten more minutes and we'll have him. Over."

"I don't like it, Reyne, but you're the one who can see it. By my wind-velocity reading, I'd wonder if you have those ten minutes. Over."

"Maybe not," she mumbled, not pressing the intercom button.

Her mind whirled as she struggled to make a decision. *Father! Father! Where are you? What should I do?* Her call guided the lives of twenty crew members. Many of them had families. All of them had parents who struggled to understand this fascination with fire, this need to go out each summer and fight it.

Reyne knew the story well. Her own parents had tried to be supportive but were obviously baffled each spring when she'd break the news that she was heading out to the fire lines after school was out. Now she was a graduate student studying fire science in the fall, winter, and spring. Come summertime, this was where she belonged. This was what she loved. Chasing the dragon. Slaying it. Celebrating afterward.

But being chased made her uneasy. It hadn't happened much in her years on the line. As she studied Oxbow and the flames that gradually grew, climbing beyond their original two-to-five feet high, she stalled. They were *so* close to finishing this job. Maybe the wind would die in a few minutes and the alarm would be proven false. Or maybe it wouldn't.

Reyne looked along the line again, counting heads through the smoke. Twenty, all accounted for. She glanced up at Stan, who still waited beside her, and then back to Oxbow. The fire was climbing trees now. No more time for stalling. They needed to get out, even if it meant giving in to the dragon this time.

She nodded curtly to Stan, and he began shouting, instantly understanding, summoning the team together. They assembled within a minute. As they gathered, Reyne radioed Thomas, telling him that the New Mexicans could still not be seen, but they had to be close. The smoke thickened as Oxbow drew near, groaning and screaming as sap-filled firs heated and exploded into flames.

Then the wind died and changed direction yet again.

"Oldre, come in. Oldre, come in," came Thomas's voice within a minute. "The line has hooked! I repeat: *The line has hooked.* Over."

Reyne forced a calm edge to her tone, aware of the crew watching her. "I copy. Can you give me coordinates?"

"I don't have current coordinates. But the New Mexicans are cut off. They're heading for cover."

"What's your call, Thomas?"

"Looking tight. If I'm reading this right, I think your only option is to get to that meadow and take cover. Get moving and let me know your plan. Over."

Reyne waved to the group, shouting over Oxbow's growing roar. Embers floated down around them, glowing red-hot. Ashes settled in a thick layer on shoulders that were still for but a moment. "Let's move!" she called, struggling to keep her voice in firm command, not give in to the sickening panic she felt inside. The crew broke from a fast walk to a jog, feeling the unspoken urgency.

The Lolo group followed Stan and her as they ran uphill in a diagonal line, in the general direction of the New Mexican crew's fire line but above it, toward the meadow. They struggled under their heavy packs, but all were in peak condition. They had to be to make it as hotshots.

In five minutes they had reached the meadow, Oxbow not far behind them. The fire, growing louder and hotter by the second, was bearing down from the ridge as well as from below.

Reyne struggled to catch her breath, to resist giving in to lungs that begged her to cough and never quit. She knew that once she started it would be tough to stop, so she swallowed hard, concentrating on the twenty yellow, fire-retardant Nomex shirts that collapsed on the hard, dry, bulbous clumps of grass that covered the meadow floor. Reyne counted the orange hard hats, each with a crew member's name emblazoned on its front, not wanting to confuse her team with the New Mexican crew, who had also arrived.

There was Zeke Johnson, who was always quick to respond in a crisis. Over there were Haley Carlson and Josh and Nate, who worked together as smoothly as train wheels rolling over new tracks. Her eyes scanned the rest. Everyone was accounted for. Reyne left them and went looking for the New Mexican hotshot crew boss.

Jojo, a short, stocky Hopi tribesman with a wide grin and a nickname of untraceable origin, pushed his hard hat back and reached out to shake Reyne's hand. "Good to see you, Oldre," he said, smiling up at the tall woman. "Seems we got ourselves in a spot."

"Seems that way, Jojo," Reyne allowed in the easy give-and-take, traditional on the lines. She forced herself to remain as calm as Jojo appeared to be. They conferred together, then set the crews to preparing shelter sites.

Reyne felt none of the calm reserve that her voice depicted as she shouted orders. This was the reason they came. The thrill of adrenaline in the heat of battle. Fighting a monster that threatened forest or grasslands or homes.

Still, none wanted to lose their lives. In all her years of fighting fires, Reyne had never had to deploy the tiny firesafe pup tent that always hung from her waistband in its yellow pouch.

Each crew member wore one of the folded tents, always at the ready. They were all trained to deploy the four-pound structure in seconds, and each knew that they would have to pray if that was all that came between them and the thousand-degree heat of a runaway fire. Yet none really thought they'd actually have to use the tents.

Reyne could see it on their faces. Maybe clear a spot. But shaking out the tiny shelters and getting under them was very rare, even among seasoned veterans.

Reyne walked by her crew, inspecting each one's progress, ignoring the few jaded members who mumbled this and that about "useless Forest Service regulations." The most likely scenario would be that they would dig their holes to be prepared, then sit with helmets or packs in front of their faces and watch the fire roll by, their shelters undeployed after all. Reyne had sat out many fires in that manner, happy to have another war story to tell at the evening campfires.

She moved on to inspect the New Mexican team, since Jojo had gone out to take a last look at how the lines were holding. But even from where she stood, Reyne could tell the wind's impact had been deadly.

Nearly three hundred feet below them, the fire was building, climbing Starburst's trees and crowning, throwing a thick black column of smoke into the air. Oxbow had spent all morning and afternoon drying out the forest canopy. Now, with the aid of a new wind, he was climbing to claim his prey.

Jojo came running back, the ashen tone to his skin barely visible under the grime of a day's fire. He had never even made it back to the place where the bulldozers had left for home base. But Reyne didn't need to see his face or hear his breathless words. She knew by his expression, from the dread she seemed to sense. *O God, this is it, isn't it? You've been trying to warn me!*

The crew seemed to sense it too. The naysayers stopped grumbling, and they all dug in more earnestly, matching Reyne's pace. The four sawyers who had no hand tools anxiously began pacing, waiting for a turn to dig their own safe haven.

Reyne glanced up worriedly and met Jojo's gaze. The crew was making little progress. The meadow, choked with thick brush, resisted their tools. Men and women, strong from months of heavy physical labor, were only able to clear small spaces with their Pulaskis. The biggest clearing was two feet square.

Oxbow was coming down the pike. A great churning noise began, as if an old steam engine were nearing, chugging, chugging, chugging.

"Dig! Dig! Dig!" Reyne shouted, unable to disguise her concern any longer. "Dig in! Give it your shoulder!" Each member kept at it, sweat pouring down their blackened faces in tiny, shining rivulets.

But it was clearly hopeless. Fat glowing embers began falling on their meadow, igniting small smoldering fires that the crew quickly stomped out. Reyne kept at them, shouting like a drill sergeant and vaguely aware that Jojo was seeking an alternative or an escape for them all. Reyne looked up. Oxbow was beyond the closest line of trees, approaching fast.

"Backpacks!" she screamed over the fire's roar. "Get rid of flammables!" All about her, hotshots threw out metal gasoline and oil bottles they carried to feed the saws and the flarelike fusees, flinging them away. On the outskirts, she saw veterans digging through rookies' packs, taking care of them like irritated older siblings. They had left the fire line barely fifteen minutes before.

Reyne heard her radio and struggled to make sense of what was coming through. Then she recognized Jojo's voice. "Up here! A road!" She glanced up and through the smoke saw him waving madly.

"Come on! Come on!" she screamed to be heard over the forest's own mewling. Without hesitation she ran, knowing that to stay in the meadow would be to end all their lives. Her crew ran with her. They reached the road—if it could be called that—thankful for at least the two ruts that were devoid of brush.

There was no time to dig away stray grasses. They had a minute, maybe seconds. They immediately began deploying the fire tents, madly wrestling the foil shelters with fingers that felt stiff and uncooperative.

It wasn't that they did not know how to use the tents. Each spring they spent hours training, learning how to use the corner straps with hands and feet, preparing to hold the narrow side flap down with elbows and knees.

But Oxbow had become a full-fledged firestorm, creating its own high-velocity winds and miniature weather pattern. Instead of rain, flaming pine cones pelted the ground. Instead of clouds, choking smoke filled the air. Instead of stormy breezes cooling their bodies, breathtaking heat robbed them of oxygen. In those conditions, shaking out the tiny folded tents, setting boots into foot straps, and ending up underneath the entire contraption was a daunting challenge.

The meadow behind them was afire.

All around her, hotshots were swearing, fumbling, not daring to watch the fire approach. But Reyne turned. Two walls of the fire met and surged even higher, a billowing wall of orange. The flames reached a hundred feet. Two hundred. She had not seen anything like it. As entrancing and electrifying as it was, she hoped never to see it again. *Dear Jesus. Dear God in heaven. Help us!* She turned to run.

Many crew members were already tucked under shelters, working to seal the edges with knees and elbows and, Reyne was sure, mentally preparing themselves for the coming onslaught. They looked like foil Jiffy Pop bags, exploding this way and that as they moved inside. Some of her team were not yet covered.

Reyne reached Janice, a trembling rookie from Tucson, and ripped the shelter from her hands to unfurl it. "You'll be okay!" Reyne shouted to her. Their hair flew madly about, and Reyne fought off the insane urge to laugh. "Remember your training! Seal the edges and ride it out!"

She turned from Janice as the rookie finally got under her shelter. Next to her was Larry, on her crew for the last three years. He looked at her in macabre resignation, gesturing toward a rip in his shelter. "No!" she shouted. "Remember what they told us! Grab the rip and tuck it under you! You'll be okay!"

The heat became noticeably worse. Reyne glanced over her shoulder. The fire was licking at her heels. With a last look around her team, packed tightly on the road—sometimes two or three in a row—she picked her spot next to two others and frantically shook out her shelter. She dove under it, tucking and praying madly.

Then the dragon came hunting.

CHAPTER ONE

*R*eyne took a last look in the Motel 6 mirror. Everything was in place on her United States Forest Service uniform. No wrinkles, no smudges.

She wiped her nametag with a tissue until it shone. She finished her pale blond braid, carefully plaited to lie close to her head and out of her face, lightly lined her round, smoky blue eyes, pressed on some concealer to cover the shadows underneath, and touched on some lipstick. She looked for her things.

Today was the day. They *had* to give her the go on her project. She had been so close last year! *I'll give them no room to decide otherwise,* she thought determinedly. *They won't hold Oxbow against me. They can't. This will make up for it.*

She left her room and hurried down the concrete walkway to the spot where her vintage '46 Chevy truck was parked. It still sported the original wooden bed but was painted only with spots of primer. She wanted to paint it forest green, but she had been busy lately.

Ignoring the admiring looks of two men standing on the walkway nearby, Reyne hauled herself lightly onto the high seat, deposited her briefcase and portfolio on the passenger-side floor, and turned the key in the ignition. The engine roared to life, and she allowed herself a satisfied smile at the smooth, powerful sound. Then she backed out of her parking spot, stepped on the gas, and headed out of the parking lot toward Missoula's Forest Service Headquarters.

Within minutes she was there, five minutes before her scheduled presentation. She carried her portfolio and briefcase into the brand-new, wood-sided building that had been built to echo national park lodges of old. The foyer towered above her, flanked by huge old trees that had been stripped of bark and capped with steel. They supported enormous beams high above her. Enormous windows illuminated the building, even on a somber cloudy day like today. The building still smelled of fresh-cut lumber and varnish.

"Reyne Oldre," she said to the receptionist. "I have a nine-thirty with Deputy Chief Alders to present my research proposal."

"Very good," the efficient woman said, nodding at her appointment book. "General Alders is expecting you. You'll find him and the other interagency brass in Room 115. Two doors down on the left," she said, gesturing toward the hall.

Reyne thanked the woman, reached the door, took a deep breath, and entered. The ten men who stood to meet her represented both Forest Service and Bureau of Land Management decision makers. Smiling, she greeted each man by name and quickly set up her portfolio on a portable stand.

The presentation began smoothly, just as she had practiced the afternoon before. She had done her homework, going through the whole spiel in front of her friend Rachel, pretending to shake hands with the room divider and couches, then setting up her materials and delivering her presentation. Rachel had helped her tear it apart and build it again, crafting a killer appeal that no one could negate. She hoped.

Her preparation was paying off. Reyne began with a field story, one learned from personal experience, that immediately grabbed the attention of all ten in attendance. They studied her face, listening intently as she segued into the crux of her request. "So, you see, gentlemen," Reyne said, glancing around the room, "the research money would be used to develop a hand-held computer that could store and accurately chart readings on temperature, humidity, wind speed—even fuel moisture levels. Crew bosses could carry it into the front lines and get an accurate reading anytime they needed it. The time factor is crucial. My project could save many lives by giving bosses the information they need, when they need it, where they need it."

Reyne's heart pounded as she sensed that men in the room were coming on board with her, understanding and getting excited about her project. Many were nodding and appraising her appreciatively— and for once the appreciation had as much to do with her thinking as with her looks. She allowed herself a brief surge of elation. *I'm going to get it!* she thought. *It's going to work!*

But the project was not yet in the bag. As the developmental time line and financial requirements for her project became clear, and as she got into the more intricate details of the experiment, Reyne could see several of the men's faces grow bored, distant, daydreamy. This she had anticipated. She was in the process of wrapping up the presentation with another story that would bring them all back around when the conference-room door burst open.

"This is where the party is?" the man's voice boomed. His expression was relaxed, unconcerned about the intrusion, and he wore a huge grin plastered across his face. "Sorry I'm late! Car broke down again!" He shook each man's hand enthusiastically, greeting each man by name as she had…although she noted that he seemed to be on a first-name basis with all of them. Each was clearly pleased to see this Logan McCabe and greeted him with smiles, laughs, shaking heads, and personal words that far exceeded those for her reception.

"Chief!" McCabe boomed as if meeting an old, lost friend. His back was to her, but she could see the general's face, warm and receptive. "When are we going to get together again and smoke some more Cubans?" Logan cracked.

"Oh brother," Reyne mumbled. The forest firefighters boys' club was always difficult for a woman to enter—even in the new millennium—but this guy was making it impossible. The tall, handsome, wavy-haired man was steadily sealing her out.

"And who's this beautiful lady?" he said, finally reaching Reyne. She bristled. *That's it! Bury me forever! Of all the sexist, egotistical, unthinking things to say in a meeting...*

General Alders appeared not to have noticed. He stood and introduced them. "Reyne, let me introduce you to one fine BLM smokejumper, Logan McCabe. Logan, this is Reyne Oldre, a fire-science researcher for the Forest Service."

"Rain? Never heard of a name like that before! Although it's a welcome word in a firefighter's ear." He smiled around the room, clearly winning each man over. He left her no room to get a word in edgewise.

"It's Norwegian—," she began her grudging reply, but he was already launching another joke.

"Did I ever tell you guys the one about Forest Service ground-pounders?"

The Forest Service officials shook their heads warily while the Bureau of Land Management brass egged Logan on. He ignored her murderous look.

"How many Service groundpounders does it take to screw in a mess-tent light bulb?"

Logan raised one eyebrow as he spoke, working the crowd like a seasoned veteran. "Twenty-one. One to hold the light bulb and twenty to break down the tent and rotate it."

The Forest Service reps shook their heads while the BLM guys groaned, slapping him on the back as if they were welcoming back a long-lost friend. Logan shrugged it off, smiling, then looked over at Reyne appraisingly. "I'm sorry. I interrupted your meeting."

Reyne sent daggers with her look. *You're ruining it, you big oaf. I've lost momentum.*

"Groundpounder, eh?" Logan quipped. "No wonder you didn't appreciate my joke—"

"Reyne Oldre is hardly your average U.S. Forest Service groundpounder, Logan," spoke up Henry Frasier, a Bureau of Land Management boss. "You've spent too much time in the Southwest with the BLM. Reyne's seen fire action from Mexico to Alaska with the Service. She made it to crew boss with the Lolo Hotshots before moving on to fire science."

"I'm surprised you two haven't crossed paths yet," Deputy Chief Alders broke in. "Reyne's one of the best researchers we have, and McCabe has made a name for himself in smokejumping. He's working on some new equipment you should take a look at, Reyne."

Ordinarily, Reyne would have appreciated the introduction and been interested in Logan's project, but she was anxious to get things back on track. Her track. "Yes, well…as I was saying, gentlemen?" She raised her voice to get the party back in order. They settled quickly, but as she wrapped up her presentation, Reyne could tell that the interruption had done critical damage. They were not all in agreement on her project. She could see it on their faces as clearly as if they were holding up numbered judging cards after watching her fall on the ice, hind-end first.

She stumbled over her words, distracted by the mental image, and lamely finished up. No sooner had she sat down than Logan McCabe stood, saying, "Great! Sounds like I missed a good presentation. You guys will have to make a tough decision. But wait until you get a load of what I want to do with the government's money..."

Reyne looked around the table as Logan began his presentation, a loosely concepted idea about some "horizontal stabilizer." They were entranced. It was like being back at high school, watching a bunch of gaga girls hang on every word that left the school jock's mouth. And his project had to do with air compression and darts. *Like something out of a James Bond movie,* she thought. *Not the more mundane ins and outs of computer science.*

As she focused, she had to admit that Logan was onto something, and something exciting, especially for smokejumpers. But could it save as many lives as hers could? And had he spent the time and effort developing the idea that she had? Obviously not. He relied on short jokes and a nudge-nudge camaraderie to get them all on board. Yet on board he got them, she grudgingly admitted.

She watched as he spoke animatedly, gesticulating in excitement, pulling each person into each word he uttered. His charisma was unmistakable, his leadership skills obvious. He was charming and handsome and buddies with every one of these guys.

Logan McCabe will get my funding, Reyne mused in disappointment. *Just as surely as Dirk Tanner will fish for the biggest rainbow trout in the Kootenai this summer.*

CHAPTER TWO

*R*eyne sipped her coffee from a deep mug and smiled as she spotted the dusty Jeep far below her on the highway. It was the Tanners' Jeep, which meant that Rachel was driving, probably after picking up Beth at the Double M. Within months of Reyne's arrival in Elk Horn, their Saturday morning get-together had become a weekly routine, and Reyne always looked forward to it.

With a happy sigh, Reyne gazed out past the still-distant vehicle to the little town of Elk Horn, the airstrip, and the Rockies beyond. It was a beautiful spring morning. And Reyne adored her new home, situated on a small hill at the southwestern corner of the Morgans' sprawling ranch—the Double M. She had saved for years to build. And now she had the house of her dreams, with a view to boot.

She smiled again as the Jeep finally pulled up in front of the cottage and Rachel, full of her usual energy, swung her long legs out. Reyne sobered as Beth emerged more slowly, taking her time, obviously not feeling well. *The cancer...* She pushed the thought away and put on a happy face as the two turned toward her.

"Good morning!" she called. "You two finally extricated yourselves from family?"

"It takes a while to get a baby situated with Dirk," Rachel said, climbing the steps to the wooden porch and giving her friend a big hug. "You know, even with Mary there, this is supposed to be strict Papa time. So I have to get everything set: clean diapers, bottles, clothes… It's almost more work than bringing the baby with me."

"Try prying a three-year-old from your leg as if you're leaving her forever," Beth said, joining them. Her smile faltered as she realized what she had said. Her friends hesitated, the words hanging in the air.

"Come on in for a caffeine and sugar fix," Reyne smoothed over. "I've been looking forward to some girl talk for days."

She hurried to the kitchen for two more mugs of coffee and a plate of muffins while her friends situated themselves in the living room. Reyne's cottage was basically just a wooden box with a wraparound porch and peaked roof. Her cozy front room featured a big picture window with a view of the town and the mountains. She had decorated the house in classic but feminine fashion—ivory walls with framed botanical prints, ivy stenciled around the tops of walls, a distressed, whitewashed screen to divide living room from dining room, and a recycled-brick fireplace with a two-sided hearth that fed heat to the sitting room on one side and her bedroom on the other.

Rachel sank into an overstuffed white chair, pulled her long, sable hair from behind her back, and pushed off her flats, propping stocking feet up on the ottoman. She was a pretty woman, as tall as Reyne, but with more exotic features. Big, oval, green eyes. Enviable olive-toned skin.

"Ahh," she moaned. "This is heaven. Pure luxury. Remember our bachelorette days, Beth? Remember our incredible apartment in San Francisco? We once went with Country French decor too, Reyne. Sadly, those years of white furniture are over. But it's great to visit. I feel like a real girl here. And listen… Not a kid to be heard for miles."

"Wait 'til Samuel starts teething on your coffee tables," Beth groused, taking a sip of coffee and placing her mug on Reyne's own low table.

"Little Hope was just giving your furniture some help," Reyne defended lightly, nodding toward the screen. "Look at that. You see? The distressed look is in."

"Yeah, right. I don't think rows of tiny teeth marks are exactly what the decorators have in mind. It's been over a year, and I still haven't refinished 'em." Beth shook her head as Reyne offered her a muffin.

"Come on, Beth," Reyne began gently. "Have you eaten today?"

"I'm not hungry."

"Beth," Rachel began, ganging up on her with Reyne. Since her diagnosis of breast cancer and her radical mastectomy the year before, Beth had continued to drop weight. "You don't need to lose any more ground."

"All right, all right," she said, giving in. "Let's not ruin the moment with lectures." She took a tiny bite of a poppy-seed muffin.

Reyne laughed as she watched Rachel give Beth a you-can't-fool-me-with-that-measly-effort look. "Boy, you have it tough, don't you, Beth? I'd hate to be in your shoes, looking at that accusatory face."

Beth smiled, and Rachel's face softened. It had been a hard year. Over the last months, Rachel and Reyne had helped the Morgans out a lot by baby-sitting their three-year-old daughter, Hope, or taking Beth in to the hospital for her checkups. But Beth was not faring well. Her cheeks, once rosy and dimpled, were drawn and sallow. Her clothes hung from her body, and even her short brown curls seemed listless.

Beth had been the first to reach out to Reyne at the tiny Elk

Horn Community Church three years ago. It hadn't been long before Reyne decided that she wanted to settle in the village permanently, not just when she was stationed there on occasion to fight fires. Reyne had wanted a home, but not on the outskirts of a bigger city like Missoula. She wanted a home in a place where people knew her on the streets, welcomed her into *their* homes. And from her brief visits to the small mountain town, she knew Elk Horn was that kind of place.

Beth was a living example of small-town hospitality, even though she was a transplanted Californian. She had welcomed Reyne at the Dub M for dinner, introduced her to her own friends—including Rachel and Dirk Tanner—made her feel like family. The high point had come when she and her husband, Matt, had offered Reyne purchase rights on a choice piece of property at the southeastern corner of their ranch. The only stipulations had been that she let cattle graze up to the fence that surrounded her acre and that they be given first option if she ever decided to sell.

The house, a dream come true, was built within six months. *This is home,* Reyne thought happily, gazing at her friends as they chatted. *I am so happy here.*

A high-pitched whirring distracted her from her reverie. She rose, looking out across town to the airstrip. "That's odd," she mumbled.

"What?" Rachel asked, rising beside her.

"That small plane. Taking off. I didn't think there were any exercises scheduled this weekend."

"Well, it's the first clear day we've had in weeks. Maybe it's a visitor. Or those new smokejumpers—"

"No," Reyne interrupted softly. "Nobody's at the airstrip yet. Very strange," she said, shrugging and turning her back to the window. "But I am *not* working today, so I won't worry about it."

"Still struggling with the working-from-home-so-I-never-get-away-from-it syndrome?" Rachel asked her.

"You of all people should understand."

"I do," Rachel returned, who had done advertising work from her home since leaving San Francisco to marry Dirk. "You have to get hard-core. Set your hours. Don't answer the phone unless it's during those hours. Leave your paperwork at your desk. Never let it get to the dining room. *Or* your bed. Let everyone know your rules. And don't let anyone break them."

Reyne nodded in agreement, then cocked her head as the Cessna sang overhead. *They never fly flight patterns in this direction.* She stood and walked to the front porch, watching in amazement as a technicolor parachute opened up high above, then slowly angled down toward the cottage.

Beth and Rachel joined her on the porch, watching the artful descent. The man landed not fifteen feet from Reyne's house. "You've gotta be kidding," she mumbled. "You! What are *you* doing here?" she asked him, fighting to keep her voice calm.

"So what do you think?" Beth said to Rachel impishly. "Should she run inside and shut the door in his face? 'Cause he's definitely not dropping in during business hours."

"No," Reyne heard Rachel say quietly. "He's too cute to turn away—and there's no wedding ring in sight. As I was saying, you have to bend the rules once in a while. Besides, he's obviously skydiving, not smokejumping. So technically, it's *not* work." She ignored Reyne's tight-lipped grimace and stepped off the porch, reaching out her hand. "Hi, I'm Rachel Tanner. Reyne didn't tell us she was expecting company."

The handsome, tall man stopped unclipping gear and flashed her a brilliant smile. "Logan McCabe," he said. "I'm pleased to meet you. I've just been detailed to Elk Horn to head up the timber company's private firefighting force as a backup for Missoula. And when I have some extra time, I'm supposed to work closely with this woman on a research project." He nodded at Reyne, ignoring her sputter and look of confusion.

Beth made her way around Reyne and went to meet the man too. Reyne looked at them both with disbelief, feeling betrayed. Then she caught herself. They had no idea what Logan had done. They only saw him as a handsome, apparently eligible guy dropping in on her—literally—during a glorious spring day. It *was* kind of romantic when she thought about it. *Wait a minute, did I just call him handsome? And think this might be romantic? Reyne, get a grip.*

She glared at Logan, who was charming her friends with another lame joke. Yes, she had to admit it. He *was* handsome, with tightly cropped, dark brown hair that waved close to his head. Dazzling blue eyes, she noted as he looked toward her, eyes the color of a Montana sky on a hot day. He was striking, strong…

Not that it was going to get him an inch farther with her. Reyne had worked with dozens of handsome, adventurous men in her years fighting fire. And this particular man had almost certainly cost her the research and development money she had worked for months to get.

She resolutely stepped from the porch and walked to him.

"What are you doing here, McCabe?" she asked bluntly.

CHAPTER THREE

*R*eyne, apparently we got off on the wrong foot," Logan said. "I need to apologize for interrupting your presentation last week."

He looked down at the woman before him, who was beautiful. Shining pale hair that spilled over her shoulders in waves. Blue eyes that smoked with anger. She couldn't possibly be as angry as she seemed. But even if she was, Logan wasn't worried. He gave her his most winsome smile.

"Fine," Reyne said, hands on her hips. "I'm waiting."

Beth and Rachel gave their friend puzzled, surprised looks but said nothing.

"I…I'm sorry," Logan faltered, unaccustomed to facing someone he couldn't readily soften up. "I was a dope. It's my immediate response to a new situation. Tell a joke. Warm up the crowd, you know." He grinned at Beth and Rachel, seeking support. They smiled in response. Reyne did not.

"That was an important meeting for me, McCabe," she said, looking at him without blinking. "I really need that funding for my pocket weather-kit project."

Logan nodded at her, sobering. "They can be tough, those guys. I'm sorry. What else can I say?"

Reyne turned and walked back to the cottage. "Not much, I guess," she said over her shoulder. "Come on, you guys," she said to her friends. "Coffee's getting cold. I assume my unexpected guest arranged for a lift home."

Logan stood there for a moment, then turned to gather his parachute. "I guess you don't want to talk until Monday," he said, just loud enough for her to hear as she opened the porch door.

"About what?" she asked impatiently.

"About our project."

"Our what?"

"Our project. I received word on Friday. I've been reassigned to Elk Horn to work with you until I start training the timber company's crew."

Reyne walked down the steps again, her gait measured, obviously pondering his words. "Are you saying that you got the funding for your project? And I'm to assist *you?*"

Logan met her gaze with a grin. "Yes! Isn't it great? They're such tightwads; it's amazing I got anything. But they stipulated I have to work with you on it. Apparently, you're the expert on things…"

He frowned as Reyne abruptly turned and walked away toward an outbuilding that matched her cottage. He tore his eyes away from her long legs in slim jeans and rushed to catch up with her.

She threw open the door, obviously furious. With one flip of a switch, counters full of computer equipment came to life. He looked at it all in amazement and then at his companion as she whirled to face him again. "Do you see this? I've invested thousands. And I've been waiting two years for the go-ahead on my project. Two years! And then you come along and—"

Logan's brow furrowed in concern, understanding dawning. "You're saying that you think they gave me the grant *instead* of giving one to you?"

"You're the one who got a call Friday, big boy. My consolation call is probably coming Monday. I can just hear them. 'Reyne, I'm sorry. Maybe next year on that computer project. But we've got another job for you...'" She shook, she was so angry, then turned from Logan, busying herself with a computer keyboard as if fighting tears.

Good grief, he thought. *Tears?* "There's always next year," he tried.

She whirled back to him, blond hair flying. His fears were confirmed. Her blue eyes had deepened to an even darker shade as they filled with tears. An impossible blue, he noted, the color of a spring sky heavy with impending rain. "You don't understand!" Reyne said, her voice tight. "My project could save lives!"

Logan took a step toward her, confused. He reached out to grasp her upper arms gently, looked down toward eyes that refused to meet his, and said, "I'm hoping my project will too."

"Don't touch me," she mumbled, shaking off his hands and stalking over to a drawing table. She leaned over it, her arms on the table supporting her in A-frame fashion. He couldn't see her face.

"Don't you even want to hear more about it?" he tried. She turned toward him as he spoke.

"No! I tell you, if I could just get some funding, my project could save lives! I'm sure of it. I've worked out enough to know that if firefighters had this on the front lines...if they were caught in a firestorm..." She faltered, her eyes distant.

"Like Oxbow?" he asked quietly, his head ducked in what he hoped was an understanding, welcoming look. It had worked on countless women before.

He had obviously caught her by surprise. "Oxbow?" she blurted. "What do you know of it?" Her voice gained altitude with each word, he noticed. *She's close to breaking.*

27

"Enough to know you *did* save lives," he said, hoping to ease the situation. Bring her tone down to one of reason.

"Or lost them," Reyne said bitterly, turning toward a window. "Depends on who you talk to."

Logan wanted to go to her, comfort her. He knew the pain of losing team members on the field, of turning a charred body over and not being able to recognize a dear friend. "I haven't met anybody who says you were to blame." He moved toward her, intending to give her a gentle pat on the back, but she turned to face him, apparently pulling herself together.

"That's our team," she said, her chin held high and a false smile on her face. "Our happy family. Never say a word against another firefighter until you've fought a mile of fire in her boots."

"Reyne, really," he tried again. He grimaced at the trace of bitterness, the anger, the sadness in her voice. But she was so graceful, even in the midst of turmoil. She held herself regally. Thin and lanky with that shiny, champagne hair and those deep blue eyes. Lips that curved up charmingly in the corners, making her look as if she were always smiling, even when she obviously was not.

Logan swallowed hard, pushing back the crazy attraction he felt toward her. He hadn't noticed her looks this much at the meeting. *But her hair had been pulled back. And she was in uniform. Not a soft sweater and jeans.* He swallowed hard again, forcing himself to concentrate. "Oxbow was a fire that legends are made of. Nobody could've guessed that he was gonna hook." *And I would never have guessed that you were the lady in charge.*

He had heard Reyne's story while he was stationed in California. The day they buried those firefighters, his team had taken the day off to mourn and pray for the future safety of all firefighters. But he hadn't remembered the crew boss's name…nor had he expected to meet her in Montana.

"Yeah, well someday I'll have to tell you more. Those four dead kids were my responsibility. And I'm going to find ways to keep it from happening again." Her tears were gone. She stared at him in open challenge.

Logan hardened his gaze. "Oh no. I can see where you're heading. And you're not getting my grant money. You help me on my project as directed, and maybe we can look at yours after. Maybe we can find some cost-saving measures that will justify your project, too. But I can be as tough as you, Reyne Oldre. And I wanted the funding for good reason. Why don't you come down to the airstrip and see?"

Her eyes fell as she looked away to the window, thinking. She sighed heavily. "Look, I've got company. I need to get back to them. I'll look you up on Monday morning, and we can talk about your project. I should be over my disappointment by then." She strode to the door, decision obviously made, seemingly not caring if he left her studio or not.

Reyne Oldre was not a woman who sat idly by and waited for someone else to make the call, he mused admiringly as he watched her walk to the cottage. She was the kind who had her fingers on the button before anyone else even thought to pick up the receiver.

Reluctantly, he walked back to his chute, packing it tightly into his bag with the ease that only experience could bring. As the cords and connections passed his fingertips, he grew gradually more irritated with Reyne. She acted as though her project was the only one of worth. Hadn't she even listened when he explained his own project at the meeting?

He glanced back at her house once more as he gave the chute a final shove, then threw his pack over his shoulder and started down her road back to town. *I guess you have one of those "groaning experiences" ahead of us, huh, Lord?* Logan prayed as his feet met the highway. *If you don't want us to kill each other, I have the feeling that you're going to have to lead the way in this one.*

CHAPTER FOUR

*S*tanding by the window inside, Rachel watched Reyne as she stalked across the room, slumped down on the couch, and threw her feet up on the coffee table. Beth went to stand beside Rachel and nudged her as Logan glanced up, finished packing, and turned.

"Is he walking?" Beth asked incredulously. "It has to be four miles to the timber company's airstrip building!"

"Good," Reyne groused from the couch. "Let him walk."

"What put you in such a lousy mood?" Rachel asked, joining her on the couch. She studied her friend, who refused to look up.

"That bozo is the one who cost me my grant in Missoula."

"Oh," Rachel said, familiar with the story of how Logan had burst into the meeting and ruined the presentation that Reyne had so carefully prepared. Beth raised her eyebrows and nodded in sudden understanding.

"So what'd he want?" Rachel asked sympathetically.

"To apologize, I guess," Reyne said, feeling childish about her anger. But she could not set it aside. "And to break the news that *we're* going to be working on *his* project, not mine."

"Was he here to gloat?" Beth asked quietly over the rim of her mug.

"No—," Reyne began.

"So he was just trying to make peace?" Beth interrupted.

"Yeah, if you can call it that. To be honest, I don't think he really understood that his project's go-ahead meant that my project was deep-sixed. I guess I'd be more open to an apology if he wasn't so showy. I mean, what was that? Arriving in my yard via parachute…it probably cost the timber company a hundred bucks."

Beth nodded, hearing her. Then, "That wasn't a BLM or timber company jumper plane. I'd say he contracted it himself. What did you say his project was?"

"I didn't…," Reyne's voice trailed. Slowly, a ragged red tinge climbed her neck and cheeks. "Oh no."

"What?" Rachel asked, obviously irritated at not being a part of the secret.

"Parachutes," Reyne said, her voice low. "He's working on a special secondary chute system in case a jumper gets hung up in the trees. He probably was here to show me something about it. Or maybe he was testing some part of it." She rose and walked to the window. Logan was already a miniature form on the dirt road, just reaching the highway.

Seeing him, her anger returned. She turned to her friends, her face tense again. "But his project is only going to benefit a few hundred jumpers! Mine would've benefited thousands of ground-pounders!"

She looked at Beth and Rachel, who simply stared back at her, waiting.

"Don't say it," Reyne moaned. "I'm whining. But don't I get to? Just a little?"

"Sure," Rachel said. "I can see why you'd be ticked at him. At first. But Reyne, have you looked at him? Really looked? The man is drop-dead gorgeous."

"And he seems really nice," Beth inserted.

"And obviously he was making an effort with you," Rachel said. "If he was a total jerk, he would've waited for you to show up or called you and bragged about getting funded."

"Did you see how he was looking at her?" Beth asked Rachel. "Like a dehydrated man on the desert spotting an oasis."

"Yeah," Rachel said, grinning and appraising Reyne. "He'd seen her in uniform last week. Even in that awful taupe she's pretty cute. But look at her today. What man wouldn't give his eyeteeth to do a little R&D with Reyne Oldre?"

Reyne pursed her lips and glanced at her friends through slitted eyes. "Okay. That's enough of that. We'll leave Logan McCabe for next week's conversation. I don't have to deal with him until Monday, so let's get back to more interesting subjects. What new trick has Samuel learned this week? Has he perfected his drooling?"

The next day, much to her chagrin, Reyne's mind was forced back to the subject of Logan McCabe. As she entered her church and greeted Pastor Arnie Lear, Logan appeared at her side.

"Good to see you're a God-fearing woman, partner," he whispered in her ear as she shook the pastor's hand.

"Logan!" Arnie intoned, obviously pleased to see him. "Hey, I really appreciated our conversation yesterday."

"Me too," Logan said. "Are you free for breakfast again this week? A certain Bible passage is really tripping me up, and I'd like to discuss it—not to mention have the excuse to eat another logger's breakfast."

How does he know my pastor already? Reyne wondered in irritation. *He just got to Elk Horn.* She tried to squelch her unreasonable feelings but used the opportunity to escape into the sanctuary and away from him. Monday would be early enough to deal with Logan McCabe.

Reyne was sitting in her pew, quietly trying to concentrate on a prayer, when she became aware of Logan coming toward her, introducing himself to everyone along the aisle on the way. She glanced back and watched as he pumped a man's hand and cracked some joke. Couldn't he be quiet even in church?

Suddenly Logan was at her side. She dragged her eyes to his. "Anyone sitting there?" he asked, pointing to the seat on her other side.

With a sigh, she moved her purse and tucked in her legs to let him by. He settled in immediately and then, to her surprise, pulled out the kneeler in front of them and knelt in prayer. Her heart warmed involuntarily, and she struggled to say a prayer of her own rather than concentrate on the man beside her. He was still there when the pastor greeted the congregation. Quietly Logan sat back and replaced the kneeler.

Reyne glanced over her shoulder. Sure enough, Beth was watching them intently; she smiled with one eyebrow lifted. *Of course,* Reyne thought. *The man prays for a minute, and Beth decides we should marry. But it's probably all for show. A political move. Show up in church and win the town. Then they won't gripe when the Sherpas and B-17s start roaring over their houses this summer.*

Reyne looked at Logan as Arnie announced the first hymn. She had to admit he seemed earnest in his actions. Logan sang without a second thought to his slightly off-key baritone and listened intently to the Scripture readings. All the while, Reyne could only concentrate on the physical nearness of him...the brush of his hand as he held the hymnbook open for them, a slight flutter as his fingertips settled by her shoulder. Several times she had to tell herself to clear her head. She was here for God, and God only.

By the time Arnie got into his sermon, she had regained some measure of composure and concentration. She tried to focus on the pastor's words, but they only convicted her heart. *Oh brother,* she mused to herself. *This is not my week. Can't you give me a break, God? Just a moment to wallow in self-righteous indignation?*

Arnie was speaking about how God worked in people's lives. "And most of all," he said, looking as many parishioners in the eye as he could, "God works through adversity. I don't know about you, but I've found that when things aren't going the way I'd like them to go, God is usually in the process of teaching me something vital. And usually it has something to do with my priorities or my attitude."

Reyne dared to look up at the pastor, absolutely sure that Rachel or Beth had tipped him off as to what was going on. But Arnie's gaze was elsewhere, and his look was innocent. *Father God, you sure have a way of timing things,* she prayed silently, a gentle smile forming on her lips.

By the time Arnie was finished, Reyne felt like standing and announcing to the congregation that yes, she had been a complete jerk and very unfair and that she owed Logan McCabe a public apology. She steeled herself to at least tell him so in private.

But as soon as the last hymn ended, Logan was introducing himself to the people on his other side, and they introduced him to others beyond them. After waiting a few minutes to be noticed, Reyne gave up in irritation and headed to the door.

Rachel met her there. "Must've forgiven and forgotten."

"Hardly. We barely spoke."

Rachel frowned, and Beth came up beside them. "I saw you sitting together," she whispered excitedly.

"Will you two stop it?"

"Didn't Arnie's sermon say anything to you?" Rachel asked, raising a brow in mock rebuke.

"It said something, all right," Reyne admitted. "And I was about to say something to Mr. Popularity, but I didn't get a chance."

"Now you do," Rachel whispered, looking over Reyne's shoulder. Rachel deliberately turned at the last minute to speak with someone else, and Beth did the same. Suddenly Reyne was alone with Logan in the alcove.

He shifted uneasily in front of her—an action that seemed remarkably odd for a man with his self-confidence. "Listen, Reyne, I think I owe you an apology—"

She looked up at him, staring into his eyes. "No, Logan. I owe you one. I was angry that I didn't get the grant, and I took it out on you. I'm sorry. I haven't really given your project a chance."

His eyes sparkled as he looked down into hers. "Apology accepted. We'll meet tomorrow?"

"At the airstrip," Reyne agreed and led the way out the door. She paused to say good-bye to the pastor and to tease him about his sermon. "Knock it off, would you, Arnie? I hate it when I'm sitting in the pews and I feel like you've been eavesdropping on my thoughts. Can't we have a message that's easy on our consciences once in a while?"

"I aim to please," Arnie said good-naturedly. "I'll work on something sweet and superficial for next week that might be more palatable." He turned toward Logan. "I see you were sitting next to Elk Horn's most eligible bachelorette."

"Arnie," Reyne began. She tried to cover her embarrassment over his comment by smoothly taking over the situation. "I'm doing fine on my own, thank you. I don't need a man to make my life complete, and I'm sure Logan has no difficulty finding dates." She gave him a smile that firmly said that's enough of that and turned to walk away.

"See you tomorrow, Reyne!" Logan yelled over the din of conversation all about them. She winced and tried not to let anyone see her dismay. The whole town would be talking. Not to mention her friends. She shook her head as she reached the Tanners and the Morgans. "Don't you all even start. I've had enough ribbing for one day."

Rachel held Samuel on her hip while Hope ran around and around the group, excited to be out of Sunday school and among the adults. She begged to hold Samuel, and Rachel knelt to help Hope pull the toddler into her lap like a huge doll. Dirk came up beside Reyne and gave her a sideways hug.

"Hear there's a new man in your life," he said with a grin, ignoring Rachel's warning look.

"In a matter of speaking," she said.

"I like him," Matt Morgan added from her other side. "A man's man."

"Great. Not that it matters. He's just my new work partner."

"Whatever you say, lady," Dirk said with a grin. He reached down and pulled his struggling son from Hope's arms. The little girl ran away, relieved to be free of the baby after the initial thrill was over. "He does seem like a good match for you though. And I was impressed—Arnie said that one of the first things Logan did when he got to town was meet with him as his prospective pastor. He's into the accountability thing."

"Oh brother," Reyne groaned. "If it's not your wives, it's you guys. You're just determined to match me up with every stray who comes to Elk Horn."

"Hardly a stray," Matt said with a shake of his head. "The man's got a lot going for him—a good job, for one thing. Full-time in fire is hard to come by, as you well know." He slapped Dirk on the back with a big, square hand. "Dirk and I both thought about it during our days as rebel groundpounders running away from life on the ranch. We could almost taste it—there's just nothing like the fire game. Logan's got a steady job in it. He must be pretty good too if the timber company's hiring him to form a private crew. And the guy's funny—he cracks me up."

"Yeah," Dirk said, laughing. "Did he tell you the one about the rancher?"

He and Matt rehashed the joke, laughing until they were wiping away tears, as if it were the first time they had heard it. "Let's have him over for supper sometime," Matt said to Beth. At her hesitation he added, "When you're feeling better."

Reyne, irritated at him for pushing Beth to entertain, griped, "I'm sure he has plenty of new friends around. I don't think you need to have him over."

Rachel gave her a puzzled look. "Reyne, that's not like you. You're the one who's always having new people over…telling us how much it meant to you when you first came to Elk Horn."

"Well sure, but…," Reyne back-pedaled. "I just don't think that Beth should be working so hard just to…" Her voice trailed as she dared to meet her friend's gaze. "Beth, you've got so much going on already," she began lamely.

"Look, Reyne. I may be sick, but I'm not dead. You just settled it. We'll invite him over. And I'll expect you to be there."

"Oh brother. I'm sorry, Beth. I was just thinking of you!"

"Thinking of me, or just using me as an excuse to avoid Logan McCabe?"

Reyne raised her hands as if in surrender. "I just seem to be digging myself in deeper here. I'm going home." She gave Beth a hug. "We're okay?"

"Fine. Just don't treat me like I'm made of spun gold," Beth said.

"I won't. And you all," she said looking about, "lay off about Logan. He's my coworker. That's it."

They smiled at her like a group of Cheshire cats, all-knowing and yet for once holding their tongues. With a sigh of resignation, Reyne turned and walked to her truck.

CHAPTER FIVE

On Monday morning Reyne pulled on her boots, wrestled her slim jeans back down over them, and walked to her kitchen. It was early, and she wanted to get some work done before facing Logan. She poured herself a tall mug of coffee and through its steam stared out her kitchen window.

For a moment the gentle white tendrils of steam entranced her, making her think of smoke wafting upward after a big fire. It took her back to that terrible day in Idaho and the aftermath of Oxbow, to emerging from her protective tent and realizing that not all of her team had made it...

She squeezed her eyes to pinch back the threatening tears and drew her lips into a grim line, thinking once again of her weather-kit project and how it might have made the difference that summer in Idaho. *If only—*

Reyne turned abruptly, cutting off her own line of thinking, and headed out to her office, stopping briefly to grab her barn jacket and pull it on over her ivory turtleneck. The spring mornings were still quite cold, and it would take awhile to warm up the outbuilding past the standard fifty-five degrees.

As she walked, trying to cast away her foul mood, the sounds of a plane drew her attention to the airfield. Reyne checked her watch: 7:00 A.M. She had to hand it to him; Logan did not seem like a slouch about his work. The forestry company's old Sherpa taxied down the runway and took off, presumably with Logan aboard.

Well if he was up, she wasn't about to let him think that she was sleeping in. It was time that Logan McCabe found out just who he had partnered up with. Reyne Oldre wasn't one to fall behind on the job either.

She ducked back into the house and grabbed her keys before heading over to her truck—her pride and joy—which now gleamed with a new coat of rich green paint. She and her brother Austin had worked tirelessly to bring the truck back to life the summer she was sixteen and Austin was twenty. Consequently, she had learned quite a bit about engines and been able to keep the Chevy in working order ever since. But it was only recently that Reyne had finally invested the money to reupholster the seats in a durable fabric that now matched the new shiny paint job outside—done two days ago—and to reface the cracked, aged dashboard in black leather. The original radio still worked, and Reyne tuned in a nearby Christian radio station after she turned the key and backed out her drive.

As she headed out, the incredible spring morning washed away her foul mood and melted her anger at Logan. Huge groves of birch that banked the Kootenai River fluttered tiny yellow green leaves in the spring breeze. Along the highway, Reyne passed newborn lambs cavorting with brothers and sisters...tiny calves attempting to nurse...colts trying out wobbly legs. The fields and hills were covered with verdant, fresh grass that waved in the wind. On the mountainside, the underbrush was once again beginning to match the color of the evergreens that towered high above.

In the midst of all the newness, Reyne could hardly hold on to her anger. "Hope springs eternal," she mused aloud, wondering where the old saying came from. And inside, she felt the same. Somehow the day gave her new hope for her work, even if she had to do it on Logan's project. *Maybe if I help him now, I'll get the funding for my project next year.*

Reyne bent over her steering wheel and scanned the skies. Where did that Sherpa go? She frowned as she thought that maybe the airstrip team wasn't skydiving at all…that maybe they had headed to Missoula and her trip to see them was all a waste. But it was too late now. Reyne was committed. She was almost there.

As Reyne turned down the road toward Elk Horn International—the ostentatious name for what was little more than a country airstrip—she caught sight of a plane. Quickly, she pulled to the side of the road and got out to watch. But it wasn't the Cessna that she was sure held Logan inside. It was Horizon Airlines' morning commuter flight. Elk Horn's newest commercial airline ran two flights a day, ferrying travelers in and out of the one-room terminal. As they landed, Reyne shielded her eyes and scanned the sky for other aircraft. Nothing in sight.

She was about to climb back into her truck and drive home when the Chevy's engine sputtered and died. Reyne frowned, tried the engine once more, then went to dig out her tool kit from underneath the seat. She walked around to lift the hood and ducked her head under it. Intent on her tinkering, she did not hear the second plane.

Through the open doorway of the plane, Logan spotted the sparkling green truck far below them and knew who must be underneath the hood. "My damsel in distress!" he yelled at the spotter, Ken Oakley. Ken rolled his eyes as Logan flashed him a wide grin and lifted his eyebrows cockily. "Duty calls her knight in shining armor to save her!" Logan yelled.

Logan tilted the radio microphone at his ear down toward his mouth to talk with the pilot. "We have our landing target, Mike. Circle around the green truck on the road."

A low chuckle rumbled in his earpiece as Mike Moser spotted the target. "You're the worst, McCabe," came Mike's voice. "You'll do anything to get a date Saturday. Ten bucks says Reyne Oldre won't let you near her truck, twenty that she won't agree to go out with you."

Logan grinned. "Can I have a few days to work on her?"

"No way. The bet is only for today. That Oldre's a tough cookie—a Forest Service legend—but you're so dang charming that there's no way I'll give you that much time."

"Ten bucks for working on her truck. Twenty if I get a date?"

"Those are the terms."

"You're out thirty bucks, my friend. We'll use it for a romantic dinner this weekend. Smokejumper away." With that he cast Ken another cocky smile and rolled out the doorway, immediately pulling his ripcord and deploying his chute.

With a fluttering roar the parachute swirled above him, spun, caught air, and canopied. The effect was immediate; it felt like an abrupt halt midair. Still, he descended, just not at the blinding speed he had been going. Reyne obviously had not seen him or heard the plane; she was apparently so involved in her work that she was not aware that he was near.

A woman of sole purpose, he mused. Briefly he thought about the myriad possibilities of what could be wrong with her vintage truck, preparing to impress her with his engine prowess. As he got closer, it became more difficult to concentrate on the car problems instead of on her attractive form leaning over the engine. He averted his eyes, deciding to think about his landing.

Sadly, she did not turn to note his perfect execution. He expertly bent his knees to be ready and then instantly rolled backward to diffuse the impact—as smokejumpers practiced doing for hours each spring. When she finally looked up, he gave her his best unassuming, friendly smile. Quickly he released his chute and left it where it lay, hopping up and then striding toward her in what he hoped was an impressive manner.

But he was the one who was impressed. She was magnificent— there was no doubt about it. Her flaxen hair was tied back again, but the breeze had worked wavy tendrils away from the knot to dance around her heart-shaped face. Reyne brushed away a strand from her eyes, leaving a spot of grease on her face. As he drew closer, he fought off a feeling of helplessness, like a sailor responding to a siren's call, heading directly toward threatening rocks in spite of himself.

"I've been having car trouble myself," Logan said.

Reyne turned to look at him and wiped her greasy hands on a rag. "What kind of trouble?"

"Big trouble. Talk about lemons! Most cars have a spare tire in the trunk; my car has a tow truck."

Reyne did not laugh, but she did allow a tiny smile to pull the upturned corners of her lips—full and rosy—just a shade higher. Deep dimples threatened.

Encouraged, he continued, "It's such a lemon that when I fill up at the gas station, I go inside for a six-pack. Of oil."

Her smile widened.

This was definitely better than Saturday. And Sunday. "You're out early," he said, giving her his most appealing grin.

"Yes. Thought we could get a jump-start on our meeting today, but you were out playing." She bent over the engine again so he could not see her face. Quickly, Logan circled the truck and looked in over the other side. She did not glance up. *You're ten bucks down, Mike. Easy money, easy money! Now for the next twenty!*

"Why don't you go start the engine," he suggested quietly, taking the wrench from her hand. She looked up at him as if to argue, then seemed to shrug internally and acquiesce.

A second later, the starter whirred, but nothing happened. Logan moved to another part of the engine and yelled, "Try 'er again!" Reyne did so, but still he could not see anything wrong. He moved again. "One more try!"

Still nothing. But everything was in working order. Logan frowned. These old engines were fairly simple contraptions.

Reyne ducked in under the hood again, and the two debated various problems. It was soon evident that she knew as much as he, and he hid his smile of approval. *A woman who knows engines. I'm going to have to marry her.*

Suddenly a thought came to him. "Uh, Reyne, I know this is probably a stupid question...but how much fuel do you have?"

Reyne shot him a fiery look as if to say, "Of all the stupid, inconsiderate..." Then she winced, looking away. "Oh shoot," she began. "I thought about it a hundred times yesterday." She walked back to the cab, climbed in, and sighed as he looked at her through the windshield.

"Out of gas?" he asked gently.

She nodded mutely, looking pained to be caught in such an

embarrassing blunder. She got out and slammed the hood shut. "I want you to know that I've never done this before."

Logan nodded, his lips clamped shut against a smile. On top of losing the research grant, this must seem intolerable. "Come on," he said, nodding his head toward the terminal and the new smoke-jumper building. "I'm sure we've got a gas can somewhere."

They walked up the road side by side, talking about trucks and engines and how they had both put vehicles back together from scratch. "I sold mine when I graduated college," he said, glancing at her. She seemed genuinely pleased to be conversing with someone who knew engines. "I've been sorry ever since."

"What do you drive now?"

"Oh, just an old sedan. Most of the time, it gets me where I need to go. But it doesn't have near the character of my '51 Chevy."

Reyne nodded in appreciation. "A '51 Chevy, huh? They're great vehicles. Split rear windows. You open the hood, and it's so clean and spare you can stand in there with the engine." She looked off in the distance as if visualizing herself doing just that.

I'm definitely going to marry this one.

"What made you sell it?" Her question jerked him back to the present.

"The right price."

She nodded. "I love almost everything about them, but I'll tell you, there are times when I'm on the road for a while that I'd give my right arm for something with a little better ride."

"Yeah, they've improved shocks a lot over the years," Logan agreed. A thought came to him. "Hey, maybe you can help me find a new '51 to fix up."

"Maybe," she hedged, raising her eyebrows.

Still, Logan thought, he had better push when he had the chance. They were connecting, and who knew how long it would last? "How about Saturday? We could head out to that salvage yard outside of Evergreen and find my next golden steed."

"Saturday? Oh no, that won't work. I...I have plans."

In his head, he saw Mike Moser's twenty-dollar bill blowing away in the breeze. "Oh, come on, Reyne. You can't get away for a few hours? I need someone I can trust to scout out half the salvage yard."

But her mind was clearly made up. "Nope. Sorry. I'm busy."

Logan stifled a sigh and opened the door to the new log building at the airstrip for her. Above them was a sign that read: GREATER NW FORESTRY CO. "Madam," he said as he gestured grandly, encouraging her to enter.

CHAPTER SIX

*R*eyne was impressed. The forestry company had spared no expense in outfitting their innovative private firefighting force. There had been talk for years about such an enterprise and musings about how it could change the face of firefighting as they knew it. But Reyne had purposefully avoided the structure up until now, content with her behind-the-scenes work in fire.

Inside the huge log building were several tiny offices, a bank of televisions and computer screens that would eventually serve as a command center during fire season, a weightroom in which person-nel could work out, locker rooms, a room full of bunk beds, a mess hall where several firefighters sat drinking coffee, a sewing room—every jumper was certified to run a commercial sewing machine to repair parachutes and protective gear—and a giant open area.

The air inside was cold and damp. The floor was concrete, and the ceiling soared a full four stories above them. A faux cliff had been constructed along one wall for rock climbing and rescue exercises. Twenty ropes descended from beams high above, useful for climbing and parachute training.

"They hope to build a hangar next summer," Logan commented as Reyne looked around. "Funding is short, even for a private forestry company." She glanced up at him quickly, and he looked as if he wanted to bite his tongue for reminding her. "I'm on loan from the BLM to help build their hotshot and smokejumper crew this summer. If the forestry company's holdings aren't on fire, we'll contract out with the BLM and the Forest Service.

"Come over here," he rushed on, eager to share everything with her. They walked over to the series of ropes and climbed up a ladder to a small platform surrounded by a large net. Grabbing a tiny remote control, Logan motioned for her to don what appeared to be a parachute setup without the chute. She took off her coat and did as he bid. He did the same in a similar setup beside her.

"Ready?" Logan asked her. He started to check all the connections on her gear himself, but she batted his hands away.

"I'm fine. Let's go."

He raised his eyebrows in concern but nodded. "Okay. Here we go."

Logan pressed two buttons, and an electric winch sprang into action, hoisting them high above. Reyne fought not to gasp as they sailed upward, her stomach flipping as they did so. When they finally came to a halt, she said, "Well, I've smokejumped enough down, but never up."

"I know," he said, grinning at her. "Isn't it great? This way we can simulate tree accidents and figure out if our equipment will work. You said you've been a smokejumper?"

"Spent a summer on a jumper crew."

"Good. Then you're aware of what danger a jumper is in when he gets hung up in the trees."

"Or when *she* gets hung up."

"Yeah. Sure," he said with a grin. "The trouble is that you're sitting up here, waiting for your buddies to find you, praying that it's before the wind changes and makes you a big smokin' hot dog on a stick, and there isn't much you can do. If your chute is caught on a branch"—he motioned above him at the fictional parachute—"that will give way when you clip your letdown gear to it, you're in big trouble.

"Up to now, as you know, jumpers had to pray that the chute would stay put or that there was a nearby sturdy branch. But with my support pouch, hopefully that will be a thing of the past."

"So what do you want from me?" Reyne asked. "You need help figuring out what to put in the pouch?"

Logan ignored her sarcasm. "I need help on a lot of fronts. We need to figure out how to build this device and then make the contents as small as possible. Obviously, the less they have to carry the better."

Reyne smiled, thinking of her jumper days. Smokejumpers traditionally donned heavy, thick apparel and wire-masked helmets as protection from the trees. The last thing they needed was another piece of equipment to carry. But Logan was right. If she was hung up in the trees, she'd want a better way out than the Swiss army knife they all carried. Reyne had been hung up before, but she had been situated in a way that she was able to cut the cords and climb down the sturdy trunk, not rely on a chute caught in flimsy branches and a letdown rope dangling beneath it.

Her friend had been lowering herself from a perch sixty feet up when the wind had changed and her chute had become unsnagged. It had taken Reyne's team hours to carry her broken, twisted body to a clearing for a helicopter pickup. And it had taken months for her to recuperate. She had never returned to fight fire.

"Okay," Reyne said slowly. "This really is not my field of expertise, but I'd say we need some trees with sturdy branches or planking in here to simulate a hang-up. And you and I can talk equipment…how we can get it down to bare minimums, where we place the pouch, and then how we modify it all."

Logan dangled beside her, smiling.

"What?" she asked, irritated by his smug look.

"You're buying into my project. Taking ownership. I like it."

"Yeah, well, I don't have much choice now, do I?"

"Nope," he said, grinning even more widely.

"I can give you three to five hours a week, tops. I've got a regular job to hold down too, you know."

"That's fine. Can you clear your desk a little so we can start next week?"

"Probably," she said. "Why don't you come to my office, and I'll show you some of the metal samples that might work for this project. I say we make it work in whatever size is easiest to develop, then concentrate on making it as small as possible."

"Okay," he said, grinning again.

Reyne tried to push away her irritation but failed. "Listen, Logan, I don't need you gloating over all of this."

His face fell. "Oh, I'm not gloating. I'm just glad to have a partner in this research. It really will save lives."

Reyne considered his words and then nodded. "Okay. Then let's get on with it. Show me what you have so far."

Logan pushed two more buttons, and the winches let them descend slowly.

Reyne unbuckled herself and walked with him to a worktable covered with various straps and climbing equipment. After they talked awhile, Logan fetched a gas can, filled it from a huge tank outside, and came back to her. "I'll carry it to your truck for you if you'll go salvage-yard hunting with me next Saturday," he said, trying again.

She took the can from him and smiled sassily back into his eyes. "No need. I can manage quite well on my own," she said. "And I already told you. I have plans for Saturday." With that, she turned and walked toward the door. As she was leaving, Logan's voice called to her.

"We'll see about Saturday. I haven't given up. Give me half a chance, Reyne Oldre, and I'll give you better things to do on the weekend as well as during the workweek!"

Shaking her head with a stifled grin, she walked out into the sunshine.

As the door closed behind her, Mike Moser called over to Logan. "So, what do you owe me, buddy?"

"You owe *me* ten," he said. "But I owe you twenty. I got under the hood of the truck, but I made no headway on the dating highway."

Mike and three other guys hooted in laughter. Logan soon learned that Reyne Oldre, although widely admired, had let few men near her. She was friendly enough, just never open to anything more than that.

"Until me," he said with bravado, straddling a chair backward and looking them all over. "I'll get her to give me a second look soon enough."

"Oh yeah?" Mike challenged. He pulled up a chair to the table and brought out a deck of cards, expertly shuffling. "From what you told me, you're fighting an uphill battle. You captured her R&D money. Now you think you can get her interested in you?"

"Better than that. Let's make our bet more interesting," Logan said quietly. "Give me until the end of the summer to marry that woman. You can give her fifty bucks at our wedding dance, or I'll give you a hundred as you walk out the door for the winter."

The guys hooted and hollered, the sounds echoing in the rafters above them. "You're on," Mike said, shaking Logan's hand. "Easiest money I've ever made, my friend. Easiest money I've ever made."

CHAPTER SEVEN

*R*eyne frowned as she drove up to the Tanners' on Saturday afternoon, wondering who was there besides herself and the Morgans. She did not recognize the other car.

Her attention was drawn away from the house by the horses in the adjoining field, who were prancing about like circus performers. Reyne laughed out loud as a large, gray stallion named Cyrano charged a dun-colored mare and then shied away at the last instant when she stood her ground, unperturbed.

I hope we can ride today, she thought as she drove by the cavorting horses. They seemed ready to get out, and she winced at the thought of sitting inside on such a gorgeous day. She pulled up beside the Morgans' new Suburban and hopped out of her truck.

She knocked briefly on the front door and then let herself in when no one answered. "Hello?" she called. "Hello! Anyone home?" She heard voices in the kitchen and headed toward the sound. That was when she made out Logan's voice and the response of her friends' great belly laughter. Hope's delighted squeals and screams rang in the midst of it all.

Reyne rounded the corner, peeking in. Logan was lifting the child high up in the air and then swooping her down in a deft move. She dissolved into wild giggles, and Logan laughed with her. For the first time Reyne noticed how his face was creased at the eyes and cheeks, obviously from smiling all the time. *What a happy man he is,* she mused. She took a few steps backward into the Tanners' living room, then moved forward again to feign recent entry.

"Hey, you guys!" she said, "Are you trying to pretend that you're not home so I'll go away?"

"Reyne!" "Hi there!" "Where've you been?" was their chorused response.

"Hi, Reyne," Logan said quietly, drawing near. "It's good to see you."

Reyne ignored her quickened pulse, playing it cool. "Logan," she said with a nod. "I didn't realize you had made my friends yours already." She winced inwardly at her own words. "I mean…I didn't mean…"

"Reyne," he said, reaching out to touch her forearm. "It's okay. Yeah, they were nice enough to invite me over for an afternoon of riding and dinner."

"We're going riding?" Reyne said excitedly, glad to turn the conversation. She glanced at Beth, who looked rather ashen. Reyne immediately curbed her excitement. "I had hoped we could. Do you feel up to it, Beth? I mean, we could sit and play cards."

"No way," Beth said, her tone brooking no argument. "It's too beautiful to be stuck inside. Matt and I are going to baby-sit the kids and work on supper while you four ride. We'll expect you back by six. Now all of you…get going!"

"Are you sure—," Rachel began, obviously feeling guilty about leaving Samuel with them too.

"Out!" Beth said, her face a mock warning. "Don't argue with someone who has cancer. Running other people's lives is one of the last things I have left to enjoy."

Beth's forced laughter encouraged everyone to get going, out of the house. They shook off the pall that had overtaken them with her words and headed to the stables.

While Dirk and Logan went to get the saddles from the barn, Rachel and Reyne climbed the corral railing to bring in the horses. "She looks bad today," Reyne said quietly.

"Yes."

"Has she said anything to you? Is she in pain? Has she been to the doctor recently?"

"In response to your questions, no, I don't know, and I don't think so," Rachel said, waving her arms to herd a mare toward the barn.

"Oh, Rachel. I get so worried about her!"

"I know. I know. She's so independent that she won't even talk to me about it anymore. I hope she's talking to Matt. She needs someone."

They grew silent, thinking. Neither wanted to intrude on Beth's privacy. But neither of them wanted her to die. They needed her. Matt needed her. Little Hope needed her.

The group spent the afternoon riding high into the mountains behind the ranch, stopping periodically to look across the valley to the towering Rockies, and talking about whatever came to mind.

"I can see why they call it the Continental Divide," Rachel said in admiration as they paused once more at a clearing. "No matter how long I live here, I'm still amazed every time I take the time to see it. It's as if you could just picture the two plates of the continent colliding and then pushing upward."

"They are beautiful," Reyne said. The men nodded, silent in their agreement. She looked up at Logan and found him staring at her rather than at the mountains. Reyne quickly glanced away, blushing at his open admiration. She was relieved to hear Dirk suggest they head back.

"Beth will have supper on soon, and I for one don't want to be late," he said. Reyne pictured Beth with a wooden spoon, feigning anger over their tardiness.

"Me neither," she said with a laugh.

They moved into single file and were heading down a narrow path over a rock-slide area when Reyne's mare slipped on the loose shale and stumbled before regaining her footing. Before she knew what was happening, Reyne was out of the saddle and struggling to keep herself from somersaulting down the mountain. She managed to finally stop her descent about forty feet from where she fell.

"Reyne!" Rachel called. "Are you okay?"

She shook her head to clear her vision and was about to answer when the crunch of rocks made her aware that someone had come after her. She squinted into the sun and sighed when she made out Logan's body and face. He knelt beside her, earnestly scanning for injuries.

Logan took her hand and cradled her face with his hand. "Did you break anything?" he asked worriedly.

"No," she said, embarrassed by his attention. "I'm fine. Just a little scraped and bruised."

"You're sure? You're bleeding all over. No neck or back problems? That was a nasty fall." He again looked her over like a paramedic on the combat field.

"Logan, I'm fine. If you'll just help me up—"

But before she was to a standing position, Logan had swept her up and was carrying her back to the trail as if she were as light as a feather. *And I'm hardly a feather*, she thought. "Logan! Really, I can walk."

"Let me do this, Reyne. I want to get you up to the trail and have another look at you. You may be in shock."

"Well, sure," she allowed. "But I'm aware enough to know that I'm not in mortal danger. Now put me down. I'll walk the rest of the way."

"No chance, Oldre. You're the accident victim," he huffed, still moving upward. "I'm the mighty rescuer," he added. "Don't ruin my big moment."

Reyne smiled in spite of herself and allowed him to carry her the rest of the way in peace. But she avoided meeting Rachel and Dirk's eyes when they reached the trail. *What has gotten into me?*

Logan set her down on the path.

"Are you okay?" Rachel asked worriedly, rushing over to her side. Logan pressed on her bleeding wounds with a handkerchief.

"I'm fine, Rachel. I think the only thing that's really hurt is my pride. I've been bucked off a horse, but I've never fallen off one." All of a sudden, she thought of the mare. "How's Cookie? Is she okay?"

Dirk nodded slightly. "She's thrown a shoe, and she's got a nasty cut on her fetlock, but it's nothing that won't heal." He looked sick to his stomach as he took in Reyne's injuries. "I'm sorry, Reyne. I was in the lead. I should've known better. We should've been leading the horses instead of riding. You could have been killed."

"Oh, Dirk, it's okay. I could've gotten off Cookie if I'd wanted to. I just thought we'd have no problem. She didn't slip a bit on the way up. It's not your fault."

Logan knelt and began checking her leg, obviously looking for breaks.

"Logan!" she said, shooing his hands away. "I'm fine! I told you, I'm all right."

He looked at her with mistrust in his eyes. "Are you sure you're not in shock and just not able to differentiate what's broken and what's not?"

Reyne clenched her lips and stood with some effort. She stepped closer to him, poking him lightly in the chest. "I'll have you know that I've reached a Class Four certification in search and rescue. I am a certified EMT, and I have made countless rescues of my own. I'm smart enough to know when I'm in shock, thank you very much, and can *certainly* tell when I've broken a leg!"

Logan backed off a step, raising his hands in surrender as she followed him, lecturing all the way. When she finally stopped, he looked back down into her eyes and began laughing silently, great belly heaves that lifted his chest and brought water to his eyes.

Reyne allowed a tiny smile to raise her own lips in response, knowing that she had finally won a round. She looked back at Rachel and Dirk, who were also laughing. "Boy, you guys pick the pushiest people in the world to be your friends, don't ya?"

Relieved that she was all right, Logan and Dirk still insisted that she ride on Logan's gelding while the rest of them picked their way over the rock-slide area on foot. Then Logan mounted behind her, strapping Cookie's reins to his saddle so that she could follow without carrying any undue weight.

Rachel and Dirk rode on ahead, wanting to warn Beth and Matt that they were running late. Logan and Reyne followed more slowly, taking their time so as not to push Cookie. As Logan talked softly to the mare over his shoulder, Reyne had to admit to herself that his strong arms felt good at her sides.

They had reached the valley floor but were still quite a ways from the house. To their left, a long line of irrigation pipe was spewing water in pulsating, circulating jets. In the early evening sunshine, it threw a shimmering rainbow against the bright green of the grazing grasses beneath. The effect was mesmerizing, and Reyne sighed happily. The earth smelled good, like the rich black soil that ran through her fingers when she gardened. It smelled of new grass and water and peat and a hint of manure.

She held the reins, but Logan held the saddle horn in front of her. It had been a long time since she had been this close to a man. As their bodies matched the easy cadence of his horse, both grew silent, listening to the *clop-clop* of the horses' hooves, the creak of their leather saddle, and the gentle buzz and whir of God's world all about them.

Logan lifted his head to feel Reyne's hair in his face, relishing the smell and the silky strands tickling his cheeks. He did not get too close, fearing he'd make her uneasy, although he longed to bury his face in the soft, blond waves in front of him. He knew without a doubt that he wanted to know Reyne Oldre better. If only she'd let him in!

"Are you doing okay?" he asked, using the excuse of talking to her to draw his face closer to hers.

"I'm fine," she said, tensing. Then after a pause, "Boy, at this rate, we'll be lucky to get to the house by dark."

Logan listened carefully to her tone, hoping to see if she really was in a hurry to be away from him or was just making conversation. He was unable to tell. "We'll get there," he said easily. He, for one, would not mind if it took until midnight.

"Logan," she said after another few minutes, "what made you want to go into smokejumping?"

He sat back a bit, startled by her first personal question. Maybe she was warming up to him after all. "Smokejumping? Well for one, my dad and grandfather were both forest-fire fighters. My dad was a jumper. He filled my head with so many war stories that I grew up thinking I wanted to wear his shoes when he left. You know…take on the enemy myself. Prove I was a man. After I felt like I had proven myself—and I took a ton of stupid chances doing so—I thought it was time to retire. But it was only then that I realized how much I loved it."

Reyne nodded, seemingly in approval.

Logan went on, encouraged. "I loved not only the rush of taking on the fire, but also figuring out where he was heading next, what he was thinking, if you will. I liked outsmarting him. And when he out-smarted me, I liked taking him on again and beating him."

"You should've gone into fire science," she said. "Figuring out what he's up to, outsmarting him…that's all a part of what I do."

"Yeah," Logan said gently, "but there's no hand-to-hand combat."

"Exactly," Reyne said, almost in a whisper. Logan had to strain to hear her.

"You retreated to the back lines because of what happened with Oxbow, didn't you?" he tried.

She stiffened slightly. "You don't know anything about me, Logan," she said defensively. "Someday I'll tell you about Oxbow. Until then, please don't try to psychoanalyze me."

"I'm sorry, Reyne. I didn't mean—"

"It's okay," she interrupted. She glanced up and said, "Ah, Timberline at last. We can finally get Cookie to some tender loving care."

At her sudden change of subject, Logan grew silent. It was obviously still a sore spot for her. He needed to let her open up in her own way, in her own time.

They rode the rest of the way in silence, both lost in their own thoughts.

CHAPTER EIGHT

*L*ogan hung up the phone with a decisive click, grinning at the familiar surge of adrenaline that always came with a new assignment. *Time to get this show on the road,* he was thinking. But then his smile drooped just a little. Almost without thinking, he picked up the phone again and dialed.

"Hello, this is Reyne Oldre." Her voice was friendly but businesslike.

"Reyne," he said, faltering, wondering why he was calling her. They hadn't spoken since their ride the day before. "I, um...I just wanted you to know that they've called me to Missoula."

"Okay," she said.

"Well, I...I was thinking that we wouldn't be able to get together on the smokejumper pouch until next week. Will that be okay?"

"That'll be fine. I've got more than enough to do." She was silent for a moment. Logan was about to say something else when she went on. "Are you going down for spring training?"

Logan felt a smile melt away the concerned furrow of his brow. Her question was an opening at least. "It's the beginning of spring training. I'm supposed to form my Elk Horn team. Half experienced. Half rookies."

"Half rookies!" she exclaimed. "Boy, I bet you'll be swamped with applications. There haven't been that many openings on a crew in years."

Logan had paced while talking with her and now paused to wind the phone cord around his arm in snake fashion. "I know it. I'm hoping to get six guys I've worked with for years to form the backbone of the team, then fill in from there."

"Sounds like a good plan."

Logan felt strangled, scanning his head frantically in an effort to find something else to say. When he remained silent, Reyne's voice came over the line again. "Well, I hope your trip is fruitful. Give me a call when you get home so we can arrange a meeting."

"Oh. Okay," he said, feeling like a teenager. Why was he so disappointed that their conversation was over? Did he think it was going to go on for hours?

"Bye, Reyne."

On the other end Reyne thoughtfully pressed the button on her cordless phone and disconnected the line. She took off her reading glasses and looked out her studio window to the towering line of the Rockies. What had Logan really been after? She smiled, wondering if he was more interested in her than their project. He certainly was acting that way. And for once, it felt all right that a man was pursuing her.

Are you speaking to me, Father? She looked outside at the tulip leaves shooting up from the black dirt, a fresh green that only spring could bring. Reyne felt as if her heart were shooting up and out, just like those flowers. She frowned suddenly. *But he's a smokejumper. A firefighter. Please, God, anyone but a firefighter.*

Once again, unbidden, came those images, the ones that haunted her dreams and drove her in her work. The charred meadow. The reek of the smoke. The crumpled, empty fire tents. And beyond them…

She leaned back in her chair, set her feet on the desk, and closed her eyes, deliberately pushing back the images. *Please God, not a smokejumper,* she prayed again. *Anything but that. I just couldn't stand to lose someone I love…*

But the urgings of her heart were unstoppable.

The next day Reyne entered her office to find a faxed note waiting. She smiled immediately, spotting Logan's name in the From section. She sat down, amazed that just his name on a piece of paper set her heart to pounding, and then read his short note:

> HI, REYNE. MISSING ME YET? WAS WORRIED THAT NO
> ONE WAS GOING TO MAKE YOU LAUGH TODAY, SO I
> THOUGHT I'D SEND THIS COMIC. HARDLY PROFES-
> SIONAL, I KNOW. BUT WHAT THE HECK.

Reyne glanced over the comic strip, smiling as Calvin set Hobbes's foot on fire, then ran to get away. She didn't know what was funnier: the cartoon or Logan's all-caps style writing. *Just like in life, Logan,* she thought. *Bigger and louder is always better.*

But she was charmed. There was no getting around it.

Five days later, coffee cup in hand, Rachel Tanner came strolling into Reyne's office. "I want to see what you're working on these days," she said. "Oh, you've got a fax…"

Reyne, just behind her, squeezed through the door and hurried toward the machine, but Rachel had already plucked the paper from its tray.

Smiling, she read the missive and handed it to Reyne. "You have some 'splainin' to do, Lucy," she said, in her best Ricky Ricardo imitation.

Reyne gave her a sly smile and ripped the paper from her hands. "I most certainly do not."

Rachel sat on the countertop and stared at her. "Oh yes you do. Are you telling me that a firefighter is courting you and you're actually allowing it?"

"What am I supposed to do? Shut off my fax? He's just being friendly," she tried, hoping to sidetrack her friend.

"Ha! That's the friendliest fax I've seen in a long while. And what are these?" She picked up the stack of previous faxes and paged through them quickly. "Every day? He's been sending you one every day?"

Reyne nodded, smiling. "What do you think?"

"I think he's terrific! And romantic! And sweet. We've already covered the handsome part. Are you telling me that you're actually giving him a chance? I thought you'd sworn off firefighters."

Reyne moved away, pacing. Her mind was a mass of thoughts, her heart a frantic mix of emotions. "I don't know, Rachel. I *had* sworn off firefighters. This is crazy." Her voice was tight, agitated.

"Reyne," Rachel said gently. "I know it was rough that day in Idaho. I know you've suffered since then. But maybe God is telling you that it's time to get on with your life. To share your heart again."

"And it would be just like him to make that person a firefighter."

"Through him all things are possible—"

"Yeah, yeah, spare me the sermon. I *know*, Rachel. But I'm scared. Scared to death. And who knows? Maybe he's just idly flirting."

"He doesn't seem to be the type. For all his joking around, from what I can see, he's pretty single-minded."

Reyne nodded thoughtfully. "Well, we'll see what happens. I'm not making any moves. We'll see what Logan McCabe is really up to."

The following morning Reyne dressed quickly and headed out to the office before the coffee was even brewed. She threw open the door and had to mentally keep herself from actually trotting over to the outbuilding. Smiling already, she crossed immediately to the fax machine.

But there was nothing there.

She fought the wave of disappointment that swept over her and chided herself for fighting back tears. *What's this, Oldre? You're tougher than that!*

She shook her head, unable to believe that she had let herself get so worked up over a silly fax. Reyne opened the door and slammed it behind her, eager to get back to her coffee now. Logan McCabe did not owe her a thing. So why was she so disappointed?

Reyne spent the rest of the morning reading firefighters' detailed reports and studying her figures. Much of her job entailed helping the interagency command center study satellite reports and deploy the appropriate troops to fight fires as they occurred. On most days, when there were few fires, she studied old data, charts, film, or footage to try and make sense of certain fire behavior.

That's what she was doing today. Studying old data, trying to develop new firefighting strategies. Or that's what she was trying to do anyway. Every minute sound seemed to distract her. Then she realized that she was listening so hard for the facsimile machine to begin transmitting that she could almost hear the blood pulsating in her ears.

Finally, three hours later, the quiet ring sang out, and the machine began to print. She sighed and then rose to wait beside the machine, laughing as she reached shaking hands to grab the paper it spit out. She felt lightheaded, delirious. *What is happening to me?*

She scanned Logan's words and doodle, giggling as soon as she saw them.

REYNE: THE PICTURE IS OF YOU AND ME HAVING DIN-
NER FRIDAY NIGHT. STOP LAUGHING AT IT. I SAID STOP
IT. I'M A SMOKEJUMPER, NOT AN ARTIST. ANYWAY, I
WAS THINKING THAT WHEN I GOT HOME I'D TAKE MY
COLLEAGUE OUT FOR A BUSINESS DINNER TO TALK
OVER OUR PROJECT. I KNOW A GREAT PLACE JUST OUT-
SIDE OF ELK HORN. DO YOU THINK THAT WOULD BE
TOO FORWARD OF ME? PLEASE ADVISE. LOVE, LOGAN.

P.S. IT'S SO HOT HERE THAT IF THERE WAS A WAX
MUSEUM, JOHN WAYNE WOULD BE THE SIZE OF
MICKEY ROONEY. IT'S SO HOT HERE THAT THE FRUIT
OF THE LOOM LABEL'S GRAPES HAVE TURNED TO
RAISINS.

Reyne giggled, but her mind was still back on his closing: *Love, Logan. Love, Logan. Stop it, Reyne! It means nothing!* But her heart pounded, and she was glad that no one was around to see the silly grin on her face.

What is this, Father? I feel your urging, but I am so scared. I don't want to lose someone I care about again. Not ever.

She sobered as she pictured Logan fighting fire this summer. Pictured him facing the dragon and the dragon winning.

"No," she said aloud. "No, Father. I can only do this if you protect him." Her voice changed from anger to pleading. "Please take care of him, Father. I can't handle it. If I do this—if I risk my heart, I can't handle losing it. I swear I can't."

Reyne sighed when no answer, no reassurance came to her. She stared outside for what seemed hours, just thinking and playing out different scenarios in her head. "Life is a risk, Oldre," she told herself. "Nothing risked, nothing gained."

Then she sat down at her computer and typed out a message to Logan:

> Logan, it would indeed be wise to spend time with your colleague. You never know what could transpire when two people talk about fire. See you Friday at six.
>
> P.S. My computers tell me it's only eighty-four degrees there. Stop your whining.

But as she faxed it through, all that ran through her head was that she was playing with fire—and there seemed to be no way to stop herself.

CHAPTER NINE

*R*eyne paced inside her cottage, anxiously waiting for the clock to tick past 5:55. She actually crossed over to the digital display at one point and tapped it, wondering if it was stuck, then checked her kitchen clock, which assured her that it was right on time. At 5:59 she spotted him on the highway from Elk Horn and watched as he turned onto the dirt road that led to her home.

Her heart skipped a beat, and she swallowed hard. "Get ahold of yourself, Reyne," she muttered, wondering how Logan McCabe had managed to get under her skin so quickly. She positioned herself by a window where she could watch his approach without being seen.

He pulled into her driveway and hopped out. To Reyne, he seemed even more handsome than before. Long, sturdy legs were encased in narrow jeans. He wore an off-white Henley under a dark green V-neck sweater and a big brown Stetson that added inches to his already impressive height. He took it off as he approached her door, and she could have sworn that he was talking to himself as he climbed her porch steps.

After he knocked, Reyne counted to five before she moved toward the front door. Then she forced herself to walk in an easy manner and opened the door with a smile.

His face lit up when he saw her. He actually took a half-step as if he wanted to take her in his arms and hug her, but then he regained control. "Reyne," he said with a nod, turning his hat over and over in his hands. "It's great, really great to see you."

"It's good to see you too, Logan," she said, amazed her voice could sound so cool when her insides felt like churning butter. "Did you want to come in? Or should we go straight to dinner?"

"Oh, you thought *you* were the colleague I was asking out for dinner?" Logan deadpanned. "No, I was talking about Ken."

Reyne gave him a sidelong look. "Well, call him and tell him you'll have to give him a rain check 'cause I'm all ready and am very intrigued with where you're taking me. There's only one restaurant in Elk Horn, and that's a pretty sad café. Is that the 'great little place' you were talking about?"

Logan flashed her a mischievous smile. "There's no pulling the wool over your eyes, woman," he said. "Let's go, and I'll show you." She followed him outside, and he opened the car door for her.

"I'm on to you, McCabe," she said saucily. She averted her eyes, trying to maintain her cool facade.

Logan climbed in beside Reyne and started the engine. He put his arm behind her on the seat and looked over his shoulder to reverse. "You know," he said idly as they backed up, "it feels great to have a woman figure me out." He stopped, shifted gears, and waited for her eyes to meet his. "To be honest, it feels terrific."

They turned out on the highway, and Reyne was so entertained by his stories of spring training in Missoula that she barely kept track of where they were going. Logan was in the midst of a hilarious story about a rookie stuck on the jump tower, refusing to come down, when they turned off the highway and headed up a side road.

Reyne had been laughing so hard that she cried. How great it felt to laugh like this again! How long had it been? She wiped her eyes, still giggling, and asked, "Okay, McCabe, just where are you taking me? We're way past the café, and I know for a fact that there are no tourist lodges or restaurants this way."

"Oh, you know that for a fact, do you?" he said. "I'm almost certain that I saw something up here the other day."

Reyne was puzzled, but she was in such a merry mood that she was not about to dispel it with an argument. He'd find out soon enough that there was nothing around here for miles, and then they would turn around. She dared to glance up at him.

He was staring ahead, carefully maneuvering past huge potholes as they climbed higher and higher on the mountain road. His burly arm and hand held the wheel effortlessly, and Reyne found herself wondering what it would feel like to have that arm around her—and not just reaching for a saddle horn. She quickly forced her eyes back to the road.

They pulled to a stop at last, and Reyne looked around at the forest that surrounded them, smiling suspiciously. "See, I—"

"We're here!" he said, hopping out of the car and coming around to let her out too.

"We're where, McCabe? There's no place to eat around here for miles!" She stood with her hands on her hips and stared at him in puzzlement.

"Oh ye of little faith," he said, stepping past her and opening up the trunk. Pulling out a giant picnic basket, he smiled at her smugly. "Follow me, madam."

Logan relished every moment of Reyne's surprise. He loved to see delight visibly spread across her face as they entered the clearing and she discovered the elaborate setup he had constructed. What woman would not be charmed?

In front of them lay a huge, old scrapped parachute, which covered the ground and provided a thin, silky carpet for them. In the middle of it stood a tiny antique oak table and two mismatched chairs that Logan had borrowed from the airstrip building. He had covered the table with a white cloth, again made of old parachute material. Its edges billowed gently in the cool mountain breeze, and Reyne shivered, rubbing her arms.

"Cold?" Logan asked. "Hold on one second. I'll be right back." He left her standing there, gazing out to the incredible view of the valley below them. Trotting back to the trunk, he unwound a length of electric cord and connected it to another cord that was hidden by the brush. Then he started up a small, portable generator that sat in his trunk and returned to Reyne.

She laughed as he uncovered a giant outdoor heater that glowed red within seconds. "Pretty snazzy, Logan, but don't you think it's a bit of a fire danger?"

"No chance," he said. "I came up here and laid a gravel foundation for it. Besides, the brush is still pretty green, and I've got this." He opened the picnic basket and pulled out a tiny extinguisher.

He raised one eyebrow in what he hoped was a suave expression. "I know what you're thinking. 'He appears to have thought of everything,'" he mimicked in a high, thoughtful voice. "But wait! There's more! Please, have a seat," he said, pulling out a chair for her.

Before he left her side again, he brought out napkins, silverware, dinner plates, wineglasses, two candles, and a tape recorder. He pressed Play, starting the instrumental music, showed off a bit by lighting the candles with a match struck on his jeans, filled her goblet, and again retreated.

Chuckling to himself, Logan went for another cord and prepared to make yet another connection. This time, however, he wanted to see her face. She was sipping from her glass, looking out at the sunset, when he stuck the metal prongs into the plastic holes. All around her, hundreds of tiny white lights lit up. In the trees, in the brush, around the base of the clearing, looped from the branches. It had taken him hours to string them all.

Logan pushed away the unwanted thought of how long it would take to unstring them tomorrow. All he wanted to think about was Reyne. He wanted to know everything about the fascinating woman before him, and maybe, just maybe, he'd learn more tonight.

Her eyes sparkled in the soft glow of the tiny lights as she smiled at him. She was worth all this and more. *How has this one remained alone?* he asked of God silently, smiling back at her. "Like it?" he asked, waving about.

"Like it? I love it!" she said. "Now please, waiter, sit down and have dinner with me. What are we having? Pizza?"

"Oh no, no, no," he said, seating himself. He had placed her where she could get the best view of the valley. But he had carefully selected his own seat earlier that afternoon, knowing that he only wanted to study her as they talked. "We have much more than that." He reached down into the basket and pulled out two salad plates covered with plastic wrap, then a covered container of dressing.

They ate their salads while Logan heated their foil-wrapped entrées on a shelf beside the heater. After a while he brought out a basket of sliced French bread and unwrapped their stuffed chicken breasts.

"Those look wonderful," she exclaimed as he served her plate. "Did you make them yourself?"

"Yep," he said with a grin, gesturing from his head to his toe. "All this beauty, and a good little cook as well. What a bargain. And I can fight fires, too."

She just smiled and picked up her fork.

The evening grew darker and darker as they ate, and their secret little wilderness room grew more and more dramatic. Logan noticed that the deepening shadows heightened the angles of Reyne's cheekbones, the gentle slope of her eyebrows, the tiny cleft in her chin. Her eyes sparkled in the light as she leaned forward, telling him a story. They reminded him of his grandmother's eyeglasses at Christmastime.

He watched her intently as she talked, enjoying the feeling of a full stomach, a romantic setting, and a beautiful, interesting, animated woman across from him. Logan found himself wanting to know everything about her, not just the surface things. Not just the fact that her hair looked like spun silk and smelled like spring breezes. Not just the fact that she was smart and passionate about her work. He wanted to know what made her tick. What made her happy. What made her sad.

That thought reminded him of the Oxbow stories he had heard. She seemed relaxed and happy now. Would it destroy everything to remind her of that terrible day? But he knew that it had changed the course of her career. Perhaps it had changed her in other ways he needed to know about.

When she finished her story and took a sip of water, she leaned back, smiling. Logan took a sip of water too, choosing his words carefully. "Reyne," he began, giving her what he hoped was a searching but warm look, "tell me about that day. Tell me about Oxbow."

Reyne's face fell, and Logan's heart jumped to double time. *There you go, Logan, rushing things! You big jerk! You've ruined everything!* He had just begun to back-pedal, saying, "I'm sorry...I, um, wanted...that is if you're ready...," when she held up her hand.

"No, it's okay. I can tell you about it. It was probably the most important day of my life. One of those days when everything changes, you know? Up to that point, I was a carefree kid with a dramatic summer job. After that day, I was dedicated to one thing: fighting the dragon and beating it. And beating it means saving firefighters' lives in the process."

Logan nodded, encouraging her. "Which also gives you passion for fire science and things like your weather-kit project."

"Exactly," she said quietly. She looked like she was a million miles away. He bit his tongue, mentally willing himself to stay quiet and wait, for once.

Reyne had Logan's rapt attention. She spun the story like a professional narrator, although Logan knew for a fact that she rarely spoke about that fateful day. *Must have rehashed it in her head a million times,* he thought. *Guess that's what I would do too.*

Reyne told him all about her crew, the seasoned veterans and the green rookies, about each one's strengths and weaknesses. She told about beating back the baby fire, moving to meet the New Mexicans in the gully, then sensing that something had changed...

It took her half an hour to reach the point in the story where they had hit the meadow. Fifteen minutes later it was as if Logan were with them—he was so caught up in her story—hitting the forest road running, madly deploying shelters as the firestorm reared behind them in a magnificent wall of orange, red, and blue.

She told him about Janice frantically trying to shake out her tent in the midst of the high-velocity winds and about Larry thinking he was doomed because of the rip in his. "And then I was finally shaking my own tent out," she went on, "and it was crazy, but all I could think of was that it was like shaking out a beach blanket in the midst of a hurricane."

Reyne paused, taking a breath as if to preserve strength for what was ahead. "I couldn't have been under the tent for more than two seconds when Oxbow swept over me. I was still tucking flaps, desperately trying to get my knees down to seal him out. All around us, the grasses were catching fire, starting miniature fires inside and under our shelters while the two-thousand-degree heat roared over us. It was like a giant wave rolling past, pushing the shelters down on our backs.

"All around me was flickering light, and I could hear Zeke Johnson still working beside me, trying to deal with his own grass fires inside and keep the seal secure. On my other side was Leanne, who was one of the first down but was green, really green. I could hear her crying." Reyne looked off in the distance, her eyes reflecting the lights more brightly as tears gathered. But her voice remained strong, steady.

"The first wave came off the trees, igniting gases ahead of it. It was so vicious, it lifted most of the tents' edges and filled them with smoke. We were beating out fires with our arms and legs, rolling over them if necessary, while fighting to breathe. The walls of our tents grew too hot to touch, and you know something? There are actually tiny pinholes that glow, just like in the training films.

"The temperature inside climbed. It was unbearable. Still, I was feeling immortal and had a distanced…fascination about the whole thing. It was like I was living out a movie. I thought about dying. But the screaming outside took my mind off it.

"We yelled at each other, begging one another not to give up, not to run. And I swear, everything in you tells you to run. We were checking in. Coaching each other, in a way. Even as people screamed, they were fighting fires, trying to reseal their edges. I was radioing Thomas Wagner every few seconds, but couldn't tell if he was responding. It was too noisy to hear. I wondered if those calls would be the last words I would ever utter.

"Inside our tents, we were all dealing with our own version of hell. We pressed our mouths close to the dirt, cupping our arms around our faces, hoping for one good, clean breath. Then, as the noise increased, we each felt alone. I wondered if I was the only one surviving. I couldn't hear anyone anymore. I started to not think straight. I dug into the earth, searching for clean air I guess. I would take a breath and hold it, then dare to take another. Each was progressively worse. I was dizzy, choking.

"Then all of a sudden, the smoke was gone. It was heaven-sent—no doubt about it." Reyne's expression was distant, dreamy. "I swear Jesus was right there beside me. For a moment I even felt colder air, just like when you're swimming in a lake and suddenly hit a cold spot. I could still hear Oxbow raging, hunting for us, waiting for any opening, but he was moving on. I could hear moaning and thrashing again. I even dared to lift up an edge to peer out. But it was still too hot."

Reyne sighed and took a long drink of water. She looked sad in the soft light, and Logan wanted to take her in his arms. But she had to finish. For herself as much as for him.

"When could you actually get out?" he asked gently.

"A few minutes later. The winds were still there, but they carried no fire. I raised up a little, and the wind took my tent. Thankfully, it was safe then. I stood up and called to Shaw and Zeke, and they stood up too. I was starting to get my hopes up again when I saw them."

She paused, looking away from him. The tears crested her lower lids and ran down her face in glittering rivulets.

"What, Reyne? What did you see?" Logan's voice was a mere whisper.

"Yellow shirts. All around us was this blackened moonscape. Nothing was left. You know how it is. And here and there were yellow shirts. The people who had run. Four were from my crew. Leanne. Frankie. Allen. Janice." She recited the names as if she were embracing each one, remembering. She wept softly and quickly wiped away the tears with the palm of her hand.

Logan went to her and lifted her up, holding her in his arms. "I'm sorry, honey. So sorry. Nobody should ever have to deal with that. Oh, Reyne…"

Reyne cried for five minutes, grieving all over again for the four of her crew she had lost, as well as the ten from the New Mexico crew. Logan left her then, taking blankets and placing them on the ground beside a tree. He sat down, motioning her over, and she silently complied, wiping her face.

She sat in front of him, leaning back against his chest with his strong arms around her. They sat there for a good hour, silently staring at the white lights all around them and the valley lights below and the dim stars far above. And for the first time in a long time Reyne felt safe, even in the swirling memory eddy of the dragon's heyday at Oxbow.

CHAPTER TEN

Over the following weeks, Reyne and Logan became insepa-
rable. They worked together two out of five days, often went
out on Friday night, worshiped together on Sunday morning, and
then spent the afternoon and evening at Reyne's house. Their routine
became comfortable, and both enjoyed it.

One Saturday morning, Reyne padded about the house, sipping
coffee and looking out her windows at another uncommonly warm
spring day. She was happier than she had ever been. She was happy
for the empty house so she could concentrate on how she loved it
when there was a man there too. The comparison felt like something
she wanted to, needed to, explore.

She traced the edge of the couch, picturing Logan sprawled out
on Sunday afternoons, playing with her hair while half dozing. She
would try to concentrate on her magazine, but his touch kept her
mind on anything but the words and pictures before her. Logan
McCabe made her feel relaxed, happy, cherished. *Thank you, Father,
for bringing him into my life.*

Reyne giggled when she thought back to that first day they had
met. How angry she had been! But what would have happened had
they not been competing for the same research money? She might
not have given him a second look, perhaps dismissing him as just
another firefighter. Over the past weeks she had come to admire his

dedication, his resolve, his way of figuring out answers to perplexing dilemmas, his ingenuity, his genuine appreciation of her own abilities. They were a good team. And they had made tremendous progress on the smoke-jumper pouch...

A movement in the yard distracted her from her thoughts, and Reyne glanced up. Beth and Rachel had arrived. Even as her relationship with Logan had escalated, still the two of them had preserved Saturday mornings for their separate friends. Lately, Logan had taken to fishing with guys from his newly formed team, since Matt and Dirk were both "stuck" doing baby care or ranch work.

Rachel rapped on the door, and Reyne padded over to answer it. She opened it, waving them in, and smiled at the old blue jar in Beth's hands. Late spring wildflowers overflowed from it.

"Are those for me?" Reyne asked.

"I guess so," Beth said. "They were sitting on your doorstep."

"A secret admirer?" Rachel kidded, heading directly for the java.

"Hardly secret anymore," Beth retorted. "The whole town is talking."

Reyne sat down, waiting for her friends to join her. She could not stop the smile that spread from ear to ear. "The whole town, huh?"

"Yeah," Rachel said. "Molly the hairdresser was pumping me for information."

"What'd you tell her?" Reyne asked, idly curious.

"All about you two, of course! I wanted her to keep away from your man. Logan is drawing females in this county like bees to honey."

"But it's just like you and Dirk, Rachel," Beth said, accepting a mug from her. "There were many women who would've given their eyeteeth for a date with Dirk Tanner. But he had eyes for one, and one only."

"Ain't that the truth," Rachel said merrily. "It's tough to be so gorgeous that you enslave a man with one mere look in his direction," she quipped, throwing a wave of hair over her shoulder dramatically. "Okay, okay. There's no need to mention the lengths I had to go to get him to take me out!"

"Oh, it didn't take much," Beth said.

"It's hard for me to imagine either one of you with anyone but your particular spouses," Reyne mused, then blurted out, "But how does that happen anyway? I mean, what exactly happens when you marry? Is there something to the two-becoming-one phenomenon?"

Beth raised an eyebrow, considering her words. "I think there is something to it. Matt and I have really tried to maintain our own identities, but there's a bond that's tough to describe. Something spiritual almost. I think God helps us join in a way that makes it tougher to drive us apart."

"Like Siamese twins?" Reyne asked, smiling.

"Something like that, I guess," Rachel said. "You couldn't separate Dirk and me without us each losing something of ourselves. And there was a time when we were like you and Logan are now—joined at the hip for a while so you can learn everything you need to know about one another."

"Yeah, remember those times?" Beth asked, enjoying the memory.

"It was great," Rachel said, smiling at her. She looked to Reyne. "You can't get enough of each other, right?"

"Exactly. Like now. I love you guys, but I can't wait to see Logan later." She waved in front of her to the wildflowers on the table. "He's so sweet. At least once a week he brings me a bouquet of flowers, usually ones he's picked himself. And we talk for hours, sometimes until two in the morning…"

Rachel sighed dramatically, putting on a moon-eyed look that was half silly, half serious. "Ahh, love. And it just gets better. Deeper. Softer."

"Ain't it grand?" Beth asked, putting her head next to Rachel's and looking upward with a similar expression.

"All right, you two," Reyne said, pursing her lips. "You just said that you've both been through this. It's so great now. But it fades, doesn't it? Doesn't that make you sad?"

"Occasionally," Beth said. "I happened to marry a man who's romantically impaired." She giggled. "I mean, Matt's idea of a romantic dinner is ham sandwiches in a fishing boat—while we fish! And yet our love has mellowed into something deeper, richer than I could've ever imagined."

"It's true," Rachel agreed. "The rush of romance does fade some in time. But as Beth says, a good relationship just seems to get better with each year. 'Like a fine wine,' my grandfather used to say. Your communication gets better. You know one another better. It all helps."

"And kids add a whole new dimension," Beth added. "Have you and Logan talked about children? How many do you want?"

"Whoa, whoa, whoa!" Reyne said, laughing. "We're not even talking marriage yet!"

"Well, what's holding up the process?" Rachel kidded her. "You two have been dating for almost a month now! Shouldn't we start planning the wedding?"

"Ooh! Another Elk Horn wedding!" Beth exclaimed. "Can't you

just see her in white, Rachel? I can see this gorgeous, soft-white gown—sort of a sleek design, I think, to show off that figure—"

"Wait, I said," Reyne interrupted, her tone firm. "This is getting a little crazy. I don't want to think about weddings yet."

"Oh right," Beth said.

"No, I mean it," Reyne said, hearing her own voice grow defensive.

Both women looked at her quizzically. Rachel spoke first. "All right, Reyne, what's up?"

Beth leaned forward, setting down her coffee cup. "Yeah, Reyne. Let's hear it."

Reyne rubbed her legs, feeling the rough texture of her jeans. She stood up, puzzled by her own agitation. "Come on, you guys. Lay off, will ya?" She forced a laugh. "I'm just not ready to talk tuxedos and gowns. What's the big deal?"

"Well, for one," Rachel said, putting her feet up on the table and leveling a no-nonsense gaze on Reyne, "I think you wouldn't want to talk weddings if you were afraid it wouldn't happen. Has something happened between you two to make you doubt it?"

"No! Nothing!" She laughed in exasperation. "What is this? The grand inquisition?"

"No," Beth said softly. "But your defensiveness makes us worried."

"He's not a man that can't commit, is he?" Rachel asked bluntly.

"No. At least I don't think so…"

"He hasn't made you uneasy, pushing you physically?" Beth asked gently.

"No. I mean, we have to really work to keep our boundaries clear. But that's *both* of us."

Her friends smiled, but they weren't about to let it go. Reyne glanced from one to the other and then out the window again. She started to pace, then stopped. "Can't we just let this go?"

"No," her friends said in unison.

Reyne sighed, gathering her thoughts. "It's just that…I've been having these awful thoughts…" She looked back at them as if seeking help. "You see, I've had these bad dreams lately. It's like I'm back in Idaho. Back fighting Oxbow."

Beth's mouth formed a silent O, and Rachel nodded, understanding at last.

"The last three nights I've had this dream that I come out from under my fire shelter and there are bodies." Her eyes grew wide as she played it out in her mind yet again. "And one of them is Logan."

"Come here," Rachel said, rising and going to her with outstretched arms. She hugged her fiercely as Reyne giggled in embarrassment.

"It's just a stupid dream," Reyne said, wiping her nose as Beth came to encircle both of them with her own arms.

"But it plays out your worst nightmare," Beth said softly.

After a moment, the three separated and sat back down quietly.

"I'll get us more coffee," Rachel said. She was soon back with the pot, pouring them each a second mug. "So tell us, Reyne. How are you going to get past this so it won't get in the way?"

"I don't know," she said miserably. "To be honest, this is the first time I've really thought it out. I mean, it's been a small nagging thought in the back of my head—especially over the last few days—but until you started talking weddings, I didn't realize how scared I was."

"Have you told Logan?" Beth asked.

"No. It hasn't come up."

"But you've told him about Oxbow?" Rachel asked.

"Yeah. The whole saga, from beginning to end. He asked."

Rachel nodded. "It *is* a big deal. You guys risk your lives when you fight fire. It would be tough for me to send Dirk off to his job thinking I might never see him again."

"But you can't let it get in the way!" Beth said, her voice uncustomarily loud. Her brows were knit in earnestness. "Promise me, Reyne. Promise me that fear won't keep you from loving Logan."

Reyne looked at her, a bit surprised by her intensity. "Okay, Beth. I'll do my best. But I'm just beginning to see that this is an issue for me. I'm not sure I'm ready to risk my heart on someone who is so constantly in danger."

Beth looked down at the floor, choosing her words. "It seems to me that you've already risked your heart. I think you love Logan McCabe."

Reyne's eyebrows shot up in surprise. "I love him?" she mused, mostly to herself.

Rachel grinned. "Yeah, there's no doubt about it. And he's mad about you too."

The three women smiled at one another, enjoying the verbal reaffirmation.

"One word about love," Beth said. "The hardest part is to risk your heart, Reyne. Don't let fear strangle your love. It's the best, most incredible thing you'll ever do."

Beth reached across the table and took Reyne's hand in hers. Reyne struggled to concentrate on her words, not the thin, frail, chilly skin next to her own. She raised her eyes to meet her friend's gaze.

"Nothing's better. No risk, no gain. Gamble it all, Reyne. Because love will see you through, one way or another."

Days later Reyne woke gasping from another nightmare. She was coated in sweat from head to toe—despite the chilly room—and her sheets were a mess. She was just contemplating a shower and a very strong cup of coffee when she heard a noise outside. It sounded as if someone was chopping wood.

She tiptoed to the bathroom, wishing she'd pulled on socks to protect her cold feet, and peeked out the window. Sure enough, Logan was out in the side yard, picking up small rounds of pine and splitting them with long, powerful strokes. Reyne smiled as she watched him work. It had been a long time since a man had done something like that for her.

Working fast, she hurried to the kitchen to put on a pot of coffee and then dashed back to the bathroom. She hopped in the shower, washing in record time. Then she toweled off, combed out her hair, and threw on some clothes. Ten minutes later she nonchalantly walked out to the porch with two cups of coffee.

"You always go chopping wood at other people's houses?" she asked, lifting a cup toward Logan.

He stood and wiped his brow, having worked up a bit of a sweat despite the cool morning. There was dew on everything, and it sparkled under the early morning sunshine. "I do when I want something from that person."

"Oh? And what do you want from me?" She took a sip of coffee to hide her smile.

"I want you to play hooky with me and go check out the salvage yard."

She nodded, pretending to consider his suggestion. "That'll cost you more than splitting," she said. "You'll have to stack that wood."

"Done."

"Well, get to it, Mr. McCabe. I can't play hooky all day."

An hour later they were in the Evergreen salvage yard, walking past row after row of junked cars. The junkyard owner had directed them to the far corner, seeming to remember a couple of vintage trucks in that area.

"How 'bout this one?" Reyne asked, pointing to a Ford F-100. "It's probably about a '54."

"Fifty-six," Logan said with authority. "Sorry. Got my heart set on that Chevy."

Half an hour later she heard him call excitedly from the next row, "Reyne! Come here!"

She moved toward the sound of his voice, noting how the sun had dried the dew and it was actually getting pretty warm out. She pulled off her cardigan and tied it around her waist. When she turned the corner, she gasped. "That's it! Logan, it's beautiful!"

"Check her out!" he said. "The wood bed looks like it's an original."

"It's in better shape than mine was, but it'll still need refinishing," she said.

"Split rear window," he said, running his hand along the side. "Let's see if she still has her engine." Logan found the hood latch and opened it up. He nodded happily, smiling up at Reyne after a moment. "I think it's the original. Just as you described it. Clean and spare."

She leaned in with him. "Just your basic, honest engine. None of that catalytic converter or fuel-injection stuff. Looks so easy, we could take it apart and put it back together again."

"Or at least change the oil," he quipped. "Come on," he said with a sparkle in his eye. "Let's check her out underneath."

They moved to shimmy under opposite sides of the truck and in their excitement ignored the dirt. "How's the rust over there?" Logan asked.

"Not too bad. Not beyond restoration, anyway," she said. "Any Bondo? Bondo means trouble."

"I'll say. No, I don't see any. Oh man, Reyne, I think we found her!" In his excitement he rammed his head trying to look at Reyne and fell back on the ground, moaning.

"Are you okay?"

"Yeah," he said, holding his head. "I'm visualizing something to get my mind off the pain."

"What?"

"You and me in the back of this rebuilt beauty—I think I'll paint her red—out on some back road, just enjoying life together. We could bring some old quilts for comfort, a thermos of something warm, snuggle down, and watch the moon rise. We'd watch until the moon sank on the opposite side of the valley and then count a million stars, talking all the while."

"Just talking, huh?" she asked with a smile.

"In between a few kisses," he said, maintaining firm control of this daydream. "We'd have Patsy Cline on the radio…" He raised his head suddenly, nearly ramming it again. "The original radio's still there, isn't it?"

"Yes, I saw it."

"Good. As I was saying, Patsy Cline on the radio. Hey, how'd it work out that you're still single? How come I'm the lucky guy who gets to listen to Patsy someday in the back of a flatbed truck with you?"

"Didn't meet the right man, I guess. How come I get to rebuild a truck with you?"

"Didn't meet the right woman, I guess."

They lay there for a minute, mulling it over.

"Logan?"

"Yeah?"

"We have a lot of work to do on this truck before we can ever listen to Patsy Cline on that country road. Unless we drag it out there behind a tow truck."

"That's okay," he said with a smile, rubbing his head. "With your help, it will be worth every minute."

CHAPTER ELEVEN

*E*ven several weeks later Reyne was still wrestling with giving Logan all of her heart. The nightmares still plagued her, memories of them coming to her suddenly in the middle of the day. *Besides,* she told herself, *he hasn't said he loved me either. Maybe it's all in my head.* But her heart knew.

They were about to throw themselves out of the Sherpa, testing out equipment, when he finally said those words. Ken Oakley had just opened the doorway and given them the all-clear sign when Logan turned to her and yelled over the deafening wind, "I love you, Reyne Oldre!" then kissed her. With that he rolled out the doorway.

Stunned for a second, she looked over at Ken, who grinned and motioned for her to follow Logan. If she waited any longer, she'd find herself hiking a ways just to meet up with Logan. She took a deep breath and then rolled out the door herself. The air met her like a welcome friend even as her heart skipped crazily, as it always did when she was insane enough to jump out of a moving airplane at fifteen hundred feet.

As Reyne fell away from the airplane, she looked up to see Ken's figure quickly becoming smaller inside the Sherpa. He saluted her and then shut the door. Thinking about Logan's words, she whooped and then pulled her parachute cord. The chute stretched out above her, twisted, and, just when Reyne was getting worried, canopied, braking her to a swift halt.

Logan wasn't far below her, having opened his chute a second before her. He waved at her and motioned toward their intended landing spot, wanting to make sure that she, too, would make it to the small clearing in the forest below. If she didn't, she might end up using their experimental smokejumper's pouch to free herself.

She blew him a kiss, smiling as she replayed his shouted words over and over. *He loves me! He* loves *me!* Reyne couldn't wait to get on the ground and kiss him, to tell him that she loved him too. They landed with barely twenty feet and three seconds separating them. Logan watched as she hit the ground, rolled, and unhooked her parachute like a pro, never stopping as she rose and ran toward him.

He smiled as he kept trying to unhook his own chute while still watching her approach. Before he was completely free, she hopped into his arms, as he laughed in surprise, and wound her legs around his waist. She kissed him soundly. When he came up for air, he smiled. "You heard me then?" he asked, grinning.

"Yes, I did," she said, staring straight into his eyes. "I love you too, Logan McCabe."

His eyes grew bigger with delight, and he took a step backward. It was a fateful error, however, since he happened to step on a parachute cord attached to his right shoulder. Unbalanced, he fell backward, and both of them collapsed on the ground. They laughed and rolled and then settled on their backs, side by side, giggling hysterically.

When the laughter finally subsided, Logan spoke first. "So, did you make a lot of scholarly notations about our research project on the way down? Our meeting with the brass is tomorrow, my lovely partner."

Reyne giggled again and then wiped her eyes. "I'm afraid the only research project I was concentrating on was you, my love," she confessed.

"Oh, I like that," he said. "I guess we'll just have to cram for the exam tonight." He stood, finally freed himself, and then helped Reyne to her feet.

"You'll be my study partner then?" she asked.

"I wouldn't have it any other way." Unable to do anything else, he again took her in his arms.

She giggled a little and allowed some space between them. "It's kinda like holding a plump snowman, huh?" she asked, gesturing down to the thick, padded gear they both wore.

"Yeah," he said, giving her another squeeze. "Except a bit more romantic."

They stood there, holding each other for a good five minutes, looking out toward the valley below before setting to work gathering up their gear.

They were on their final check of their research project, and everything had worked out fine aerodynamically. Now they joked that the only thing that would've made it better was landing in a tree and actually having the excuse to fire off their horizontal stabilizer to descend. They had tested it countless times, simulating every way possible for a jumper to be hung up. But this last dive had really been planned in celebration of their success and as an excuse to hike together. And they would certainly have the opportunity to hike. They were miles from civilization and were carrying full smoke-jumper gear.

In tandem they stripped down to their Nomex shirts, khaki slacks, and boots; crammed their padded outfits, helmets, personal gear, and chutes into heavy packs; and hoisted the packs onto their backs.

Reyne groaned. "Now I remember why I got out of jumping.

My wimpy fire-scientist bod has a hard time dealing with these sixty-five-pound packs anymore, and I'm not even carrying tools."

"Hardly wimpy," Logan appraised, looking her over.

"Logan! Get your mind back on work, will ya? How far are we from town?"

"It's over that next ridge and eight miles down. About nineteen-point-three clicks total."

"Twelve miles, eh?" Reyne asked, swallowing a groan. "Well, let's get to it. I want to have time for a picnic lunch on the way down."

"Sounds good," he said. "Lead the way, milady."

They hiked a good distance before settling on the next small ridge for lunch. They made their way to the base of a large, flat boulder that ended abruptly, with nothing at its far edge but a thousand-foot drop. Logan climbed on top of it and spread his arms out. "I'm on top of the world!" he yelled.

"In more ways than one," Reyne said, grinning up at him. He jumped down beside her and gave her a quick kiss. "Lunch?"

"You bet. I'd wager that our peanut butter sandwiches have seen better days though."

"Better than MREs any day," Logan quipped, referring to the army-style Meals Ready to Eat that smokejumpers usually carried. "Even squished," he said, sounding less sure as he looked over the oddly shaped sandwich.

Reyne smiled over at him and took a big bite of her own misshapen sandwich. Then, looking beyond Logan, she stood and went to the edge of their little clearing, pushing brush away to get to the largest of the saplings. Taking her Swiss army knife from a back pocket, she sawed away at the biggest branch until it fell and she could study its core.

Her face sobered. All around them, the underbrush of the forest was this dense.

Logan looked at her, understanding what she was after. "How old? Four, maybe five years?"

"That's what I'd guess," she said. "We've had incredible rainfall in the last five years."

"And good summers, too," Logan said, taking another bite. "The bad news is that we're behind in precipitation this year. Things are too dry already."

"Record-breaking rain and hot summers only spell one thing," she said, lost in thought.

"An excellent fire season," Logan finished for her, grinning.

She stared at him. "An excellent fire season means something else, too," she began.

He looked at her, puzzled. "What?"

"A lot of separation for us," she said, hating the neediness that climbed onto her words and rode them. "Which will give us more time for our research," she rushed on, knowing her follow-up was lame.

He nodded, chewing, thinking it through.

"The Kootenai used to set these woods on fire," Reyne said, referring to the native tribe that had once lived in this part of Montana. "To clear land for farming, to chase out game, even for entertainment at times."

Logan nodded, still walking. He grabbed a leaf from an aspen as he passed, smashing it in his hand. "This still has good water content, at least," he said.

"It's not the aspens I'm worried about," Reyne said. "It's all this underbrush. These woods are like a giant tinderbox just waiting to explode."

"From what I hear, so is everything west of the Mississippi."

"That's comforting."

"Yeah. What's worse is that these forests haven't seen a major fire in twenty years. They're due."

"Was that part of the impetus in establishing the Elk Horn smokejumper and hotshot crews?"

"I assume so," he said. "Aside from not wanting to pass up the opportunity to allow my masterful hands to mold a new generation of firefighters."

Reyne snorted, rolling her eyes. "Oh yes, that of course was a large part of their decision."

"You've got it. I think the execs with the timber company pulled some strings with the BLM to get me to head it up for the summer. I know some guys who work for them."

"I'm glad," Reyne said. "Or else you might've been stationed far from me." He turned to flash her a grin, and then they walked for a bit in silence.

"So tell me more about those crazy, fire-happy Indians," he said flippantly.

"They were hardly fire-happy," Reyne said. "By setting a few well-placed fires, they cleared underbrush, which created grazing areas that drew game. They made their camps more defensible—or threatened their enemies. To me, it's all very logical."

"Yeah, if you had been in one of the torchers' camps and not their enemies'," he laughed.

Reyne nodded, smiling.

"I was studying some old settlers' journals last year," Logan said, choosing his next step carefully as the trail narrowed. "They wrote of how the valleys were wide and treeless and how game was much easier to hunt. To them it seemed like a paradise. Then after forty or fifty years, the forests grew dense again, making hunting more difficult and forest fires more dangerous. The Indians were no longer maintaining the forests."

"And forest fire entered a new era," she finished for him.

"Exactly. So here we are." They spent the rest of their hike debating the benefits of prescribed burn, changing subjects eventually to the effectiveness of the Incident Command System. Reyne thought it was the saving grace of firefighting. Logan thought it was the bane of their existence.

"Are you telling me that you'd rather do without it in the midst of a major conflagration?" she asked incredulously, breathing a sigh of relief as they reached level ground much later that afternoon. Her calves and thighs were aching and threatening to cramp with every step.

"All I can say is that nothing drives me crazier than watching a fire gain force while we sit around waiting for the proper commander to give the proper command. What's so confusing? 'There's a fire; put it out,' seems obvious enough to me."

Reyne guffawed. "Come on, Logan, you know it's much more than that. You've told me yourself that some guy in a tent with a weather computer with satellite linkup has saved your bacon. More than once."

"Well, yeah, but—"

"And how at that one fire, if it wasn't for the reading and smart command at headquarters, your crew would've been square in the middle of a firestorm."

"Yeah, but—"

"And how that one commander ordered you to run through a

wall of flame because he knew it was your only way out, and you had to trust him. And then later you discovered that he had saved your life with that crazy order."

"Reyne! Stop! Okay, I admit it, sometimes you people in the command center give us orders that make a whole lot of sense. But that's a small percentage of our time. A lot more of it is spent playing Frisbee or Hacky Sack in the camps, waiting for the order to put out the fire."

"It takes time and coordination—"

"I know. Listen, Reyne." He stopped and grabbed her arms as they neared his "new" parked truck, which was waiting for them at the base of the mountain. Reyne hoped it would start. It wasn't close to being in perfect shape yet.

"I know what you do is important," Logan said. "I didn't mean to put a bee in your bonnet. But you have to admit that the system can get a bit bureaucratic at times."

"I suppose so." She was feeling irrationally irritated by his words. But his complaints were common; she had heard them hundreds of times before and voiced them a few times herself. What was really eating at her?

Then it hit her. Fire season was coming fast. The man in front of her, the man for whom she had just proclaimed her love, would be spending most of the summer away from her. And it promised to be a "good fire season" from the looks of it.

"Come on, God," she muttered heavenward, pulling open the cab door after throwing her pack in the back. "A little rain would be great about now."

CHAPTER TWELVE

*D*id you remember to put mustard in the potato salad?"
Reyne asked Logan absently as they pulled up in front of the
Morgans' ranch house one Saturday night in early June.

The three couples had been trading off houses, each taking a
Saturday evening to entertain the others. They would typically eat
and then play cards until the wee hours, often laughing until tears
came to their eyes. But Reyne hadn't felt much like laughing this past
week, and now she felt her stomach clench in its familiar tight knot
as Logan slapped a hand against his forehead.

"Oh man! I forgot. I'm sorry, I was thinking about that call
today. I guess things in Colorado are reaching a peak—"

"Logan! You forgot? I told you at least three times!" She got out
of the truck and slammed the door, so angry she was shaking.

What is this? she asked herself. Even at that point she knew that
it was about more than the missing mustard.

He pulled her to a stop as she stalked toward the front steps of
the house. "Reyne! What's going on? You're this ticked because I forgot some dumb mustard? We can add it now! I'm sure Beth has—"

Reyne shook off his hand. "It's not the potato salad!" she said.
"Don't you see?" Pain overwhelmed her, and tears sprang to her eyes.
"Logan, it's almost over! This whole, wonderful, romantic time is
about to disintegrate!"

"What are you talking about?" he asked, enunciating each word as if willing control into his voice.

"It's June already," she said. "We haven't had a drop of rain in months, the fires are already rolling, and you're going to get the call to go out any day now. So how are we supposed to keep our relationship intact with you gallivanting all around fighting fires and me moving from place to place with the Service?" She paced back and forth, feeling unreasonable, but unable to curb her angst. "We'll be lucky to see one another by September."

"Reyne," he began, rubbing his hands over his face and then through his hair. "You knew what I was about all along. You know I love fighting fire. I thought you had coped with things. Figured 'em out. I didn't think you would've started up with me if things weren't straight in your heart." He moved toward her as if to take her in his arms, but she moved away.

"No. Don't, Logan." She held the potato salad between them like a shield. "Obviously, it wasn't straight in my head." Reyne looked up to see Matt open the front door and wave at them. She forced a smile and waved. "We'll be right there!"

Reyne moved back toward the truck a little, gathering courage for the words she had been working on all week. It was better to get them out now than fret over them for another seven days. Her words were rushed, urgent. "Logan, I've been thinking. Why don't you think about interviewing for that full-time fire management position with the BLM? Many of us end up on the front lines part of the time anyway. Why not do that and get out of the line of fire for at least part of the time? You'd still be in the game."

Logan's eyebrows went up in surprise. "You want me to become part of the bureaucracy?"

"Now, Logan, I—"

"No," he shook his head. He moved toward Reyne and took the salad from her, placing it firmly on the hood of his truck. Oddly, she felt defenseless without it. "Reyne, you know that I love what I do. I *love* it. I'm excited to go in there and fight the dragon again. You have to believe that I'll be okay. That I'll do my best to make wise choices."

"This doesn't have anything to do with wise choices. You could be the wisest firefighter around and still get killed. I've seen it, Logan. And I know you. You'll get caught somewhere being a hero. It won't be your foolish choice that will take you down. It will be someone else's that you try and fix."

"Reyne, you gotta put more trust in me."

"I do! I do trust you! I just said it. It's like not being afraid of you driving—it's all the drunk drivers that make it scary. You'll be out there with your crews—half of them are green! Someone's going to make a mistake!"

Logan sighed heavily and, without warning, took her in his arms. She struggled, feeling angry, but he wouldn't release her. Reyne was horrified as tears came unbidden and she succumbed to his embrace. Logan simply held her, stroking her hair. Then he whispered, "It's gonna be okay."

She wiped her eyes and nose. Her words were barely more than a whisper. "I'm so afraid, Logan. I'm so afraid that I'll lose you. I love you too much."

"I know, Reyne, I know. I love you too. But this is what I do." He paused and kissed her head. "I'll think about the management position. I will. But you have to accept that this is my life for now. Maybe always. And you have to decide if you can deal with it long-term."

She backed away and wiped her eyes, then nodded. "I know," she murmured. "I'm working on that."

⁓

She did work at it all weekend, but by Monday, Reyne's stomach still felt tied in knots. When Logan called to tell her that his group had been activated under their Forest Service subcontract and was heading out to fight their first fire outside of Denver, she was barely civil.

He didn't call her again for days. By Friday, she was nearly out of her mind with worry. She had been monitoring the ICS reports coming out of Colorado and knew the eighty-thousand-acre brush fire was nearly out of control.

Hating it, but unable to stop herself, Reyne sent an e-mail message to Thomas Wagner at the Denver command center, asking how the Elk Horn crews were faring. The response came in ten minutes. The crews had been on five consecutive patrols through the week, apparently desiring field experience and getting their share. The smokejumpers had parachuted into remote regions and combated five separate fronts that threatened to break loose. Even the small groundpounder crew had proven themselves, digging fire line day after day. Many had hailed the rookie team as one of the best they had seen.

Then came the personal inquiry. "Why the sudden interest, Oldre? Are you really interested in a certain hometown boy?"

She had to nip this one in the bud. "Many people in town ask me what is happening. I told them I'd ask," she typed in. A half-truth. A couple of people had asked.

"Uh-huh," came Thomas's reply. She rolled her eyes as she read it. A defensive statement now would read as clearly as an affirmative answer. The fire camp would be abuzz, and Logan would not be pleased. The teasing would be merciless.

"Thanks for the information, Thomas. I'll inform the mothers."

"And the girlfriends," came his reply. He was not fooled by her evasiveness. "Why don't you come down here and join us?" the message went on. "We could use the help."

"From what I see on my screens, you're doing fine," she typed in. "Oldre out."

Logan called that evening. His voice sounded tired, yet wary. "Reyne, I hear you're checking up on me."

It stung that they were his first words. "I've been keeping track, Logan. It's part of my job. I'm supposed to keep an eye on all crews in the States. And so what if I checked up? I haven't heard from you all week!"

"Reyne, you know how it is." She could hear the exasperation in his voice. "Five consecutive duties. We've been sleeping on ridges, maybe three hours a night, and hiking out. They dropped in cargo rations on one particularly fun day. I haven't exactly been in a motel room ignoring the phone beside me."

Reyne closed her eyes and swallowed hard. She visualized him at the base camp, in a temporary phone booth, with firefighters in line behind him waiting to make their own calls. She remembered the exhaustion. "I'm sorry," she said quietly. "I was…worried."

"I know," he said, sounding a million miles away. "I've missed you. I think about you all the time."

She smiled. "That's good to hear. I thought you'd be concentrating so much on your first fire of the season that there'd be no room left in your head for me."

"Not a chance, Oldre. You've captured my heart." She grinned wider as she heard the men behind him giving Logan a hard time. "Listen, Reyne. I'm not keeping us a secret. Wagner was onto us anyway after your e-mail. Is that okay with you?"

"It's fine. I thought you'd be the one to object."

"Object to being known as the one who gets to call Reyne Oldre the love of his life? No way! I'll be the folk hero of all the fire camps. In fact, I've been bragging about it already. My chest is so big, they have to get a new tent for me 'cause I ripped the first one coming in last night."

She laughed, visualizing that scenario. "I'm glad you feel that way, Logan. It's so good to hear your voice. I'm sorry I let you get out of here without a proper send-off. I…I just get so worried."

"I know, babe. Listen, why don't you come down? Wagner said they were swamped and could use you. Said he'd name-request you from dispatch, if necessary."

"Yeah. I just don't want to come down unless they really do need me. I don't think I should use a professional excuse to see my man, as much as I want to."

"Gotcha. Well, I suppose they'll call you and order you down when the need arises."

"That's what I was thinking." They stood there, silent on either end, done with their conversation but reluctant to sever their connection.

"Well, the guys want a piece of this phone line," he said at last. "I love you, Reyne. And I am being careful."

"I know, Logan. And I'm working on this fear thing."

"Good. I'll call you again as soon as I can."

"I'll look forward to it. Good-bye." Reyne hung up quickly then, unable to stand teetering on the edge any longer. She stood there for a long time, just staring at the phone and thinking.

CHAPTER THIRTEEN

*T*he next morning Reyne opened the door to welcome her friends but stopped short, her smile fading fast. Rachel was physically helping Beth from the Jeep. Reyne ran to help.

"What's wrong, Beth?" she asked anxiously. "What's going on?"

"Let's get settled inside, and I'll tell you all about it," Beth said wearily, placing her other arm around Reyne. Always tiny, she seemed almost weightless now.

The two women got her inside. Rachel's face was drawn and gray, almost as pale as Beth's.

With shaking hands Reyne poured the mugs of coffee and rushed into the living room. "What is it, Beth? What's going on? You shouldn't have made yourself come over if you were so sick. Did you go to the doctor?"

"Yes. I went. Yesterday." Beth raised her eyes to look directly into Reyne's. "He didn't give me good news, Reyne. The cancer has spread. It's in my bones. My chest. Even my legs."

Reyne set her coffee cup down so hard the liquid splashed over the edge. The coffee stayed where it had spilled, forming tiny rivulets that rounded and rolled for a second, then stopped. Reyne stared at it, not caring that it might damage the finish. She was sure that if she saw herself in the mirror she would be sporting the same pale shade of gray-green that her friends wore. "I…I'm so sorry, Beth. What else did he say? What do you do now?"

Beth wearily took a sip of coffee and leaned back. Each movement was evidently torture for her. "I'm not going to do anything. I'm going to die. And I don't want to be in the hospital during my last days."

The trio was silent for several minutes. Reyne felt confused, angry at her friend's words. "How can you say that?" she asked, her tone pleading. "You've fought for so long..." Her mind raced, searching for the right argument. "What happened to the Beth who fought this back the first time? A year ago you told me you'd do anything to have more time with Matt and Hope."

Beth closed her eyes as if she'd received a physical blow.

"I'm sorry, Beth," Reyne said, "but have you thought this through? About what you're giving up?"

Beth took a deep breath before responding. "I think you know me better than that, Reyne. You know I'd do anything to stay with Matt...with Hope. With you guys." She looked at them both, her brown eyes bright with tears. They looked enormous in her thin face. "I did want more time with you all. I prayed for it. And God answered that prayer. I've had a whole year."

Silence enfolded them like a stiff curtain. Then Reyne finally ventured another question. "How long, Beth? How long did he say you had?"

"Two, maybe three months."

"And there's nothing you can do? You're not going to do any more chemotherapy?"

"Matt and I are talking about it. But at this stage they can't promise it'll do much good, and I'm not sure I'm willing to spend my last days going through all that for nothing. I'd rather spend every second possible with Hope and Matthew and you two."

Tears came to her eyes and spilled over at last, her face shrouded in pain. "I don't want to say good-bye," she managed through her tears. "I have so much more I want to do!"

Tears ran down Reyne and Rachel's faces, too, as they nodded, listening. Reyne reached out to hug Beth, and Rachel went around the sofa to stroke her hair. For a long time, the three just sat together, holding one another and sniffling.

"It's just not fair," Reyne said at last. "We thought you had beaten it. It's just not fair." Her voice cracked as more tears came.

Beth sat up suddenly and wiped her face. Rachel brought a box of tissues from the bathroom, and they all sat there trying to get control of themselves.

"Sorry, Beth," Reyne said, grabbing yet another Kleenex from its box. "We're supposed to be the strong ones, right?"

"Yeah," she said, smiling through her own swollen eyes, "I think that's the way it's supposed to go."

"So, my friend," Rachel said, "what can we do to help?"

And for the next two hours, the three did nothing but pray.

CHAPTER FOURTEEN

*R*eyne wasn't surprised when she didn't hear from Logan during the next few days. She knew that the Colorado fire was spreading, eating up new acreage as the dry summer wind drove it onward. And she was even less surprised to hear Thomas Wagner's voice on the phone by midweek.

"We need you here, Reyne," Thomas said over the crackling of the phone line. "Get your bags packed, 'cause I've just name-requested you. You can expect your orders shortly. We've got four new fronts to battle, and I need more hands on deck."

"I'll be ready," she said without hesitation. She was excited to see Logan—if indeed she managed to find him in the chaos of the fire camp. But the adrenaline was pumping through her veins at the prospect of going to *work*. She had always hated the dragon and welcomed the chance to help pound him out—even from the relative safety of the command center. And now he was more than just a nameless monster. He was a constant threat to the man she loved.

A helicopter took off from Elk Horn International three hours later, whisking Reyne and more supplies off to the base camp south of Denver. A slim, tall rookie was there to meet her. He stooped under the helicopter's whopping blades to help her out and carry her things.

As they exited the immediate area, he introduced himself. "Hello, ma'am. I'm Jamie Pickering, temporarily assigned to the general at this fire camp."

She held out her hand. "Nice to meet you, Jamie. I'm Reyne Oldre. Who has ICS assigned as incident commander here?"

"Commander Wagner, ma'am."

Reyne grinned, picturing Thomas eating up his new title. Back when they had fought Oxbow in Idaho, Thomas had been fire boss, and later she had heard he had been made operations chief. Obviously, Thomas had gained numerous points on his ICS red card—the method by which the ICS kept track of experience and assigned duties—since that fateful day years ago. Making it all the way to Type I Incident Commander qualified him and his team to take on the largest of fires.

Reyne pushed memories of Oxbow out of her mind, focusing on the huge fire camp in front of them. She scanned the area for Logan, ignoring the slim chances of actually seeing him, and noted the hundreds of yellow Forest Service–issue tents as well as the numerous personally owned tents beside them. It was practically a small city, a typical sight for firefighters at the height of fire season. *But it's only June,* she thought.

Jamie showed her to her private tent, where she quickly dropped off her personal belongings. She kept her soft-sided briefcase with her.

They reached the Incident Command Center, and Reyne smiled as she ducked inside and caught sight of Thomas. Jamie sighed audibly beside her as they watched the grizzled commander blast another rookie for messing up on some duty. "Welcome to Incident Command, ma'am," Jamie said, glancing from her to Thomas. He clearly did not want to get any closer to his boss than necessary. "Is there anything else I can do for you?"

"No, Jamie. Thank you. I think I can take it from here." She watched the young man scramble away, then looked back to find Thomas still chewing out the other youth. "Hey, Wagner," she said loudly, hoping to distract him from his obvious displeasure. "I hear there's a way to earn an honest living here!"

All eyes turned to her, the tent growing momentarily quiet as they checked out the new arrival. Reyne was the only woman in a crowd of twenty or more men.

"Oldre! Finally!" Thomas turned to meet her halfway and swept her up into a huge bear hug. "So I have to pull rank and order you here to get a look at ya now, huh?"

"I just want to feel needed, Thomas—you know that," she said with a grin.

"Yeah, right. Well, you're needed, all right," he said, nodding toward the bank of computers, shortwave radios, telephones, and the team of men who had already returned to their duties. "We've reached Type I status," he said, referring to the escalating nature of the fire. A Type I fire was a major conflagration. "We've got the extended team—including yourself—arriving today, and more ground troops."

They walked over to a wall covered with maps. Thomas picked up an infrared aerial shot of one blaze among many that made up the fire they were fighting. They had dubbed it Devil's Head—after the campground in which it started. Already the name was being shortened to "the Devil."

Thomas handed Reyne the infrared photo. "It's old—last night's." He motioned toward the Pike National Forest topographical map in front of them. "As you know, the fire's been burning for over two weeks," he began, looking grim. "We thought we had it sealed up last week, but then we got this infernal high-pressure system, and the Devil's had *us* by the tail since then."

"How many ground troops do you have in?" she asked, studying the map and then looking at the aerial photo again.

"We'll have a thousand by nightfall."

"And how many smokejumpers?" It was odd that there were smokejumpers left here at all. Typically, jumpers were used in remote places to ward off small fires, not on a Type I fire running over a couple of weeks. Silently she prayed that the Elk Horn crew had not been moved on to another fire.

Thomas gave her a quick glance. "Four squads of six. Logan McCabe's heading 'em all up. We've got so many remote flanks and startups on this one that we still need 'em."

"And you have fire like this on all fronts?" she asked, gesturing toward the photo in her hands.

"On two fronts it's that bad. On the two others, it's worse."

Reyne nodded, staring down at the photo, knowing what it meant. Fires typically died down at night as low-pressure systems moved in. But last night, according to the photo, Devil's Head had been driving fires to crowning in places, creating a spectacular, if deadly, bonfire of the forest.

"I assume we're going to have a command team meeting shortly?"

"At 2100 hours. Until then, I'd appreciate it if you could man the field radio and monitor the west flank division. I lost my red-carded man to a flu bug this afternoon."

"You've got it. Show me where to sit."

Thomas got her situated, filling her in on the crew bosses, their teams, and their current situation, then handed her the sick man's transmission log. Within minutes she was up to speed and radioing the crew bosses to introduce herself. As she talked with each of them, joking and laughing like an old friend, Reyne had to admit that being back on the fire scene felt good. *No place like combat to connect people.*

She was quickly immersed in her temporary duty, studying the maps and monitoring her teams, advising them as advanced reports came in to the command center. The hours melted away like minutes until it was time to grab a quick, late dinner and meet with the command team.

As she walked into the "cafeteria," or mess tent, she was greeted by a shout. She looked around and spotted Buddy Taylor, an old friend from her college days on the fire line. In his typical adolescent exuberance—even at age twenty-nine—he had stepped up on his crowded picnic table and was quickly making his way toward her, dancing around plates and glasses and leaving a wake of chaos behind him.

Buddy was about six foot two and weighed a sturdy two hundred pounds, so his delicate prancing was all the more hilarious to onlookers. When he finally reached the end of the last table and jumped to the ground in front of Reyne, the entire cafeteria full of men and women were looking their way, laughing and cheering for Buddy. He was obviously the clown here, as he had been everywhere she had known him.

Egged on by their applause and shouts, Buddy picked Reyne up in his arms and introduced her. "Have no fear, boys and girls!" he shouted. "Fire Specialist Reyne Oldre has arrived!" The entire tent erupted into louder applause.

"You know what a fire specialist on the scene means?" he yelled, looking at Reyne proudly as if she were a hard-won trophy.

"TYPE ONE FIRE!" the crowd yelled as one. Their battle had

become a full-fledged war, and the title change was fuel to their fire.

Reyne felt the creeping blush on her face and begged Buddy to put her down. She was laughing, half in enjoyment, half in embarrassment, when he whirled her in a circle, gave her a smacking kiss on the cheek that would make Bugs Bunny proud, and then carefully set her down. As she gained her equilibrium, leaning heavily on his arm and laughing at his next words, she glanced up to her left.

Logan stood there, surrounded by his team. His look was grim. It was one of those moments where the world seemed to stand still—where only two people existed on earth.

Logan looked exhausted. Soot coated his face where his hasty washing had missed, and his eyes looked strained and red. But to Reyne, he looked like the handsomest man on earth.

Until he turned his back and walked out without a word to her.

Reyne glanced at Buddy, confused, then embarrassed. The rowdy mess tent had fallen silent as everyone watched the spectacle at the entrance. Was it Buddy that had upset him? Or something else?

She walked out after Logan, determined not to run after him, but just as determined to get to the bottom of the problem immediately. As soon as she cleared the tent, she yelled after the broad-shouldered, Nomex-shirted man who strode away from her. "Logan!"

He stopped short and looked up, as if saying a quick prayer for patience, then turned. Reyne felt her brow furrow and her heart pound. She walked right up to him, her anger building. "What was that? We haven't seen one another for two weeks and you can't say a word to me? What is going on with you?"

"I could ask you a few questions myself!" he said, obviously struggling not to shout. His expression was furious. "I was thinking about grabbing a bite to eat and then giving you a call, and then what do I see? Buddy Taylor's hands all over you, and you leaning all over him!"

Reyne sputtered, aghast at his unfair assessment of what had transpired. "What are you talking about? Did you see the whole thing? Or did you just walk in for the last part?"

"What did I miss?" he spat out. "Did he kiss you first? And why are you here, anyway? To see your *boyfriend* or to check up on me?"

Reyne shook her head as if to shake out the incredible things she was hearing. She took a deep breath. "Look, Logan, you are obviously very tired and unable to be a good or reasonable judge of what's going on." She sighed, unable to believe that their reunion was spoiled. "I was so looking forward to seeing you! I've missed you so much!"

She looked up at him. His face softened, but she was not ready to let him off the hook. "But you are being a total jerk right now, so when you're ready to apologize, you can look *me* up."

With that, she turned her back and walked back to the cafeteria tent, grabbed an apple from the stack at the end of the line, then left to find a quiet place to eat it before her meeting.

After three bites, she was unable to eat any more. She threw the half-eaten fruit into a nearby trash can and walked to the command center for their scheduled meeting. She would need concentration and poise to counteract what they had all undoubtedly witnessed at the cafeteria. *Help me, Lord,* she prayed silently, then entered the brightly lit tent.

In one corner, away from the chaotic flurry of activity, a long table had been set up along the side, and on the walls were more maps and a marker board. Everyone was in place, and Reyne was quickly introduced to the leadership team, made up of the day- and night-shift operations chiefs, a logistics specialist, a meteorologist, an air operations commander, two mappers, a public information officer, four medical unit managers, a helibase manager, two dispatchers, and a food unit leader. Thomas had called in a full-scale team. He intended to put a stop to Devil's Head, and fast.

Within an hour, they all had a good idea of what the commander's plan was. After the meteorologist and Reyne conferred, studying weather patterns and current fire behavior on all flanks, they agreed with his plan. "As you all know," Thomas concluded, "you don't fight fire. You herd it. I want to herd it into this valley here," he said, gesturing toward a remote valley that surrounded a high mountain lake. "And when the weather gives us a break, we're going to give the Devil some of his own."

After wrapping up the meeting, the command team exited the control center, and Reyne wearily made her way to her tent, glad that her elevated position had rated a private tent. Hopefully Jamie had found the foldaway cot she always carried with her to fire camps. Even Thomas slept on the ground, but Reyne did not fare well doing so. As soon as she could justify it—and had her own tent—she had invested in the small camping cot. Her days of waking up with a knot in her back were over, thank God. And tonight she really needed a good night's sleep. She hoped that she and Logan could work things out after they both had caught some shuteye.

Reyne paused ten feet from her home-away-from-home, stifling a laugh as she made out Logan's form draped across the entrance. He had obviously been waiting for her but in his weary state had fallen asleep where he sat.

As funny and sweet a picture as he made, Reyne was still angry at him for his unfair assessment and jealous words. Gingerly, she stepped over him and quietly zipped up the tent, wincing as every tooth met the other and made a sound.

But Logan was out cold. He had to be exhausted. Still, memory of his words stung her heart as she silently undressed, pulled on a nightshirt, unfurled her sleeping bag on the cot, and climbed in. She was soon asleep, oddly comforted by Logan's proximity and yet still relishing the idea of the camp awaking to find the fabled and respected Logan McCabe camped out in her doorway.

CHAPTER FIFTEEN

Logan awoke to the snickers and stifled laughs of passersby. He opened his eyes, wincing at the crick in his neck and the bright light above. People were giggling or glancing away in embarrassment for him as they walked by.

Oh no, he thought. *I slept here all night!* He rubbed his face and sighed heavily, thinking about what a jerk he was, then sat up.

He could hear Reyne's soft, even breathing through the thin mesh weave of her tent sides. *How can I apologize, Lord? I really did it this time.* He drew a deep breath and unzipped the door, peeking in to make sure she was still asleep. She was.

Logan made his way over to her, then sat down beside the cot, simply staring with nothing but love in his heart. *What a fool I was,* he thought. *How could I have greeted her like that?* He stared at her face, admiring her long, dark lashes, the gentle contours of rounded cheeks that gave way to dimples when she smiled, a cute nose that sloped to a slight peak at the end, full lips that begged for a kiss…

Slowly he bent down to take the kiss and awaken her, but then he stopped himself. He did not deserve it. He owed her an apology first, and a public one at that. Feeling a near-physical twinge at having to tear himself away, Logan quietly stepped out of the tent and zipped up the door behind him.

Reyne listened as Logan turned away from her, zipped the door back up, and walked away. Then, feeling grumpy, she sat up and swung her feet to the floor of her tent.

She had not slept well, as usual, and she had been groggily awake when she saw him stand up outside her door, but she had closed her eyes and pretended. He, after all, needed to come to her, regardless of the spectacle he made of himself. When he entered her tent, Reyne's heart had pounded as she waited for him to kiss her. She had felt his breath on her face, tickling her skin in his nearness. But then he apparently had changed his mind and exited.

Miffed that he had not awakened her, she got up, brushed her hair, and dressed. She hoped that a cup of coffee would clear her fuzzy head. She had had an intense night of wild, bizarre dreams— when she did actually manage to sleep—and nights like that always left her feeling more weary than refreshed.

Reyne stooped over, walked to her window, and unzipped the flaps. Devil's Head had painted the sky a sickening yellow-brown, with thick smoke choking out any hint of blue. She dropped the flap, grabbed her briefcase, and then moved out of her tent to go to mess.

Breakfast was still going strong, and waves of firefighters kept arriving at their scheduled times to keep things rolling. As part of the leadership team, Reyne was allowed access at any time. When she entered, she immediately saw Logan standing with a sheepish expression on his face. Buddy stood beside him.

"Hear ye, hear ye!" Buddy yelled. "Quiet in the court! Quiet in the court! This gent has a public proclamation to make!"

Logan stepped up on the table and looked around the room, then directly at Reyne. "Last night," he yelled, "some of you witnessed me being a complete fool. I'm fortunate to be able to spend time with that incredible woman over there, and I made a serious blunder by being a jealous idiot. I am sorry, Reyne. Will you forgive me?"

The entire mess tent was silent, witnessing yet again a very private moment. But that was common in fire camps, as in any sort of camp. Private moments became community property.

"Well, Oldre?" Buddy yelled. "What say you? Off with his head?"

She smiled and nodded once in what she hoped was a regal manner. "He may keep his head."

The crowd laughed and cheered and immediately went back to their food. Logan made his way to Reyne, said a quiet good morning, and then went to save her a seat at a nearby table.

Afterward, Logan and Reyne made their way out of the cafeteria and hiked about a quarter mile into the forest behind the base camp. Finding themselves a sufficiently private location, Logan again took Reyne into his arms and kissed her deeply. After several long minutes he drew back with his eyes closed, as if still appreciating the feel of her lips on his.

He opened his eyes and gazed down lovingly at her. "I *am* sorry, Reyne."

"I know," she said, wanting only to put it behind them. "You more than made your apology."

"I was still out of line. I don't know what got into me. I was tired. The shock of seeing you here…seeing Buddy holding you…"

She smiled smugly. "You were jealous."

He shifted, obviously uncomfortable about her assessment. "A little," he admitted. "I don't want anyone but me to touch my girl."

"I hardly had a choice."

"I know. I should've known better. Buddy is a wild man. But I couldn't help myself."

"Yeah, well, don't let it happen again. Our time together is too precious to waste on stupid things like this."

"Agreed." He pulled her closer, resting his chin on her head. "It feels so good to hold you."

"It feels great to be held. I've missed you, Logan."

"And I you," he said, tenderly reaching to tilt her chin up again to receive his kiss. Afterward he asked, "Do you know how much I love you, Reyne Oldre?"

"A lot?" she asked, tilting one eyebrow up.

"An incredible amount. Like I've never loved before. It's never been like this for me." His Montana-blue-sky eyes stared into hers for a long time, never wavering, as if he was willing her to believe him.

"It hasn't been like this before for me either," she said softly. Her heart pounded as he pulled her to him again, feeling his strong hands on her back and his hard-muscled arms tighten at her sides. He kissed her yet again, then slowly, reluctantly, released her. "It's probably a good thing you have a meeting in three minutes," he said, checking his watch.

"And that you take off on an assignment in an hour," she said, smiling.

He leaned in for a final kiss. "I think you're amazing, Reyne. Thank you for loving me, even when I'm a jerk."

"Anytime."

With a soft groan he let her go again, then took her hand in his and led her back down the path toward the camp. He left her at the command center tent. They released each other's hands, slowly dragging them apart from palms to fingertips as if each second of touch was precious.

"Be careful out there, Logan," Reyne said softly. She hoped her gaze was intense enough to telegraph her concern.

"I will, Reyne. I love you. I'll see you in a couple of days," he whispered, then walked off.

"Oldre, you're late!" Thomas's voice rang out from the tent, interrupting their love-swept reverie.

"Coming!" she yelled over her shoulder. "Good-bye, love," she said softly to Logan's back as he walked away. "Dear Father, please protect him. Set your angels all around him. Before him, behind him, beside him. I commit his safety to your care," she whispered.

Merely uttering the words gave her comfort. With a sigh she turned and walked in to face the commander's glower.

CHAPTER SIXTEEN

*T*homas had begun the meeting without her. Feeling like a chastened schoolgirl, Reyne quickly took her seat, opened her notebook, and picked up a pen.

"We're sending in six sets of jumpers," Thomas said. "Teams of four jumpers each. They'll land here," he said, gesturing toward numerous spots on a mapped mountain ridge. "We cannot allow these little fires to hook up with each other and become another flame front. We're having enough trouble managing what we have. As you can see, Winter's Ridge is isolated and difficult for road crews to reach...the few access roads available have been cut off."

He looked at the meteorologist beside Reyne, then gestured back to the map, pointing as he spoke. "Larry and Reyne have assured me that the Devil won't be climbing Winter's Ridge today. Let's hope for the jumpers' sake they're right. If they are, which we're banking on, the teams should be able to contain all these tiny arms of fires you see banking here and heading down the watersheds toward Woodland Park and these other communities."

"No pressure," Reyne quipped.

"None intended," Thomas tossed back, obviously forgiving her tardiness.

He probably figures I'm suffering enough sending Logan in there, she mused.

"We have about four thousand people in these communities," he said, gesturing again toward the map, "and about ten thousand more below. Let's stop Devil's Head, people, before he reaches that first subdivision." He looked sternly around the room, studying each team member's face. "Any questions?"

The Greater Northwest Forestry Company's old military Sherpa circled the giant convection plume of smoke, bouncing and swaying in the quixotic winds. Logan looked out the open doorway, searching for the proposed drop site for the next team of four. The spotter found it and pointed it out first to Logan, then to the next team leader. "It's about as big as a postage stamp, Anderson," he shouted, pointing toward the minuscule landing spot above the fire.

"Thanks for the encouraging words," the woman beside Logan yelled back. Jill Anderson was a kindergarten teacher in the off-seasons; this was her fifth year as a Forest Service squad leader. She looked out, watched as the spotter's weighted streamer descended, and then nodded in grim agreement when the spotter gave her the signal to go at the next pass.

Jill motioned to the three on her team to be ready, preparing the first two to jump, then the third to go with her. She walked past them, doing last-second checks and watching as they hooked up their static lines to the plane's bar above. The other end of the line was attached to their deployment bag, what Forest Service jumpers referred to as the *d-bag*. Finally they were ready, poised to go in the classic two-by-two formation jumpers called *sticks*. This formation often allowed jumpers to talk on the way down and land within a few feet of one another.

Just before the first stick rolled out, the plane lurched and dropped in the crazy mountain winds. Leaving the bumpy plane and entering the air would actually come as a relief to most of the squad. Logan watched as the first two jumpers, then Jill and her partner fell away from the plane, pulling the small rings on their backs that deployed small chutes called *drogues*. The drogues pulled the smoke-jumpers to a vertical position and the main chutes out of the packs so they could open—leaving the line and d-bag dangling beneath the plane.

The spotter brought the mike to his mouth. "Smokejumpers away," he reported.

"Roger," came Mike Moser's voice from the cockpit, which Logan could hear over his own radio. "You boys are next, McCabe. We'll be over your drop site in about three minutes. Ready your team."

"Roger." Logan nodded to his team, two rookies from California and an old smokejumping partner, Alfred Jensen. Logan was glad that Alf was along to partner with one of the rookies. It was the expertise of men like him that was shaping Logan's forestry company crew into a group of professionals.

A huge updraft swept past the plane at that moment, sending the little gear that was not stowed flying. Logan pitched and caught a handlebar, narrowly missing an impromptu departure from the plane. His heart pounded as he looked up and saw the white faces of his rookies and the huge grin on Alf's long face.

"McCabe's not quite ready to go fight the fire alone!" Alf shouted to the young men, laughing as he did so.

"Smokejumper target in sight," Mike's voice came over Logan's radio.

Logan looked out the doorway again, this time with a firm grip on the bar above. "Where exactly does Wagner think we'll land?" he shouted to the spotter, scanning the acres of trees below him. The arm of fire that they were to put out was clearly visible. The proposed landing zone below it was not.

"Looks like an unbroken timber landing for you boys," the spotter yelled, still scanning for a suitable site. When none was found, he tossed his crepe-paper streamer, and both men watched as it fell.

"I'd say you have about a ten-mile-per-hour cross wind," the spotter said. Because mountain winds could make it difficult to keep a parachute upright or could throw smokejumpers into an unscheduled patch of trees, any winds above fifteen miles per hour negated a jump.

No excuse now, Logan said to himself. *But at least Anderson had a postage stamp.* He rose and walked back to his team, speaking mostly to the rookies, but giving Alf a meaningful glance. "We've got unbroken timber!" he shouted above the aircraft noise. "We'll take it on, just like in training. Remember, be ready for your landing, keep your eyes open, and find the best landing spot. We'll reconvene on the ground!"

They exited the Sherpa in a professional manner, with Alf leading and Logan in the rear. Logan watched with satisfaction as his three teammates' drogues deployed below, with the huge rectangular chutes not far behind. He looked up and watched as his own chute opened, and he sent up his customary prayer of thanks for every inch of the 350 square feet of nylon above him. Then he turned his attention to the trees that were rushing toward him and began to plan his landing.

Reyne was busy, very busy. She and Larry, the meteorologist, were working to prepare a special weather forecast for the fire command center, checking with the National Weather Service on the hour as well as conducting their own studies. They were in the process of sending up weather balloons when Thomas bellowed at her. "Reyne! What do you have for me? I need answers!"

"We're trying to get a read, Thomas. Give us five minutes."

"You've got four."

Reyne scowled and looked over at Larry, who immediately checked his portable forecast unit. The temporary setup could still give a cursory read on humidity, temperature, air stability, and wind speed and direction. By factoring in long-term factors like the fire's climatic influence on forest fuels, they would be able to give Thomas a summary on the fire environment and Reyne would be better able to make judgment calls on the fire's behavior.

She frowned as they made note of the hot, dry weather with gusty winds. "Perfect, just perfect," Reyne said sarcastically. "All we need now is for the Weather Service to call with a forecast of lightning storms."

The phone rang, as if on cue. "Maybe that's them," Larry quipped, smiling at her. He shook his head to dispel her fears when the person on the other end began speaking.

Reyne turned her attention to a new batch of aerial shots. The fire was building, all right, even beyond the average major conflagration. If they kept up at this rate, the ninety thousand acres that had already been burned would seem like child's play. Larry hung up.

"Tell me you have good news for me," she said.

"I do." Larry was jubilant. "We were right on our readings. It's bad now, but we've got rain on the way. In twenty-four to thirty-six hours we'll be doused."

"Excellent!" Reyne paced, thinking fast. "So our initial plan to herd the Devil into the valley is right on target. If we can get him in and keep him there, then all we have to do is wait for Mother Nature to put him out."

"Sounds right on to me. Now, the only other concern I'd have is the potential for other lightning fires to begin. The Weather Service isn't forecasting thunderstorms, just showers, but I think we ought to be prepared for anything. I'd hate to kill this fire just to begin fighting another one. Let's plan to nip any others in the bud."

"Good," she agreed. "Let's go tell Wagner."

Logan grunted as the trees rushed up at him, bracing for the inevitable impact. He hit, rolled, and stood, muttering a prayer of thanks for the thick, fire-resistant Kevlar material from which their suits were made. It was the same material that bulletproof vests were made of, and Logan had had many opportunities to be thankful for its protection.

Quickly stuffing his chute into his pack, Logan paused to look around. He had managed to land in a relatively clear spot among the trees. But he was worried about one of the rookies, Andy, who had drifted into a thick stand of lodgepole pine.

When Logan found him, he grew more concerned. The man's parachute was caught in the canopy, but not firmly anchored, so he couldn't clip his letdown gear and descend. To complicate matters, Andy thought he had broken an arm, so he couldn't get a decent grip on the tree trunk to cut and climb.

Logan picked up his radio and pressed the intercom button. "Command center, this is smokejumper team six. We have an injured smokejumper, command center. Repeat, we have an injured smokejumper, over."

Logan studied Andy's face, noticing the grim look of pain. "Command center, we will need a medevac chopper. Do you read? Over."

"We read you, McCabe. Medevac chopper will meet you a half-mile east at the ridge clearing in half an hour. Over."

"Very good, command center. We'll see you there. Over."

Logan stripped off his Kevlar suit and climbed the tree. In the pouch that he and Reyne had developed and that he now carried on his chest was an air compression system that, when activated, shot out a harpoonlike dart and rope. He reached Andy's level, aimed at a nearby tree trunk, and shot off the dart. It entered the ripe bark and, when Logan yanked on it, shot out several spokes that firmly embedded it in the tree.

"What's that?" Andy asked. "Looks like spy paraphernalia."

"Yeah," Logan said with a grin, tying off the other end of the rope on his tree and creating a firm letdown line for Andy's descension hardware. "Ain't it great?"

Logan climbed back down the tree and watched as Andy painstakingly made his way down one-handed. In addition to his broken arm, Andy had injured the ligament of his right knee. But he got down safely, at least.

Their pouch had saved the day! Logan cheered inwardly. All his work with Reyne had paid off. *In more ways than one*, he thought with a grin.

When the helicopter touched down at the fire camp, Reyne raced to meet it. As soon as Logan disembarked, she ran to embrace him, and never had his arms about her felt better. She had heard the radio reports about the rescued smokejumper and had been so worried that Logan was the injured party. They stood there, just the two of them, holding each other while their hair blew about in wild fashion and workers unloaded the helicopter.

Reyne drew back and looked up into Logan's bright blue eyes. He looked very dashing with a smudge of soot across his cheek and an exultant expression upon his face. "It worked!" he yelled over the helicopter's noise. "The pouch! That's how I got Andy down!"

"Great!" she responded, feeling no enthusiasm. She was more concerned with the prospect of panicking every time she heard that a smokejumper was injured. Of being apart most of the coming months. "How are we going to do this all summer?" Reyne shouted to him. But her voice did not carry. And she already knew the answer.

"What?" he yelled, bending to hear her.

"Nothing!" she said into his ear. "We can talk later."

He studied her with concern but nodded. Then, placing his hand on her lower back, he ushered her away from the helicopter, which was being refueled. The blades never stopped whirring; the chopper took off on another assignment within fifteen minutes.

CHAPTER SEVENTEEN

*T*hat night the entire fire camp celebrated. The smokejumper teams had been most effective doing what they did best—serving as initial strike teams to stop minor fires from becoming major. They had put out each arm of the fire that threatened to overcome the line. A nearby team had hiked in after Logan evacuated Andy and had taken care of their assignment in their stead. With the coming rain and with Devil's Head being successfully turned toward the valley, it looked like the month-old fight was all but over.

As an impromptu band congregated and the weary firefighters began singing and dancing in the camp's "streets," Logan pulled Reyne close for their own slow dance that ignored the crazy, fast rhythm of the current song. She did not care that they were a spectacle, a glutton for punishment among the ranks. She only cared that Logan was close and safe and that he was holding her.

Reyne leaned her head back to look up into his eyes. He gave her an intense look, staring back at her, not saying anything. There was no need for words. They said everything with their steady, unwavering gaze.

She was the first to break their loving glance, bending to rest her cheek on his chest. She felt safe. Loved. Exhilarated. And she could think of nothing but returning to Elk Horn. She wanted to spend hours tinkering under their trucks or gardening or hiking. Or spending evenings on her front porch with their friends, laughing, playing, talking. *Our friends...* Reyne resolutely pushed thoughts of Beth's illness from her mind. She wanted to focus only on Logan, for the moment anyway.

"I was so worried," she muttered, not quite sure she wanted to broach the subject at all.

"What?" he asked tenderly.

"I was so worried," she said, looking up at him and speaking more clearly. "When I heard a jumper was injured, I immediately assumed it was you." Reyne shook her head as Logan began to speak. "I know it doesn't make sense. After all, you're the one that's leading those crews up there. But Logan, I'm just so scared. I have these dreams...these awful dreams."

He tilted her head back up so he could meet her eyes. "Of what?"

"Oxbow," she said with a sigh, dropping her chin, unable to meet his gaze. She looked away but pulled him close, listening to his heartbeat for a moment before going on. "I dream that when I emerge from the fire shelter, you're there. You're one of the guys that didn't make it. It's so vivid, so real to me, that it's like it actually happened. I wake up crying, all sweaty sometimes."

"Oh, Reyne—"

"No." She broke away from him, setting her hands on her hips with her back to him. "I know it's stupid. Somehow my worst fears have fused with my worst memories. It makes sense. And yet it doesn't. You're the best at what you do," she said, looking back over her shoulder. "I know you are, Logan. But you've made your way into my heart, and I'm scared to death that something is going to happen to you."

Logan took a step toward her, placing his big hands on her slim shoulders. "Nothing's going to happen, Reyne. You're just going to have to trust. Who knows? Maybe dispatch will send us both home tomorrow and we'll while away the summer planting trees for the forestry company and working on your pocket weather kit."

She turned to him, embracing him fiercely. "Sometimes I think we should both retire from fire," she said softly, "Walk away. Find another line of work."

He pulled her arms from him and looked at her. "No way, Reyne. We both love this. You do; I can tell. You've got to get hold of this fear thing and get past it, or it will rip us apart. 'Cause I'm staying in the game. I've got to."

She swallowed hard, trying to decipher all that she was feeling. "What if it's not just fear, Logan? What if God is telling me this? Asking us to get out?"

"Whoa," he said. "I haven't heard that." He sighed heavily. "I'm not saying that it isn't possible, Reyne. But until you can tell me that yes, you're sure that the Lord is telling you this and it's not just old nightmares plaguing your present life, or until he tells me the same thing, I can't honestly consider it."

She bristled. "Are you telling me that you'd shut out God's leading?"

"No," he said quickly. "Didn't you just hear me? I said that God would have to tell me the same thing or you would have to stand there and tell me that you're sure, not just mention it as a convenient excuse to avoid dealing with your old issues."

"Is that what you think this is? You think I need to see some therapist or something?"

"Maybe that'd be a good idea. Reyne, I—"

"I get concerned about the man I love, and you think I should see a counselor?"

"Reyne, that's not fair. I was only—"

"Look," she said, holding up her hands. "We're not getting anywhere here. Let's just talk tomorrow."

Thomas had reconvened the command team the next morning, passing on the interagency's dispatch assignments. They met outside, enjoying the milder weather that the rain had brought and the partially blue sky. Briskly, he made the announcement. His core command team would be heading to Idaho with him to fight a Type II fire near the Oxbow burn of two years ago. Reyne swallowed hard when she heard the location. Others were given alternate details.

Reyne was going home to Elk Horn. Alone. She left the meeting and saw Logan waiting for her nearby. With some trepidation, she approached. Would he be returning with her? *Please, God.* Could they spend some time just being together instead of fighting some infernal fire away from home?

He looked down at her tenderly and drew her into his arms for a brief hug. "I'm sorry we argued last night, love. I'm not quite sure *why* we were arguing."

Reyne could only nod, feeling responsible for her harsh words but not quite ready to admit it. "They're sending me home." She took a deep breath. "What about you guys?"

He looked her straight in the eye. "We're going to the interagency fire command center in Boise to be on standby for more assignments. That will give my rookies the opportunity to be around a pro BLM jumper base, learn some tricks of the trade. I've heard that there's a good one going outside of Idaho Falls—"

Reyne's head swam. Boise. Idaho Falls. Oxbow. The correlation was too much. Logan was heading straight into her worst nightmare, and there was apparently nothing she could do to stop him. She turned and walked away as if on autopilot.

He ran after her. "Reyne!" he yelled.

She did not stop.

"Reyne!" he tried again. In the back of her mind it registered that his voice was nearer this time, that he was coming after her. Still she did not stop. Everything in her told her to run away, to flee, to get away from this man who loved fighting the very monster that could kill him.

Logan reached her and grabbed her arm, swinging her around to face him. "Reyne, what is going on? Why are you so angry?"

"Angry?" she repeated. "*Angry?* I'll tell you why I'm angry. I'm angry because I've finally fallen in love with a man, and he's in love with someone else! Some*thing* else!"

Logan's brow furrowed, and he brought his face closer to hers, recognizing that their argument was once again drawing curious stares. "Listen, Reyne, I know this must be tough—"

"Tough? This isn't about something that I just have to be strong enough to deal with, Logan. This is about smarts. Plain old smarts. I've seen the dragon do his stuff. I know you think you have too. But you haven't been there, Logan."

She paced in front of him, feeling the tension draw her face into a taut mask. But she couldn't stop herself. "You haven't seen flames shooting five hundred feet into the air, ready to come and swallow you for breakfast. You haven't waited it out in a tiny silver taco that they call protection!"

With that, she strode away again, furious, fearful, not sure whom she was really angry with. But her choice was made. It made her miserable, but everything had been said already, and she was going to stick to her guns.

In a moment Logan was behind her again, swinging her to a stop once more. He started to speak, stopped himself, ran his hands through his dark hair, and started again. "Look, love. It's because I'm going to Boise, huh? It brings it all back? We've talked about this. I know it's going to be hard, but—"

"You don't know anything, Logan McCabe," she spat out. "Go and fight your dragon. But don't think I'm going to be the grateful princess waiting back at the castle for you."

Logan watched as she strode away, stoic in his thoughts as she disappeared among the tents. Her words had stung, but he knew she hadn't meant them—not in the way they had come out anyway. She was plainly scared to death. And part of him could understand how she felt. Realizing she was in love. And that the man she loved fought fire, her worst fear. He wouldn't like it if she was on the fire line. He wouldn't like it at all.

But Reyne had come into this relationship with her eyes open. She knew his life was fire and he was consumed with the desire to fight it. And if she'd just admit it to herself, she still loved it as much as he. They had talked it all through, over and over. Even though she had been emotionally wounded fighting Oxbow, she still felt the passion—he would bet money on it. If she didn't, she would have removed herself from the fire scene entirely. Study something else.

But she had returned to fight fire—albeit from the relative safety of the command center. But even those in the command center had to face the dragon occasionally, to lead a team on the line or to study the conditions firsthand. The way the season was shaping up, Logan was sure that Reyne would find herself facing the monster head-on more than once or twice in the coming months.

Logan left the campsite and walked into the woods. Finding a fallen log in the clearing among the trees, he sat down and stared up into the morning sky, studying the cloud formations and the occasional hawk for several long minutes. "God," he whispered. "Only you could be the instigator of this one. I've fallen in love with a hardheaded woman who has one huge fear in her head…and in her heart. Only you can change that. Please be with us, Father."

He appreciated the cool morning air with its welcome hint of moisture. To Logan, it felt like a tangible promise from the Savior that he was on his way to personally put out the fire. The gentle breeze caressed his cheek, and he was thankful for his faith. It gave him strength when his world felt upside down. *Or when the woman you love is angry at you.*

He looked around at the dark trees, thinking about how easy it would be to get lost in the forest. He continued his conversation with the Father after a moment's rest, a moment's thinking. "Show us your way, God, and how to go about getting on that path. Because right now, I'm feeling pretty lost."

Chapter Eighteen

*R*eyne had left camp without seeking Logan out or saying good-bye. Now, back home, she was paying the price. He was on her mind every minute of the day, and she closely monitored the progress of the various fires via computer in Boise, hoping for word about Logan and his team without making a direct request for information.

She gathered that the fire near Idaho Falls was almost out after more than ten days of work, but she was still worried. She had said things to Logan that she regretted. She had been unfair and unfeeling in her anger. And she could not wait to apologize. She missed him. She loved him. *Will he forgive me?* she wondered for the thousandth time. He had not called.

Unable to concentrate on her work, she left the studio to grab a late breakfast and then do a little gardening. After a quick piece of toast, Reyne stopped by the cottage entrance to don a straw hat from the rack, glanced at her image in the hall mirror, then went outside. She surveyed the plants from her porch.

The early summer heat wave—and Reyne's absence—were hurting her garden efforts. The English garden around her cottage was withering, and she needed to act fast to save it.

Still, here and there were the beginnings of beautiful antique annuals, her favorites. Reyne had carefully planned her garden, beginning with a picket fence she had left unpainted so it would weather quickly. Over it climbed dark green vines with dangling pink blooms called kiss-me-over-the-garden-gate. Interspersed with the vine were glorious purple-black morning glories on perfect, heart-shaped leaves, and a nearly preposterous snake gourd vine sported quaint little white flowers and gourds that would eventually grow as long as seven feet. Reyne planned to sell the gourds to local crafts-men who specialized in making them into eye-catching containers, birdhouses, even musical instruments.

At the fence's base, below the soft, velvety leaves of the gourd vine, stood the white angel's trumpets, Reyne's favorite. Last night their perfume had wafted through her open bedroom window as she tossed and turned, reminding her that she needed to tend the gar-den. Above them, spilling out and over the edges of an antique wooden wheelbarrow, was a stand of tiny golden feather. Over by the porch and lining its latticed front were delicate purple-pink balcony petunias. All around her were building banks of painted tongue, Chinese foxglove, flowering tobacco, and local varieties such as red Indian paintbrush, purple pasqueflowers, pink bitterroot, and deli-cate harebells. There were even pastel sweet peas struggling to make their way up a trellis, although those especially seemed to be fighting a losing battle with the heat.

All in all, it was becoming quite a beautiful, tranquil setting. *If I can just keep it alive,* Reyne mused, squinting and glancing up at the sun from under her hat's brim. After pulling weeds for an hour and watering the thirsty plants, Reyne took off her hat and wiped the sweat from her forehead again. It was only the beginning of July, but the Elk Horn Valley was already sweltering. It had to be over ninety degrees.

Replacing her hat, Reyne gazed out over the valley to watch the thunderheads build in the distance. Large areas of pastureland looked parched and brown, a sad contrast to the almost unnatural green of the irrigated fields. The forested hills looked tired and dusty, and Reyne found herself remembering the acres of dry underbrush. *One good lightning storm,* she decided, *and we could be in real trouble.*

Pushing the unwanted thought from her mind, she searched for others. Finding a pleasurable one, she hurried into the cottage and picked up the phone.

"Rachel!" she began as soon as her friend picked up on the other end, "Listen, let's grab Beth and go to the swimming hole! I'd kill for a dip in that water right now!"

"Oh, that sounds great," Rachel said wistfully. "But I've got the baby, Mary's out grocery shopping, and Dirk is who knows where."

"Bring Samuel along! There's shade there under the big oak, and we can take turns watching him."

She could hear Rachel's excitement grow. "Well, if you're sure you wouldn't mind watching him some…"

"Mind? I would love to. I need to get out of here. Away from my fax and my computer screen."

"And the phone?" Rachel ventured.

"Yeah. And the phone. I'm sick of worrying about it all. All I want to think about is my friends, your babies, and a nice, cool spot on the river."

"Sounds good to me," Rachel said. "Let me pull together some lunch. You pick up Beth and then us. We'll be ready by then."

"Great!" Reyne said, feeling enthusiastic about something for the first time since she left Colorado.

Beth sounded tired when Reyne called her, but she was unwilling to miss out on anything. She said she would leave Hope with the new cook and be ready within a few minutes. "But I don't know if I'm up for swimming," she warned.

"No problem," Reyne said readily. "It'll still feel good to be down by the water—with your incredible friends, of course."

"Of course!" Beth said.

Reyne could almost picture the weak smile on her friend's face. *Please, God, give us as much time as possible with her,* she prayed silently. "I'll pick you up in ten minutes."

"Good enough," Beth responded, then hung up.

Reyne rushed around getting ready. She threw on her deep blue swimsuit, a pair of cutoffs, and a T-shirt and, at the last second, tied a sweatshirt cardigan around her waist before climbing in her truck and heading for the Double M to pick up Beth.

When they reached Timberline, they all piled into Rachel's Jeep, which was already packed with the picnic and the baby. They pulled up to the swimming hole on the Kootenai River fifteen minutes later, giggling like schoolgirls on some errant escapade.

Rachel parked not eight feet from the water, directly under an old shade tree so the baby could stay in his car seat, where he had fallen asleep. The river was wide at this point, perhaps thirty feet across, and more quiet and shallow than in other places. An eddy had formed long ago, creating a deep pool that was a perfect green blue. Tiny pieces of bark and creek grass floated here and there on the surface, swirling upstream in a hypnotic display, as if inviting the women to join them. Rich, green grasses lined the river's bank, and the rushing sound of the water immediately made them feel cooler.

"That water looks delicious," Reyne said. "I've been so hot for so many days that all I care about eating is that pool."

"I haven't been swimming here in ages," Rachel said. "It's been two, maybe three, years, hasn't it, Beth?"

Beth laughed as she carefully pulled herself from the backseat. "Yes. It has to be three years. It was that day we came here after our food fight in the kitchen. Remember? You stripped and jumped in the water, and you had just dried off and redressed when Dirk rounded the corner on his horse."

"That's right!" Rachel said, shrieking with laughter at the memory. "Talk about timing!" The three women spread out their huge picnic blanket and took off their shoes to dangle their feet in the water while they ate their sandwiches. Afterward, they leaned back on the blanket, looking up into the barely wavering leaves of the towering birch above them.

"Where are you, Beth?" Rachel asked, finally broaching the question that had been on her and Reyne's minds since they got there. Their friend had been very quiet. "How are you feeling?"

Beth stayed where she was on her back, simply staring upward. "Physically, each hour is a battle. Emotionally, I'm up and down, really feeling like I'm grieving all over again. It's like last time I prepared myself for this. But after the mastectomy and the all-clear report from my doctor at three months, six months…even a year later, I relaxed. I told myself that I was going to live a full life. I was going to have lots of time with Matthew and Hope. So now I have to deal with saying good-bye all over again."

Neither of her friends responded. They could hear in her voice the need to talk.

"Mentally, it's like God's been whispering the truth in my ear all along. The news that the cancer had suddenly spread far and wide didn't come as a surprise. It didn't. It was like he had been preparing me so I wouldn't waste precious time on the why-me's but rather concentrate on things that are eternal. Like this. You two will always remember our playing here by the pool. At least I hope so." She paused, thinking, apparently gathering strength to go on.

"Every day is so precious. I wish I could give you the gift of this feeling without the price I'll have to pay. Do you understand what it might be like to think you'll die within the next few years…the next few months…the next few days? Time is no longer endless…it is absolutely priceless. There's no more waste in my life. That's why I went ahead and redecorated the dining room; I've always hated it. That's why Matt and I have been traveling more, trying to do the kinds of things we've always wanted to.

"When you finally realize that each day is a gift, you live your life differently. You spend your time on family and friends, giving them every ounce of love possible. You give yourself permission to take care of yourself, to celebrate all that God has graced you with." Beth sat up with some effort, pushing her brown wavy hair away from her face as if it were interfering with her momentum. She looked down and over at her friends. "Do you guys get it? Can you grasp what I'm saying?"

"I think so," Rachel said. "How do we know? I mean, really? You're facing something that we can only begin to imagine."

"Yeah," Reyne put in. "You sound like you've turned this living nightmare into something wonderful. I don't know if I'd have the strength to do that. I'd be back in the why-me's you talked about."

"Like you are with Logan?" Beth asked quietly.

Reyne frowned and turned to look at her. "What do you mean?"

"I think you know, Reyne. 'Why does it have to be a firefighter I've fallen for? Why does he have to jump out of planes for a living? Why does he have to fight the thing I am most scared of?'"

Reyne sat up, pulling her knees to her chest and holding them like a physical barrier. "Enough with the lecture already. Let's go swimming!"

"Uh-uh," Rachel said. "You're not getting off that easily, Reyne. You've been fretting about Logan since you got home."

"You've got to let go of your fear, Reyne," Beth urged. "It will get in the way of one of these priceless, rare things that God sends our way. Do you know how many women would give their eyeteeth to find a love like you and Logan have discovered?"

"Well, I'm going to take a dip," Reyne said, ignoring Beth and standing up. "Come on, you guys. Come with me." She pulled off her T-shirt and was pulling off her shorts when Beth rose with some effort and came very, very close to her.

"Reyne Oldre, do you hear me?" Beth looked angry, an emotion that her friends had seldom seen on her. Reyne looked to Rachel in confusion, taking a faltering half-step backward. "Do you hear a word I'm saying? You've got to stop wasting time on this fear of yours. Explore it. Make yourself deal with the agony of that day in Idaho. *And get beyond it.* This is your chance. Don't you see?" Beth's voice took on a note of pleading. "Do you think it's a coincidence that God has placed a firefighter in your heart?" She shook her head. "No way. He wants you to deal with Oxbow. Once and for all."

Beth turned, taking a couple of steps away from Reyne and looking out at the river. With wisps of hair flying in the slight afternoon breeze, she turned to look back at her friends, and all Reyne could think of was that she looked like an angel. Her voice was softer, more powerful somehow, when she began again. "Reyne, you *have* to go back. Go back to that day. Remember. Mourn. Be angry.

But get past it. Each moment is a precious gift, and your fear is keeping you from one of the most glorious gifts there is: love. Logan loves you."

Beth stepped closer and took her friend's hand. "Let him love you, Reyne. Let him. Please."

Reyne dared to look into her eyes, which shone with an unfamiliar brightness. There was a hint of eternal knowledge in their depths; Reyne felt as if Beth could see into the very center of her being, as if God was speaking through her. And all Reyne could see in those fathomless eyes was love. For all of Reyne's stubbornness and fear, Beth…God loved her. As Logan apparently loved her.

Reyne broke their intense gaze, looking out across the river and nodding slightly. She was silent for a full minute. Pride kept her from acquiescing entirely though. "Can we swim now?" she asked with a quiet smile and a raised brow.

Beth's lips turned up in response, and she finally let her off the hook. "You two go in," she said. "I'll stay up here and keep an eye on Samuel."

Rachel and Reyne spent a good hour laughing and playing after their intense conversation. Beth looked on, chuckling with them from the bank and even shrieking a bit when they splashed her. She was holding the baby while Rachel and Reyne took turns swinging out above the water on a long rope and then dropping into the pool. Beth was scoring their descents, giving them points for artistic finesse and especially for avoiding belly flops.

Reyne had just dived in, barely making a splash as she arced into the pool. She even pointed her toes. She emerged at the surface, smiling and smugly expecting a big score from Beth. But what she saw she didn't expect. Beth and Rachel were still sitting on the bank with little Samuel. But behind them stood Dirk Tanner…and beside him, Logan McCabe.

Logan and Dirk had heard the women from a quarter mile away, their laughter carrying along the water. "I told you we'd find them here," Dirk had said smugly. When Logan had finally reached Elk Horn and couldn't find Reyne, he had been nearly frantic that they had missed one another. He was due to fly out on assignment again tomorrow. He had to see her before then. He had to know where they stood.

When they reached the pool, the sight of her took his breath away. Suddenly all his well-planned words escaped him. He couldn't even remember one of his standby jokes to break the ice. All he could think about was how lovely she was, her pale hair waving about her on the water as she surfaced, her shapely form barely hidden in the depths. He was glad Dirk was a happily married man. Logan wanted this woman for himself.

Reyne exited the pool gracefully, taking hold of bunches of reeds on the bank and using makeshift steps in the muddy wall to rise from the water. Logan tried not to stare, focusing on her eyes. Reyne smiled at him shyly, an uncommon expression for her, which made it all the more fetching. But he supposed he would deem any look she gave him at this moment as heartstopping.

As if they were in a tunnel, their friends just seemed to fade away. Beth gathered up Samuel and carried him to the car, presumably to change him. Dirk welcomed his wife from behind the protection of a proffered beach towel, and they walked a ways down the river. Logan did not care why. He only cared that he was alone with the woman he loved.

Silently she gathered a multicolored towel around her body, fastening it under her arms sari-style. Tentatively, she moved closer and closer to him. Her face was wet, her long lashes clinging together under the weight of the droplets. Without a word, she tilted her face upward, and he bent to kiss her deeply.

Reyne leaned against him, and he could feel her damp towel seep moisture onto his shirt and pants. But he did not care. All he cared about was that she was here, in his arms. There was no place he would rather be.

When they finally broke off their kiss, she encircled him with her arms and gave him a fierce hug. "Oh, Logan," she began, "I am so sorry."

CHAPTER NINETEEN

Logan and Reyne separated the next day on better terms, but then they did not see one another again for weeks. It seemed that every time Reyne got home from the field to check her messages, wash clothes, and water her garden, Logan was away on assignment. And whenever Logan returned to check and repair equipment, sift through paperwork, and continue training his crew, Reyne was called out.

They communicated through lengthy letters sent to various smokejumper bases, trying to convince themselves and one another that the separation was good for them in many ways. They had the chance to get to know each other mentally and emotionally through writing without having to deal with the physical challenges of intense attraction. They had the opportunity to pursue their work whole-heartedly instead of trying to divide their time. But all their excuses sounded feeble on paper and to their own ears. Still, they repeated them over and over.

In letters, Reyne learned all about Logan's family. His grand-father had been a full-timer in fire for fifty years, even serving with the great Pulaski himself. Logan's father had followed in his footsteps. His mother had borne the brunt of raising the kids over summers when he was gone most of the time. And two of his three brothers claimed to be "messed up" because of their father's periodic absence. For Logan, on the other hand, his father had provided a goal, an ideal, a hero figure. Still, he maintained that if he and his "future wife—whoever she may be" ascertained that it was better for his children to have their father stay home more, he would find a way to do so.

"Yeah," Reyne mused, looking over his letter for the second time. "If you live to make that decision." She looked forward to his daily letter, rushing to greet George, the old, stooped-over mailman. Each day that she was home, George handed her a new missive with an insider's grin. Sometimes after being away, there would be numerous letters for Reyne to open, and she would carefully separate them by postmark to know which one to open first. Everything was deemed junk mail compared to the sweet letters that were always written on white, college-ruled legal pads, and carefully marked with Logan's terrible, illegible script that she enjoyed deciphering.

Still, the letters dredged up all kinds of emotions. She liked getting the firsthand news of the fire Logan was currently fighting, the paragraphs of love prose, the tidbits of information that let her know Logan better. But caring about him, getting to know him more deeply, made Reyne's fear of losing him all the greater. And his absence did not help. There were no tender hugs to shore her up. No gentle kisses to push away her fears.

So it was with some surprise that the two actually found themselves in town at the same time in late July, just in time for Elk Horn's annual Sweet Pea Festival. Logan showed up one afternoon, knocking on her studio door and calling "FedEx" to throw her off track. When Reyne opened the door, she gasped and then threw her arms around him. It had been about three weeks since they had seen each other, and having him in her arms again made her want to never let go.

"Oh, Logan," she said happily, nestling her head under his chin and listening to the steady thump of his heart, "it is so, so great to see you."

"And you," he said. Logan bent his head, searching for her lips, and tentatively she raised hers to meet his. Their kiss began shyly, then grew more searching, passionate, as the seconds ticked by. Finally she ducked away, feeling the niggling need to break their intense embrace before things got out of hand.

Logan grinned at her, looking like a model in his collarless denim shirt and cream Henley underneath. "Oh, I almost forgot," he said suddenly, bending over to reach down beside the door. "This is for you." In his hand was a single, delicate pink sweet pea flower, already withering in the heat. Reyne briefly wondered where he had found it; the ones in her own garden had succumbed to the brutal summer weather weeks ago.

"Will you be my date tomorrow for the dance?" he asked.

"If we're both in town," she said, angling her head sideways and shooting him a you-never-know-with-our-schedules look.

He raised one eyebrow, throwing her a mischievous grin. "We will. I made sure of it."

"You did, did you?" She moved into his arms once more and gazed up at him.

"Yep," he said proudly, "I did. Took us off the active lists for twenty-four whole hours. We deserve it. And there's no fire that's more important than a little time with my lady."

Reyne laughed lightly and grinned up at him, unable to stop staring. How had this big, adorable man made his way into her heart? "Well, since you've gone to such great lengths, I guess I'll go with you to that dance."

"I'm mighty glad to hear it, ma'am," Logan said with his best John Wayne imitation. "Mighty glad."

The next evening cooled to a glorious seventy-five degrees, finally breaking their streak of hundred-degree days and eighty-degree nights. Reyne moved from room to room in her cottage, unable to keep from smiling as she readied herself for the dance. "For goodness' sake, Reyne Oldre," she said to her mirrored reflection, forcing a frown to her face. "You're acting like a girl getting ready for her first prom."

But even her own condescension failed to dim her bright mood, and she continued to pace happily, reveling in the feelings of love. She was barefoot, and the cool wood floors felt good to her toes. Forcing herself to concentrate, she moved in her robe to the kitchen, where she haphazardly ironed a cream linen sheath, then pulled it on.

Looking in her full-length antique mirror, she reached for artsy gold hoop earrings, then a gold pendant on a long black necklace. Reyne looked herself over again. *Still missing something.* Raising one eyebrow, she walked to her bedroom closet and threw things over her shoulder, searching for her woven sandals, and then the right bracelet.

Then she sat down in front of her vanity mirror, touched up her makeup, and braided her hair. *Too young,* she decided, pulling it apart and glancing at the clock in alarm. Carefully, she wove her blond tresses, rolling them at the neckline and winding them around her head. When the last pin was in place, she had to admit that her hair looked great. Fresh. Sophisticated. And just in time. Logan's knock sounded at the door a second later.

When Reyne opened the door, she took Logan's breath away. Unwilling to let a comic moment pass him by, he staggered backward, clutching his heart and audibly gasping for breath.

Reyne gave him a patient smile, waiting for his theatrics to end. Her eyebrows went up in concern as he neared the porch steps and teetered for a moment, almost falling. When he had regained his balance, he sheepishly looked back at her.

"Great, just great," she quipped. "This is the man who jumps out of airplanes for a living. Is that supposed to make me feel better?"

"You notice, of course," he said, drawing near her again, "that I regained my balance. Another near accident averted because of the supreme balancing ability of Logan McCabe." He puffed out his chest and struck a heroic pose.

"Bravo," she said blandly.

He turned back to her, quickly looking her over from head to toe. "You, my love, are stunning."

Reyne gave him a genuine smile then. "And you're not half bad yourself. I like that shirt."

Logan fingered the heavy, hand-woven cotton. "This li'l ol' thing?" he asked in a silly imitation of a Southern belle.

"The cowboy boots, too," she said, pointing to his feet.

He grinned and looked down. With the extra height of the boots, he realized, he was a good six inches taller than she. She was gazing up at him, her face bright in its halo of pale gold, and he fell silent, cherishing the look of love in her eyes. *Please Father,* he prayed silently, *let that love always be there.*

Logan could not imagine anything better than this feeling between them. It was exhilarating. Sometimes when he was fighting a fire, he entertained thoughts of quitting just to be with her. What could be more important? Lately he had considered her suggestion of serving on a command center team. That way, they would be far more likely to end up together at a fire than they were now. Or maybe the forestry company would eventually hire her, too. It all depended on a lot of unknown factors.

He considered telling Reyne right then what he was thinking. Then he shelved the idea, deciding to wait for the perfect moment. *If I really want to do it,* he wondered.

"Madam," he said, offering her his arm, this time taking on the voice of a distinguished English gentleman, "it would be my distinct pleasure to escort you to the ball."

"Lead on, my good man, lead on."

Reyne and Logan joined their friends at the dinner tables outside the grange hall half an hour later, immediately joining in the merry fun of the barbecue dinner, the loud, raucous conversation, the un-bridled laughter. As usual, the entire town had turned out for the annual event of the summer. What was unusual was the general absence of the festival's hallmark, buckets of fragrant sweet peas. In the near-drought conditions, there were few to be found in Elk Horn's gardens. Many gardeners had brought roses instead, which were prospering in the heat. The townspeople had happily dubbed the roses "temporary sweet peas" and gone about their festival.

Reyne reached over to hug Rachel and Beth and to give their husbands quick kisses on the cheek. She ignored the fact that Beth was as white as her cotton dress and smiled into her friend's eyes as if willing strength into her body. But as they sat down to eat, she could not help but notice the slow manner in which Beth approached her meal, as if every motion was agony and even lifting the rib to her mouth to eat was a burden.

Still, Beth was smiling, and the general mood was upbeat. They finished eating and then joined others who were filtering into the grange hall to dance off their supper.

Inside, the temperature rose a good ten degrees, and Reyne was glad she had chosen her sleeveless linen dress. She moved into Logan's arms for a fast dance where he whirled her about, teaching her the country-western steps as they went. She felt like clay under the potter's deft fingers, easily finding her way with the dance as if she had known it all her life.

"You're quite a dance instructor," she said into his ear, almost shouting to be heard over the noise of the country band. "Is there anything you don't do well?"

Logan clamped his lips shut and furrowed his brow, apparently thinking while he continued to lead her across the dance floor. When they came together again in a subtle move, he whispered into her ear, "My chocolate cakes are pretty sad."

She laughed, feeling alive and happy, truly happy, for the first time in what seemed like ages. Dance after dance, Logan taught her new steps and kept her on the floor, discouraging her many admirers from cutting in. Clearly, they were a couple and interested in no one but each other. Their eyes often met and held, creating "eternal moments," as Beth would have called them.

Surely this is the handsomest man I've ever met, Reyne thought as she gazed into his sparkling sky blue eyes. She laughed out loud.

"What?" Logan asked, taking her hand and expertly swinging her around.

"Nothing," she said evasively, still smiling.

"What?" he asked again, giving her a mock-threatening look.

"I was just thinking about the first time I saw you," she said.

"And?"

"And I thought you were the biggest jerk in the world."

"And the most handsome and intelligent, right?" he said, smiling down into her eyes for a moment before they separated and went on with their dance.

"That came later. Definitely later."

"As long as it came. I, on the other hand, knew as soon as I saw you that you were beautiful and intelligent."

"Oh, so it's a contest now who discovered whom?"

"There was no contest," he quipped, smiling smugly.

She shook her head and smiled, feeling her cheeks ache from all the grinning and laughing. *Thank you, Lord,* she prayed suddenly. *Thank you for this incredible happiness.*

It was with some consternation that Reyne watched Beth accept a friendly neighbor's invitation to dance. She had been sitting with Matt, storing up energy for a slow dance with him, but could not refuse the sweet, well-meaning invitation. It was so like Beth to go the extra mile just so she wouldn't hurt anyone's feelings. *If it were me, I would've just said no thank you.*

Furtively Reyne watched her friend, glancing occasionally to Matthew's worried face.

"What's wrong?" Logan asked at their next turn.

"Oh, nothing. It's just that—" She broke off, watching Beth more closely. Was something wrong, or was Reyne just imagining things?

"What?" Logan looked over his shoulder, following her gaze. "You worried about Beth?"

"Well, yes. She hasn't been feeling great, and she's as white as—" This time she broke away from Logan, running to the spot where Beth lay slumped on the floor, her bewildered partner kneeling beside her. A crowd gathered, and the music trailed off as people rushed to help. Matthew shoved his way through, checked his wife's pulse, and called, "Beth? Can you hear me? Beth?"

The group grew silent as they waited in vain for her answer.

CHAPTER TWENTY

*T*he news wasn't good. At the county hospital, Logan and Reyne had sat with the Tanners and their pastor while Matt stayed in the emergency room with Beth, awaiting test results from the lab. Beth had come around while still on the dance floor, protesting that she had fainted and nothing more, but Matt had insisted on taking her to the hospital to check things out. Much to Beth's dismay, the Tanners, Logan and Reyne, and Pastor Arnie went with them.

They were glad they were there though. Hours later, when Matt came out to pass along the report, he looked gravely ill himself. But he managed to keep his composure for a time, carefully explaining what had been explained to him. Beth was dying. The cancer was so pervasive that it had spread throughout her body—the lymph nodes, her liver, even her brain.

"Looking at radiology reports," Matt said, finally daring to look into his friends' compassionate eyes, "the doc says it's a miracle she's alive now." His last words were choked with agony, and then he finally let go. Watching the big bear of a man dissolve into tears immediately brought the rest of them to their feet. Logan moved to him, embracing him in a fierce hug. Then Rachel gently led Matt to a couch and sat down beside him.

Matt kept saying, "I gotta be strong," chanting it as if saying it would make it true. But the words just made him teary all over again.

"We need to pray," Arnie ventured softly to the tightly knit group when Matt finally gained some measure of control. "What would you like us to pray for, Matt?"

His suggestion just seemed to aggravate Matt's pain, and his tears turned into giant, quiet sobs. *O God,* Reyne cried silently. *This can't be happening! Tell me this is not happening! Please, Father, where are you? Not Beth! Not her!*

Matt's friends waited, with tears streaming down their own faces, until he regained his composure. He swallowed hard, wiping his eyes and nose with a large handkerchief. "Time," he said at long last. "Let's pray for every minute that God will spare her to be with us."

And right there they knelt about him, praying for as much time as possible.

Logan and Reyne rode home in silence, each thinking about Beth and Matt and little Hope. Reyne was the first to speak as they exited the highway toward her home. "Surely this can't be God's way," she said softly.

"His ways are mysterious," Logan answered. "What doesn't make a whole lot of sense now will make more sense years from now."

Logan's answer angered her, as if he were dismissing all of the pain with his easy, trite words. "I don't care about the future," Reyne said, sniffling and looking toward the reflected dashboard lights in her dark window. It was late, about eleven o'clock. "How can you say things like that?"

Logan continued driving, apparently mulling over his response. "I don't think they come easily. I mean, I'm almost thirty-one, and I have learned some hard lessons. In the end, it seems that afterward I can always see more clearly where God was than when I'm in the middle of the muck of life."

Reyne nodded, still sniffling. "Sorry," she forced herself to say. "I'm not mad at you. It's just hard for me to see how Beth's dying would be a part of some divine plan. And I'm mad at Beth's body for not fighting off the cancer. At God for not stepping in. She doesn't deserve to die, Logan. She's such a good person. She has so much to teach me as my friend! She and Matt—they're great together. And Hope…how fair is it for a three-year-old to lose her mother?" The tears came fast, building with each new thought.

Logan pulled to a stop in front of her house, unfastened Reyne's seat belt, and then drew her to him. He sat there, silently waiting for her to finish crying, not pushing, not making her feel stupid for doing so, just understanding and waiting and holding her.

When she had wiped her face again and gained some measure of control, he spoke. "Reyne, we have to think about all the things we can do to make Beth's last days the best possible. I think that's what God wants of us. To bow our heads and accept whatever's ahead, make the most of it. And to celebrate every moment that we have with Beth as a gift. That's what the Morgans are after. We should be too."

Reyne nodded, tearing up again. "That's what she told me that day by the creek," she said, fairly croaking. "'Every moment is precious,' she told me."

Logan opened his door. "Why don't you invite me in for coffee? I think we both need to talk. And pray."

Chapter Twenty-One

*D*espite the fires that were raging from Washington to Mexico, Reyne requested a leave of absence. The officials at Forest Service headquarters were gracious but reluctant to let her go. She was needed, they said. But Reyne gave them no choice. To her, there *was* no choice but to stay near Beth. To Reyne, there *was* no greater need than that of the Morgan family.

Rachel and Reyne took turns spending the afternoon at the Double M. They fielded phone calls from neighbors and church friends, suggesting ways to help. They helped Beth bathe as she grew too weak to get in and out of the tub, brought Hope to her bedside so she could read to her daughter, and picked up the stories when Beth fell asleep in the middle of them. And then, gently, they would ease the little girl away from her mother, often distracting her with games outside the house. All the while, every adult was counting the ten days that the doctors had allotted as Beth's probability at life.

One afternoon four days after Beth had come home from the hospital, Reyne was playing with Hope outside while Beth rested. Hope was giggling and being so silly that it caught her father's attention and he went to retrieve the video camera to shoot some footage. While they went on playing, Reyne suddenly stopped, looking from Matt to the bedroom window upstairs.

"Hey, Matt," Reyne said. "I just had a great idea."

"What's that?" he said, looking at her through the camera lens.

"I'll tell you in a minute." She rushed by him, eager to get to Beth and see what she thought.

It seemed like hours before Beth finally awakened. When she did, Reyne was right there. "Beth," she said, kneeling beside her bed, "I just had a brainstorm."

"Uh-oh," her friend managed to joke, her voice little more than a whisper. "What are we in for now?"

"Stop it," Reyne said, nudging her arm playfully. "Matt was out there videotaping Hope, and I got to thinking. What if we set up a camera and taped you? You know, make a series of tapes for Hope from her mom. For her eighth birthday or her eighteenth. For her baptism! Her wedding day!" She stopped herself from getting too excited about the idea before Beth agreed to it. The last thing Beth needed was pressure.

Beth turned her head on her pillow and gazed outside. A single tear escaped her eyes and trickled down her left cheek. "That," she said, taking a deep breath, "would be wonderful." She thought a bit more and then said, "But I don't want to look like an invalid. You and Rachel would have to make me beautiful and then get me into a chair in the living room. No bedridden, last-messages stuff."

"It's a deal." Reyne smiled. It felt good to have a plan, a purpose. She took Beth's hand in hers. "I'm so glad you like the idea. I think those tapes will become priceless to Hope as she gets older."

"It's a good way to reach out to her, even after I'm gone."

Her words frightened Reyne. How could they be talking this way? How had it come to this? It seemed unreal. Surreal. Intolerable.

"To show her how much I love her," Beth was saying, "how much I miss her. How dearly I wanted to be a part of her life." Beth paused to take a breath, apparently forcing tears away. Reyne waited patiently, trying hard to ignore what felt like an elephant sitting on her chest. She swallowed hard against sudden tears. "Call Rachel, will you Reyne?" Beth asked in a whisper. "Ask her if she can come first thing tomorrow. I usually do better in the mornings."

"I'll call her right away," Reyne managed, but her words fell on deaf ears. Beth was already fast asleep.

They began the following morning. After helping Beth bathe, Rachel and Reyne combed out her hair and dried it into soft waves. The bath seemed to sap Beth's energy though, so they had to wait for an hour while she napped. But when she awoke, she was a woman on a mission. There was a sparkle in her eyes and more energy in her movements than her friends had seen in weeks.

They helped her put on some makeup, especially blush to give her some color and concealer to hide the shadows under her eyes. Then they brushed out her hair again. Beth picked out a light-colored, classy dress, and then they helped her down the stairs and settled her into a large, comfy living-room chair.

Matt came in with Hope and smiled as he saw his wife. "You look so pretty, honey," he said, bending down to kiss her and then hand Hope over. The little girl gave her mother a fierce hug.

"Are you going to town with us, Mommy?" she asked, touching Beth's hair as if it were her Barbie's.

"No, sweetie. Aunt Rachel and Reyne are going to help me with some special movies." She looked down to watch Hope tentatively nod. "Remember what we talked about last night? That I have to go away soon and live with Jesus?"

Little Hope nodded again, this time more slowly. Reyne had to turn away to hide the tears that sprang to her eyes.

"Well, I'm making some movies for you to watch on special occasions, so you can feel like I'm part of those special times." She pulled the little girl to her and stroked her hair. Her voice was choked with emotion. "Because I don't want to miss those times, baby." Tears came and flowed down her cheeks. She sniffled, obviously trying to regain her composure and be strong in front of her daughter.

Reyne moved in to help. "Would you look at that?" she asked Hope brightly. "Your mommy is the star of our movie, and she's ruining her makeup! Do you think we should fire her?"

"No!" Hope said gleefully, jumping at the chance to escape the heavy moment.

"Are you sure? Maybe we should make Aunt Rachel the star." Reyne stood back and looked Rachel over as if she were truly considering it. Rachel played along, striking a glamorous pose.

"NO!" Hope shouted and giggled. "Mommy's best!" Beth smiled through her tears, wiping her nose with a tissue and giving Hope another quick hug.

Matt moved closer. "Time to go, pumpkin. Let's go see Mr. Laramie at the hardware store. Maybe he has that Big Wheel out you like to ride."

"Yeah!" Hope scooted off her mother's lap and ran to the door. "C'mon, Daddy!" she yelled, her mind already occupied with a new adventure.

"Bye, honey," Matt said, bending low to kiss his wife tenderly. "Make us some movies so we can always remember how wonderful and beautiful you are."

Reyne glanced at Rachel, wondering if she had heard his heart-wrenching words, too. Apparently she had, because she swallowed hard and squeezed her eyes shut.

Finally the three friends were alone.

Reyne steeled herself for the hard moments ahead and then looked through the lens of the camera, set up on a tripod. "Perfect," she announced. She looked over the tiny Sony to grin at Beth. "You look mahvelous, dahling."

Beth merely smiled and nodded, as if she were saving every ounce of energy for what was ahead. Then she looked down for a moment, thinking. "Will you guys pray with me?" she asked.

"Of course," Rachel said.

"What are we praying for?" Reyne asked, coming to kneel beside Beth.

"For the right words," she said. "For my final words."

Somehow they got through the next few days, taping for several hours at a time and then getting Beth upstairs to rest. Often Rachel or Reyne would have to leave the room. At times they left Beth alone with the remote control to tape herself. It was easier if one of them was there, however, because Beth was so weak that she often dozed off in midsentence.

By the third day Beth had made many tapes for Hope and had hand-lettered each of the labels. Reyne read through them: "Your First Day of School: Kindergarten, First Grade, Junior High, High School, and College; Your Grade School, Junior High, High School, College, and Grad School Graduations—"

"No low expectations from this mother," Beth quipped as Reyne read them.

"On Your Baptism Day & Questions About God; Your First Job and Your First REAL Job; A Word About Sex, Your First Date, Broken Hearts, and So You've Met Mr. Right; Your Wedding Day & a Word to the Groom; When Life Gets You Down & You Miss Your Mom; You're Going to Have a Baby!; and birthday messages for every year through age thirty."

On the birthday tapes Beth often talked about what she herself had gone through or experienced that year, thus leaving a legacy of memories as well as advice and warm wishes for her daughter. Beth included favorite Bible verses or quotations as well. One afternoon, Reyne watched through the camera lens as Beth taped Hope's final birthday message.

"So, sweetheart," Beth said into the camera, "you're thirty years old. Hard to imagine for your mom, who at the time of this taping is only thirty-two. I think that turning thirty made me think I was really an adult. Responsibility hit me like a ton of bricks," she said with a smile, her eyes alight. "You were a year old. I was cooking for the ranch hands—twelve of them—and raising you. It was only when I got sick and had my mastectomy that we hired a cook.

"Thirty was an age of discovery for me too. In fact, I've always been thankful for my cancer. If that sounds strange, think of it this way. If you were to find that a life-threatening disease was living in you, would you not cherish each day? So many times we plan on our future—'If I can just earn this amount of money I can get this' or 'If I can just accomplish this, I can do that'—you get the picture." Beth paused, looked down at her hands, then back at the camera. She leaned forward to emphasize her next words.

"Don't wait, Hope. Make the most of every single moment God has given you. Life is precious. Celebrate it. I've loved this life. You've made it all the more rich for me, as has your father, my friends. That's what Christ calls us to do. Don't sit back and accept what comes. Go out there and *take* it. Life really is what you make of it. Don't you want yours to be an incredible adventure? That doesn't mean you have to trek through the Himalayas. You can be a housewife on a remote Montana ranch, raising a daughter alongside your husband, and still be incredibly satisfied. I have been."

She paused, emphasizing again each of her next words. "You deserve the best, my daughter. I'm sure you would have been my friend. Make the most of your years, Hope. And know that through all of your happy and sad moments I'll be right beside you. I love you."

Reyne willed her fingers to find the stop button. She struggled to find the right words, but failing, remained silent.

Beth was nodding off again anyway, exhausted from the emotion of her taped messages. Rachel moved from her perch in the corner and brought over an afghan to cover Beth. Then she and Reyne went into the kitchen to force themselves to eat some lunch.

As they made sandwiches, Rachel looked at Reyne. "Have you noticed something?" she asked.

"What?" Reyne asked, scooping some mayonnaise out of the jar.

"These last few weeks—ever since Beth was diagnosed really. And since you came into our lives and we started our Saturday morning coffee klatches."

"Yes..."

"Our conversations. I've never really had friendships like this. I mean, Beth and I were as close as sisters before, but the cancer... It's like we talk differently because we know we don't have forever, you know? I wish we had talked this way before, that we hadn't let life itself impede us. It's as if the threat of death has made us all live life more fully."

Reyne nodded, understanding. "Yeah, I know. I noticed it right away. I thought it was just you two—like you were special or something and just waiting for me to join you. But as I think back, it probably had more to do with the fact that Beth had been diagnosed beforehand. She led the way, set the pace. I was just fortunate that you two included me in your friendship." She reached out to give Rachel a tender hug. "I wouldn't have missed this time for the world."

"Me neither," Rachel said, her eyes dry for once. She was excited from translating her vague feelings into clear thought. "We've talked about things we've always talked about before," she said. "It's just that we've gone deeper; we're more honest. And more intimate, unafraid to share, you know?"

Reyne nodded. "It's the kind of friendship women prize. The kind we always search for."

Rachel studied her for a moment. "I'm glad you moved here, Reyne. I'm glad I'm not alone in this. I need you." She choked up and once again moved to hug Reyne.

Reyne smiled through her own tears. "No kidding. This is grueling. I couldn't do it without you either. She gazed solemnly at her friend. "Of course, you know, chocolate helps too."

Then suddenly they were giggling. Relieved by the levity, Rachel moved away and finished making her sandwich. "You do know we're using humor to mitigate the pain."

"Hey, nothing wrong with that," Reyne said, smiling. "Beth does it too. Like when she put that PATIENT: CANCER CARE CENTER sign in her car while she was going through chemotherapy?"

"Yeah," Rachel giggled. "So she could park for free."

Reyne laughed louder, remembering. "And she said that if a cop pulled her over and saw it, he'd feel too sorry for her to ticket her."

Rachel shook her head and laughed.

Beth shouted feebly from the other room. "Hey, you guys! No having fun without me!"

"Well, look who decided to wake up and join the party!" Reyne said, wiping her eyes quickly and pushing open the kitchen door. "Want something to eat?"

"Maybe a little. Can you bring it out here?"

"Coming right up," Rachel called.

CHAPTER TWENTY-TWO

*W*ith the videos completed, Reyne and Rachel resumed their previous routine at the Morgans', taking care of Beth and trying to make it possible for her to spend every waking moment with her husband and daughter. The cook took care of meals, but they often cleaned or did wash, not wanting Matt to waste precious time on the mundane.

Gradually, Beth got out of bed less and less. When she did, her gait became unsteady and slower by the day. She spent hours reading to Hope or sitting on the porch swing, watching her daughter play with Rachel and Reyne. She also spent a lot of time talking with Matt about the future—possible problems, situations, "girl things" he would need to know about.

Matt took it all in gravely, finally shushing her with tender kisses and cuddling with her on the couch. Those were the times that Reyne would have to look away. She could not bear the thought of Matt without Beth or vice versa. And seeing them together made her ache for Logan's arms.

Logan had been called out to Wyoming the previous week and hadn't been back since. He tried to call as often as possible, eager for word of Beth, and Reyne was quick to recognize that he was checking on her, too. He was as worried about her as he was about Beth.

"I'm sorry I'm not there," he told her over the phone that

evening. The call had come just as she walked in her door and kicked off her shoes.

Reyne leaned her forehead against the living-room window, watching her breath fog it up as she listened to him breathe on the other end of the line. "I need you, Logan. This...this is becoming unbearable."

She listened, waiting for him to respond. Part of her worried that he thought her weak for asking.

"I think I can get home in about six hours. By tomorrow afternoon definitely. Would that be okay, love?"

"Yes," she said softly. Not the "Well, don't come if it's a problem to get out of work" that sprang to her mind like a reflexive thought. Not "If you want to." Simply yes. It felt like a concession from Reyne, but she could not help herself. She needed him with her. She needed his arms around her, his comforting voice in her ear. And in the back of her mind, she admitted to herself that this would get him off the front line of fire.

"I have a surprise for you, Reyne," he said gently.

"Oh?" Reyne's voice was trailing in exhaustion.

"I'll tell you tomorrow, love. Get some sleep."

"Okay. I love you."

"I love you too. Tomorrow then. I can't wait."

"Me neither," she said. "And Logan?"

"Yeah?"

"Thank you."

The old BLM bus was feeling its age. As it chugged asthmatically along the highway that climbed toward the mountain pass, Logan found himself chanting "come on," under his breath, as if he could will the ancient vehicle to go faster.

Every minute of the trip from Wyoming seemed like hours to Logan. Reyne's voice, and the uncharacteristic naked need within, had seemed to wrap tendrils around his heart and give it a big tug. Everything in him wanted to be near her, comforting her, encouraging her, loving her.

And he was almost there—arriving home, just as he had promised. After telling the command center he needed to leave because of a "family emergency," he had organized the next mission for his crew, briefed the next person in line, and boarded a plane that was taking BLM troops home to Missoula. From there he had taken the bus hauling other personnel home to Elk Horn. At the time it had seemed the fastest way. Now Logan wasn't so sure.

The old bus finally made its way through the mountain pass and started its descent into the pristine valley. Logan was waiting by the door when it finally pulled into the airstrip, and he stepped off the minute the doors folded open, calling a quick *thanks* to the driver.

He took a deep breath. It seemed it had been ages since he had been able to do so. The air was fresh and clean, despite the heat, with not a trace of smoke. Logan sheltered his eyes with his hand and peered upward. The sky was light blue, draped here and there with thin, wispy cirrus clouds. Briefly he wondered how long Elk Horn could escape the choking smoke that was steadily spreading in so many Western forests.

Logan shoved the thought from his mind. He was eager to fill his thoughts with Reyne and Beth and Matt and the others. He felt needed, and that empowered his every step with purpose. He hurried toward the barracks for a shower and change of clothes, then hopped in his '51 Chevy to drive over to Reyne's.

She was out on the porch before he had even turned off the engine. Logan stared through the dirty windshield at her, wishing he had washed it so that even this first, brief glimpse of her would be unhindered. He thought her a vision, even with her blond hair pulled back in a messy ponytail and dark rings shadowing her eyes. These last weeks had been tough for her; he could see it. Still, there was no other who equaled her beauty in his eyes. Reyne was a caring, loving, brave, beautiful woman. And she needed him.

Logan stepped out of the truck and welcomed her into his arms.

"Oh, Logan," she said softly, her voice muffled. "Thanks for coming home."

"I'm glad to be here, babe. Thanks for asking me to come."

They stood there, holding each other, for several long minutes. Logan relished the feel of her body against his, cherished the intimacy of the moment. He stroked her hair. The burning late-July sun was making the golden strands hot to the touch.

Reyne pulled away first. "Hungry?" she asked.

"Thirsty," he said, but kissed her before she could step away. When their lips parted, he grinned down at her. "Powerful thirsty," he added.

Reyne gave him a playful swat and then led the way to the porch. "Then I guess you need a very tall glass of iced tea."

"I need a tall drink of something," he said, studying her shapely form as she climbed the porch steps.

"You wait here, cowboy," she said, gesturing toward the porch swing. "We'll want to sit out here and talk. It's sweltering inside."

Logan sat and waited for her, wishing she would hurry. It had been too long since they had seen each other, and he was impatient with even one more moment's separation.

Finally Reyne appeared with two tall, slim glasses brimming with ice cubes and lemon wedges. She sat down beside him with a smile. They toasted. "To finally being together again," Reyne said.

"Regardless of the circumstances," he added. They took a sip of tea, and then he asked, "How's Beth, Reyne?"

"Terrible. I'm thinking Matt's going to have to take her to the hospital. She doesn't want to go, but she's so terribly weak. It's tough for her to even eat. Rachel and I have tried everything we can think of—even milkshakes made with real cream—to keep up her energy and stop the weight loss. But it's hopeless. The most we can get down her is a couple of ounces."

Logan sighed and pulled Reyne closer to his side. "And how are you?" he asked tenderly, studying her face from the side.

"Exhausted. These last weeks have been tough, really tough." Her eyes became glossy with tears. "I just got to this point last night where I couldn't think of going on alone. I hope you don't think I'm a complete wimp for asking you to come home." She looked down and wiped her eyes with her hand.

Logan lifted her chin. "Reyne, your asking me to come meant a lot. It was the first time, really, that I felt like I was half of a couple. I want to be here for you in good times and bad. We've had some good times, so I guess what's coming is the bad. And I'll be here as long as you need me."

"Thank you," she managed to say softly. From her, it sounded like a painful admission. He folded her gently to him, determined to handle this new vulnerability carefully but also celebrating the new aspect to their relationship. This was the kind of trust they needed if they were ever to be together the way he hoped they would be. As man and wife.

Thank you, too, he prayed silently, as he held Reyne tenderly in his arms. *And help us to trust each other even more.*

After dinner the phone rang, and with some trepidation Reyne went to answer it. She prayed it wasn't the dispatch center, calling her or Logan off their leave, but she did not want it to be bad news about Beth either.

It was Rachel. Her friend was all business. "Reyne, Matt had to take Beth to the hospital. I think they're there now."

Reyne took a shallow breath. Logan came up behind her and slipped his arms around her waist. "Do they need us there?" she asked. Unconsciously, she leaned back against Logan's chest.

"I'm waiting to hear. Matt said he'd call."

"Beth doesn't need us there. She'll just worry about us."

"But I want to be there for Matt. Maybe I should call Arnie, too." Rachel's voice was giving way to the weariness that Reyne felt to the core of her soul. Reyne could hear the baby crying in the background. Briefly, she thought of how difficult these last weeks must have been for Rachel as a mother and wife.

"You're needed at home, Rachel. Why don't I go to the hospital and then report? Logan is here with me. We'll call you if you need to come, and then you can call Pastor Arnie."

"Okay," Rachel said finally. "But please, Reyne, call me the minute you know anything, will you?"

"I will. And I'll give her your love as soon as I see her." They hung up without saying good-bye, their hearts heavy, their worst fears finally realized.

Logan had picked up his keys before she said another word. "Ready?" he asked.

"Let's go," Reyne said.

Matt came to meet them in the waiting room several hours later. He looked haggard. Reyne rose and went to him, with Logan right behind. "Matthew, are you okay? What's the news?"

He sat down heavily on a blue couch, stretching out his work boots and clunking them down on the terrazzo floor. He rubbed his face as if he would gain energy from the action. His voice was uncharacteristically quiet. "This is it. She's dying."

Reyne and Logan waited for him to go on.

"The doc says she's got maybe two, three days left. He wants to keep her here, keep her medicated so she'll be comfortable, you know. Beth wants me to take her home." He swallowed hard. "I don't know if I can take it, you guys. I don't know if I can handle taking my wife home to die."

Reyne wondered where her tears came from. She thought of all the times she had cried these past weeks and thought there should be none left to shed. But Matt's obvious anguish cut to the heart. She took his hand with both of her own, waiting for him to regain control. Then she said, "We're going to be right here with you, Matt. Me and Logan and Rachel and Dirk. We're your friends. We won't let you down."

Matt shook off her hands and rose. "Aw, you guys all have stuff to do." He ran his hand through his hair, and paced. "You've got fires to fight. The Tanners have a ranch to run and their own kid to raise. The last thing you all need is us on your hands."

Logan and Reyne rose as one. Logan spoke first. "The last thing you three are is a burden. We want to be here for you. We want to help you any way we know how, man."

Matt stood there, thinking for a moment, and then nodded slightly. "Well, okay. I guess the first thing I need help on is deciding what's best to do about Beth."

In the end they decided that they should comply with Beth's wishes. With some coaxing, the doctor agreed that he could send them home with enough medication to keep Beth comfortable but still coherent. She had insisted that she wanted more from her last hours than being a zombie. But first she needed to stay in the hospital overnight so the medical staff could work on stabilizing her. Reyne saw her briefly, but she was asleep. All she could do was squeeze Beth's hand, carefully avoiding the IV, stroke her hair, and whisper to her that Rachel and she were thinking about her all the time.

She called Rachel when they returned home, and they agreed to meet at the Morgans' the next morning to prepare the house for Beth's final homecoming. As soon as Matt and Hope were out the door, they set to work getting meals ready and cleaning the house. They changed the sheets on the beds, dusted, vacuumed, and opened the windows to air out the house. They fluffed pillows and beat rugs, working like crazy to be done within the two hours that Matt had given them before returning.

Dinner that night was a celebration of sorts. Beth, energized by her brief stay in the hospital and perhaps realizing that there would not be many more dinners with her friends, even insisted Matt carry her to the table. They feasted on casseroles from the freezer—a selection from the bounty that had been left by church members during Beth's illness—and talked and laughed until eleven at night. Finally the Tanners and Logan and Reyne bade them good night, leaving them to tuck their sleeping daughter into bed and find some rest themselves.

Beth's rallying was temporary. Two days later, Reyne entered her room and noted with alarm the grim expression on Rachel's face. Rachel was beside Beth's bed, holding her hand. Matt was on the other side of the bed, holding her other hand. Hope lay in bed with her mother, cuddling.

Beth still managed a faint smile for Reyne and for Logan, who had entered the bedroom behind her. "Well, you're all here," she said in a voice barely more audible than a whisper. "This must be it."

"Not a chance," Reyne said quickly, instinctively wanting to abolish any negative thought. But even she could see the folly of it. Beth was right. She was nearing the end.

"Please," Beth said to Matt, "help me sit up." He moved to place some fluffy pillows behind her, raising her to a semisitting position. When she was settled, she raised her hand to Logan and Reyne as if beckoning them. Reyne sat beside her on the bed, and Logan knelt.

"Logan," she managed, "take care of Reyne. She is a wonderful, dear woman." Beth paused to take several breaths as if shoring up for an important task. Reyne noticed that her skin looked almost like porcelain, translucent. "And Reyne, you remember what we talked about by the pool that day."

Reyne nodded, staring into her eyes. For once, her own eyes were dry. Inside, she tried to reconcile what was happening with her feelings. *Please, God, tell me this isn't happening. Please tell me this isn't the end. Tell me it's not good-bye!* "I will," she told Beth. "I'll always remember your words. I'll always remember *you*."

Beth smiled again, softly, and Reyne fought off the desire never to leave her side, not to let her go. Beth looked at her with such tenderness, such understanding, that she suddenly felt a shiver along her spine. Once again Reyne noticed that Beth held something of the eternal in her gaze. As if she could see the other side and, therefore, saw those around her with even more vivid clarity.

Reyne tore her eyes from Beth's, knowing deep down inside that she was not going to look in them again. Logan bent down to squeeze Beth's hand and kiss her softly on the forehead before turning to put his arm around Reyne. They moved to the corner of the room, making room for the others.

Beth and Rachel spent several long minutes talking quietly, and then Dirk knelt by her side. With tears slipping down his cheeks, he thanked her for her friendship and for bringing his wife-to-be to Elk Horn. As Logan had done before him, he kissed her on the forehead and looked into her eyes for a long second before leaving her. "You'll be well cared for there, Beth," he said softly. "You won't have any more pain."

"I know," she whispered, looking at them all with eyes bright with tears.

She was slipping away. They all held their breath, as if waiting, feeling the tangible presence of the Spirit there with them.

"Mommy," Hope said, raising her head from her mother's chest, "I don't want you to go away."

"Oh, baby," she said, tears falling. "I don't want to go. But I'm not going far. I'm going to live where the angels sing. I'm going to be well enough to run and laugh and play again. And you've got to remember, I'll always be near you and your daddy. Loving you from the other side."

Reyne swallowed against the lump that choked her. She gripped

Logan's arms around her waist as if to gain strength from them.

"Now, you go to Daddy, sweetheart. He loves you very... much and will take good...care of you. You be a good girl. And you watch those...love tapes I left for you."

Hope nodded, her eyes big, trying to understand what was transpiring. She reached for her father, and he pulled her into his lap, moving to sit beside Beth on the bed as he did so. He took her hand.

"My love," Beth said. "I can't tell you...how thankful I am...for the time we had together." She paused, visibly losing strength by the moment. "You go on and live a full life. Find love again—"

"No, Beth," he interrupted. "Never."

"Matthew," she said, gasping for air now. "Know that I want you to love again. And...I'll be...waiting. For you. On the other side."

Matt, crying now too, bent to kiss her lips tenderly. "I know, Beth. I know. Are you leaving us now? Are you going home, baby?"

"Oh, Matt," she said, her voice suddenly stronger than it had been for days. "He's here. Jesus. *He's here.*" Her eyes were shining, glorious in the love and excitement that she alone could see. "I'm here, Lord. I'm here."

And then, as they all watched, the light in Beth's eyes faded, and her lids closed for the last time.

CHAPTER TWENTY-THREE

They buried Beth two days later on a picturesque, grassy knoll high in the century-old cemetery outside Elk Horn. It was only then that Reyne truly recognized how many lives her friend had touched. Beth's parents had arrived the day before, as had Rachel's parents. Their good friends, Jake and Emily Rierdon—now doing missionary work in the inner city of San Francisco with the intent of one day returning to Elk Horn—wanted desperately to come, but couldn't get away. Matt had spent a good hour that morning on the phone with them, reminiscing.

Earlier they had gathered inside the stifling hot country church to sing, pray, and remember Beth and the gift she had been. They dressed in bright colors, as Beth had requested. Person after person had approached the lectern, faced the congregation, and testified what Beth's encouragement, friendship, or faith had meant to them.

This is what it's all about, Reyne thought. *To have lived life and be remembered intimately in the hearts of many.* In small ways and in big ways, Beth had reached out and touched people. And behind her she had left a legacy.

There had been several moments when the group had laughed through their tears, remembering sweet, tender times with Beth. The hymns Beth had chosen for her own memorial service were upbeat, full of hope and praise. *Just like you, Beth,* Reyne thought softly, speaking in her mind to her dear friend.

The burial was swift, and they moved through it in a blur. Matt placed a red rose on the casket, and Hope laid a tiny, soft-pink rosebud on top of it. Then she turned away and lifted her arms, silently asking to be picked up, and Matt swiftly complied.

"Ashes to ashes, dust to dust," Arnie said, throwing a handful of dark, rich dirt. Reyne's breath caught at the poignancy of the moment. *That's what you were to us, Beth. Rich, fertile soil to our souls. Thank you. Thank you for all you taught me, shared with me.*

"We are sorry that Beth has left us," Arnie said as they lowered the casket in front of him, looking about the group gathered there. A light wind blew his hair into his face, and he reached up to push it back. "She leaves a huge void in our hearts, but friends, let us celebrate for her. Let us be happy, knowing that her pain has ended and she is in paradise."

He was silent for a minute, pursing his lips and bowing his head, letting them all ponder the thought. Then he continued, "Let us finish this day in prayer. Please lift up your own thoughts and thanks as you feel led to do so. I'll close us when we're done."

For half an hour the group prayed and praised the Lord for all the good things that Beth had shown them, shared with them. And in the end, they all agreed that the service had been just as Beth would have wanted: a celebration of her life and the hereafter, not a mournful farewell.

Gradually the group dispersed, each stopping to hug or speak to Matt in soft, hushed tones. When they were all gone, only the Tanners, Logan, and Reyne remained with him and Hope. Hope had skipped off, dragging a long branch over tombstones that lay in the ground and stopping to run her hands over the cool marble of various monuments while her grandparents numbly watched over her. Matt remained at the grave, staring down into the hole and at the glossy cover of Beth's casket.

Before long, his shoulders shook with gut-wrenching sobs. Reyne looked from him to his little girl, wondering about the best way to help them. Dirk was right there. "Why don't you and Rachel take Hope home?" he suggested. "Beth's folks have to take Rachel's parents to the airport, and I think Hope'll need a little mothering about now. Matt's not in great shape. Logan and I'll take care of him."

Reyne nodded, glancing up toward Matt again. She moved toward Logan for a brief, encouraging hug and kiss, then motioned to Rachel. Reyne told her what they had discussed, and her friend quickly agreed.

"Come on, Hope, honey," Rachel called to the little girl. Hope skipped over to her, and Rachel gathered her up in her arms. "How about an ice-cream cone?" she asked.

"Okay," she said, watching over her shoulder as the women carried her out of the cemetery. "Is Daddy coming?"

"No, pumpkin. Daddy's got to have some time to be sad about your mommy. He's going to miss her, just like you."

Reyne walked beside them, listening. "But you know what your mommy would want you to do?"

Hope looked at her with a slight frown and shook her head.

"She'd want you to cry when you have to, but also to smile and hold your head up high."

"'Cause she went to live with Jesus?"

"That's right. And if she were here, she'd order a triple-scoop ice-cream cone and make your Aunt Rachel pay for it."

"You'd better believe it," Rachel said.

"Can we bring Daddy a cone too?" Hope asked doubtfully.

"Sure, sweetheart," Reyne said. "I think he deserves a whole gallon of ice cream today. You can pick the flavor."

Logan went to Reyne's that evening, stopping in town to pick up hamburgers and french fries from the Elk Horn Drive-in. He had spent the afternoon with Matt and Dirk up in the beautiful prayer chapel Dirk Tanner had built at Timberline, asking the Lord to sustain Matt and to grant him wisdom in parenting a little girl on his own. Matt seemed to gain strength from the fellowship with his brothers.

Reyne opened the door, looking as exhausted as Logan felt. "I took a chance that you hadn't eaten," he said, walking in.

"No way. After our triple-scoop ice-cream cone at noon, I felt sick all afternoon." She collapsed on the sofa and then raised one eyebrow. "But I have to admit that smells great."

Logan walked over to the kitchen counter, unloading their dinner onto plates and stealthily taking the phone off the hook. Outside the kitchen window, a storm was brewing. Great big cumulonimbus clouds gathered in a bank that billowed and swirled as if angry at the mountains at their feet.

Reyne joined him at the window. "That looks like I feel," she said.

Logan nodded and pulled her into his arms. "Let's eat outside. Watch the storm build."

"Okay. We can pull the wicker chairs around from the other side of the house. Why don't you do that, and I'll bring out the food."

Logan went out to the porch, and after surveying two broad chairs and a small sofa, he decided on a chair for two. "McCabe, you *are* a scoundrel," he said under his breath, smiling at the thought of sitting near Reyne.

Reyne came out with the food, looked up at him with a quick grin to say she had noticed his chair choice, and then settled in with him. They ate in companionable silence, their minds swirling with thoughts, much like the skies above them. The waning day cast its remaining sunset on the clouds, making them seem to live with an eerie, burnt orange light. Heat lightning flashed deep inside the largest cloud, and a shiver of foreboding shot down Reyne's spine.

"This is no ordinary storm brewing."

"No."

On and on the storm roiled, becoming more dramatic as the surrounding skies grew darker and its own light intensified. The sunset's reflection soon faded, but the lightning continued. The air was becoming blustery as the two finished their quiet dinner, and Logan drew Reyne closer beside him. The wind came as a welcome respite to their ongoing heat wave, breaking the humid stillness with a hint of coolness.

"You realize that this means fire," Reyne said as the first lightning bolts broke free of the clouds and cut their way down toward the earth. In seconds, thunder pealed, so loud that they could feel the reverberations inside their chests.

"We should go inside to watch," Logan said, ignoring her statement and shoving away guilty thoughts of the intentionally off-the-hook phone inside. "We need some time just to think about Beth and remember. Let's not think about fire. There will be time enough for that later."

"Agreed," Reyne said. They grabbed their plates and glasses and napkins before the wind could rip them away and made their way inside.

Logan moved to turn on the lamp by Reyne's overstuffed, high-backed chair, but Reyne's voice stopped him.

"No, Logan. No lights. Let's just watch the show."

Logan shot her a surprised smile, then moved to help turn her sofa around to face the living-room picture window. He sat down, and Reyne snuggled in beside him. With the wind blowing through the open kitchen window, the air turned surprisingly brisk. They could smell the rain coming.

But the cool air was refreshing, and they left the window open, deciding to cover up instead. Reyne pulled an afghan over them and tucked a corner around Logan, playfully exaggerating her fussing. Logan drew her closer, and they kissed softly.

When she moved back, Reyne looked deep into Logan's eyes. "I'm so glad you're here, Logan. I don't think I could've made it through these last days without you."

He tenderly traced her jaw line. "Sure, you would have. You're strong, Reyne. So's your faith. You would've made it just fine. But I'm glad I was able to be here too. For you. To say good-bye to Beth. And for Matt."

Reyne listened to Logan intently, then settled even closer to him, resting her head on his chest and wrapping her arms around him. Logan reached up to stroke her hair, staring out at the murderous storm and wondering how many fires it might start.

The small trees that Reyne had planted were nearly doubled over, no match for the ferocious wind. Finally, when it seemed that the storm was directly overhead and shaking the cottage at its foundations, the rain came…blessed, giant drops that met the roof and splattered.

It came down so suddenly and so hard that Reyne raised her head, peering out the window. "Is it hailing?"

"I don't think so. Just big rain."

"Great. I've asked for rain for weeks. And now, when we finally get it, it comes down like bullets bent on killing every flower in my garden."

"Maybe it's not as hard as it sounds," he tried.

"Maybe." She thought for a moment. "But it's somehow appropriate, you know? For as much as I put on a happy face for Matt and tried to celebrate as Beth asked us to, I'm really sad. I don't feel like ever planting another flower again."

"You will, love," Logan said, stroking her hair again. "And even if you don't, God will take the flowers you've planted and bring them back year after year. Love is like that. It goes through seasons, but if it's strong, it comes back 'round."

She glanced up at him, her eyebrow raised in gentle surprise.

"What?"

"Nothing. It's just that I'm surprised to hear you speak so poetically."

"What? My love hast not seeneth my heart's deepest desire? Lo! It is near! Thou must only looketh for it!" Logan said dramatically in mock Shakespearean, jumping at the chance to make her laugh.

"Oh, Logan," Reyne giggled, "that was *really* bad."

Logan smiled and let her comment go, pleased that he could still make her grin on such a dark day. *Maybe, just maybe,* he thought, *something good will come out of all this pain. Maybe we'll end up with a real celebration after all.*

CHAPTER TWENTY-FOUR

*D*espite Logan's protest, Reyne replaced the phone on the hook as soon as she discovered it was off, and just as he had feared, it rang within a minute. Reyne answered. With a grim look on her face, she handed the receiver to him.

"Logan, this is the interagency dispatch center," said a formal-sounding man. "We have obtained permission from the Northwest Forestry Company to utilize your team as boosters for our Missoula crew. Can you mobilize by tomorrow?"

Logan looked over at Reyne, searching her face. The adrenaline poured through his body at the thought of another big fire. Yet everything in him made him want to stay. *If this keeps up,* he thought, *it's gonna tear me in two.*

He looked away from Reyne and concentrated on the dispatcher, who was describing the numerous fires in Oregon and Northern California. They needed smokejumpers, and they needed them now. "Okay," he said, making his decision, "I'll rendezvous with my crew and move 'em out. Where do you want us?" He grabbed a pen and paper, shutting out the image of Reyne's crestfallen face.

When he hung up, Reyne remained where she was, waiting. "Reyne, I, uh…"

"You said you'd be here as long as I needed you."

"Hey, you were the one who decided to hang up the phone. I told you—"

"You told me you'd be here." She did not sound petulant, just adamant.

Logan circled the kitchen counter and sat beside her. "Listen, love. If you ask me to, I'll stay. I think you know by now that you're my first priority. But they need me. And I'd bet a thousand dollars that they'll be calling you any minute too. They've got fires from Mexico to Washington. Don't you think that it would be good for both of us to concentrate on something else?"

Reyne rose and walked to the window, staring as raindrops crawled down the pane. "You said you'd be here for me. For Matt."

Logan sighed, thinking. Then he went to stand behind her. He placed his hands on her shoulders. She did not move. "And I'm asking you if it's okay to leave. I'll call Matt. But I want an okay from you first."

They stood there for long seconds that seemed like hours before she spoke. Then she said, "I'm trying, Logan, I really am. Beth talked long and hard to me about trusting and living every moment to its fullest, and I want to do that. I do. But Logan, I just lost one of the dearest friends I've ever had. And now you're telling me I have to risk you too."

Logan swallowed, willing away the trite, easy answers that sprang to mind. He wanted her beside him. But Oxbow had created a major hurdle for them. *Dear Father, help me. Help me help Reyne. Give me the words that will shore up her heart.* "I've found," he began carefully, "that when I risk, I gain. You have to go with your heart, go where God's leading. But do you hear me, Reyne?" He paused to turn her around to face him. "I'm asking you to let me go. I won't go without knowing you're okay with it."

She turned away, avoiding his gaze, then finally met his eyes.

"And how am I supposed to tell you no? Tell you not to go after the very thing you love to do?"

He thought about his conversation with Thomas Wagner a week prior. The United States Fire Service had offered Logan a full-time job in fire management. He would supervise smokejumping operations across the country during big fires, and in between he could continue to train and shape the Elk Horn hotshot crew for the forestry company. But the position wouldn't be opening up for another year. For now he had a job to do, if the woman he loved did not stand in the way.

Suddenly it hit him. What would happen if it came down to a choice between her and fire? Could he honestly walk away?

Logan searched Reyne's eyes, willing her to give him the freedom to pursue his passion. He prayed silently that God would strengthen his love for Reyne so that if he had to, he could make the right choice. But he also prayed that God would strengthen Reyne, abolishing her fears about the front lines of firefighting.

"Go," she said quietly, turning from him.

"What?"

"I said go." Her voice was a little stronger this time.

"Reyne, I can't go without you really meaning what you're saying."

She turned back to him, gathering anguished fistfuls of his shirt in her hands as she spoke. "Logan, you obviously have to go—"

The phone rang, interrupting her speech. She ignored it, staring into his eyes. "You're probably right. Now they're calling me. And we have a job to do. You go and do yours, and I'll do mine. But promise me—"

"Anything, Reyne."

"Promise me you will take the extra second to make the wisest choice you know how."

"I will, love. I'll take extra care." He grinned and pulled her to him while the phone rang for the seventh time. "My woman's counting on me."

Reyne let the tiniest smile edge her lips before leaving his embrace to answer the phone.

CHAPTER TWENTY-FIVE

*T*he call had been for Logan again, not her, with information on where he was to report, where his crew was, and what shape they were in. He had left immediately for the airstrip to welcome home his weary crew, help them clean, repair, and pack their equipment, and prepare them to head out again. They were gone in twenty-four hours.

The storms continued for days, and as predicted, the lightning touched off countless fires. Most were held in check by the rain, and because of the crazy antics of fires across the West and the chaos they were causing in the ICS, crews from New Mexico ended up fighting Montana fires while the Montanans flew to New Mexico to fight theirs. It was precisely what Logan railed against, Reyne thought; the bureaucracy often made incongruous decisions to play the game of jurisdiction and first rights. She did not envy her bosses and the choices they had to make.

By the time Logan left town, Reyne had taken herself off leave and received her own orders days later; she was to help manage a team outside Wenatchee in central Washington.

When she arrived, Reyne had to admit that it felt good to go back to work. Her last days with Beth and the time afterward with Matt and Hope and Beth's parents had taken their toll, and concentrating on something tangible—their collective battle against the fire—came as a relief. She needed an enemy she could get hold of and strangle, pouring out all the anger she felt inside. More than ever in her life, she needed to destroy the dragon.

First, however, she had to outsmart him. And that meant she had her work cut out for her. Already this fire had eaten up more than thirty thousand acres.

The fire camp was located on the south shore of Lake Chelan, normally a pleasant spot for campers and vacationers, with boating and sunning and swimming. Now the entire south end of the lake was surrounded by a huge tent city that housed more than three thousand firefighters.

Reyne had been to the lake once years before to visit Holden Village, a church camp on the north end. Campers had been picked up at the ferry landing, now just visible through the smoke, and dropped off at the camp, which Reyne even at sixteen had deemed "just this side of paradise." But Holden Village had been evacuated two days before, and they all feared that there would be little left of the fifty-year-old refuge. The ferry had even been pressed into service to carry firefighters northward.

Reyne remembered giant mountains ringing the lake valley, mountains that plunged from high in the sky down into the blue black depths of the lake. Yet with all the smoke that choked the skies now, the mountains were obliterated. Reyne could barely see across the water and make out the other side, let alone the ridges that she knew towered high above.

She rolled up her sleeves and grabbed her duffel bag and brief-case. As usual, a rookie was waiting to show her to her tent.

In Central Oregon, Logan had been digging chains for five hours and was just wondering what he saw in this line of work when his hip radio crackled to life. "McCabe, this is headquarters. Come in."

Logan wiped his brow and pulled the radio from his belt. "McCabe here, over." He squinted, listening for the medical unit manager's voice to come back over the sporadic connection.

"McCabe, we've got a jumper in trouble. He's…" Their connection was breaking up. "He landed square…pretty much came right through his thigh…team is carrying him out…you meet him at these coordinates…clear a landing so we can evacuate him."

Logan looked over his shoulder at his partner, Wyatt Franklin, a rookie from eastern Montana. He nodded, beckoning, pressed the intercom button again, checking to make sure he had understood the rendezvous coordinates, and then told headquarters that they would meet the team as requested.

He and Wyatt began moving right away. They had limited time to hike the two miles over the ridge, and they still had to clear a site in which the emergency helicopter could land.

Several hundred miles away Reyne went into action herself. The fire was nearing the picturesque German tourist town, Leavenworth, and across the mountains appeared to be closing in on Lake Chelan from several different directions. Three separate lightning fires had broken free of initial attempts to contain them, then gone on to join forces and wreak havoc. Within minutes of arrival, Reyne was ordered onto a helicopter to observe the three fronts firsthand and report back accordingly.

The short, stocky pilot introduced himself as Ray Firigno, looked her over appreciatively, and then handed her a headset so they could talk over the noise. They shot upward and then tilted forty-five degrees, banking toward the west.

Ray nodded to the steaming natural hot springs just over the hill from camp. "Maybe you and me can take a dip after our shift ends," he said suggestively.

"I don't think so, Firigno," she said. "Don't think my boyfriend would like it." *I wish Logan were here. A dip in a hot spring with him would be fun.*

Ray glanced over at her. "Reyne Oldre has a boyfriend? Since when?"

"Yeah, it's possible. Just concentrate on the job at hand, will ya, Ray?" Reyne pushed away her own thoughts of Logan. Better not think about him right now. She needed to concentrate on the job at hand too.

Ray quieted and did as he was told, working to keep control of the chopper in the quirky winds stirred up by the fire. Within ten minutes the ride grew even more precarious, however, as the helicopter responded to the near-storm conditions created by the heat of the big front they were studying. Up and down they went, and Reyne had to will herself to focus on their task so that she would not lose her lunch. She took photo after photo, hoping to study them further back at base camp.

Reyne disliked this part of her job as a fire behaviorist, but such trips were often invaluable in deciphering the fire's intentions. There had been many occasions where her advice to the command had been a key element in getting the fire put out. It was worth all the bouncing and the jolting and the smoke.

They hovered as near to the front line as they dared, within a quarter of a mile of the furious wall of flames. Then she nodded curtly to Ray. He banked the chopper, and they headed to the second front.

Logan and Wyatt reached the ridge, coughing hard after their physical exertion in the smoke-laden, high mountain air. Within minutes, the other team arrived with the injured man. Two carried the makeshift stretcher—a tent held at each corner with sticks tied through knots—and the third carried the downed jumper's pack alongside his own, a combined weight of over two hundred pounds.

"Glad to see you, McCabe," Jill Anderson said, as soon as she spotted him from around a tree. They laid down the unconscious man, who moaned in pain, and Anderson rubbed her neck as she talked. "This is Ned Price. He caught some surprise down air and went straight into a grove of dead lodgepole pines. They were like huge impaling poles. One of the branches came straight through his thigh like a lance."

Logan winced as he heard the story, and Ned groaned again. The stob remained where it had broken off—a two-foot section of limb that emerged on either side of his thigh.

"This lucky guy," Jill continued, "somehow avoided hitting an artery. He was woozy and shocky, but he didn't seem to be losing much blood. Still, we were afraid to move the stob in case it's just blocking the artery. Thought we'd leave that to the guys on the medevac."

"When did he pass out?" Logan asked.

"About half an hour ago."

"Well, we've been working on this clearing for about an hour. As soon as you all catch your breath, we could use your help. The chopper will be here at about 1600 hours."

Anderson checked her watch. "We've got a whole hour, huh? Boy, nobody can ever call us loafers."

Reyne was eating with the crew in the mess tent when she first heard of the injured smokejumper.

"The way I heard it," one hotshot shouted over the din, "he had half a tree coming out of his stomach!"

People groaned and threw pieces of rolls and other food at the guy.

"No way. It was a tree through his arm!"

"His leg!"

Reyne's heart was pounding, and she had lost all her appetite for the food on her plate. *Oh no, not again.*

"Please," she said, leaning across the table to the woman in front of her. "Do you know the real story?"

The woman studied Reyne, undoubtedly recognizing the strange urgency on her face and in her voice. "Smokejumper. A boss, I think. Caught a crazy cross wind and some down air that blew him into some dead lodgepole. Impaled him through the thigh, as near as I can gather."

Reyne sat back, feeling dizzy. Her companion leaned forward. "I think they got 'em out."

"Where? Where was this?" Reyne managed to ask.

"Central Oregon, I guess. Somewhere outside Bend."

Chapter Twenty-Six

*R*eyne paced in front of the computers in the command center, waiting for any word about Logan or his crew, until the commander ordered her out. "Oldre, you're off-duty, and you're distracting those of us who are working this fire.

"I'll send for you as soon as we hear," he added as he ushered her to the door. "But right now you're supposed to be getting some shut-eye so you can be of use to me at 0600 hours."

She stood outside the tent, sputtering, wanting to return despite the direct command. What if they didn't watch the monitor for news of Logan? What if they didn't let her know? She paced outside the command tent for a while. Then, when the commander caught her eye with a disapproving glance, she turned and walked to her tent. After pacing inside it for several moments, Reyne knew she had to get out. Get away. It might be a day or two before she found out about Logan anyway. But it was after midnight. Where could she go?

Suddenly the image of the shimmering hot springs appeared in her mind. She would go there and soak. But not with Ray. Alone. Spend some quiet time with God. Just the thought of it was like a balm to her irritated soul, and she quickly changed into shorts and a T-shirt.

She exited her tent and looked this way and that, then made her way out of camp and toward the place where she judged the springs would be. There had been three narrow pools. Hopefully, the camp had not discovered them yet. Weary firefighters would love a soak in that steaming water.

Reyne passed through a forested grove and crossed a grassy meadow, glad for the waxing orange moon that shone brightly even through the thick blanket of smoke. After some poking about, she thought she caught a whiff of sulfur and headed in its direction. Before her was a rocky wall, and Reyne picked her way carefully among the boulders, choosing each footstep with care.

She was just squeezing through a particularly narrow slit and wondering if the nighttime jaunt was worth it when the narrow crevice opened up into an idyllic little bowl of a room with a steaming pool at its center. Walled round with boulders, it looked cozy and inviting, as if it had been created only for her.

Reyne smiled and sighed. The sulfur smell was stronger here, but it wasn't unpleasant. The only sound was that of gentle bubbles rising and breaking on the surface of the spring and the quiet *hoo-hoo*ing of a night owl nearby. The moon reflected off the water in a wavering orb of light, as if beckoning her.

Reyne's grin grew wider. It was perfect, and apparently undiscovered. Quickly she pulled off her shirt and shorts and felt her way along the sloping edges of the pool. She kept her Keds on, aware that hot springs often had craggy edges or mineral deposits that could cut a person's skin clean open. But as she eased her way in, she discovered that this was an uncommon pool.

As she looked around, she decided that once this had been a river's way. The boulders and the crevice through which she had climbed were like large river stones, mostly worn smooth except for where they had cracked and opened under the harsh, central Washington sun. She felt along the bottom of the pool and finally found the opening that allowed the hot, nourishing waters of the spring through to her basin. All along it were the rough mineral deposits she had expected. But away from it, where Reyne found a nestling place, the stone was as smooth as her bathtub at home.

She giggled aloud, feeling as if she had entered Eden through a secret passageway. "Thank you, Father," she whispered. "For showing me this place."

Reyne closed her eyes and listened only to the bubbles cresting and popping open, feeling the warm waters ease away the tension in her shoulders and neck. She slipped lower, resting her face in the water up to her nose. Even her jaw muscles needed relaxing.

Whenever she moved, the moon's reflection broke up into a thousand shimmering shards of light. When she stilled, the orb gradually pulled itself back together into one image, like a mother hen tucking her chicks under her wings. She raised her hand, cupped full of water, and watched as the sparkling droplets fell, met the spring, and disappeared. She contemplated the images for a while.

"That's what it's all about, huh, God?" she whispered. "Our lives scatter and we leave your side, but eventually we all come home."

There was no audible answer, but in her soul, Reyne thought she heard what her Creator was trying to tell her. "I just get so worried. What if it is Logan who's been hurt?"

Do not worry.

"Easy for you to say. You know it all. Couldn't you let me in on part of it? Just part of it? I'd like to see the next few years of my life mapped out. Logan's life. Then I could rest easy."

The owl hooted again. *Look at the birds of the air.*

"Yeah, yeah," she said with a giggle.

Who of you by worrying can add a single hour to his life?

The verse filled her mind like the hot water filled the pool in which she sat. Reyne thought of Beth, remembering her last words to her. Her entreaties.

"I want to trust, Father. I want to rest in the knowledge that you are here with me and there with Logan, wherever he is." She rushed on, feeling the urgent need to express her soul's cry. "That you know the beginning and the end and that you're going to carry me through the middle when it gets tough. But I'm scared. Dear Jesus, I'm so scared. I'm scared I'm going to lose Logan like I lost those others."

Reyne could not tell if she uttered these words aloud or not. In any case, she was sure that God was present, hearing her. His Spirit was palpable. A tear left her eye and made its way to the pool and disappeared.

"I've wanted to lean on you, Lord. I know you've been waiting. But God, it was my fault. It was my fault that those kids died. I let Oxbow get them."

It was not yours to control. Nor is Logan yours to control.

She sat there a long time, rubbing her puckering palms together as the waters continued to work away her stress and God worked on her heart. An awful thought sprang to mind. "If you let them die, how do I know that you won't let Logan die?"

There was only silence in her soul for long moments afterward. Reyne anguished over her own accusation. She knew that her Oxbow crew had made their own choices. But still, her God was *God*. He could've stopped them had he chosen to.

Finally the tender words came. *I am your Lord God, Reyne. Trust in me. Trust in me. I have good things in store for you. And for Logan.*

Trust in me. Trust in me. The words beckoned to her heart like a candle in a dark window. *Trust in me.*

How long had it been since Reyne had truly trusted in God? She knew this was a weak spot for her. She took a deep breath and slipped all the way under the water, feeling the water cover her scalp and her hair spreading out around her. And there, as she was surrounded and buoyed by the healing water, an image ran through her mind.

She pictured Logan injured, hurting, somewhere out in a forest. And then she pictured God standing between the man she loved and the roaring, consuming flames. But not just standing between. Surrounding him, embracing him, shielding him. It was as if Logan was in a protected cocoon where nothing could touch him.

Reyne's heart swelled. *Yes, Father. I will cling to that image. Go before us. Beside us. Behind us. I will trust in you. I will let go and trust our lives to you.*

Her lungs were fairly bursting for air. She broke the surface gasping, her tangible communion with the Spirit over. But she felt more free and at ease than she had felt in years. *This is what it feels like truly to hand something over to God.*

Then once again she thought of Beth, of how her friend had accepted her lot and made a gift even of her last days. "You taught me so much, Beth," she whispered to the night sky. "I'm still learning from you."

She stopped at the command center's tent on her way back to camp. "Hey, Oldre, glad you stopped back by," called the commander, ignoring the fact that he had been the one to order her out. "Turns out McCabe's okay. Fella named Price was the one who got a stob through his thigh. And he's going to be okay too."

Reyne stood in the tent's doorway and breathed a quiet prayer of thanksgiving. But she didn't feel the wild rush of relief she had expected. And then she realized, *It's because I already knew everything was going to be all right.*

She smiled, realizing that the good news had come only *after* she had made the decision to trust. She took it as affirmation that she was on the right track.

And it's so much easier than the other way. Reyne smiled. *Well, it's about time, Oldre.*

The next morning Reyne learned she had been reassigned to Libby, Montana, where firefighters were in even more dire straits than in Wenatchee. The fires were everywhere; it almost seemed that the entire western half of the United States was aflame. Reyne hastily packed her duffel bag and her briefcase and boarded the chopper for Libby. On the way, she found herself wondering when she'd have a chance to see Logan again. She didn't even know where he was stationed. *Well, Father, I'm glad that you know. Guess that's just another thing I'm going to have to trust you for.*

The fire camp at Libby was in chaos. Thomas Wagner, also newly arrived, was scrambling to get equipment set up and the command team organized. Pitching in, Reyne found herself a Fire Service Jeep and headed toward town for some supplies. All along the highway she saw sandwich signs with handwritten entreaties: *Firefighters needed. Inquire at base camp.*

They were desperate for help. It had been twenty years since the West had seen fires this bad, and everyone was feeling the strain. Supervisors sniped at one another as crews became more and more difficult to obtain. Power plays abounded among those in the interagency command center as personnel were stretched to their limit. Some fires were abandoned simply to run their course. Others were fought grudgingly simply because of the political pull that subdivision homeowners threatened. Everyone was working eighty-hour weeks, sleeping when they could.

Reyne pulled into a convenience store and hopped out of the Jeep. After entering the store and taking off her sunglasses, she smiled ruefully around her, observing empty shelf after empty shelf.

"They plumb cleaned me out," said the clerk with a shrug of his shoulders. "Were ya lookin' fer anything in particular?"

"Well I was on a general snack-food run for the command center. I guess they'll have to grab something from the mess tent just like everybody else. Unless there's someplace else in town…"

"Nope. From what I hear, everybody's in about the same state o' affairs ya see here."

"Oh well. My more important mission was batteries. I need Ds."

Again he shook his head. "Cleaned me out of them, too."

"Anyplace else in town?"

"You could try the general store about a mile south o' here."

Reyne hurried out of the store. Usually, the ICS handled supplies as efficiently as it did anything else, but there was nothing usual about this summer. Supply lines were down, and the people in charge had to scramble to obtain what the troops so desperately needed—such as batteries, which were needed to run some of the command center's equipment and radios until the generators could be set up.

Reyne sighed and hopped in the Jeep. It was going to be a long day.

Chapter Twenty-Seven

Logan hopped out of the plane directly behind his teammate, and their exit was nearly perfect. The winds were tolerable, and they chatted calmly as they watched the ground come toward them at twenty feet per second. Logan liked Jeffrey Shanks, had been glad to see his ruddy face when he arrived at the Libby camp last night. He was a friend from way back, and after a summer of working with rookies, it was a treat to serve with a pro.

In an unanticipated turn, the Mount Snowy fire—as the Libby crew had named it—had woven its way around the base of a mountain, then abruptly turned and swept uphill. It had crossed the mountain saddle and within hours had closed off a tiny town called Haven, torching the bridge—the only way out—and taking many people by surprise.

Most of the residents had heard the earlier reports and evacuated as suggested. But others had been more adamant about the folly of "BLM bureaucrats" and opted to stay, hoping to protect their homes. Now, with the flames lapping at the town's outskirts, Logan and Jeffrey had been assigned to run through the settlement and make sure everyone got out immediately.

After landing and stowing their chutes, they started on the point highest up the mountain, running past homes on the only street and hoping there were was no one in the houses beyond. Their mission was to canvass the town, hitting every house they could, and then return to the uphill end to be picked up by helicopter crews. They moved fast, using their bullhorns and banging on doors. Judging from the view they had on the way down, there was little time. Mount Snowy was not behaving like a normal fire, and they did not like what they sensed in the air.

It wasn't long before they had reached the downhill edge of the tiny town, getting closer and closer to the fire. They had only come across eight people and had sent them up to the landing site first. Over the roar of the fire, they could make out the sounds of helicopters and tankers that were working to control the flames and buy them evacuation time.

At the east end of town, the street dipped and turned. It was there that Logan heard Reyne's voice.

"Haven crew, come in. Haven crew, come in."

Logan stopped in his tracks, grinned at Jeffrey, then pressed the intercom button. "I'm right here, baby. Where've you been all my life?"

There was a pause, undoubtedly as Reyne prepared to whip the impudent firefighter into shape with a quick lashing of the tongue and reminder of rank and respect. Then she said tentatively, "Logan?"

"You betcha! What are you doing here, babe? What are you doing on the radio with a jumper crew? Fire behavior becoming boring?"

"Not a chance. As you may have noticed, it's all hands on deck. We're all doing everybody else's job like you are now. Listen, Logan. We're monitoring the fire above the highway, trying to get tourists off the road before they're incinerated. But we've heard there's some old man on the far side, caught between the fire and the river. We can't get to him. Check it out and report, will you?"

"Consider it done," Logan said, all business now. He and Jeffrey moved into a jog, sensing that time was running out. "I will most definitely see you later."

He could hear the laughter in her voice. "Oldre, out."

Just as Reyne had said, an old man stood amid falling, burning embers at the edge of Ross Creek, at the bottom of the hill. Behind him, his cabin was in flames, and above it the hill that banked the highway was burning too. The bridge farther up the river had been so damaged by fire that it was impassable.

They paused, observing the scene as if it were in a movie. There was something impossible about it: the old man staring at the uncommonly deep creek while the embers came down about him like gentle snowflakes encasing a cozy winter scene.

Jeffrey looked at Logan with the question in his eyes. Both men looked to the swift water, their minds racing. How would they get him out?

"No way but to go across, as I see it," Logan said first.

"Yeah. This the best place?"

"Good as any. We don't have much time." With that, Logan trudged in, tossing the end of his rope to Jeffrey and wrapping the other end of it around his waist as he fought the numbing glacial waters. "Just my luck that this is one of the few running waterways left in the West," he quipped.

Jeffrey continued to dole out rope as Logan reached chest-level in the creek, gave up trying to walk across, and swam with all his strength. In a minute he was able to touch on the other side, struggling to gain purchase with his waterlogged work boots.

The old man just stood at the water's edge, staring across at

Jeffrey. He looked ancient, eighty or ninety years old. Would he survive the crossing? *Sweet Jesus, please help me make the right decision,* Logan prayed silently as he touched the man's shoulder.

Old eyes shielded by the film of glaucoma turned to look at him. "Oh, young man. Can you save my home?"

Logan wiped dripping water from his face and looked up behind the man. The heat was so intense that it was already drying his skin and his Nomex shirt. "I'm afraid not. I think we'll be lucky to get you out. What's your name, sir?"

"Ollenstad," he said vaguely. "Eric Ollenstad."

"Are you ready for a dip in the river, Mr. Ollenstad?"

"I suppose," he said. "I was just saying to my dear wife, Katherine, that it was so hot out we oughtta consider a swim."

Logan glanced up at the cabin in consternation. The roof was one big flame, the burning beams exposed and the whole structure on the verge of collapse. "Sir! Is your wife in there?"

"Oh no," Mr. Ollenstad said. "My Katherine went on to glory some years ago. I still talk to her though."

Logan took a deep breath, relieved. He raised a hand to shield his face from the heat. "I see. Well, come on, Mr. Ollenstad. We had better take that swim now, or we're not going to get the chance at all."

It was that night when Reyne turned to see Thomas Wagner, asleep with his head resting on his hands, still sitting at a command radio station as the buzz of night transmissions went on. She went to him and gently touched his shoulder. He stirred a bit but did not waken, ignoring her and the radio buzzing before him.

"Thomas," she whispered, "wake up. Thomas!"

Finally he opened his bloodshot eyes and blinked at her. "You better go take a nap," she said. "You're obviously no help here."

He rubbed his face, embarrassed. "You too, Oldre. You've been on as long as I have."

"I'll finish up what I'm working on and be right behind you. But first I want to look in on a certain smokejumper..."

Thomas smiled wearily. "Gotcha. See ya at 0600."

"I'll be looking forward to it," she said, with little pleasure in her voice. As soon as she was out of the command tent, she looked around for Logan. Officially off-duty, she could now concentrate on the one thing on her heart: the gut-wrenching, heart-pulling, incredible urge to see him. Ever since his voice had come over the radio, all Reyne had been able to think of was Logan, and the stories that drifted in about his rescue of Eric Ollenstad had just made things worse. It had taken a supreme effort for her to continue to concentrate on the tasks at hand. But she had stayed on the job and tried to focus. Lives depended upon it.

Already the tent city at Libby resembled the one at Wenatchee. Here and there groups of weary firefighters played Hacky Sack or listened to someone strum a guitar. Others played cards. One group had even set up a makeshift half-court for basketball, using a bottomless waste can nailed to a tree for a hoop.

Reyne reached her tent and walked in to change before going to the mess tent to grab something to eat. There on her pillow was a small bouquet of wildflowers, slightly withered. Smiling, she raised them to her nose, but all she could smell was smoke. *Ah well, it's the thought that counts.*

She turned around, half expecting Logan to be in the tent with her. He was not. Reyne opened the tent's window flap and glanced out at the walkway directly in front, but he wasn't there either. She felt her sudden, eager smile fade away. Her need to see him was achingly urgent now, and she stripped off her clothes and changed in record time.

Reyne looked from side to side as she walked to the mess tent, scanning the "streets" for any sight of Logan. She couldn't wait to look into his laughing eyes...had trouble thinking of anything but walking into his arms...wanted nothing but to talk with him, walk with him.

The mess tent was deserted by the time she got there, the food long since stored away. She looked at her watch. Twenty-two hundred hours. Reyne looked around and unconsciously rubbed a hand over her suddenly grumbling stomach. *Gotta credit fire season for one thing at least,* she mused. *Weight loss.*

"Looking for some dinner?" Logan's voice suddenly sounded directly over her shoulder. It was as if his voice melted and settled over her like a warm blanket—it was so welcome.

"Logan!" Reyne squealed as he picked her up and swung her around, throwing his head back and laughing with joy.

"It is good to see you, too, my love." Gently he set her down, but she remained in his arms.

Reyne reached up to run her fingers through his short, wavy hair. "It's only been a couple of weeks, but I swear, Logan, every day seemed like months to me."

"It is good to be missed," he said tenderly, nodding. "I hope you realize it's been even worse for me."

"Ha! How would that be?"

He raised his eyebrows and cocked his head to one side. "Well, because I was missing *you,* of course."

She smiled wisely. "I'll take that. Cheap flattery will get you everywhere."

"Everywhere?"

"Within limits."

"How about a dinner date with the woman of my dreams?"

Reyne's eyes grew big. "Dinner? I'm starving! I was just wondering how I was going to make it to breakfast when you came in."

"I saw you working in the command center and guessed you wouldn't have time to eat. Come with me, madam, for a dinner you won't forget."

Smiling, she took his hand, relishing the feel of his rough palm and fingers enfolding hers. Together, they walked out of the mess tent. Reyne let him guide her. She loved the feeling of being cared for, protected, as much as he obviously liked caring for her.

On the outskirts of the tent city, they entered the forest and made their way to a little clearing by the light of the crescent moon.

Reyne smiled and looked up at him. "This looks like that little spot near the fire camp in Colorado. You know, the place we went after you apologized…"

"I thought so too," he said, moving to the edge. "And maybe this will remind you of somewhere else." Logan flipped a switch on a tiny portable generator, and one strand of tiny lights lit up their dinner site.

Reyne grinned. "Hmm. What does it remind me of? There's some vague image…"

Logan moved to take her in his arms, smiling smugly.

She couldn't resist. "Christmas?" she asked innocently.

He threw back his head and laughed again. Reyne could feel his laughter reverberate in her own chest. "Really, Logan," she said, growing more serious. "This was really sweet. I mean, I can't even find batteries at camp anymore, and you've managed to round up a generator and a string of lights."

He led her to a log, and they sat down together. "Well," he said, "I could only get one strand, but I thought it would be enough to conjure up images of our first date."

"And do you have dinner like you did that night?"

"That," he said, standing again to pull her toward the folded parachute making up their "dining-room" floor, "will take some imagination."

"I'm game," she said. She sat down where he had indicated and waited for him to rummage around in a large paper grocery sack.

Logan pulled out a can of peaches, a paper plate full of cold macaroni and cheese that he had grabbed from the mess tent, and four carrot sticks that looked as if they had been dried on the front lines. He was glad for the darkness as he ruefully handed the shriveled vegetables to Reyne.

"Sorry. It was the best I could do," he said.

"No apology needed," she said between bites. "Food is food. The best part is being with you." In the soft light, her eyes were luminous, and Logan fought off the urge to toss the food aside and kiss her hungrily. *Control, Father,* he prayed silently, still smiling back into Reyne's eyes. *Help me keep control around this woman.*

"Would you like some of Kraft's finest?" he asked, handing her a fork.

"Mmm," she said, taking a bite. "Haven't had macaroni and cheese for, let's see, maybe three days?" Fire camps were notorious for serving heavy quantities of carbohydrates and protein to weary, ravenous firefighters.

"They had steak, too," Logan said, sorry he hadn't picked up one. "I thought it would be too hard to cut."

"Oh, that's fine. All I care about is some food and, as I said, some time with you." Within minutes she had polished off her dinner, with a little help from Logan. Truth be told, he had stopped to eat a steak and salad with friends while waiting for Reyne to get off her shift.

"Logan," Reyne said softly, "I have something to tell you." She looked so joyful, so appealing, so at peace, that he could not resist the urge to reach out and touch her hair softly.

"What, love?"

"I...I think I'm over my fear. I think I've finally put that day with Oxbow behind me once and for all." She looked down at her feet, then back to him. "I really thought about what Beth had told me and concentrated on handing all my worries and fears to Christ. And suddenly, last night, it was as if they had disappeared."

Logan could feel the smile spread across his face. "So you're okay?" His heart leaped with excitement. Suddenly he could see their future together, their jobs and lives intersecting and intertwining in more ways than one. Forever. For him, Reyne's words served as confirmation for something he had wondered about for a long time.

He casually moved a hand to his jeans pocket and felt the familiar small lump of a tiny plastic bag that he had kept with him for weeks. He looked back to her. "You're okay with us? This?" he asked, waving about their forested fortress. "With me working the fire lines, jumping?"

"I think," she said, measuring her words, "that you need to go where your heart takes you. God has brought us together, Logan. That's enough for me right now."

He sighed, smiling at her, utterly content. Reyne's words made him feel free, trusted. Logan reached up to trace her jaw line, staring into her eyes without moving his own. Then slowly he pulled her to him, kissing her in an agonizingly tender way.

When they parted, he smiled again, then reached down to his pocket. "You said this reminded you of Christmas."

"Yes…"

"Well, I got you a present."

She gave him a puzzled look. "A present? What? A fire extinguisher? A new Nomex? A fusee?" Reyne asked with a laugh.

He laughed with her, picturing himself bringing out an old firefighter's backfire torch and grandly presenting it to her with a big red bow. He cast aside the thought, intent on what was at hand. "I hope…I hope that you'll think it's even better than that."

"What could be better than a new Nomex?" she cracked. "Maybe some batteries…"

Logan pulled the plastic bag from his pocket. "Close your eyes."

Reyne cast him a suspicious look and then complied. "Okay. They're closed."

He pulled apart the tiny zippered opening and dumped the delicate ring into the palm of his other hand. "Don't peek," he said, moving to kneel in front of her.

"I won't," she said.

She was so beautiful, sitting against the log, her shiny hair glimmering in the pale moonlight. Just looking at her seemed to make him ache inside. "Reyne," he said, his voice low.

"I can open them?"

"Yes." He watched as her smoky eyes fluttered open and she looked at him with wonder. He moved his hand, and her eyes followed.

"A ring?" she asked at last.

"A ring."

A smile spread across her face. "Does this mean we're going steady?"

"I hope. For a long, long, time. Reyne Oldre, would you consider being my wife?"

A shadow fell over her face. "I would. I mean, Logan, I...I would love to. Consider it, I mean." Her features contorted as she struggled to get the words out now. "Logan, isn't this a bit soon? I mean we've only known each other for a few months."

His gaze never wavered. He watched her and smiled. Somehow he had known this wouldn't come easily. But that was all right. Logan planned to bring her along, convince her, for as long as it took.

"Reyne, I know. I know I love you and want to spend every day possible with you. I want to take you to bed and wake up with you in the morning. Heck, I want to wake up in the middle of the night and watch you sleep. Somehow I know you'd be even more beautiful in the middle of the night. Peaceful. Like an angel."

She shook her head. "I'm afraid I'm not such a peaceful sleeper," she murmured ruefully. He reached up to cradle her cheek.

"Doesn't matter," he said. "I adore you, Reyne, and I know I want you to be my wife. Don't you know if you want me as your husband?" His voice was not wheedling. Logan wanted only to push her to the truth that he knew was in her heart. It had to be. God could not let him get to this point without giving him some sign that his feelings were not reciprocated. Certainly not...

"Logan McCabe," she said quietly. "I've made a decision."

"You can think about it if—"

"No. I'm through living my life dictated by fear. Isn't that what I just told you? Oxbow is gone. He tried to do his damage, but I'm living with the confidence of Christ now. He's going before me. And here you are," she said, looking up at him with shining eyes, "a handsome, courageous, loving, happy man, wanting to take me as his wife."

She smiled at him indulgently. "I consider it a gift that you're considering a lifetime partnership with me."

Logan, unable to stop himself from continually smiling, asked, "Then we have a deal?"

"I think we can shake on it."

Logan stood and lifted Reyne to her feet. He looked away, trying to stop smiling, then looked back at her from under a mock furrowed brow. "I consider a person's handshake a seal on her word."

She looked away and then managed to glance back at him with a similar expression. "As do I."

"Then shake my hand."

They did.

"And let me put this ring on."

She did.

And afterward he pulled her into his arms, and they dissolved into celebratory laughter.

Chapter Twenty-Eight

News traveled fast in a fire camp. By the time Reyne entered the mess tent the next night on Logan's arm, the whole camp knew of their impending marriage. When they walked through the front entrance, the raucous crowd suddenly hushed and then started stomping their feet and pounding on the tables as one.

Reyne laughed as Buddy Taylor climbed up on his table and nodded his head in time with the collective beat as if he had orchestrated it all himself. "I should've known!" Reyne shouted to Logan above the din. They waited where they stood, certain that their firefighting comrades were not finished.

They weren't. Buddy raised his hands to quiet the stomping, and the tent grew still. He hummed, as if to find his key. He ran through an operatic *mi-mi-mi-mi,* then started humming and snapping his fingers. As if they were consummate professionals, the table around him began humming along, accompanying their leader.

"Go-in' to the chapel and they're goin' ta get ma-a-a-ried, they're go-in' to the chapel and they're goin' ta get ma-a-a-ried." He walked down the tables toward them, much as he had walked toward Reyne a few months before. Each time he got to an extended "married," he swiveled his knees and swung his arms as if he was doing the twist. Reyne giggled and glanced up at Logan. This time he was enjoying Buddy's antics too.

Their minstrel kept singing, walking on tables all the way, until he got to the mess-tent entrance. As a grand finale, he paused in his song to motion them back and did a gymnastic flip off the table, landing on his feet. The crowd exploded into hoots and applause, but Buddy frowned and shushed them. Then, kneeling and spreading his arms wide, he finished singing, "Goin' to the chapel of l-o-v-e!"

The crowd erupted with applause and laughter again, moving as one body to carry the happy couple and Buddy to the front of the buffet line. Laughing, Reyne looked at Logan and shook her head. Never, ever, had she felt this happy.

When they were back on their feet, Buddy nudged Logan's back. "You know you're getting the most gorgeous firefighter in the biz, don't ya?"

"I do," Logan said, smiling at Reyne like a king surveying his storybook kingdom.

"And the brainiest?"

"I prefer *smartest,*" Reyne put in.

"Okay, smarty-pants, *smartest.*" Buddy took the opportunity of being in line to heap up a second helping of dinner for himself.

"Yes, I'm aware of that fact."

"And one of the best firefighters to ever go after the dragon?"

"Yes, I know," Logan said, still smiling.

"Hey, I'm liking this," Reyne said. "Go on, Buddy, go on. Surely you can think of more good things to say."

"Not in front of this hulking fiancé," Buddy quipped. "What do you think I am, an idiot?"

Reyne finished loading her own plate with pasta, barbecued chicken, bread, and salad. The cooks had outdone themselves today, but it mattered little to her. She decided that she could eat macaroni and cheese for the rest of her life and die a happy woman because the things that mattered were in order. Her faith. Her life, for the most part. Her love. She glanced back at Logan with a smile meant only for him.

"Yes," Buddy said, catching a glimpse of Reyne's smile and slapping Logan on the back, "you're a lucky, lucky man, McCabe. Be careful. You're not to the altar yet. I just might try to steal her back from you."

Logan looked back at him, his eyes narrowing. "Now, Taylor…"

Buddy threw up his arms in surrender and laughed. "Joking! I was only joking! You two kids," he said, putting an arm around each of them, "are clearly destined for one another."

Reyne and Logan were able to grab snatches of time together over the next three days, but rarely alone. They had an early breakfast the next morning, a late dinner the following day. On the third day, Reyne awakened to find Logan sleeping on the ground next to her cot. When he woke up, she was still in her bed, looking down on him with a big smile.

"Hey," he said sleepily, rubbing his face, "I'm the one who's supposed to be watching you sleep."

"I like to watch you. Your nose twitches like you're smelling something funny in your dreams. Besides, you're the one who sneaked into my tent."

He took her hand, studying the simple gold band on her ring finger. "I'm sorry. I should've asked. But I came to see you and then couldn't bear to wake you when I saw you sleeping so peacefully. Just like I thought," he said, smiling up into her eyes. "No matter what you say, you do look just like an angel. I couldn't stand leaving you again."

She smiled at him, knowing just how he felt. The idea that they might be torn apart, sent to separate fires at any moment, was torturous. Reyne watched as Logan played with the ring on her finger, twisting it around and around. "Why'd you pick this ring, Logan? Why the braid?" she asked, referring to the three golden strands that wove themselves together to form the band.

"Three strands," he told her. "You. Me. And Jesus. I want God to be a part of our relationship always."

Tears sprang to Reyne's eyes. "Oh, Logan. If Beth could hear that, she would dance in the streets." She turned away from him and held her hand up in the air to look at her ring. "She was always telling me that her and Matt's faith helped make their marriage strong. I love it that it's as important to you as it is to me to have Christ as our foundation."

"Couldn't get any stronger," he murmured. Reyne turned to look at him. He was dozing off again.

"No we couldn't," she whispered.

"Oldre," Thomas barked at her as soon as she entered the command center. "You've been reassigned. Home post duty. Get your gear and head out to the heliport."

Reyne's heart skipped a beat. "What? Home post? What's going on?"

Thomas glanced up at her from over his clipboard, which was choked with papers going every which way. "Elk Horn. The hotshot team that Logan left there can't control the fires anymore, and Missoula's team has already been split up into too many subgroups to count. There's no one left. The Northwest Forestry Company has ordered their whole crew back to Elk Horn. And Boise's trying to get you help soon. Somehow…"

He looked around, already distracted. "Reyne, it's bad. Everywhere. I don't know, realistically, if the forestry company will get much governmental assistance until the town itself is threatened. I'm amazed they're letting you go. So run, before they think twice."

Reyne was still back on the news that there was a big fire in the Elk Horn Valley. Her heart sank as she thought of the beautiful forests surrounding her home going up in flames. And then her mind started working. She nodded briefly at Thomas. She'd put out other dragons. This one was no different.

Reyne picked up her notebook computer, sorted out the cord from the tangle of others, threw her logbooks, notes, and cellular phone in her backpack, and headed out the door. Reyne cast one last look over her shoulder. The crew here was getting the Mount Snowy fire under control, but they looked the worse for wear. The summer was taking its toll. And it was only late August, with two potential hot months ahead.

But her mind was already on Elk Horn as she turned away from the command center and headed toward the heliport. *Logan...*, she thought suddenly. *I wish Logan were going with me. Now.* Without another thought, she turned and walked back into the command tent.

As soon as he saw her, Thomas knew. He held up his hands and gave her a look as if he were dealing with a whiny kid on a softball team. "They're already scheduled on the next flight out. Just as soon as they get back from their mission."

Reyne flashed him a smile and turned back around. With Logan at her side, she could conquer the dragon anywhere he chose to show his face.

"And Oldre!" Thomas called. "I want an invitation to the wedding!"

CHAPTER TWENTY-NINE

*E*lk Horn Valley was in trouble.

Reyne knew it as soon as Mike Moser took her up in an old twin-engine plane to see the fire for herself. The rolling acres of ranches, the grain and other crops, the cattle, the majestic homes, the tiny town, the forests that rose up from the valley floor and blanketed the mountains—all of it was in peril from the flames that were licking at the ridges surrounding the southern end of the valley. The fire Reyne saw below her had the potential to grow into the biggest one she had faced so far this season. And with the chronic shortage of personnel and supplies, she knew they were ill prepared to fight it. There were no extra crews to obtain, and few fresh ones.

Reyne leaned forward, peering out the windshield, and then fell back against her seat, moving the microphone away from her mouth and blowing out forcefully. There was a lot of work to do. A lot. She closed her eyes and whispered, "Dear Father, please help me in this. I am overwhelmed. This is bigger than I am."

Nothing is bigger than I.

She smiled at her heart's response. *Thank you, Jesus. Thank you for being with me every second of the day.* She lowered the microphone to her mouth again and glanced at the pilot. "Get me on the ground, Mike. We have work to do."

Reyne took charge of the command ready room in the airstrip barracks like a woman born to lead. There were six hotshots remaining at the base, and Reyne picked up the phone immediately to enlist friends and neighbors in the cause. She sent Rachel off to obtain the most up-to-date topographical maps possible; she asked Dirk to start rounding up supplies that she knew by now would run short: batteries, sleeping bags, toilet paper. For Matt Morgan, a longtime member of the community who enjoyed friendships with influential Montana politicians, she had a special mission. For good measure, Dirk would follow up his calls. Two prominent ranchers were better than one.

"Matt," she said gently, hearing him pick up. Reyne ducked away from two other team members who were already on the other phone lines carrying out her orders. "How are you?"

"I'm doing pretty well, Reyne, considering. We've missed you around here—and not just 'cause we're all about to go up in flames."

"I've missed you guys. We have some big news for you when things settle down. But, Matt, I need your help right now."

"Anything."

"Logan and I've been out on several big fires these last weeks, and everywhere it's the same. There are too many fires and too few bodies to fight them. Getting adequate crews in here is going to take some doing. We've only got one tanker, and it's grounded right now. We're going to need at least two, and a chopper would be great too. I thought you could make some calls."

"You've got it."

"And also do some recruiting. No one could say no to you. And if you take that darling girl of yours along, they'll really turn out."

Matt laughed. It felt terrific to hear his big laugh again. "What are you saying, Oldre? Exploit my baby girl for the sake of the cause?"

"You're onto me, Matt," she said, grinning. "I was thinking a big neon sign above her that says, 'Don't make my baby fight fires herself,' might be in order."

He groaned. "Now, that's really bad."

"Okay then," she said, needing to wrap up the conversation, "you get me people on your terms. Preferably young men and women in good shape. And then come down here. I need you to help train them."

"But Reyne, it's been about thirteen years since I dug chains."

"Do you ever forget?" she demanded.

"How could I forget? I've wanted to—"

"Okay, then. See you at 0600 tomorrow." With that she hung up, grinning as she imagined the look on his face at the other end. She hoped her clipped commands amused him.

And she hoped their friendship and a cause gave Matt Morgan yet another reason to go on living without Beth.

Two separate fronts were converging on the Elk Horn Valley, each coming from a different direction. This presented the thorny problem of having to divide up her already inadequate crews. The regional fire coordinator center called her every two hours for an update but still had not assigned her command-center help. Each time she inquired, the answer was the same. "Sorry. We're tapped out. Everyone is assigned to fires in which lives are endangered," or something to that effect. If she heard it again, Reyne thought she'd have to scream.

Never had she seen a fire situation like this.

Never had she thought that she'd be the one in charge.

Still, it came naturally, as instinct. She was able to keep her head, sort out the tasks that needed completion first, and move forward. Within twenty-four hours, Matt's requested chopper arrived, an incredible blessing. Best of all, Logan was aboard.

Immediately he was beside her, hearing out her plan, helping make decisions, sending her to bed ten hours later for a few hours' rest. Matt and Dirk, old groundpounder buddies, were outside training crew after crew recruited from around the valley. Reyne came in to give a three-hour lesson on fire behavior, practically yelling so all could hear. She was intent upon scaring them to death so they'd lose the innate bravado that came with young, inexperienced people excited about fighting off the fire and saving the town.

Many of the recruits weren't young at all. Middle-aged ranchers turned out in droves, and Reyne thought of the early firefighting days when crews looked very much like those before her. In the old days, men had routinely been pulled away from their crops to fight fire, and they had gone willingly, feeling obligated to save the land on which they made their living.

But a good third of the crowd was female, a distinct difference from the past. Reyne was especially glad to see the women in the room. From her experience, female crew members often seemed to give the men the desire to work harder and show off, but they also pressed them to make wiser decisions that might save all their lives if a problem arose. Women were stabilizers on fire crews, and they would certainly need stability to fight effectively under these conditions.

Within twelve hours their crash course on fire safety and firefighting was over, and Dirk and Matt were leading two rookie teams to the front lines to train behind their scant veteran crews for a day before taking on fire alone. Logan began training a new team of perhaps a hundred. With those and the reinforcements they expected to arrive at any moment, they would have a revolving supply of firefighters. When team one came off duty, the second could go in, and so on.

Now Logan and Reyne began planning strategy on how they could best use his small team of six smokejumpers, the helicopter, and the seasonally contracted A-20 tanker plane, which the mechanic assured them could be up and running in eight hours. They set the chopper to work right away, attaching a huge water bucket.

"Fill her up at Dancara Lake," Logan told the pilot, Gene Edmonds. "You're going after this arm of the fire here," he added, pointing at the color-pencil sketch of the fire on the topographical map. He also showed him several satellite shots of the same arm, indicating the toughest part of the fire for groundpounders to reach.

"Got it," said the pilot with a cocky smile, putting his aviator's glasses on. "Time to rock 'n' roll."

As the third crew loaded up on big flatbed trucks requisitioned from farmers, Reyne thought again of the Depression-era pictures of Civilian Conservation Corps going out to fight fires. She breathed a sigh of relief as they grew smaller in the distance. All the preparation time had slowed them down, and Reyne knew the fire was gaining ground. Now, at last, they were going out to meet the enemy head on.

The battle had begun.

CHAPTER THIRTY

*R*eyne was in the top of the airstrip barracks in the miniature weather station when Logan found her. As soon as she spotted him, hot tears sprang to her eyes. She wiped them away quickly.

"Sorry," she said, feeling foolish. "I guess I'm a bit tired."

"I wonder why," Logan said, sitting down beside her. "Come here," he said, pulling her out of her chair and into his lap on the floor.

She giggled. "What are you doing?" she asked but complied with his request.

"I haven't held my fiancée in my arms for a good two, maybe three, days."

"We've been a tad busy."

"Still, there's no excuse." He gave her a quick kiss and then studied her intently. "I don't want a day to go by in our marriage without at least one hug," he said, squeezing her.

"Sounds good to me. I'm so tired I think I'll pass out, Logan. How are you doing?"

"Well, I never thought I'd say this, but I'm about ready for fire season to be over."

Reyne laughed. "Me too. I'm pretty sick of worrying whether we'll run out of TP. I'd rather think about our wedding ceremony."

"Oh yes," he said, wiggling his eyebrows, "and the wedding night…"

"Logan!" she said, swatting him playfully.

"What?" he asked, pretending to be hurt. "You're not looking forward to the wedding night?"

Knowing she was trapped, Reyne changed the subject. "Back to the fire…"

"Ah yes, the fire," Logan said wearily. He eased his grip on her, and Reyne edged away.

"Let's go look at the maps."

"Ah yes, the maps."

"Logan! Are you with me?" she asked, already at the door.

"Right behind you."

Their battle against the Great Bear fire, named for the wilderness near the flame's source, was a daunting one. Day by day the fire crept closer to Elk Horn, eating up precious forested acres while the makeshift command team vacillated on what to do. Finally Reyne brought up the solution they'd been avoiding.

"We've got to light a backfire. From here to here," she said, indicating a ten-mile-wide swath on the map. "And from here to here," she added, pointing to the other side of the valley. "Without it, we're toast. Weather reports indicate we're in for wind and more dry weather. No lucky low-pressure system either. Ol' Bear's just gonna keep on rolling, and even our volunteer corps can't stop it. We'd need ten thousand troops on the line. We've got maybe a thousand. And I've given up on the system sending any more our way until Great Bear's right on top of us. But they'll be only too happy to grant approval for the backfires. Forest, they have. Personnel, they don't."

Logan nodded, thinking. The few other experienced fire commanders at the table agreed. They planned the backfire, then separated to make the appropriate calls and get some sleep—and pray that the backfires would do the job of protecting Elk Horn from the Great Bear's rampage.

Matt was outside the barracks, flipping hamburger patties like a mad Viking chef. Reyne and Logan approached him, enjoying the view of him and five others at work on their makeshift grills—metal oil drums cut in half and placed on concrete bases.

"Ingenious," Logan said, indicating the grills.

"Hey," Matt said with a small smile, "gotta feed the troops. And Weber doesn't make 'em big enough." He glanced around, looking for Hope. Spotting her eating with a group of female firefighters, he visibly relaxed.

"How are you holding up, Matt?" Reyne asked with concern.

"Good. No, great. It's good to get my mind off things and get away from the ranch. I have some solid men there who can take care of it all as well as I can. And working here gets me away from everything that reminds me of Beth." He glanced up at them guiltily. "Not that I need…or want—"

Reyne shook her head, cutting him off. "We understand, Matthew." She moved under his free arm to give him a sideways hug, stretching to reach around his wide, muscular middle. "*Beth* would understand. She'd be happy to see you able to smile a little. And if taking a breather from the memories does it, so be it. It goes without saying that you all are a godsend to us firefighters."

"You'd better wait until you taste this burger before saying that," he warned, waving his spatula over the sizzling patties.

"No need," Reyne said. "You've proven to be invaluable, with or without the burgers!"

CHAPTER THIRTY-ONE

*T*welve hours later the winds picked up, and Logan and Reyne made the decision to move up the backfire burns. They loaded some crew members with fusees and drip torches. The plan was to burn a ten-mile swath on one side of the valley and an eight-mile swath on the other. Each would be at least a quarter mile wide. In this way, they hoped to deprive the Great Bear of fuel and turn it away, denying entrance to their precious valley. Just in case they failed, Rachel and Arnie had already been detailed to begin evacuating the ranches nearest the valley's mouth.

Logan was grounded with his smokejumpers, cleaning and repairing equipment, when the hotshots left to set their plan into motion. At the appointed time, Reyne radioed each team captain with the command to clear the fire lines of brush and debris, then set the lit fusees to the dry tinder just on the other side of the lines. Then she looked at the helicopter pilot.

"Gene, are you willing to take me up?"

"I've been waiting all day."

"The wind's bad."

"I like a challenge. Where're we headed, boss?"

"I want to see the front. For myself," she said, walking beside him toward the helicopter. "Up close and personal. Make sure this is going to work."

Logan, who was across the huge room from her, glanced around and saw her. Reyne smiled and blew him a kiss as she left the building, ignoring his call. She knew he wouldn't want her to go up. The winds were dangerous. But she had to see; their equipment here was more rudimentary than at any command post in which she'd ever served. In person the fire could look a lot different from what showed up on satellite.

And a lot was at stake here. Her home. Her future with Logan, in a way.

They were inside the cockpit when she saw him next. He stood outside the barracks door, hands on his hips, clearly disapproving, but she nodded to Gene to start the engine. The blades above them soon whirred to a seamless blur. They rose up and away.

Half an hour later they had observed the entire southwestern front of the fire line. The backfire there was already lit and well under way, eating its way back to the Great Bear fire as if it were a small child rushing to meet its father. The southeastern flank was trickier, and crews were still struggling to clear the fire line. The rocky soil was scattered with tough, clumpy grass that resisted their efforts to pull it out. But they were getting very close.

That task accomplished, Gene suggested going to the Great Bear flank nearest them to check it out, and Reyne nodded her approval. They dipped and shot over the trees at breakneck speed. Reyne, in her weariness, stared transfixed at the view under the bubbled cockpit.

Within seconds it seemed, Great Bear was directly in front of them, just over the ridge. Then suddenly the chopper dipped and turned crazily.

Gene had paused over a low saddle in the ridge—not thinking for a crucial second about the impact of such a decision—and the combined airflow from the cooler valley with the hot fire before them created havoc with the already stiff winds. Reyne gripped the bar above her right shoulder and the seat with her left hand. Back and forth the chopper waved as Gene swore under his breath and fought for control.

For a half-second the wind died, and Gene sighed as he regained control of the helicopter. But it was to be a brief respite. The turbulence resumed, and they swung crazily to the left, spiraling out of control.

"Mayday! Mayday!" Gene screamed into the radio.

They crashed before he could finish his transmission.

CHAPTER THIRTY-TWO

*C*hopper down! Chopper down!" the air-operations manager shouted to the stunned firefighters sitting in the command center room. He flipped a switch, frantically trying to connect with the helicopter again. "Gene, this is command center, do you read? Edmonds, this is command center, do you read?"

Logan felt queasy as he watched the man try to raise the chopper pilot again. *No. Please God, no. Reyne! Reyne!*

A steady hand clapped his shoulder and remained there, and Logan turned to find Dirk to his right.

"Gene, this is command center. Do you read?"

"It's going to be okay," Dirk said softly to Logan.

"Gene, this is command center. Do you read?"

"I'm going after her, Dirk. We'll take the plane up…" He stepped into motion with his friend right on his heels. Matt appeared on his left and quickly gathered what was going on. He had met Logan's eyes as Reyne took off in the chopper less than an hour earlier.

"I don't think that's a good idea," Dirk was saying. "I mean, I don't know much about winds, but if Gene can't stay aloft, you don't belong up there in some tiny plane, jumping out to try and save her."

"You might both be killed," Matt said.

Logan paced for a second or two and then went to find the Forest Service meteorologist, assigned to the Great Bear fire just the day before. "Joe, what do you have for me? What's it lookin' like?"

Joe, already aware of the downed chopper, looked up at him with a frown. "It's not flying weather. It's gotten worse since Reyne and Gene went up."

Logan rubbed his eyes, frantically searching his weary mind for the answer. He was aware of Matt and Dirk flanking him. With them close behind, he walked to study the bank of computer monitors, studying the latest satellite and firsthand information from the groundpounders. Then he hurried back over to where the air-operations manager, having given up on raising the helicopter pilot, was scanning the radar for their signal.

With some turns of the dial he finally spotted the faint blip of their emergency beacon on the screen. "There," he said, pointing. "I've got 'em! I've got a location!" He grimaced and looked up at Logan's face, seeming to know what he was thinking. "But McCabe, there's no guarantee they're alive."

Logan fought back the desire to punch the man out for even suggesting such an idea. Deep down, he knew the guy was just trying to protect him from doing something foolish. And he knew what he was about to do was just that: foolish. But if Reyne was in trouble, he saw no other option.

"Mike! John!" he barked to a group of smokejumpers and plane crewmen who were lounging on old couches in a corner. "I need to go up. Can you guys take me?"

"Yes sir!" they said in unison, hopping up.

"It's risky!" Logan warned.

"Best kind," Mike Moser quipped, immediately grabbing his gear and heading toward the command center so they could discuss their game plan. "The Sherpa or the Cessna?" he asked.

"Sherpa. We'll need her weight against the wind."

"Now, wait a minute," Dirk said, stepping between Logan and the pilots. "Just what do you think you're doin', Logan? This is crazy, and you know it."

"Step aside, Dirk. I'm going after her."

"And do what? Get yourself killed in the process?"

"I'm going after her," he repeated, pushing past his friend's shoulder and striding toward his locker and gear.

Matt tried too, once they reached the lockers. "Logan," he said, reaching out to take the other man's arm, "you have to consider she…she might not have survived the crash. Or she might've gotten out and is hiking home right now. You might skydive in there and find no one but yourself to fight the fire. What's the sense in that?"

"You of all people should understand why I have to go, Matt." Logan winced inwardly at his sharp tone. "I have to go try and save the woman I love."

Matt held his unwavering gaze. "Sometimes there's no way to save 'em, Logan," he said softly.

Logan grimaced and looked down at the floor, picturing Beth's bright smile, her gaunt face. Then he looked back up to face his friends. "I have to try," he told them. "I just couldn't live with myself if I didn't at least try and help her when she was in trouble."

Dirk and Matt glanced at one another and then back to Logan. Dirk was first to speak. "Then let's make sure you have the best plan possible," he said, turning toward the command center.

"We've got the east flank here," said Ken Oakley, indicating a place on the map that was being gradually colored in as the fire moved toward Elk Horn. "Team eight lit their backfire before we could get to 'em," he added grimly, daring to glance up at Logan.

"And the bad news is that we think Gene and Reyne went down here," the air-operations manager said, circling an area dead center between Great Bear's southeast flank and the backfire.

"Winds are at fifteen miles per hour, sometimes gusting up to twenty or thirty," Joe put in. Logan ignored Dirk's meaningful glance. He knew it wasn't smokejumping weather.

"Best we can tell," Joe went on, "is that you have maybe thirty minutes to get to them and get them to a clearing where we can land. We've called in the chopper from the local hospital. They'll be at your clearing in forty minutes, as scheduled."

"What if we dump some retardant here," suggested the tanker pilot, pointing over Ken's shoulder toward the map. "Give them some sort of backup in case they can't make it to the clearing."

"That's a good idea," Ken said. "You better take a chain saw and three fire shelters with you, Logan. If you've got two injured people in there, you'll have no choice but to ride it out."

Logan nodded, pushing away memories of Reyne's last ride through the dragon's mouth and what it would do to her to ride it out again.

"As soon as you pinpoint their location, Logan, we'll start digging chains in your direction," Dirk said. "We could try and make some sort of path out in a T formation between Great Bear and the two flanks of the backfire we've lit."

"I don't think that'd work," Joe said. "Winds are too fast. You'd never stay ahead of 'em, and you all might get caught."

"So this is it," Logan said, nodding. "I have to get to Reyne and Gene, clear a landing spot, and get them to it or under shelters before one or both fires converge on us."

The group all stared back at him, affirming his synopsis. "Well, people, let's get to work. My fiancée's in there, and I intend to get her out."

They took off eight minutes later. Logan had insisted on going in alone, not wanting to endanger any of his crew on the perilous mission. Mike understood the risks. As the Sherpa lumbered up into the sky, Logan glanced around the empty cabin and shivered involuntarily. It was eerie to be in the big, cold compartment without any of his crew along.

As soon as they leveled off, Logan stood and, holding on to the various rails above him, made his way to the open doorway. His equipment seemed bulkier, more unwieldy than usual, and he clenched his teeth as the plane dropped thirty feet, then rose, already encountering turbulence from the firestorm dead ahead.

Logan studied the huge plume of smoke behind them, to the west, that was the color of creamed coffee and represented the other flank of Great Bear. They were flying through a thin layer of smoke, presumably from the backfire lit only hours before. Logan leaned out to study the line, pleased to see that it was making good headway and was right on target to end Great Bear's western front.

To the east, however, Great Bear was having his heyday. The rocky slopes were too tough in many places for groundpounders to reach, and when they did get close to the fire, the terrain fought them with every step in their efforts to dig chains. The result was a haphazard, sloppy line that he and Reyne had eventually called off.

Reyne had been right. The backfire was a far better plan—to move closer to Elk Horn, where the terrain smoothed out, dig a fire line there, set the backfire, and get the heck out of Dodge, as Thomas would say.

But now that same fire that Logan had helped her engineer was threatening her life. *If* she was still alive. Logan swallowed hard, pushing away the unthinkable possibility.

She was alive. She had to be.

Reyne willed her eyes to open, feeling as if there were heavy weights on each. She couldn't imagine where she was or why she had such a pounding headache. "I don't have time for migraines," she muttered, cradling her head in her hand and finally managing to pull one lid to half-mast.

When the image before her registered, both eyes flew wide open. She was in a helicopter, and the windshield had shattered into a blue cracked montage that reminded her of a winter frosted window. But it was too hot. Much too hot. Suddenly it all came together, and she eased her head toward Gene, forcing herself to look.

He was slumped over, his helmet askew, his aviator glasses in his lap. Not breathing. Feeling as if she had been drugged, Reyne leaned toward him and pulled her hand toward his neck to seek a pulse. Finding none, she let go, as relieved that that effort was over as she was grieved to find that Gene was gone. *O God*, she thought, *is this it? Am I to die in a helicopter crash?*

But then she caught her first glimpse of Great Bear, directly in front of her, tiny flames dancing eerily in the million separate pieces of the helicopter's windshield. *Oh no. Please God, no. I can't fight him today. I can't do it.*

I give strength to the weary. Hope in me, and I will make you soar on wings like eagles, walk and not be faint.

Her version of the Isaiah verse popped into her head, repeating like a broken record. She moved her hand to the seat belt in uneven, jerking motions and, after working at it for a while, managed to free herself. Then she opened the tiny, rounded door and leaned out, wincing at the pain in her head but seeking an unfettered view of Great Bear.

He was headed her way, a giant of a fire. Maybe ten, twelve miles away at the most. And coming fast down the mountainside.

"O God," she mumbled. "I can't do it again! I can't!"

I am your fortress. Your refuge in times of trouble.

She sighed, trying to get hold of herself. Then she leaned forward, opened the cockpit's emergency kit, and managed to remove the tiny emergency beacon and a bottle of water.

Reyne rested for a moment, gathering her strength, checked once more for a pulse on Gene's neck, then swung her legs outward. Slowly, ever so slowly, she eased out. She was half standing, half leaning against the helicopter wreckage when she saw it. *The backfire,* she thought, her memory suddenly clearing. She whipped her head in consternation back to Great Bear's front, and the movement was too much. As fear forced a cry to her throat, a wave of black encompassed her.

CHAPTER THIRTY-THREE

I 've got 'em," Mike said over the radio, his voice suddenly crackling into Logan's ear. "Dead ahead. We'll do a low cargo flyover and then return for your jump."

"Roger," Logan responded. He leaned out of the doorway, anxious to spot the wreck site and plan his dive. Within seconds it came into view; Logan swallowed hard against a wave of nausea and shoved the cargo chute out. He leaned to watch as his chain saw floated toward the ground ahead of him.

They were maybe three hundred feet above the ground when he saw her. "There she is!" he shouted into the helmet microphone, wincing as the plane's belly again blocked her from his view. "Did you see her? Did you see her?"

"Roger that, Logan." Mike's grim tone made Logan stop and think. Seeing her outside the chopper was not necessarily a good thing. If she had been thrown from the vessel upon crashing, her chances were certainly slim. The Sherpa banked sharply, and Logan concentrated on his jump.

He saw the helicopter again just before having to concentrate on nothing but the approaching trees. Or he thought he saw it; he wasn't sure. Then all of a sudden, a new wind picked up, blowing him to the west. In seconds, he was hanging in a tangle of lines and chute and tree branches. When the ripping and crunching sounds ended and Logan at last felt himself come to a stop thirty feet above the ground, he swore mildly before he could stop himself. "Sorry, God," he growled. "But even *you* have to admit things aren't exactly going my way."

An upright man gives thought to his ways.

"Yeah, I hear you," Logan muttered. "I'm sorry, I'm sorry." Not wasting time, he clipped his descender hardware to the chute fitting, then looked around for a branch that would hold the horizontal stabilizer. That deployed, he released the chute lines and swung underneath the canopy, holding his breath that either the stabilizer rope or his backup line would hold. They did. Slowly, he rappelled downward on the letdown rope.

Once he reached bottom, Logan looked up to see the bright blue of the chute rippling in the wind. The sky beyond it was dark brown. He squinted, wiping away the sweat on his brow, and studied his surroundings, getting his bearings.

Logan could hear him. The Great Bear. He was maybe five, six miles away, judging from the huge, thunderous plume of smoke rising forty thousand feet into the air. Logan turned around. The backfire was closer, maybe three miles away, but moving more slowly than its larger counterpart. With either fire, they had precious little time.

He spotted his chain saw while he shrugged off his bulky Kevlar outfit, leaving only his Nomex shirt and BLM-issued pants. If he had to carry one or two people out of this mess, he couldn't deal with the suit, too.

Then he shouldered his bulky pack and the saw, glanced down at the compass he wore on his wrist, and without hesitation headed out.

By his figures he had drifted more than a quarter mile off target. He jogged along the rocky path of a small ridge, grunting as the pack and saw bumped against his back. He was carrying a combined weight of more than a hundred pounds.

It took him ten minutes to get to his intended location and another five to spot the downed helicopter. Logan glanced behind him. Great Bear was coming fast. The evacuation chopper would be arriving in twenty minutes, expecting a cleared location. And he didn't even know yet if Reyne was alive.

The wreck site lay at the base of a tiny valley, directly under a saddle in the ridge that Logan surmised was the cause of their accident. *The cool air came up from here,* he thought as he picked his way down a dry creek bed, *and met the hot air from Great Bear. Venturi effect.* He paused to look around and get his bearings. There she was. Not fifty feet from him. And very, very still.

"Reyne!" he shouted, unable to say more because he was panting so hard for breath. He neared her and paused to drop his pack and chain saw, irritated by the precious seconds it took. Unencumbered, he ran to her side.

"Reyne!" he repeated. "Can you hear me?" He glanced up again toward the approaching fire and grimaced at its pace. It had closed the distance to about three miles already, and it was crowning. That meant it had found ladder fuels—tall brush and lower branches that allowed the sweeping ground fire to climb to the tops of trees. Higher up, the winds blew faster, and therefore the fire came on faster. Too fast.

There. A pulse! He turned back to Reyne, quickly running his hands over her body to check for broken bones. She was unconscious, but he could find no major injuries; she had probably climbed out of the chopper herself before passing out. He willed himself to leave her side and check on Gene, who was still strapped into his seat.

While he jogged around the front of the chopper, bending low to avoid the huge blades that had hit the ground at an angle and stuck, Logan radioed the command center. "Home base, this is McCabe. Do you read me?" The radio buzzed with interference. Logan pried open the pilot-side door and scanned Gene's ashen face. Grimly he checked for a pulse. "Home base, this is McCabe. Do you read me?"

Finding no pulse, Logan clenched his teeth and shook his head. "Come on, God, we need your help here," he said, looking around at the two walls of flame moving in on them from either side.

"Roger, McCabe, we read you loud and clear. Over."

"Good. Chopper on its way? Over."

"Winging its way toward you right now. Estimated TOA is 1750 hours. And McCabe, I doubt if you'll have ten more minutes to get out of there. Over."

Logan checked his watch. "It's gonna take a miracle to make it. I've got one unconscious and one dead—Gene. You tell that chopper pilot to wait for us until the last second. You got that? Over." He unstrapped Gene and pulled him out of the cockpit, wondering how he'd ever get his body and Reyne to the helicopter in time. He winced as he made the immediate decision to abandon Gene's body. He and Reyne were still alive. And their only chance to stay that way was for Logan to make hard, fast, good decisions.

"Roger that," the air-operations manager said.

He ran around to the other side of the helicopter and checked Reyne's pulse again. "Reyne! Honey, wake up!"

She didn't move.

"Reyne, sweetie," he said, pushing back sudden tears that took him by surprise. "I've gotta leave you for a few minutes. Clear a spot for the chopper. I'll be right back for you. I will. I promise. And we're going to get out of here." He kissed her forehead lightly, then scrambled to his feet and back to his backpack and chain saw. Loading both up, he cast one last glance toward Reyne and then ran up the creek bed. Their lives depended on his speed, and he knew it.

Logan left the creek bed, crested the ridge, and ran another six hundred feet to the agreed-upon location for the evacuation chopper. Deciding he was far enough away from the small valley to avoid the same downdraft that had killed Gene, Logan fired up his chain saw and began cutting. Pine after pine went down, and the area was cleared when the chopper emerged from the wispy clouds of smoke above like an angel of deliverance.

He didn't bother to watch it land. Instead, Logan glanced up at the fire, now maybe two miles away, and sprinted back toward Reyne. He nearly broke his ankle as he slid over the rounded rocks in the creek bed and fell, tumbling for a perilous moment before righting himself. But he didn't stop running. Logan was determined to reach Reyne and get her back to the chopper in time. No dragon was going to cheat him of a life with her.

He nearly laughed in relief when he finally spotted her again and managed to clamber over to her. Pausing for a second, wondering about neck injuries, he decided that there was no time to do anything about it anyway.

He picked Reyne up and carefully slung her over one shoulder. With one last, sorrowful glance back toward Gene's body, Logan muttered a prayer over his choices and set off in a half jog up the creek bed toward the ridge high above. He could hear the *whop* of the chopper blades in the distance, and he knew their time was short. Great Bear was nearly on top of them. Logan could feel his hot breath.

He stumbled twice as he climbed, nearly dropping Reyne to the stones at his feet. When they reached the ridge, he was so out of breath that he had to set her down, gasping. He turned to face the dragon, which was edging ever closer, the flames shooting higher than three hundred feet in the air. He could allow himself no more time.

He picked Reyne up—cradling her this time in his arms—and glanced around. The smoke was getting thicker, and the A-20 tanker was banking back toward them to dump the planned fire retardant as a precaution. They were still a good four hundred yards from the chopper.

The winds were picking up—the fire again creating its own weather pattern. Logan scowled. By the time they made it to the chopper now, it would be a miracle if the pilot could get them out. He set Reyne down and waved his arms madly at the pilot, motioning to him to get out while he still could. He and Reyne would have to ride out the firestorm in the retardant-drenched area nearby.

The chopper pilot remained where he was, hovering just above the ground for a second as if vacillating about what to do. Logan leaned toward the radio strapped to his shoulder. "Home base! This is McCabe! Get that chopper out of here! We're taking cover in the retardant area! Over!" He screamed to be heard over the wind and prayed that the message would be audible on the other end.

He assumed they had heard him because a second later the helicopter took off, bobbing crazily in the wind. Logan prayed that the brave pilot who had tried to save them would make it. Then he concentrated on saving themselves.

The wind picked up Reyne's hair and blew it like straw in a wind tunnel. Logan felt as if he were leaning forty-five degrees into the fierce gale. And against every instinct in him, he had to head toward the fire—toward the clearing that lay between them and Great Bear. "Come on!" he roared at the flames towering above them, not a quarter mile away now. "Come on!"

His words sounded braver than he felt inside. But they managed to reach the clearing that the tanker had doused in retardant and waded through the thick, red muck to the very center. Logan set Reyne down, her back against his legs so she wouldn't slump into the foam and suffocate. Then he undid the tiny square of foil to deploy one fire tent that would serve as their flooring.

The fire was almost upon them, the heat nearly unbearable as he gently laid Reyne stomach-down on the first tent and, with trembling fingers, worked to deploy a second. He looked up to see the firestorm coming toward them at breakneck speed, gobbling the brush near the edge of the clearing. He had to get them covered.

Logan set his mouth in a grim line, squinting to avoid the irritating dryness as the fire seemed to lick the moisture from his eyes. He leaned his head toward the closest flames, hoping his hair might buy him seconds. Miraculously, the second tent was deployed in record time. Logan waved it out before them and was reminded of Reyne's description of it being like a beach towel in hurricane-force winds.

Then he was under it, tucking it around Reyne and himself, struggling to keep the flaps sealed. But before he sealed the final flap, before lying down beside Reyne, he was looking up into the face of the dragon. He had faced big fire before, but nothing like this. At last he could see what had taken her so long to get past.

There it was, towering above him in a swirling, crimson dance of flames. Its movements were hypnotic, transfixing.

It was the face of the devil himself.

CHAPTER THIRTY-FOUR

*W*hen Reyne regained consciousness, she blinked to make sure she wasn't dreaming. The first thing she saw were the bright orange dots of a fire shelter—just as she had seen in her nightmares of Oxbow. Then she heard it—the familiar roar of a dragon cheated of its prey. And from the sounds of it, he was right on top of her. Instinct prodded her to flee, and in her fuzzy state of mind she moved to obey it. She tried to rise to her knees, to run, to escape the monster that threatened her.

But somebody stopped her. "No!" he yelled, leaning more heavily upon her.

She turned her head and found herself staring into Logan's blue eyes. Shaking her head as if still dreaming, she looked around as best she could. It appeared that they were sharing a fire tent, and Logan was half shielding her with his own body.

"It's good to see you're awake!" he shouted, smiling at her as sweat dripped into his eyes. He seemed oblivious to the fact that a fire was raging outside.

"Where are we?" she yelled back to him.

"Riding out Great Bear!"

It all came back to her. She frowned and glanced back at Logan. "Gene?" she asked in a single shouted word.

Logan grimaced and shook his head slightly. "I'm sorry!"

Reyne laid her head back on the foil material beneath her cheek, suddenly very, very weary. She gave in to the sudden desire to slip back into the blackness without a fight.

Logan studied her thirty minutes later as the fire abated. Periodically, he would lift a corner of the tent to check, but it was still too hot for them to escape their flimsy shields. At last she roused, coming back to the land of the living, and Logan smiled, wanting his grin to be the first thing she saw.

She opened her eyes as if it pained her to do so and then wearily smiled back. "Is it over?" she asked, now able to speak in a normal voice.

"The worst of it." He kept smiling.

"And what's making you so happy? That we lived?"

"That we lived through it together. Reyne, we just survived a firestorm together. If we can get through that, we can get through anything. I have high hopes for our marriage, Mrs. McCabe-to-be."

Reyne lifted her head and brought a hand to her cheek. The retardant had managed to seep through the minuscule holes of the tent below them and had coated their bodies in red. She wiped away some of the sludge. "I think I'll need a bath before we go to the altar, Mr. Oldre-to-be."

"Uh-oh," Logan groaned. "We haven't discussed the whole name issue, have we?"

"I don't think it will be an issue," she said with a small smile. She grew more serious. "Logan, I would've died back there... If you hadn't come..."

Logan nodded silently. Then he said, "I couldn't do anything else, Reyne." Their eyes held for a long, intense moment. Then he looked away, again checking a corner of the tent. "I think it's safe to get out," he said. "You feel up to standing?"

"If you'll help me."

Logan rose and tossed away the foil shelter. All around them was a charred wasteland that would have smelled overwhelmingly of smoke had it not been for the pervasive detergent odor of retardant all about them. Logan helped Reyne to a sitting position, then leaned toward his radio. "Home base, this is McCabe. Over."

Ken's excited voice popped over the line a second later. They could hear laughing and yelling behind him. "McCabe, is that you? You made it? How about Reyne? Over."

"We're both well and accounted for. How about a lift home? Over."

"You've got it," Ken said jubilantly. "We'll have a chopper at the original clearing in twenty minutes. Over."

"Sounds good. Over and out." Logan switched off the intercom and then knelt beside Reyne to study the blackened landscape before them.

EPILOGUE

*W*ithin days, the last tendrils of Great Bear's smoldering fire had been stomped out by groundpounders, and not a moment too soon. Due to the supreme effort put forth from the valley's people, even the evacuated ranches had been spared. There would be more fires to fight that fall, but none were as big and dangerous as Great Bear.

As fire season finally drew to a welcome close, Reyne and Logan found more and more time to plan their wedding and recuperate from the summer's exertions and losses. It was a lovely autumn, crisp and cool, and they relished it after languishing in the excruciatingly hot summer climates that supported their livelihood.

They spent many days puttering around Logan's '51 Chevy, fussing about details, and Reyne even got him to help her in revitalizing her battered garden, planting lots of autumn flowers that sported various shades of gold, orange, and red. The beds of chrysanthemums and marigolds gave her cottage a warm, welcoming look.

One day they went for another drive into the back country, wanting to survey Great Bear's damage from the inside out.

Another day they drove Logan's truck far out on a country road and parked. They snuggled under several old quilts in the back as they watched the harvest moon rise, and then they made their way back to town when the moon sank over the opposite horizon.

On a lovely October evening, in the quiet forest clearing where they had enjoyed their first dinner date, they had their wedding. Logan had painstakingly recreated the scene, stringing strand after strand of tiny white lights. Only a small group of fifty or so close friends and family members were invited, and even they filled the small clearing to capacity, edging into the forest in places.

As a hired violinist played, Reyne smoothed her simple raw-silk gown and waited for her mother to settle the short veil over her face. She smiled at her mom, then took her place between her parents to walk down the "aisle." She looked down the pathway and spotted her handsome husband-to-be standing beside Arnie Lear. Beside them stood Thomas Wagner, Mike Moser, and other grinning fire-fighting friends dressed in their bright yellow Nomex shirts, which were clean for the occasion. As she drew near her groom, heart-stopping in his black tuxedo, Dirk and Rachel Tanner smiled at them from one side, Matt Morgan from the other. Little Hope stood beside him clutching a little basket, having done her duty as flower girl. And somewhere, Reyne was sure, Beth was looking on and smiling.

When she reached Logan, he stepped to her side, and the rest of the group circled them. It felt to Reyne as if they were enfolded in a circle of love. Arnie spoke eloquently of love and trust and the holy bond of matrimony, and Logan's fingers were steady as he slipped a narrow band of diamonds onto her ring finger, next to the woven engagement band. The rings met and meshed, and Reyne resisted the urge to stare at them again. There would be plenty of time for that later.

She took Logan's ring from Rachel—a matching band of three woven strands—and smiled up into Logan's eyes. "With this ring, I thee wed," she repeated after Arnie while gazing steadily, tenderly, at

Logan alone. And as the sun set in a fiery display of orange and red, Arnie Lear pronounced them husband and wife.

At the grange hall reception, after eating a huge, catered meal outside, the firefighters present pulled out hidden Pulaskis and saluted the couple military style, crossing them between two rows and creating a tunnel for Reyne and Logan to rush through. As soon as they were through, she and Logan started the dancing with their own private whirl around the floor, and afterward Reyne was swept from one man's hands to the next as the men lined up to dance with her.

More than an hour later, when Mike Moser's turn was finished, he handed her a crisp fifty-dollar bill. "What's this for?" she asked, her spirits high. "You don't have to pay me to dance with you. You're really not that bad."

"It's a bet I had with your husband!" he yelled over the band's music. He gave her a merry smile. "Last spring he told me he'd marry you by fall or pay me a hundred dollars!"

"Oh he did, did he?" she asked, planning to give her husband a bad time as soon as she caught up with him. She turned and glanced around the hall, looking for him. He obviously had had one eye on her, and when Reyne met his gaze, she got his full attention.

She cracked the bill like she meant to make Logan pay for every dollar of it. He laughed, seeing Mike's shrug behind her, and then strode toward her to collect his own dance.

"Would you accept another dance with your new husband?" he asked with one eyebrow jauntily tilted upward.

"That depends," she said, hands on hips. "The going rate is quite high."

"How much?" he asked, crossing his arms.

251

"Fifty bucks, it seems."

Logan fished around under his jacket and pulled out his wallet. He frowned and showed her the contents. "I'm afraid I'm running short. Would you accept twenty?"

She pursed her lips. "I guess you've earned a family discount," she quipped, taking the bill from the wallet.

"Such a deal," he said, pulling her into his arms. "All I had to do was marry the woman, and I get more than a fifty-percent discount on dances."

"Someday," she said, "you can dance with me for free."

"A dance with you, my love," he said, looking down at her tenderly, "is worth any amount. And a lifetime of loving you is a priceless treasure."

Reyne smiled happily back into his eyes. "That's so sappy, it's perfect. I won't try and top it."

"Please don't," Logan said merrily.

She hugged him fiercely to her, and as they swayed to the music, they glanced around the room at their well-wishers. When Reyne spotted Matthew, dancing solemnly with his daughter's tiny feet on his, she thought again of Beth and how great it would have been to have her there. And then she thought of the moonlit spring and the Eternal One who had brought them all together in his own, sweet timing.

Beth had been the one who had urged her to take this step. To trust and love and live each moment for all it was worth.

For you and my husband and my God, she promised Beth silently. *I will never let fear get in the way of loving again.*

Thank you, my dear friend, she whispered. *Thank you.*

Sandcastles

CHAPTER ONE

*M*atthew Morgan perused the menu and, for the second time, peeked over the top of it at his brooding five-year-old daughter, Hope. It was Mother's Day, and despite his best efforts to get around it, the precocious girl knew what she was missing. Or, more specifically, whom she was missing.

The waitress, the quintessential southern California blonde, came and asked if they were ready to order.

"I'll have the special," Matt said.

"Good choice," the waitress said as she wrote. "I think it looks, like, *majorly* delicious."

"Great," Matt said, not truly caring what he ate today. Hope wasn't the only one who missed Beth. Mourning her death for almost two years had not filled in the gaping hole she had left in their lives. For him, the pain had lessened, and to a great extent the grief had subsided. But he was at a loss trying to be both mother and father to his little girl.

"What do you think, pumpkin?" he asked Hope. "What about the chicken piccata? You always like that."

Hope continued to peruse the menu as if she could read every word. "Umm. Okay."

The waitress gave the girl a sunny smile, obviously feeling bad for anyone not out with his or her mom that night. "Perfect. Do you two want our house special for the dressing on your salads?"

"Which is…?" Matt asked.

"Balsamic garlic. We also have a terrific orange vinaigrette."

"Do you have Thousand Island?" Hope asked.

"I don't know. I could try and, you know, rustle up some somewhere."

"And I'm afraid I'm pretty old-fashioned when it comes to dressings," Matt said apologetically. "Is there a bottle of ranch somewhere back there too?"

"Probably," the waitress said with a smile. Now he was feeling like the object of her pity. He studied her as she left them and then glanced around. Was he just imagining it? Or were all the other families looking at them and wondering where the mother in their family was? He told himself he was just being paranoid and watched as Hope picked out a sugar packet and popped it in her mouth.

"Now, Hope," he began, "I've told you not to do that."

"Whaa?" He managed to make out her grumbled challenge around a mouth full of sugar and paper.

"Because it's disgusting and rude. Now spit it out, please."

She frowned down at the table, then let the collapsed sugar packet fall off her tongue with all the grace of a cat ridding itself of a hairball.

Matt grimaced and glanced around to see if they had offended anyone. Fortunately, everybody else appeared to be otherwise involved. He sighed deeply. Fatherhood took more patience than he had ever expected. Especially on Mother's Day. He took a sip of his water and watched as his daughter reached for another sugar packet.

"Hope—"

"What? I'm not putting it in my mouth," she said saucily, tearing open the packet and pouring it into her water.

"Hope Emily—"

"What?" she repeated. "I can't help it. The water tastes bad here. I want to go home to the ranch."

Matt thought longingly of their beloved ranch in Montana and halfway considered the idea but then dismissed it. "We'll be back soon enough. Besides, this is supposed to be a vacation. Your idea, if I remember right. We'll be heading back on the plane before you know it."

"I want to go now."

Their discussion was interrupted by the waitress, who placed their salads in front of them with a "Here you go," then disappeared again. Matt bowed his head to say grace and peeked at Hope to make sure she had done the same. Thankfully, she had. "Father, thank you for this food and this day to remember Beth by. Thank you for the time we had with her, and we ask that you be with us as we continue on without her. Amen."

Hope did not join in with her customary "amen" but instead picked up a piece of arugula from her bed of European salad greens. "I hate this stuff. I wish I could just get a normal salad."

Matt hid a grin by taking a huge bite of salad. Beth had expanded his limited vegetable-eating repertoire during their brief years together, but in his opinion, what the population of southern California deemed edible was bordering on ridiculous. Still, he ate it. It didn't taste half bad most of the time, and at least he wasn't cooking.

"Would you please pass the butter?" Hope asked in her best adult imitation.

"Sure," he said, hiding another tiny smile. *Oh, Beth, she's growing up so fast. And looking more like you all the time.* He watched as his daughter stabbed a tiny, hard butter floret and tried to spread it on her roll. Giving up, she popped the whole thing in her mouth and followed it with a French-roll chaser. This time Matt snorted, unable to conceal his amusement.

"What?" she asked.

"Nothing," he said with a smile. "I just always wrestle with those little butter doodads myself." He cleared his throat. This was as good a time as any to broach the subject. He felt it was his responsibility to check with her once in a while to see what was going on in her little head. If he could get that far.

"Honey?"

"Yeah?"

"Honey, how are you feeling about your mama today? Are you missing her?"

"I don't know," Hope said noncommittally. She reached for another butter floret.

"I bet you miss her more today than most, huh?"

"I don't know." She bit into her roll, avoiding his gaze.

"Well, I know I miss her. It just doesn't seem like there should even be a Mother's Day if your mom isn't around to enjoy it with you. If she were here, she'd be telling you to put that butter on your plate, break off a chunk, and then spread it on your roll."

Hope gave him her best pained expression, but he went on. "And you'd probably give her a handmade card, and she'd love it. She loved you so much. You remember, don't you?"

The little girl barely nodded. She was looking down at her plate, and her short brown hair covered most of her face. Staring at her chocolate-colored locks, Matt recognized for the first time that a slight wave like Beth's was emerging.

After a moment she spoke. "I can barely remember what she looks like. I mean, I see her pictures and what she looks like on video, but I don't really remember myself."

Matt swallowed hard. He knew the feeling of an image that was beginning to fade, the panic of losing the hard-edged facts of a person's being, as the three-dimensional faded into two. "That's okay, honey," he reassured her. He cast about for the right words. "Your heart kinda paints a picture of people you love, so that even though you can't remember what someone looks like on the *outside*, you remember how much you loved them on the *inside*. You remember that about your mama, don't you?"

"I guess," Hope said. She didn't look at him as the waitress removed their salad plates to make room for their entrées.

By the time they finished their dinner, Matt felt exhausted but relieved. As they topped off their meal with ice-cream sundaes, they actually laughed together, remembering how Beth had loved home-made ice cream and how when she first tried it, she had put the rock salt inside the metal can instead of outside with the ice.

Hand in hand they crossed the street to their eight-story condominium building, which faced busy Pacific Coast Highway on the east and the glorious Pacific Ocean on the west. He had chosen the spot because he was uncomfortable with the idea of Hope's living in a hotel for the entire length of their three-week stay. At least here there was some semblance of hominess.

Matt was just thinking about relaxing on the deck with a good book and a cup of decaf when they entered the elevator foyer. There, in front of the one working lift, was a couple in the midst of a heated conversation. Feeling uncomfortable, Matt led Hope around the pair and pressed the button, mentally begging the sluggish elevator to speed its way down for once.

"Look," the woman said, her voice betraying her agitation. "For the last time, our date ends here. I'm sorry if you got a different impression."

Mercifully, the elevator dinged and the doors slid open. Matt quickly made his way in with Hope, then turned to hold the door for the woman. She obviously needed an escape. But when he looked up again, her much larger date had grasped her arm. He was flushed from collar to jaw line. The guy was obviously ticked.

"Ma'am?" Matt intervened gently. "Goin' up?"

"I am. Good night and good-bye, Jack. I think we've had our first and only date." She nodded down at his hand as if cueing him to let her go. Jack glanced furiously from her to Matt, who still patiently waited. Inside, Matt felt every nerve tense with unspent energy. As he stood there, forcing a disinterested look, he admitted to himself that pounding the guy would just be a convenient excuse to get rid of some frustration. *Help me out, Father. Give me control.*

Fortunately, Jack let the woman go, and she entered the elevator without another word. The doors slid shut at what seemed to the occupants a leisurely speed, finally cutting off their last view of Jack's sulking back as he turned and walked away.

Matt and Hope's elevator companion collapsed against the elevator wall. "Thank you. I appreciate it that you waited for me." She looked into Matt's eyes for a brief moment, her look telling him the story that she could not repeat in front of a child. It struck him that she was pretty, in an unconventional sort of way. The color of her eyes was a brilliant green, the exact color of birch leaves submerged under the Kootenai River, he mused. Uncommon.

"Was that your boyfriend?" Hope asked bluntly, staring up at her.

"No way."

"Did he take you out on a date?"

"Hope—"

"If you could call it that," the woman said, clearly amused. "Jack was my diversion for the night because my mom's on a cruise and I was missing her. It was a bad choice. I'm Ella O'Donnell," she said, introducing herself, "and I'm on the sixth floor."

"Hmm?" Matt asked, not connecting with her.

"Sixth floor. The button."

"Oh!" Matt said, embarrassed. *Smooth, Morgan. Way to go.* He quickly pushed numbers four and six. The elevator gave a little start and moved upward.

"You two new neighbors?" Ella asked.

"Temporary visitors," Matt said, nodding at the illuminated sign for the fourth floor as the elevator dinged. "This is where we get off."

"Oh, well, thanks. It was nice meeting you. Should I just call you my knight in shining armor and his short attendant?"

Matt grinned as they exited, then looked back. She really was pretty. All eyes and a big, toothy grin that left a person with no choice but to join her in a smile. He found his voice as the door shut. "We're Matt and Hope."

"Nice to meet—" The door clamped shut, muffling the rest of her sentence.

The two paused for a second, then were silent as they walked to their condominium's door. "Did she look like Mama, Daddy?"

"Wha—no. You know that, Hope. Your mom had short brown hair and big brown eyes. That lady was much taller. I mean, her hair was longer. Different colored eyes." He fumbled with the key in the lock and then rushed on. "Not as pretty as your mom," he added lamely. The lock clicked, and the bolt slid open at last.

Matt recognized his last comment as a lie as his daughter walked behind him, directly into her room. Ella was every bit as pretty as Beth, just in a different way. And his comment had rushed out because for the first time in a long time he was looking at another woman, and he felt guilty. He pushed the guilt away. *Beth told me to look for love again.* But it seemed too soon, somehow. As if he were being unfaithful.

Moments later, Hope appeared in the kitchen doorway as he brewed himself a cup of decaf. "I wasn't talking about Ella's hair. I meant she looked like Mama. There was something about her…something about the way she looked at me that reminded me."

Matt managed to give her a nod, slightly sticking out his lower lip as he thought about what she said. Now that she had mentioned it, there *was* a familiar spark, something that reminded him of Beth. He pressed the Mr. Coffee's On button and listened as the water started to bubble and drip.

"You want to read with me out on the deck, pumpkin?"

"Yeah!" She ran off to her room to pick up the latest in her series of early-reader books about girls and their horses. Mostly, she just liked to look at the pictures.

"Look at this one, Dad," she said, pointing to her book beside him. "It looks just like the palomino we saw today on the beach."

Matthew nodded and smiled. "Do you want to go riding some-day, sweetheart? I think the stable offices are just up the road."

"Maybe," she said with a shrug, moving away from him. "I'd rather just go home and ride Cookie." She settled into the lounge chair beside him on their tiny deck and looked over at him seriously. "Dad, this really wasn't a *bad* Mother's Day. Last year was worse."

"I'm glad, pumpkin," he said, reaching over to ruffle her hair, deciding to take her comment as a compliment. Maybe this whole California thing was not such a bad idea for an old Montana cowhand. At home it had seemed far-fetched—especially as things got busier at the ranch—but Hope had grabbed the idea of going to the beach and run with it. He'd almost said no to her, but then their friend Rachel had started in. "Matthew Morgan," she had said, pointing her finger and jabbing him in the chest. "You have a competent foreman, an efficient housekeeper and cook, and an able accountant. Go. It's the first time I've seen your kid so excited about something since her mom died. Do it for her. For yourself. You need some time to find that spark again."

"Spark?" he asked blankly.

"Yes. Spark. You're moping. Go away and find what God has in store for the rest of your life. Your daughter needs you. Not to mention a trip to Disneyland."

Rachel and Reyne, his deceased wife's best friends, had harassed him until he agreed. Matt had to admit that the extreme change of scenery *had* lifted his spirits, especially over Mother's Day.

"Hey, look at that," he said to his daughter. "The sun is going down for the night." And together they watched as the last tiny bit of the sun edged into the water and disappeared.

Two days later Matt agreed to give his daughter long-promised help building a sandcastle. It was late morning, and the sun was just beginning to get hot when Ella approached and examined their work, obviously just coming in from a walk on the beach.

"My temporary neighbors!" she greeted them enthusiastically. "You call that a sandcastle? Where are you from, Idaho?"

"Close," Matt said, looking apologetically at the castle and his daughter. "Montana. I'm afraid I haven't had much experience in castle architecture."

"I don't think it's so bad," Hope said defensively.

"Well, no. It isn't bad. You need more water. Hold on, I'll go get you my bucket. Hey, where's your mom? Moms are usually great with castles. Much better than dads…sorry, Dad." She grinned at Matt, then frowned slightly at the look on his face.

"My mom died of cancer," Hope said, turning back to her digging.

"I…I'm sorry, honey. I never thought… Hold on. I'll be right back."

Matt watched as she walked away, noting legs that were tanned even this early in the season. Five minutes later, Ella was back. She briefly smiled into Matt's eyes as she handed him a trowel and Hope a bucket. "You can return them to me anytime. I'm in number 642."

With that she started to back away. "Gotta run, neighbors," she said cheerfully. "My shift starts at noon." Ella pointed at Hope. "You watch out for sand elves."

"Sand elves?" Hope said doubtfully.

"You haven't heard of them? If you start a sandcastle and leave it out overnight, they'll either level it or build on it, depending on how good they think it is."

CHAPTER TWO

*L*ife as an oncology nurse was rarely easy, but some days were more horrific than others, Ella reflected. Like today. Sitting in the darkroom after reviewing x-rays with the oncologist, Ella could not find the strength to move. It seemed impossible that yet another loving, otherwise healthy and happy woman of faith was about to die.

Cheryl Montane was not especially beautiful, but Ella had learned enough from their brief conversation to know that she was gorgeous from the inside out. She had arrived for a routine mammogram that had been put off for a few years—"Kids, a move, you know," she explained uneasily—and was immediately referred by her doctor to the oncologist on call. The staff had wasted no time, but they were already too late. It was as if a death sentence were written across the x-rays, spelling out that this young mother had not long to live. Her children...her husband... Images of Cheryl holding tightly to her husband's hand flashed through Ella's mind. What would he do without her? *God, God, where are you? How can you let this happen over and over?*

"Can I have a minute? I don't know what's wrong," she managed to say to Dr. Anders's back as he continued staring at the films. Ella felt strangled by sudden tears. She was expected to serve as moral support while Dr. Anders confirmed the Montanes' worst fears.

Dr. Anders searched her eyes for a brief moment before curtly nodding. "I need to make a phone call. I'll come back for you in a minute."

Ella nodded as she turned away, unable to stop the tears and not wanting to cry in front of a doctor. Even the most sentimental nurses rarely cried. They saw too many tough cases to break down over each one. Usually she was right with them. Wasn't she the one patients relied on to spread good cheer with an occasional doctor joke? The one who always had a smile at the ready and a word of hope to share? Not today. Today, suddenly, it was all too much.

She sank to a bench and stared bleakly at the x-rays above her. Oh, why, why did it have to be this young mother? Why anyone? Why couldn't they find the cure? *Why, Father? Why?*

After several moments the flood of tears was over, and Ella took a few deep breaths before rising and walking to the tiny sink to splash her face. She was just toweling off when Dr. Anders ducked his head back in. "Ella? Ready?" He averted his gaze, clearly uncomfortable with tears.

"Yes," she said, forcing a small smile. She pulled the films as she walked by, placing them in a large Manila folder and handing them to the doctor as they walked down the hall to Cheryl's room.

She was resting as they entered, but she opened her eyes as soon as the door squeaked. Her husband set aside his book and stood to take her hand. Both looked as though they knew what was coming. Ella moved to the bedside and took Cheryl's other hand as Dr. Anders spoke. She hoped her expression was encouraging.

"Cheryl, Gene," Dr. Anders said, nodding to the Montanes in greeting, "I'm afraid we have bad news." He moved to the mini light box in the room and slid the films up against it as he told about the war going on inside Cheryl's body. Briskly he noted where the cancer cells had metastasized deep inside her first, pointing out the huge tumor and dropping his tone a notch to explain that there was no reason to operate. He then clipped up the second set of films and pointed out the tumors in her lungs and the evidence of bone cancer. There was no reason to try radiation or any other therapy. The cancer was too fast, too effective at its executionary mission. She had months, maybe weeks left to live.

The Montanes nodded numbly, taking each word Dr. Anders uttered as if bearing physical blows. Ella swallowed hard, trying to concentrate on the doctor's words so she could answer the Montanes' questions after he left. Patients always had questions a bit later, after the diagnosis had sunk in. But Ella could not concentrate. The doctor's well-meaning words were a monotone drone to her, and she was unable to make sense of them. All she could think of was one more motherless, wifeless family, robbed by cancer. The Big C, patients called it. Briefly, she thought of her neighbors on the beach. Had they gone through a similar moment?

Dr. Anders reached past Ella and gave Cheryl's forearm a gentle, perfunctory squeeze. "I'm sorry," he said lightly. "Let us know if we can do anything." With that, he walked out, as usual leaving Ella to pick up the pieces. She dragged her eyes to meet Cheryl's, then Gene's. "I'm sorry," she said gently, sitting down on the bed beside Cheryl. Ella waited for a moment, and when neither one of them spoke, asked, "Do you have any questions for me? Or would you like me to give you some time?"

Gene nodded and glanced at his wife's face. "If you wouldn't mind—"

"Not at all," Ella said soberly. "I'll check back in with you in a bit, and we can go over your immediate plans." She swallowed against the knot in her throat and forced a small smile. "You won't be alone in this."

"Thanks, Ella," Cheryl said, as if in a fog.

Ella left the room and walked straight to the hospital chapel, ignoring the stack of paperwork and calls to be answered. She needed a break, a chance to breathe. Maybe a talk with the chaplain. In minutes she was sighing in relief as the heavy, soundproof wooden doors of the chapel thumped shut behind her. Cued by a bell in his office, Father Frank ducked his head in. "Ella!" he said, obviously glad to see her. "What can I do for you?"

"Maybe a prayer or two, Frank," she said quietly. She saw his face fall at her tone. Ella sat down in a pew and stared at the beautiful stained-glass window above the chapel altar. It depicted Jesus as a shepherd, tenderly holding his lost lamb and surrounded by others.

"Where is he?" she asked Frank in an accusatory voice, pointing her finger at the glass.

"Jesus? Why he's everywhere. Here, right now. You know that, Ella. You tell your patients every time they give you half a chance."

"I know that. I mean, where is he now? When a young mother of two down the hall is dying? Where are his miracles now?"

Frank sadly returned her look. "Hit a wall, Ella?"

"No," she said in irritation. "I'm just frustrated! I spend all this time, spreading the gospel, the Good News, and yet where is he? We need a miracle here. Make that *miracles*. Tonight. In about five different rooms on this ward."

Frank rose and paced, mulling over her words. She knew she had taken him by surprise. Ella had been voted Most Eligible for Candy

Striper by her fellow nurses last Christmas because of her seemingly endless reserve of energy and smiles.

"You know God moves when he chooses to. There seems to be no formula. It's a mystery that we have to accept and something we need to constantly pray will be done again. How about Josephine?"

Ella's mind raced as she remembered the sprite of a woman miraculously cured overnight of a cancer as widespread as Cheryl's. "Yeah, but she was one of a thousand women I can think of who prayed for healing."

"Still, Ella. Remember, we still have to pray that it will happen again. For each and every person in your ward. And others," he added softly, reminding her that she was not the only one who dealt with death day in, day out.

Ella sighed. "I'm sorry, Frank. I'm just dumping. I know you're right. I'm just beat, you know? Even the happiest nurse in the cancer ward gets down once in a while."

Frank sat down beside her and took her hand in brotherly fashion. "It's understandable. I worry about you sometimes. Worry that you don't dump enough."

Ella smiled ruefully. "And who do you get to dump on? You have to get as tired as I do of seeing good people die."

"The Shepherd," Frank said, nodding at the window. "He probably hears more of it than he wants to. In fact, I know he does. But he understands. And venting keeps me in a place where I can serve others faithfully."

Ella glanced at the floor, understanding his point.

"Ella," he said gently, "you need to let go of some of the pressure. More often. Before you break. You're an excellent nurse. Your patients need you. But you need to be healthy in order to serve the sick."

She nodded and squeezed his hand. "Will you pray with me, my friend?" she asked.

"With pleasure."

That night another patient in Ella's ward died. Her name was Jana. Ella had known her for months. The woman left behind her grieving husband of twenty years and three children in their teens. Ella barely made it to the car before she gave way to the sobs that racked her body. She felt choked with grief and found it difficult to breathe. Then she thought again of her neighbors, Matt and Hope. They too had said good-bye to someone dear to them. *How long ago?* she wondered. It made her grieve all over again. *Help me understand, Father. Help me to be strong. To show people the hope of you. Help me, Father.*

Ella suddenly remembered the castle and her admonition to Hope to watch out for sand elves. This was one way she could bring a smile to someone's face. It would be like magic to the little girl when she discovered it the next morning.

She wiped her eyes and took a few deep breaths, then turned the key in the ignition. It never failed to amaze her when her old Honda Civic continued to start after three hundred thousand miles. "We oughtta be in a commercial, Jeffrey," she said, patting the cracked dashboard. "Now take me home. We have work to do."

It was after one in the morning when she reached the condo, but Ella was unfazed. Her most common shift was noon to midnight, so she had become accustomed to living as a night owl, often sleeping in until ten. She hurried to her bedroom and changed into sweats, then rummaged through her kitchen cupboards and recycling bin for castle-building supplies. She emerged minutes later with several cans of varying sizes, a pie server, a small knife and a larger one, loaf pans, and another bucket. At the last moment she reached for her plant sprinkler.

Ella could barely get the door closed and locked, her hands were so full. But she was all smiles for the first time that day. "Sand elf-dom, here I come," she mumbled, wondering if Jana, her patient and friend, was looking down from heaven with a smile. The thought of it pulled the corners of her lips even higher. She was home. At peace. And whole again.

Dear Jesus, Ella prayed as the elevator sank toward the lobby, *please be with Jana's family. And help others to reach out to them as I'm reaching out to Matt and Hope now.*

CHAPTER THREE

The next morning Matt awoke to his five-year-old jumping on his bed. She was dressed in her customary jeans, boots, and western shirt, and judging from the sand all over her pant legs, had already been to the beach. "Now, Hope, I told you not to go out alone—"

"Dad! You have to see it!" She was squealing and still jumping all around him, bouncing on the bed. "Wait till you see it! It's a...a miracle!"

Matt was feeling a bit cross with her disobeying him and then bouncing all around on the bed, but her words disrupted all sense of order in his head. A five-year-old using the word *miracle*. "What, pumpkin?" he asked her with a grin, sitting up and running his hands through his hair. "What's a miracle?"

"The castle! The castle! The castle!" she said gleefully, springing off the bed. "Come on! Come see it!"

"The sandcastle?"

"Yes, Dad! The sandcastle! Wait'll you see it!"

He laughed and lowered his eyebrows at her as if she were crazy, but he obediently got up and began to dress. "Let me just get some coffee—"

"No, Dad! Now! Somebody might tear it down! You have to see it *now!*"

"All right, all right," he said in a fatherly tone. He laughed as he watched Hope bounce up and down like a Tigger to his lethargic Eeyore. "This really must be something."

"*Come on!*" She was getting impatient as he pulled on his cowboy boots and tucked them under his jeans.

"I'm *coming.*"

She grabbed his hand and dragged him along, making him feel like a lumbering, reluctant elephant behind its trainer. He headed toward the elevator, but Hope insisted it would take too long. They took the stairs.

Minutes later and slightly out of breath, they reached the sand dunes. Matt's eyes widened in astonishment. Their castle—what yesterday had been three-foot-wide mounds with finger holes for windows—had been expanded into a six-foot-wide, three-foot-high deluxe castle, complete with parapets and towers and guard walls. There were even bricks drawn into the walls and a tiny drawbridge over the moat.

Gleefully, Hope asked, "Do you think it was really sand elves or just Ella?"

"Maybe both," Matt said with a smile. His eyes scanned the sixth floor for any sign of her, but he spotted nothing.

"What do you think this is for?" Hope asked, holding up a small red plastic spritzer. Just then a small corner of the wall gave way.

"I bet it's to keep it wet because the sand crumbles if it dries out."

Hope immediately headed to the water's edge to fill the bottle, then came back and began spritzing. After she had given the castle a thorough once-over, she looked at Matt. "Let's build a village around it, okay?"

Later that night, when Hope was watching television, Matt walked to the front door. "I'm just going to run to Ella's and return this," he said, holding up the bucket and trowel. He looked at his little girl and smiled. She was exhausted after a full day on the beach. "Don't let anyone in the door except me, okay? I'll be back in five minutes."

"Okay. Ask her if she did the castle or if there really are sand elves."

"Okay." Matt turned and closed the door, locking the deadbolt behind him. For the hundredth time, he wondered how Ella had done the whole castle herself and even whether she had been the one to do it. Even after several hours of work, his and Hope's surrounding village paled in comparison to the castle above it.

He whistled a little tune as the elevator whisked him up to the sixth floor, then he confidently walked to 642. Just as he was about to knock, he faltered. Maybe she wasn't alone. Matt didn't really know her. He cleared his throat and willed his confidence back, then knocked.

Matthew could hear her on the other side of the door. He hoped he looked okay. He knew people looked loony though a peephole, like a reflection in a Christmas ornament. In spite of that fact, she opened the door and smiled up at him.

"Sorry I'm dropping in unannounced," he said uncertainly. "I wasn't sure if you were working tonight or not…"

"Not today. Tomorrow." She leaned against the door. Matt thought she looked friendly. Better than friendly. *Fetching*, his mother would say.

"Well, um, I think a certain sand elf was missing her bucket."

"Ah, I've been found out."

"I wanted to thank you. It made Hope's day."

"I'm glad," Ella said, smiling genuinely. She gently took the bucket from his hand, then looked at him as if waiting.

"Ella," he began, suddenly feeling like a teenager, "I'd like to ask you out for coffee or something, but Hope's in the condo alone. I need to get back," he said, nodding over his shoulder.

"Oh sure," she said, nodding. "I understand."

"Would you mind having breakfast with the two of us?"

"That'd be great," she said, raising her eyebrows.

"And then maybe…sometime…you and I could go out."

"Maybe," she said with another big smile. "Let's start with breakfast."

Matthew nodded quickly and smiled back at her. "Well, good night, Ella. See you at the coffee shop across the road at eight?"

She groaned. "Too early for me. How about nine?"

"Nine it is. Incidentally, how did you get so good at sandcastles?"

"Laguna's Sand Blast. Each year, I take part with my team from church. We've done pretty well. Third place two years ago, second last year."

"At that rate you should win it all this year."

"One can only hope," she said, flashing him another grin. Matt looked into her green eyes and realized it was her spark that had reminded Hope of Beth. It was as if Ella carried a light inside that made her happy and whole, regardless of the circumstances around her. It was the flickering light of the faithful. His heart sped up a bit. He swallowed hard. "Well, I'll see you at nine in the morning."

"I hope you realize that nine is still a sacrifice for me."

"We appreciate it. Thanks again."

Hope and Matt had been waiting for five minutes when Ella showed up. "Sorry," she said, as she approached the booth. She slid in across from them. Matt noticed that she was dressed in slim jeans and a red cotton sweater that brought out the vivid green of her eyes. She wore very little makeup, and it pleased him. He wasn't a heavy-makeup kind of guy.

The waitress came up, and Hope immediately ordered a hot chocolate. "Double, tall skinny latte, hold the cinnamon," Ella said in a tired voice.

Matt snorted. "Californian," he said, ribbing her. "Just plain coffee, straight up, for me," he said to the waitress. She left immediately, fairly uninterested in her customers. Matt glanced down at his daughter and was brought up short by her look of concern. Clearly, she had noted the element of playfulness with Ella and did not approve. Matt swallowed hard, determined to ignore Hope's reaction. His intentions were innocent. Hope would just have to get used to Matt's getting to know new people. Even if it was an attractive woman.

He looked over at Ella, but she seemed to be taking the whole scene in stride. "I heard the sand elves had a heyday with Pippin Palace," she said to Hope in a friendly manner.

"Pippin what?"

"Pippin Palace. Your sandcastle. It must've been very special if they took on a project of that scope. It's not every castle attempt that gets the king's treatment. Or in this case, should I say queen's treatment?"

Hope shrugged her shoulders, and her eyebrows settled a little lower as she glanced over at Ella. "Why didn't they do anything to my village? Do they only work on castles?"

"Not always." Ella looked at her as if thinking over something quite serious. "Did you work very hard on your village?"

Hope nodded.

"Maybe you need to work on it a bit more. They don't come out for just anybody. Only for the people they think have done their share."

"Are you just saying all that? Have you ever seen sand elves?"

"Why, no," Ella said, meeting Hope's serious look. "Haven't caught a glimpse of one myself. But my dad told me all about them when I was about your age. Even had a close encounter." She leaned forward, as if she were about to share a secret. "One night, I was determined to see them, so my dad and I camped out on the beach near my castle. It was sad though." Ella shook her head dramatically and set her lips in a line of resignation. "I fell asleep sometime during the night, and that's when they appeared and did all their work."

"Why didn't you try again?" Hope's eyes grew narrower.

"Well, we woke up all wet from the sea spray. Our sleeping bags were soaked. I got a terrible cold, and my mother wouldn't let us do it again. I called it the Mom Block."

The waitress arrived with their drinks, and Hope immediately set to spooning the tower of whipped cream directly into her mouth. Ella went on, "I told her it was like being a fairy princess locked up in one of the castle parapets."

"What'd your mom say?" Matt asked.

"She said I'd just have to wait for my handsome prince to rescue me, because until then, I wasn't going out on the beach at night."

Matt and Ella shared a furtive, warm look that was interrupted by the clink of Hope's mug spilling on its side. "Whoops," the girl said dully. It was apparent that it was no accident, but Matt treated it as such, determined not to ruin their breakfast with a confrontation. He threw more paper napkins to Ella, who laughed and kept saying "whoa" as she caught one brown rivulet after another from dripping into her lap.

It was Ella who caught the waitress's eye and ordered Hope another hot chocolate. "What do you say, Hope?" Matt asked.

"Thank you," she said, obviously not meaning it.

He ignored her and asked Ella another question. She launched into an animated story, and in watching her, he almost forgot the troublemaker beside him. As they continued to talk through breakfast, Matt found himself smiling more and more.

Ella was funny, spirited, amiable, and up-front about her spiritual life. Soon enough he knew that she was devout in her faith, very close to her parents—who lived a few miles away—and gentle in her touch with kids, judging from how she handled Hope, who seemed strangely testy this morning. Maybe she had not slept well last night.

One thing was clear as they parted after breakfast. Matt wanted to see Ella again.

All afternoon he battled the urge to call and talk with her. That night, he finally left a message, and she called him back the following afternoon while Hope was watching cartoons. Smiling after a half-hour conversation, Matt hung up the phone and almost tripped over his daughter when he turned to exit the kitchen.

"Are you going out on a date?" she asked in an accusatory voice.

"Not yet," he said, not wanting to hedge but also not wanting to blow things out of proportion. After all, what could come of it? He and Hope were in California for only another week and a half. He was just flexing his emotional muscles. Opening doors to see what

God would do. It felt good to have a little female companionship, and he hadn't felt this alive in months.

"We might get together for dinner some night," he said, walking past Hope. "Don't worry about it," he added over his shoulder, shoving the image of her disapproving face from his mind. "Let's go work on your village. There might be a chance that the sand elves will approve and add their bit tonight."

Chapter Four

*B*y the time the Morgans went for their walk the next morning, the sun was swiftly rising toward its noon haven. Hope
was still out of sorts, having slept until ten, and labored through her
breakfast cereal as if eating it were a chore. If this was the way she was
going to react to women in his life, Matt decided, he was going to
have to sit her down for a talk or resolve to live alone. Feeling angry,
he started to snap at her but stopped short, paused, and took a deep
breath.

Dear God, he prayed, *give me strength for this. Give me patience.
For my daughter's sake, give me the words to comfort her.* He looked at
his daughter and sat backward in a chair beside her. "Do you want
to talk about anything, pumpkin?"

"No," she said miserably, toying with the soggy squares in her
milk.

"Well, if you want to, we can. Want to check out your castle and
village? It was pretty windy last night. If it's still intact, you should
spray it down."

"Okay," she said, sliding off the chair and moving toward him.
She slid her small hand into his and looked at him seriously. "I just
really miss Mama."

He cradled her face with his free hand. "I know, sweetheart. So
do I." He struggled to find the right words. "But, honey, Mama's

gone. And she really didn't want us to be alone forever. There's nobody who could replace her. But let's give Ella and anyone else we meet the chance to be the special people God created them to be, and see how they fit into our lives. Okay?"

"Okay," she said softly, not meeting his eyes.

Hope left him and went to dress. When they stepped onto the sand minutes later, her spirits seemed to lift. And as they drew nearer the castle, they noted that several people were staring at it and pointing.

Much like the castle, the village had been transformed. There were tiny thatched roofs on what looked like adobe walls and pebbles for fireplaces and chimneys. There were cobblestone streets and tiny fences around some of the homes. The castle was even bigger than before. Hope was astounded, her face transformed by delight as clearly as the castle had been transformed. Matt laughed out loud. How had Ella accomplished all this?

"This is the best vacation ever, Dad!" Hope hugged him fiercely around the thighs and fell to all fours to examine the village more closely. "Look at this chimney! There's a little white shell that looks like smoke! And look! This shell looks like a sheep in the front yard!"

Matt was amazed too. He looked on with Hope, noticing all the details and changes, then settled down on the sand to look at the waves building, crashing, and sliding as he thought about his enchanting neighbor. Who else would get off a shift at midnight and come build sandcastles to please a kid? It had been a long time since he had met someone like her. Since Beth, he admitted. Beth might've done something like this.

Hope spent a good hour playing in and around the castle with little plastic figurines. She was still at it when Matt spotted Ella walking toward them. As soon as she was near, Matt rose and thanked her with a big smile.

She smiled back at him, flashing what he noted were very white teeth against the backdrop of a pretty, welcoming face. "Hey, neighbors," she said. "I see the sand elves were busy last night," she said to Hope.

"Yeah!" Hope said, momentarily unable to withhold the glee from her voice. "I'm going to play on the other side now," she said to her father.

"If you were a sand elf," Matt said to Ella with an insider's grin, "where would you live in that castle?"

"That castle?" Ella asked, feigning offense. She adopted a high-brow accent. "Why that, dear sir, is none other than Pippin Palace! I need not see myself as a sand elf, with it being what it is to me."

Matt smiled, playing along. "I take it I should know the place? And your station in life?"

"Know of it?" she asked incredulously, her eyebrows raised. "It's famous throughout the land. *You've* heard of Pippin Palace and the righteous O'Donnells, right, Hope?"

From across the castle, Hope reluctantly shook her head as if admitting defeat.

"Ah. Foreigners, I take it?" She crossed her arms and looked over the Morgans.

"'Mericans," Hope confirmed sadly.

A hint of a smile crossed Ella's lips, but then she turned away. "I see I'll have to tell you the story of Pippin Palace."

"There's a story?" Hope asked.

"Ah yes. You see, once I was small enough to live in this castle.

We were a happy family and kingdom. But then my sister got married and moved away. I, unhappily, am the forgotten sister, sadly waiting here in this parapet for her knight." She pointed to a small, skinny tower to her right.

"Still kept under lock and key by your evil mother, eh?" Matt asked, intrigued with his companion and her creative, fanciful ways. They shared a brief look that told him Ella was just having fun. He glanced at Hope. She was as mesmerized as he.

"Oh no," Ella said. "My mother has been imprisoned in the dungeon for years now, and my evil uncle has taken over the kingdom. My father is off in the Crusades, fighting for God. Someday he'll come back and chase away my evil uncle and set me and my mother free."

Matt paused a moment before risking an offer. "Well, I think anyone so into a magic kingdom should go with us to Disneyland. Do you think that you could escape your parapet tomorrow?"

"I could," she said with a smile.

"How?" asked Hope.

"I know secret passageways," Ella said with a wink.

"Can you get up by eight for breakfast?" Matt asked. "We want to be there when the gates open."

"Well, that's asking a lot," she said, pretending to mull it over. "But I guess I could do it."

"Great! It's a date." The words were out before he could stop them, and he looked up quickly to see if Hope had noticed.

The little girl was standing stock-still, studying them both. She said not a word.

CHAPTER FIVE

his is my favorite," Ella said, ducking under the chain fence to join Matt and Hope in the Matterhorn line. She distributed the other two chocolate frozen bananas. "It's just not a trip to Disneyland without one of these," she said. Matt smiled at her as he took his, and once again she wondered why it had taken so long for him to enter her life.

To her, Matthew Morgan was a prince, maybe the one she had been waiting for. It was as if she had known it as soon as she stepped into that elevator. No, before that. She'd known it when she looked over at his adorable, concerned, protective face as Jack grabbed her arm. It was a face a woman could trust. But how was she going to win Hope over? The little girl seemed not to like her. And Ella and Matt would have to get past that serious problem if they were to discover whether they were meant to be anything but friends.

The night before, Ella had called her mother. "Mom, I don't know what I'm thinking. They're *leaving* soon. To *Montana*. I can't just drop by there to see them. I think he's terrific, but he's only visiting! How can God do this to me? I finally meet a terrrific guy, and he lives a million miles away!"

"Calm down, Ella," her mother had said sensibly. "Are you sure this isn't just a crush?"

"Mom, I'm thirty-four years old! I think I know when it's a

crush. But…maybe. Oh, you're right. I've only known him… What am I talking about? What has gotten into me?"

Her mother had laughed at her. "Take a deep breath, Ella. It will all work out for the best."

"For the best? What if we fall in love? Get married? What about my job? I really feel like my work is a ministry, Mom."

"I know it, Ella. And you're great at it. But that doesn't mean that God can't use you in ways other than oncology nursing. Your skills are broad based. Don't limit your Father in what he can do for you."

Ella was struck silent at the thought. She loved her job, didn't she? Sure, she had been down and tired lately, but that didn't mean she wanted to quit. "I don't know if I could leave nursing, Mom."

"I didn't say leave nursing. Just don't look at your life as a long tunnel. Inevitably it will twist and turn. Look forward to those changes. They keep things interesting. As far as Matt's concerned… Well, maybe he's the one. Then again, if he's too dense to see the beautiful woman in front of him, maybe knowing him is just an experience that will help prepare you for someone else."

Ella snorted. "Or maybe I'm just getting all worked up for nothing. Maybe he and Hope will leave next week and it will all be over."

"Enjoy it for what it is," her mother urged. "Let God do the rest."

"Easy for you to say," Ella said. "When you've been married for over forty years, you think every relationship just happens. Dad's told me and Lynn what he had to do to win you over. Maybe I have to take drastic action here."

"Maybe, maybe not."

"That's your sage advice? 'Maybe, maybe not'?"

"Ella, I'm telling you to let God take the reins on this one. I know it's not your nature, but if you sit back and really let him lead you—and if he's truly in this—he'll give you your heart's desire."

"Yeah, I've heard that one before. I want to believe it, Mom, but I'm afraid. What if I risk my heart and Matthew just flies off to Montana never to be seen again?"

"Then you'll pick yourself up off the floor, brush yourself off, and move on. If he's so thickheaded that he doesn't want your heart as badly as you want his, he's not worth it."

Her mother's words rang in Ella's ears as she watched Matt take a bite of banana and smile at her. He sure seemed interested. Her heart lurched with hope as he continued to stare at her warmly, speaking to her without words.

"I don't like this," Hope interrupted, handing her banana to her father. She turned away to hang on the chain as if it were a jungle-gym rope.

"Sorry," he said, looking at Ella. "I like mine. Hope," he said, "you can go throw this away. And you can thank Ms. O'Donnell anyway."

"Thank you," Hope said mechanically.

"You're welcome." She watched as the girl ducked under the chain and ran to the trash can. Just before she threw it away, she turned her back to the adults and sneaked another bite.

"She thinks she's so smart, hiding it from us," Matt said with a shake of his head. "It's tough, you know. My showing interest in another woman. She's usually a great kid."

"I think she is great, Matt," Ella said, looking into his blue eyes. She longed to reach up and brush his light, sandy-colored hair from his forehead. It looked as if he needed a haircut. Had Beth always reminded him? "I think she's just trying to adjust to me. Let me guess. Haven't been dating in Montana?"

Matt shrugged as Hope drew near again. "Not since Beth. Haven't ever been interested." His eyes penetrated hers with another meaningful look.

She smiled back at him, keeping her lips closed. Ella hated her big mouth. Was it a turnoff to Matthew? She hoped not. Altering her smile would be tough. *Just be yourself,* her mother had said. Matt turned to move forward with the line and gently, casually placed his hand at the small of her back. It was a small gesture, an idle gesture, Ella told herself. But his hand had lingered just a moment.

All morning Hope had insisted that she would be the one to go on the rides with her father, and Ella had agreed, anxious not to give the girl something else to hold against her. But when they got to the front of the line, a little redhead about Hope's age was looking around, obviously hoping to find a partner. She smiled over at Matt's daughter, and miraculously, Hope smiled back.

"Why don't you ride with that little girl?" her father urged.

"Okay," Hope said amiably, momentarily forgetting her mission to keep her dad and Ella apart. She skipped over to the redhead and asked her a question. The redhead smiled and nodded.

"Whew," Matt said over Ella's shoulder, his breath warming her ear. "I thought I'd never get a chance to get close to you today," he said softly.

Ella could not contain her grin this time. She let go until every pearly white was in view, and Matt smiled back at her, apparently not turned off in the least.

They kept going all day, stopping only for the occasional sugary drink or junk-food break. Ella could tell that Hope was impressed with her knowledge of the park, which enabled them to get to rides faster, but she remained distant. Finally, as the last float in the Main Street parade disappeared, Ella looked over to Matt—who sat beside her on the sidewalk—and the sleeping girl in his lap. The last lights of the float shone in his eyes, and he held his daughter so tenderly that it brought tears to Ella's own.

He looked over at her then, saying nothing, only staring back at her. To Ella, his eyes said it all. He wasn't thickheaded. He was interested. He was definitely interested.

CHAPTER SIX

*T*he next day Ella alternated between berating herself for falling for someone who lived so far away and praying that he would show up. Countless times she paced to the patio window and past the telephone. *Come on. Pick up the phone, Matt.* She gave up trying to reach him with her experimental mental telepathy and sighed. *Please, Father. Please don't let me risk my heart for nothing.*

She called her mother, then her sister, Lynn. She even phoned friends she had been out of touch with for over a year, just to distract herself. As the period of silence between her and Matt grew, so did her doubts.

When she returned from a late afternoon matinee, she rushed immediately to her answering machine to check for messages and collapsed on her couch in despair when there were none. Just then, there was a knock at the door. She checked her watch. Seven. It took him this long?

"Hi, Ella," Matt said with a grin, leaning against her doorjamb with his arms crossed. "I got a baby-sitter for Hope. I know this is late notice, but would you like to go to dinner with me?"

She took a deep breath and squared her shoulders, willing herself to find the courage for her next words. She needed to get things straight. After all, she had thought about it all day! "Look, Matt, I think you're terrific," she said. "But let's be frank. Realistically, how far can this go?"

He looked surprised but, curiously, not offended. "Dessert?" he tried.

She laughed and looked down at the ground before meeting his look again. "I'm sorry. I just don't want to waste your time."

He tipped his head a bit toward her, and Ella's heart gave a little lurch. "If we're going to talk marriage plans, don't you think I should sit down at least?"

Ella felt the deep flush rise from her collarbone. "No…that's not what I…um…sure, come in." He didn't wait for another invitation. In seconds, he was sitting on her couch, an expectant look on his face.

"Look, Matt," she began, searching for words as she walked toward him. This was all much easier during her afternoon practice sessions. "I wasn't proposing—"

"I know, Ella. I was just giving you a hard time. But to be honest, I'm not one to mess around much myself. I can't risk heartbreak after Beth. For me or my daughter." He stood, then began to pace, wringing his hands as though he ached for a hat with which to occupy them. He looked at her, and it was as if he suddenly found inspiration.

Silently he stepped forward, gripped her shoulders, then slid his big hands down her arms to take hers. He looked deeply into her eyes. "But there's something about you that I think is irresistible. You're kind and fun and pretty. And something inside tells me that I should get to know you better. There. I said it. When God pushes me like this, I usually find it's in my best interest to follow through."

Ella sat down on the couch, hard. She had never expected such a frank confession from him, even after her direct statements. Had she ever met a man so willing to discuss things up front? She could not recall.

His voice brought her back to the present. He knelt in front of her, still holding her slim hands in his own. She was still relishing the feeling of being held when his words brought her back around. "So Montana would never be an option?"

Now she was really stunned. They weren't talking about marriage, and yet they were. To Ella, there was a very thin veil between their conversation and poring over invitations with her sister. And they'd been around one another a total of, what? Fifteen, sixteen hours?

He gently released her hands and went back to pacing, occasionally pausing to look meaningfully into her eyes. "I know this is fast, Ella. But I feel as if I know you. At least the main important stuff. I know that spark that lights a fire in your heart. I don't believe in coincidences, and I don't believe in playing games. I'm here with my hat in my hands—well, it'd be in my hands if I had one— because I'm interested in courting you. I'd like to try out for that prince position you talked about on the beach."

"Let's just start with dinner," she said, finding her voice at last.

Ella and Matt spent a good two hours over dinner, cherishing the time to learn about one another's lives. There was so much she wanted to know about him, and apparently he felt the same. She liked what she heard about Matt and his life on the ranch. It was more conventional and old-fashioned than her own in some ways, but she found the differences refreshing. His life seemed like one that could meld with hers.

It was an uncommonly balmy night, full of the promise of summer's heat. As they exited the restaurant, Matt took her hand. Ella cherished the feeling, wanting to memorize it so she could remember it when he left.

"I don't want this to end," he said.

"It doesn't have to," Ella told him.

"What do you mean?"

She smiled at the element of consternation in his voice and playfully pushed away from him. "I'm not coming on to you, you big lug. I'm asking you to join me in a bit of sand elfdom. I'm giving you the chance of a lifetime. A walk in Oz. The sprinkle of fairy dust. If you're man enough."

Matt grinned and crossed his arms, a habitual gesture, she noted. "Well, I usually keep a good distance between me and mythical creatures," he said, "but if it means spending a little more time with you, I'm game."

"Good," she said, linking her arm with his. "Let's go change and convince your baby-sitter to sleep a couple of hours on your couch. You have a lot to learn."

By the time they finished at two in the morning, Pippin Palace had been repaired where it failed, and expanded in other places. At first, Matt had resorted to old techniques, but Ella had set him straight.

"No, no," she said, as his wall crumbled almost from the get-go. "You need more water. Come here, I'll show you the consistency you're after." They went to the water's edge, bringing one of the battery-powered lamps with them. In a large tin bucket, Ella slowly added water to the sand until it was the right consistency, as liquid as possible while still holding its shape. "It's kind of like egg whites, when you get them to hold a peak."

He stared at her blankly, and she laughed. "Let me guess. You have a cook?"

Matt shrugged his shoulders and flashed her a guilty grin. "As charged. No way to take care of a ranch and a five-year-old *and* cook."

"That's okay," Ella said. *I could get used to having a cook.* She had just turned to walk back to the castle when she felt the cold spray of water seep through her shirt. She glanced over her shoulder with what she hoped was a superior look. "I hope you don't call that a water-fight challenge."

Matt's grin grew. Once again he crossed his arms. "I do. What do you intend to do about it?"

"Nothing now. I'm too smart to get all wet at two in the morning. I'm liable to wind up with pneumonia, and my mom will come down and forbid me to go out on the beach at night." She walked a few feet and glanced back to see that he was following. "Oh, but don't think it's over. Expect it when you least expect it."

She spent the next hour honing Matt's sand-castle-building skills, while trying to ignore his proximity and casual, glancing touches that sent shivers down her spine. Matt was warm and wonderful and seemed to be perfect for her. The thought of kissing him made her tingle down to her toes.

They were finished with their work and packed up to go when she spied the half-full pail of water. Casually she picked it up and glanced over at Matthew. His arms were full of equipment and, smiling, she judged him incapacitated. Without hesitation, she let the salty water fly, giving him a satisfactory drenching. She laughed as he blinked and the water continued to run down his face. He looked down at his soaked shirt, then back at her, and gave a playful little growl.

Her heart skipped a beat, and she jumped into action, knowing she was on the defensive now. She turned and ran with every ounce of strength she had, but she could hear the pail and other metal equipment clanging as they dropped from Matt's arms. Unencumbered, he would get her in seconds. She gave a little shriek and kept running, but suddenly his arms were around her and lifting her off the sand. Matt threw her over his shoulder with all the finesse of a miller with a sack of flour. Ella stifled a scream, reminding herself it was the middle of the night. But Matt was heading directly back down to the water.

"No! Matthew!" she laughed hysterically. "Please! I don't know what came over me!"

"Yeah! You sound very sorry! In you go." He pulled her off his shoulder and into his arms. She took the opportunity to grab fistfuls of shirt and hair, again begging him to stop.

"No way," he said with a grin, setting her down in front of him to pry her fingers from their holds. He held both her freed hands easily with one of his own and dragged her into the water. When the waves were swirling around their knees, he paused and pulled her to him. She giggled, half expecting him to kiss her, half expecting him to shove her into the next wave.

It was dark away from the lamps, and she could barely make out his face. He paused, as if vacillating on what to do, then finally turned her around so her back was to his chest, still managing to keep her hands in check. She felt helpless in more ways than one. Matt bent his head toward the side of her own and spoke softly. "Look at that," he directed. She glanced up to see a waxing moon. "By the time it's full, in three days, I want to kiss you."

His words alternately thrilled and relieved Ella. He wanted to kiss her but was biding his time, letting the feelings between them grow naturally, not rushed by the physical. "And," he said, turning her around, "if I kissed you now, how could I throw you in?"

She laughed and shook her head. "You're not going to throw me in. You couldn't. You're too gallant."

"Like a prince?" he asked softly. He dropped her hands, and they stood together as several waves crested and swirled around their knees.

"Possibly," she managed to say, breaking their lingering glance and moving toward shore. She spoke over her shoulder. "But don't think I owe you anything for not throwing me in. We're even now. Even-steven."

"Yeah, right," he said, following her uphill. "Think what you must to put your mind at rest. But someone wise once told me to expect it when you least expect it."

Together they collected the equipment where it had been strewn about, smiling all the way.

They stopped off at Matt's rental, laughing and shushing, trying not to wake Hope. As they set their sandcastle equipment in the closet and Matt awakened the baby-sitter, Ella thought she heard a sound in the hallway. She looked up but saw no one there. She checked her watch. "Two-thirty! Good grief, I'd better get going," she whispered. Hope was surely sound asleep, but *Ella* needed to get to bed.

"I had a great time, Ella. I can't wait to see you tomorrow." He looked down at her as if he wanted to say something really impor-tant.

"You mean today," Ella said, smiling up at him. After a moment, Ella stuck out her hand, and Matt shook it with a wry grin.

"I'll look forward to the next three days passing."

"As will I."

CHAPTER SEVEN

At ten o'clock Matt trudged out to the kitchen in his bathrobe, exhausted after his short night's sleep. He had been in bed by three, but he had tossed and turned until six, unable to get Beth and Ella out of his mind. Was he being unfaithful to Beth by pursuing Ella? His wife had begged him to find love again, and he had to admit he loved every new aspect of Ella that unfolded. But he could not get rid of the niggling guilt. Finally, he had cried out to God to give him direction and peace and had fallen asleep at last.

He poured himself a cup of coffee and looked through the kitchen doorway to the living room. Hope was sitting directly in front of the television set, entranced with cartoons. "Good morning," he said to his daughter and took a swig of coffee. Matt grimaced. The timer had obviously gone off at his customary 7:00 A.M. The coffee was cold and bitter by now. He was considering brewing a new pot when he noticed that Hope had not even looked up. "Hope? Are you okay?"

"Yeah," she said, not looking away from the TV.

"Whatcha watching?"

"Cartoons."

"I can see that. Which one?"

She refused to look at him. "I don't know."

"You don't know or don't want to tell me? Isn't that one we decided wasn't good for you to watch?"

"I don't know."

"Well, I do. Either turn the channel or turn it off."

"Why?" she asked, her voice at once accusatory and whiny.

"Because I said so."

"So?"

Matt could feel one of his eyebrows go up in consternation and his pulse pick up. "Hope Emily, what has gotten into you today?"

She stood up and faced him, her hands balled up into fists. "I saw you two last night! You're going to marry Ella! I think that's just mean!" With that, she ran toward her bedroom, a blur of Winnie the Pooh p.j.'s.

"Hope! Stop right there." Even to him, his voice sounded unnecessarily loud. He brought it down a bit, hoping to breathe some calm into the situation. "Come here."

His daughter trudged back into the room, resisting every step, as if unwillingly drawn by a huge magnet. Begrudgingly, she sat down. "And you guys are the sand elves. You lied to me," she said softly. "That wasn't nice."

Matt sighed and rubbed his forehead, suddenly battling a headache. He sat down next to Hope on the couch, casually putting his arm around her. "Okay, let's take this bit by bit. First off, it was not nice of you to spy on me and Ella. Please do not do that again. Second, we have not agreed to get married, just to get to know one another better. Sweetheart, I think you've been as lonely for your mama as I have. I'm hoping that someone nice will fit into our lives again—for both of us. I'm not trying to replace your mama. No one could do that. She was wonderful. But she knew we'd be lonely. And that someone else might be able to be a part of our lives in a different way that would still make us happy. Do you understand that?"

"Maybe," Hope said miserably. She looked very small to him as she pulled her legs up to her chest and tucked them under her pajama shirt.

"Well, we'll probably have to talk about that some more. But I want you to give Ella a chance, okay?"

Hope said nothing.

"Look, you're right. Ella has been the sand elf, and last night I helped her work on Pippin Palace some. She did not do it to make you feel stupid. She did it to make you smile. Which she did," he said, reaching out to pinch his daughter's cheek. Hope pressed her lips together and averted her gaze, obviously determined not to grin back at him. "She never really lied to you. I would guess that if you had asked her a direct question, she would've told you the truth."

Hope sighed heavily, as if carrying the weight of the world on her shoulders.

"Come on. It's a beautiful day. Let's get dressed and go for a walk. You can see what Ella and I did to Pippin Palace last night." He rose and headed back to the Mr. Coffee machine.

Slowly Hope slid off the couch and obediently made her way to her room.

When Ella showed up at their door that afternoon, Hope opened it.

"Hi, Hope," Ella said. "Is your dad at home?"

"Yeah. Did you make Pippin Palace yourself?" the girl asked, crossing her arms like a smaller version of her father.

Ella studied her for a moment and decided on the honesty track. There was something about the girl that told her she had better not try to pull the wool over her eyes any longer. "I was about your age when I figured out it had been my dad all along. Yes, it was me. Sand elves are just family folklore. Can I come in?"

Hope studied her for a moment, then stood aside to let her pass by. Just then they heard the shower turn off and Matt calling from the bathroom. "Hope? Did I hear someone at the door?"

"Yeah," she said in a low voice that her father was not likely to hear.

Ella studied her, and Hope looked right back.

"You don't want me to see your dad?" Ella asked softly.

Hope slowly shook her head.

"Oh," Ella said, nodding. "I'm really sorry you feel that way. Because I really like you both." She decided to ignore the girl's obvious slight. "What if all three of us went roller-skating this afternoon?"

When Hope did not immediately decline, Ella decided to push. "We could go to Balboa Island. You can skate on big, wide sidewalks. We could get cotton candy and ride on the Ferris wheel, and, come dinnertime, we could talk your dad into a burger at Ruby's. Doesn't that sound like fun?"

Hope studied her, unsure what to do.

"Hope? I asked if someone was at the door." Matt's voice was closer now. Ella guessed that he was in the bedroom dressing.

"Yeah," Hope said. "It's Ella." Her gaze did not leave their neighbor's. "She wants us to go skating."

Matt finally appeared in the doorway, looking handsome with wet hair and a freshly shaven face. His nose and cheeks were a bit sunburned, and the color made his blue eyes sparkle. "Oh, hi," he said to Ella, giving her a tender smile. "And you want to go, Hope?"

"I guess so," she said.

"Great. How soon?"

"About five?" Ella asked. "Let me just change out of my uniform, and I'll be ready. I told Hope that we could eat dinner down there."

"Sounds good to me."

"To me, too," Ella said, looking at both the Morgans with a pensive gaze.

They spent the evening canvassing the island just off Newport's peninsula. An hour of laughing together at Matt's trying to stay upright was the best thing for Hope and Ella. It seemed to Ella that some of Hope's walls came down as the five-year-old warmed up to her.

They were on the boardwalk, skating side by side behind Matt, when Hope hit a crack in the cement and nearly went down. "Whoa!" Ella cried, grabbing her hand to try to save her. She failed, however, and they skidded to a stop on the ground instead, thankful for the long pants and Polarfleece jackets that saved them from scratched knees and elbows. When Matt fell himself, after looking over his shoulder and trying to turn around, Hope and Ella dissolved into giggles. There was something hilarious about the big man on wheels. To Ella, there was something endearing about a Montana rancher willing to try skates at all.

After another hour Ella and Matt pleaded with Hope to let them go back to street shoes, promising to follow her around for as long as she wanted. After that, unbeknownst to Hope, they walked hand in hand behind her, enjoying the sunset on the harbor as they passed tiny beach house after tiny beach house.

Finally, even Hope grew tired of the skates, and they returned to the rental shop for her sneakers. "That was great!" she said as they emerged from the shop. "What's next?"

"How 'bout the Ferris wheel and a cotton candy hors d'oeuvre?" Ella asked.

"Yeah!" Hope yelled. The next second, she took Ella's hand to pull her along. Her eyes were wide, and she looked as surprised by her own action as Ella was. Ella looked over toward Matt and caught his grin, but when Hope spotted their pleased smiles, she dropped Ella's hand and grew quiet.

"Back to the sour dowager," Matt whispered in Ella's ear. "Can't get too excited about the new woman in Dad's life. It might actually encourage him."

Hope glanced over her shoulder to see them whispering and frowned. "Come on, you guys! Hurry up! We'll never get to the Ferris wheel!" she said grumpily.

"We'll get there," Matt said merrily, taking Ella's hand in his again. "Don't worry. Ella said it doesn't close till midnight."

They turned a corner, and Hope spotted the ride. She took off running. "And don't you worry," he said to Ella. "We'll teach Hope that it's okay to love again."

Ella's eyes widened. "Love?"

"Love," he said, smiling back at her. "I can smell it a mile away."

They had just purchased burgers and fries at Ruby's, a fifties-style diner at the end of a pier, and settled on a bench when Hope let her feelings be known.

"I like you, Ella," she declared, taking a big bite of hamburger.

Ella grinned at her and then at Hope's father. "I'm so glad, Hope. I like you too."

"Yeah," the little girl went on. "It's sad."

"What is?"

"That you can't have more dates like my dad."

Ella laughed out loud and met Matt's merry grin. "Yeah. I'd agree with that."

"When we go home, you'll just have men like Jack to date."

Ella sobered immediately. The girl was casual in her manner but was clearly making a statement. She saw her father's relationship with Ella as temporary.

"What if Ella came to visit us, honey?" Matt broke in.

"Oh, she won't do that. She works here. Besides, at home we can get back to normal. Just you and me and the hands on the ranch. I like it that way. I miss home, Dad. Can we go home soon?"

"Soon enough," Matt said, gently stroking Hope's hair. "Too soon," he said softly, meeting Ella's look.

CHAPTER EIGHT

*E*lla trudged off to work two days later, painfully aware that the Morgans' time in California was drawing to an end, and feeling the effects of her short nights. It seemed as if there should be some sort of temporary leave available at the hospital for someone in love, Ella thought. *Not sick leave, but... "love leave," that's it.* She snorted under her breath at her train of thought and resolved to concentrate even harder on her work that day. Her patients deserved the very best, not a woman in a trance who watched the clock as each minute lumbered by.

Still, despite her best efforts, Ella had to berate herself for wanting to plead illness and head home. *What has come over me?* When she almost made a mistake in distributing medications, she sighed, turned directly toward the nurse's desk, and went to talk to the charge nurse, an older woman with graying hair and kind eyes.

"Eleanor," she said without preamble, "here's the scoop. I am falling head over heels in love with a man who is in California for only a short time. I'm trying to concentrate, but I am doing a poor job of it. I'd keep on going, but I just caught myself about to inject Mrs. Hanson's IV with six cc's more med than was ordered. Can I take some personal leave?"

Miraculously, Eleanor laughed at Ella's excuse and told her to go. "I've been wondering what's been wrong with you these last few days," she said, still laughing. "It never occurred to me that you were in love! Get out of here. It's slow and I'll get John to cover your shifts the next few days. He's been wanting to pick up some extra money."

"Thank you! Thank you!" Ella said, squeezing Eleanor's hand in appreciation. "I'll make it up to you next month!" She was out the door in minutes. It wasn't until she was starting her old Civic that she remembered Matt had taken Hope down to San Diego for the day. "Well, let's get on home anyway," Ella said miserably to Jeffrey.

All the way home she fantasized about going down to San Diego and trying to find the Morgans at the Hotel del Coronado or Sea World but then acknowledged that the idea was crazy. "Okay, God," she said aloud, "I got out of work. Do you think you could arrange a little time with Matt even though he thinks I'm busy?"

Unfortunately, her prayer went unanswered. Ella spent the afternoon watching time tick by, just as she had at work. "At least I'm not endangering anyone's life," she mumbled to herself as she cleaned the kitchen counter for the second time. Needing to keep her hands busy, she dragged out her portable vacuum and ran it over the carpet throughout her condo, pulled down her living-room curtains to wash them, and cleaned out her refrigerator.

She was in the middle of scouring her stove when there was a knock at the door. Her heart skipped a beat as she glanced at the clock. Six. Was it Matt? He and Hope could be home! She hopped up off the kitchen floor and was practically running for the door when the sight of her image in the hallway mirror stopped her short. She looked terrible! Her hair was a mess, pulled back with an old handkerchief, and she had dirt all over her.

Whoever was at her door knocked again. Ella tiptoed to the door and peeked through. It was Matt and Hope. Even distorted by the keyhole, they looked better than she. She flinched as a big fist came up to knock again. "Ella?" Matt said, his voice muffled by the door. "Ella, are you home?"

"That was her car in the lot," Hope said with some authority.

"Are you sure, honey? She's supposed to be at work."

"I'm sure."

"Well, I thought I heard some noise in there. Maybe she's sick and can't hear me knock." The buzzer rang inside the condo.

Drat. I can't let him think I'm sick. She tiptoed back and stomped toward the door as if just arriving, then opened it with as much confidence as she could muster. Matt and Hope blinked at her with some surprise.

"Hi there! Back from San Diego already?"

"Yeah," Hope said. "You shoulda seen Shamu and the baby penguins!" She marched into Ella's condo uninvited, and Ella stood back to let Matt in too.

"I thought you had to work," Matt said. "Are you okay?"

"Yes. I might look like I've been run over by a Mack truck, but I'm fine. I got off early." *I'm on love leave.*

"Great! We just stopped by to change. We're going for fish and chips at Dana Point. Want to join us?"

"Sure," Ella said. "Can you wait fifteen minutes? I'll just hop in the shower and then be ready."

"We can wait," Matt said, smiling down at her. Seeing that Hope was distracted at the window, he whispered, "I don't think you need to change. You're kinda cute with smudges of dirt on your cheeks."

"Dad! You should see the view from up here! It's much better than our condo!"

"I'll be back in a few minutes," Ella said, grinning too. "Despite what you think, the world will be happier if I scrub up." She left them then, glad that she'd had the afternoon to clean her home. Hope had moved on to her picture table, and Matt was looking at her books. "There're drinks in the fridge," she called over her shoulder.

Twenty minutes later she returned to her guests, dressed in jeans, turtleneck, and a slim wool sweater. "Fifteen minutes, hmm?" Matt asked with a smile.

"I'm always about five minutes off, it seems," she said.

"It was worth the wait," he whispered as they left her home.

They drove in the Morgans' rented sedan down the Pacific Coast Highway. Traffic was picking up as summer approached. "You should see it in July!" Ella exclaimed after Matt made a comment. "I avoid PCH at all costs when the tourists arrive."

"Maybe you should go away in July and avoid it all together."

"Where?" Ella said blankly.

"I don't know," Matt said, glancing in the rearview mirror at his daughter. She was absorbed in the view outside her window of busy shops, galleries, restaurants, and strollers. "Someplace north. Far north."

"Ah," Ella said, understanding his meaning at last. "I'll have to think about that."

"I wish you would," he said, shooting her a look.

Ella just smiled.

They reached the harbor and walked along the docks, admiring huge cruisers with names like *What's Your Pleasure?* and old wooden sailboats called *Mary's Pride* and *Sweet Horizons.* Finally, they reached a favorite shop of Ella's, a fish market simply named Sam's. Huge fillets of freshly caught cod and salmon and halibut lay in the ice. The shop's specialty was fried fish and chips, which customers purchased and ate outside on the picnic benches. More extravagant meals like half a lobster or crab were also available. Ella thought to herself that it would be fun to pack a picnic with all the fixings and bring Matt back down for a romantic—and relatively inexpensive—dinner.

If only they had more time.

The Morgans were due to leave in just a few days, and the thought saddened her. They needed more time together! She needed more time to gain Hope's trust, to show her that loving another woman did not mean being unfaithful to her mother's memory. Each moment seemed to confirm that Ella and Matt were kindred souls, but how could they be sure? It was a whirlwind courtship, yet Ella did not want to rush into anything. They had not even kissed! The thought brought her up short, and she searched the sky as Matt arrived with their food.

"There," she muttered in awe. Just above the horizon was a huge, full, cream-colored moon.

Matt followed her gaze as he distributed their dinners, then smiled. "Let's say grace," he said smoothly. "Would you like to bless the food, Ella?"

"Sure," she said, her mouth suddenly dry. She took a quick swig of water and then said grace. By the time she said *amen* the moon seemed to be rising visibly into the sky.

Later Matt tucked Hope into bed and closed the door behind him. A teenage neighbor had agreed to baby-sit, and Matt felt jubilant. He had left Ella earlier with a simple request. "Come out on your deck at ten o'clock. Dress warmly."

Now he had work to do. He checked his watch. Nine o'clock. He had just an hour. And despite what needed to be accomplished, he felt that was sixty minutes too long. He smiled, thinking again of Ella's face as she spotted the full moon. She had looked excited, embarrassed at being caught. It was like sharing a wonderful secret. And tonight…tonight he would take her in his arms and meet her lips with his own.

Matt was pulling on a sweater when he heard Hope's first cry. Concerned, he went to her room. His daughter moaned again. She seemed to be half asleep. "Hope?" he said gently, shaking her shoulder. She came awake at once and cried out, more loudly this time. "What's wrong?" he asked.

"My tummy hurts."

"Where?"

"I don't know," she said, tears welling up in her eyes.

"Now, Hope," he said sternly. "Are you just saying that so I won't go out with Ella?"

"No! Ouch! Daddy, it hurts! It hurts really bad!"

"Where, pumpkin? It's important that you tell me where."

"Over here," she said, motioning toward her lower right side.

Her appendix. "Do you feel sick to your stomach? Do you think you just ate something that didn't agree with you?"

"No!" She moaned in pain. Matt could see that she was not faking it. A burst appendix could be serious. Even fatal? He couldn't remember. All at once, the agony of losing Beth came rushing back. He couldn't do anything to risk Hope. The hospital! He needed to get her to the hospital! Debating about calling an ambulance, he decided he could not risk the extra time. He knew right where the emergency room was. They had passed it earlier on the highway. Gathering her up in his arms, he mumbled an explanation to the baby-sitter, threw some cash on the couch for her, and ran to the car.

Ella nervously paced the floor, well aware that it was almost ten. What did Matt have planned? How would it feel to finally have him take her in his arms and kiss her? Maybe she had built it up too much in her mind. Maybe it wouldn't be anything special. Or maybe it would.

She sat down hard on a dining-room chair, determined not to walk out on her porch until five minutes after ten. No use in letting him think she was desperate. It was good to let a man wait a bit. Besides, it was only fair after he made her wait all evening for whatever surprise he had planned.

Ella tapped the floor in time with the second hand. At four minutes past, she could not wait any longer. She opened the sliding glass door slowly and walked out on the porch with her head held high. She hoped she made a pretty picture for him. The moon was climbing in the sky, a brilliant milky white against a royal blue–black night. Ella swallowed hard and then searched the beach below for Matthew.

He was nowhere to be found. Disappointed, she stood at the railing for a good half-hour watching the foam on the waves swirl and surge, then she paced the miniature deck. Had she misunderstood his directions? Was he waiting for her somewhere else? No, he had been pretty specific. Finally, she sat down in a lounge chair and somewhere around midnight dozed off. She awakened an hour later. Bitterly disappointed and genuinely concerned that something was wrong, she went to her telephone and dialed Matt's condominium. The phone rang and rang with no answer. "There has to be some reason he didn't show," she told herself. "There has to be." But inside, her doubts grew.

Ella awoke to the doorbell buzzing and groggily looked at her clock. Ten o'clock, twelve hours after their promised date. If it was Matt at all. She ran her fingers through her disheveled hair and padded to the door, past the two empty pint cartons of ice cream and her shoes, which she had pulled off without untying them.

Her eyes widened with surprise as she looked through the peep-hole. Not Matthew. But flowers. She opened the door.

"Ms. O'Donnell?"

"Yes." Ella took the proffered pen, signed for the gorgeous bou-quet, and reached for them. She pushed the door shut with her hip and walked to the coffee table, inhaling the sweet scent of Casablanca lilies. They were a favorite of hers. How did he know? And there were six, seven, *eight* stems of the huge, picturesque white flowers fastened in the low, sleek vase, with a total of twenty-two blossoms or pods waiting to open. It was so big it took up half the coffee table.

With trembling fingers she reached for the card. Had he changed his mind? Was this his version of a Dear Jane letter? Or some excuse? She opened the tiny envelope and pulled out the card.

> Sorry doesn't begin to say what I feel about missing
> our date last night. Does an emergency appendec-
> tomy count as a good excuse? Hope we can take a
> rain check on that full moon. In the meantime, I
> thought these might help make amends. With love,
> Matthew

An appendectomy! Her heart soared as she deemed it as, yes, a good excuse. But was it him or Hope? Which hospital had they gone to? Who was their doctor? The protective nurse in her emerged as she ran around the house getting ready to check on the Morgans. She felt needed, useful, wanted again. And she was going to them just as soon as Jeffrey could get her there.

CHAPTER NINE

*E*lla found Matt in a hospital waiting room dozing beside a plastic foam cup filled with cold coffee. When she sat down beside him, he awakened and pulled her to him in a fierce embrace. After he released her, she said, "Whew! I guess you missed me."

"I did," he said with a smile. "I'm so sorry about our date. You got the flowers?"

"I did. They're beautiful. I take it Hope is the patient. How is she?"

"Good. She got out of surgery hours ago, and the doc said everything went well, but I felt uneasy leaving. Being in a hospital brings back some bad memories."

"I can imagine." She sat beside him in silence, doing just that. What had he gone through in saying good-bye to Beth? He had been largely silent about the whole experience. Ella took his hand and placed it in her lap, stroking it with the other. "You know that you'll have to tell me about her sometime."

He nodded wearily. "I guess. What do you want to know?"

"What she had, how she died. More important, what she was like and what it was like to say good-bye."

Matt sighed heavily. "It's tough, you know? Talking about it gets easier as the years pass, but it still is like reliving a bad dream when I go through it again."

"Let's start with the good stuff. What was she like? Where'd she come from?"

"Beth was this miraculous woman who walked into my life after I placed a personal ad in *Rancher's Journal.*"

"*You* placed a personal ad?"

"I did." There was no remorse in his voice. "I was a lonely bachelor in a place where there aren't a lot of eligible women. My ad brought me over three hundred interested parties."

"Of which Beth was the best?"

"Hers was the only one I answered. From the moment I read her letter, I knew she was special. She thought it was by God's design that she happened to receive a copy of the magazine at her job. Beth worked in some high-powered marketing firm in San Francisco. She got *Rancher's Journal* in one of a thousand media kits. But for some reason she paged through it that day. And wrote. The rest is history."

"Hmm," Ella said with a smile. She did not feel threatened by Matt's obvious love for the woman. His devotion encouraged her, made her feel more secure that he was indeed a man who could feel things deeply. Maybe he would have similar feelings for her someday. "Sounds romantic."

"Yeah," he said, pulling her hand to his lips and smiling at her tiredly. "Kinda like a chance meeting on an elevator, huh?"

"Kinda."

"Beth gave it all up for me. Left the city, her family, her friends. Except for her friend Rachel, that is. Beth got her to come visit one summer, and Rach fell for my buddy Dirk."

"They should call the Elk Horn Valley the 'Hitching-Post Valley.'"

Matt chuckled. "They could do that. It's a romantic place. I hope you'll come see it."

Ella smiled at him, glad for the repeated invitation. She would call a travel agent as soon as she got home.

"Beth and I got married soon after meeting. After that we lost a baby in an accident, then Beth got pregnant with Hope. Having our daughter was like a miracle." His eyes shone as he traveled back in time. "I thought everything was back on track in life. I was wrong. A couple years later, we found a lump."

"What kind of cancer?"

"Lobular carcinoma."

Ella nodded.

"We didn't fool around. I loved her body, but I loved the woman more. She had a modified double mastectomy. Once again we thought we were back on track. She went a whole year, cancer free. Then we found out it was back."

"How many lymph nodes were involved?" Ella asked softly.

"By the time we found out, eighteen. It didn't take long for the cancer to spread. Everywhere." He swallowed hard, and his eyes glimmered with tears. Matt looked at Ella with a little shake of the head. "I really have dealt with this. I got counseling for me and Hope. Beth made sure we'd do it. Made us promise. So things are in order. I just don't know if I'll ever get over being sorry for losing her."

His words choked Ella. She stroked his face. "Oh, Matt. I don't know if you ever get over losing someone precious to you. The pain fades, the sorrow, too. But people special to you leave little spaces in your life when they leave."

"I guess you've seen a lot of this."

"I have. Too many to count. Fortunately, most of the terminal patients I've known have gone on to a life without pain. A place where they can be whole and free again."

Matt grinned and nodded. "Beth did the whole death thing right, ya know? Made sure she told everyone what she needed to. Even left Hope a series of videotapes for important occasions in her life so she'd know her mother cared. That was the toughest thing for Beth. She knew I'd be okay. But she was so sorry that she wouldn't be around to mother Hope."

Ella smiled softly. "She sounds terrific. I think I would've liked her."

Matt looked at her meaningfully. "No doubt. I think you would've been friends."

Ella agreed to stay at the hospital in case Hope awakened so that Matt could grab some shuteye. She sneaked him into a dark staff room and left him snoozing on a cot practically as soon as he was horizontal. Then she went to talk with Hope's nurses. As Matt had reported, the girl had been fine throughout surgery and seemed to be doing well in recovery. She would be released in a few days.

Ella grabbed a cup of coffee and sat down to read an old *Reader's Digest* in the waiting room. But her mind was not on the magazine articles. It was on Matthew and Hope. Was she really ready to be an instant mother? For years she had longed for a baby, agonizing over the time passing by and wondering if she would be able to have a child by the time she found a decent husband. But a five-year-old? Kindergarten. Brownie troops. Sunday school. Now *that* was instant motherhood. And the girl was clearly not convinced that Ella should be given the job at all.

To be fair, they had met only a couple of weeks before. And while Matt and Ella were able to recognize possible partners in one another, Hope obviously had not spent much time thinking about what it would be like to have a stepmom. Indeed, it sounded like Matthew had not dated at all. *Ella, you lucky dog, you're the one to break her in.* Was that all she was, really? A groundbreaker? Was it truly realistic to think that this relationship could go on once they parted? Sure, he had invited her to come see them. But was he thinking beyond the visit?

All the insecurities of being ditched the previous night resurfaced. It did not matter that Matt had a more-than-adequate excuse for not appearing. Somehow, when he did not show, Ella lost some of her confidence. She felt every one of her thirty-four years and the nearly twenty years of fruitless dating. She wanted to be a wife and mother. Was Matt really ready to have someone step into Beth's shoes? Was he really ready for another relationship? Maybe Ella was just getting her hopes up for nothing.

She stood and paced, feeling her brow furrow as she concentrated. *Dear God,* she cried, *please don't let all this be in vain. I'm too old to get worked up just to be disappointed!* She paused and sat, leaning over to fold her hands and pray. *You know the desires of my heart. Please order it as I trust you will—in the best interest for us all: me, Hope, Matt. Give me direction, Father. Confidence. Ease my doubts unless I really have something to be concerned about. Thank you for this, God. I'm falling in love, and it's great. But please, please don't let it be for nothing. Amen.*

When she looked up, Matt was standing beside her, watching her. "Praying?"

She looked down and nodded. "Yes. You didn't sleep long."

"An hour. It was just enough to make me feel better than the walking dead. Thank you for standing guard."

"You're welcome. They say she should be released in a few days."

"Yes, I know. Ella, how 'bout—"

"Mr. Morgan?" a nurse interrupted.

"Yes?"

"Your daughter's awake. She's asking for you."

"Great!" He stood up quickly and then looked back at Ella. "You'll be here for a while?"

"As long as you want me here."

He smiled, then turned and made his way toward Hope's room.

By that afternoon Matt was convinced that his daughter was out of the woods and comfortable in her room. Unlimited TV access was her kind of vacation, so she was not overly sorry to see him go for the day. He followed Ella home in his own car, and they parted for a few hours. Matt went home to sleep. Ella went home to pace.

At the appointed time, Ella was again out on her deck. The moon was still large and bright, with just a hint of the waning darkness claiming its right edge. Far below her, at exactly ten o'clock, Matthew galloped up on a white horse, towing a brown-colored mare behind him. He waved, dismounted, and bowed deeply. Then he motioned for Ella to come down.

He didn't have to ask twice. She turned and hurried out the door. Discarding the idea of waiting for an elevator, Ella scurried down the six flights of stairs. She arrived breathless on the central deck but immediately went to the last rock stairs that led to the beach. "My prince!" she quipped with a laugh.

Matt grinned as he caught sight of her. "Hey," he said, moving to join her and take her hand, "it's not a white stallion, but it'll have to do. The rental stables only have mares."

"Close enough," she said. "But I just want to point out that you give me a hard time about running five minutes late. You're twenty-four hours behind."

"Better late than never," he said, swinging up onto his horse. "Come on. Let's ride. We're escaping, remember? The evil uncle and all. Now's your chance to leave the ivory tower behind. Not to mention get us back over to the private beach where these horses are allowed. You do know how to ride, don't you?"

"A little." She managed to place her sneaker-clad foot in the stirrup, grab the horn, and swing herself up and over. Sitting there in the saddle, she was flooded with memories of her countless lessons at the equestrian center.

"It's a beautiful night," Matt said, pausing so she could draw alongside him.

"It is," she agreed, looking at the moonlight shimmering on the ocean waves. After they had settled into an easy pace for a while, Ella looked over her shoulder. "Oh no," she said worriedly.

"What?" Matt asked, following her gaze. Far, far down the beach, the lights of a lifeguard Jeep were making their way toward them.

"The castle guard! They're after us! Follow me!" She dug her heels into the horse's flanks and raced off on the hard, dark sand where the water ebbed and flowed.

Laughing, Matt took off after her. It seemed like years since his heart had felt so light. Ella's expertise on the horse surprised him, as did the speed of the two horses, which had looked too old to move at more than the slowest walk. He was half disappointed, having visualized a lesson that might draw them closer together. But this was more fun. Matt dug his own heels into the white mare's flanks and soon matched Ella's stride. Carefully, he held back, so as not to get pelted with the sand her mare was kicking up. Where was Ella going, anyhow? The beach looked as if it were coming to an end.

Ella slowed, and Matt could soon see why. The sand ended, and the beach gave way to hard rocks. She let her mare pick her way through, then ducked as she entered what looked like a cave at the point. Matt followed, turning into the cave and spotting what she was after. Around the point, the passageway gave entrance to a quiet, idyllic cove.

In front of him, Ella left the cave and sat straight in the saddle, turning to see if he was coming. His breath caught, and he was glad his horse kept moving since he was not concentrating on the path. Ella was a vision, sitting straight on her mare, her long hair waving in a gentle breeze and shining in the moonlight. She grinned, and her smile brought tears to his eyes. *How could I be so lucky, Lord? How could you give me two such women to love in one short life?* He knew. He knew she was the one. Did she?

Suddenly he could not wait any longer. Free of the cave, he urged the mare toward Ella, gently herding her own docile mare toward the back of the cove. She backed up and laughed nervously. "What are you doing?"

But he did not answer. He just kept moving toward her, unable to think of anything else. Her mare, apparently sensing the approaching wall behind her and the other horse crowding her, stubbornly refused to move any farther. Matthew dismounted and was at Ella's side in less than two seconds, reaching up to pull her off her horse. In his arms, she looked up at him, well aware what he was after. But still he backed her up, up, up, until her own back was against a smooth boulder. He leaned close. "Is that a full moon?" he asked, nodding back toward the bright orb in the sky without looking away from her eyes.

"Close eno—" Before she could finish her sentence, Matthew leaned down to pull her to him and kissed her soundly. Her mouth tasted sweet to him, and he could smell the sea air in her hair. After the kiss ended, he held her for a long time, not wanting ever to let her go. After Beth, he thought he would never desire another. He was wrong. This woman could drive him crazy. And it was more than her beauty. It was the way she had about her. The way she spoke. The way she looked at him. The way she dealt with his daughter.

"Ella," he said quietly.

"Yes?"

"I know we haven't been together long, but I feel like I had better tell you something."

"What's that?" she asked, leaning closer to rest her head on his chest.

"I'm in love, Ella. I'm in love with you."

His heart skipped a beat as she paused, as if not knowing what to say. Maybe she did not feel the same. Maybe he had misread—

"Oh, Matthew. I'm so glad," she said, apparently finding her voice. "I've been so afraid that my feelings were one-sided. That I was building it all up in my head."

"No, sweetheart," he said, cradling her cheek in his strong hand. "You are definitely not alone in this."

After a while Matt pulled out a bundle of wood, a blanket, and a small bag of food and drink.

"What'd you bring?" Ella asked, looking over the crook of his arm into the bag. "Champagne and caviar?"

"Close. How 'bout hot chocolate and makings for s'mores?"

"Even better," she laughed. "I'll go look for roasting sticks while you build the fire."

Matt had a small, warm fire rolling in no time at all. He beckoned to Ella to join him under a blanket. Sitting side by side, they huddled together, staring into the fire.

Ella was the first to speak. "What are we going to do, Matt?"

"What do you mean?" he asked, knowing intuitively what she was after.

"I mean, we live a million miles apart. How can we see if this is really what we think it is?"

He turned to her slowly, studying her in the firelight as if she were slightly crazy. "I know what this is. Don't you?"

Their remaining days together flew by, mostly because after three days of love leave, Ella's personal days were used up and, miserably, she had to trudge back to work. On their last night together, Ella hurried home to share a late night cup of tea in Matt's living room, and they talked about what was ahead of them. "We'll find a way, Ella," he promised her. "God didn't bring us together just to say good-bye."

She clung to those words after he was gone, mulled them over countless times as she waited a week to hear from him. Ella spent that time fighting the fear that it was all a farce, he really wasn't falling for her, and crying out to God to bring them back together. Sometimes she just cried. Was it really fair for this to happen to a thirty-four-year-old woman? After all, she wasn't just some teenager caught up in an infatuation. Or was she? How well did she know Matthew Morgan, anyway? Why didn't he call her? Didn't he know that she couldn't call him?

Finally a letter arrived for her, carefully penned in awful, scrawling script that seemed choked with the emotion it tried to convey.

> I miss you, Ella, terribly. Won't you please come to
> visit us? Enclosed is a ticket. You can stay with my
> friends. Come see us. See our valley. And decide for
> yourself if you could see yourself here for a year—ten
> years—maybe even a lifetime. Love, Matthew

And once again Ella wept.

Chapter Ten

There it is," Matt said, pointing through the dirty windshield. "That's our home."

Ella smiled and looked through the drenching rain at the sprawling ranch about her and what she could make out of the big log house. "You say it like the Double M is a castle."

"Well, you know a man is king—"

"Don't say it."

Matt laughed and they pulled up in front of the house, which was bordered by a huge deck. Ella smiled as she spotted the porch swing and the big peeled logs that supported the roof above it. She would enjoy spending time out there with Matt, rain or shine.

Even now she could not believe she was here. The Elk Horn Valley was a long way from southern California, but something felt inherently right about it. It wasn't just being with Matt. It was the place itself. Matt had told her that when the clouds lifted she would be able to see the towering Rockies on one side of the valley and the high hills to the west. The gorgeous green valley already made her feel safe, protected. How exciting it would be to see natural gates around her!

"There's my girl!" Matt said, grabbing Ella's hard-sided suitcase from the back of the truck. Ella turned to where he was gazing but caught only a glimpse of Hope as she entered the house. "I guess she's not as excited to see me as you were," Ella said.

Matt paused to bend down and give her a quick kiss on the nose. "Take courage," he said. "That is just the court jester, determined to give us a run for our money."

They ran up the steps and shook off the rain as best they could before entering the house. "Oh, Matt," she said in awe, taking a sweeping glance of the huge, tastefully decorated home. "It's gorgeous."

"Thanks, but I can't take all the credit. I built it. Beth decorated it."

"It's perfect. It could be in a Ralph Lauren ad."

"Ralph who?"

"Never mind." She moved to the gigantic picture window that started at the floor and soared high above her. Behind was a massive fireplace and big cushy chairs. "I could sit in here and read all day."

Matt came up behind her, enfolding Ella in his arms and kissing her on the cheek. "Or day after day after day."

She grinned and turned to face him. She was about to pull his head down for a solid kiss when she spotted Hope on the stairs beyond him. "Hope! There you are! It's good to see you!"

Ella no longer needed to wonder about being ignored. Hope kept moving up the steps, disregarding Ella's call.

"Hope Emily Morgan!" Matt thundered, obviously angered and amazed by his daughter's behavior.

"Matt—," Ella began. Forcing Hope wasn't going to win her over. Ella would end up like the countess in *The Sound of Music*.

"No, I can't let her be so rude," he muttered. "Hope, get down here right now!"

"No!" Hope cried, openly defying him by stomping her foot. "I don't want her here! She doesn't belong here! She lives in California!" She turned and took off for her room.

"I'll be right back," Matt said, his face exposing his fury.

Ella reached out to grab his arm. "Wait. Matt, you can't force her to like me. This is a tough situation. Why don't you sit down here for a moment and calm down before you talk with her? If you go up there angry, you'll accomplish very little. We need to make progress with her if there are to be no barriers between us."

Matt sighed and ran his beefy fingers through his hair. "You're right. Okay, let's talk about something else for a bit, and then I'll go up. Tell me what you've been up to the last couple of weeks. I want to hear everything. I've missed you."

"Oh, Matt, I've missed you terribly."

"If only Beth had left a tape entitled *When Your Dad Gets a Girlfriend*," Ella moaned as she slumped down on the couch two days later. "Things aren't getting better. Any suggestions?"

Matt shook his head and slumped down on the love seat beside her. The rain had continued nonstop, and it seemed to match his mood. He knew Hope was against his relationship with Ella, but he had thought that with time she would be won over as he had been. How could his daughter not like the woman beside him? It made him feel furious at his daughter and torn between the two.

"Lunch was horrible," Ella said, voicing his thoughts exactly. "We can't keep on this way. She and I need to have it out. Would you trust me to take a chance with your daughter?" she asked.

He looked at her sharply. "Chance?"

She took his hand, and Matt noticed the spark of excitement in her eye. "I think it's the only way."

"Just what are you planning to do, Ms. O'Donnell?"

Ella knocked on Hope's door and entered without an invitation. Matt was right behind her. "Hope," Ella said, "you and I need to do something together. We can't go on like this, not speaking. Please get your rain slicker and boots on and meet me in the yard. I have the perfect project."

"I don't want to."

"I'm sorry you feel that way, but I still want you to come." She moved to the bed. "Will you dress yourself, or do I need to do it?"

Hope frowned and stuck out her lower lip. "I don't want to go. You can't make me." She turned to her father. "Daddy—"

"No way. You've been respectfully asked to do something by an adult. You know the rules, kiddo. Into your slicker and boots. It won't kill you."

"Daddy, I—"

"Now!"

Hope moved quickly off the bed at the sound of her father's tone, then more slowly dragged open the closet door and reached for her yellow slicker and galoshes. "Daddy, why—"

"No questions, sweetheart," he said. "You just have to do this. For all of us." She looked confused and glanced at Ella. "You are to respectfully mind Ella as you would any adult, got it?"

"Got it," she said miserably.

"Come on, Hope," Ella said, putting her arm around the girl and nudging her out of the room. "We're going to go have some fun if it kills us." But Hope shook off her hand and ran ahead of her, apparently determined to put as much distance between them as possible.

Once outside, Hope turned to her on the porch. "We can't go out there. It's raining."

"It's perfect," Ella said, picking up a couple of pails and trowels from the deck. "We're going to build another little village."

"How?" Hope pouted. "There's no sand here."

"No. There's something better. Mud."

Within two hours they had built a riverbed underneath a canopy of bramble bushes, adding waterfalls and bridges and dams here and there. Hope got into it in spite of herself and fashioned small log homes out of sticks. She wasn't talking to Ella much, but she also wasn't pouting.

Ella was digging more trench to lengthen the river, when her trowel caught on a root. She pulled, and a small clod of dirt went flying, spattering Hope's yellow jacket. "Hey!" Hope said. Seemingly without thinking, she reached for a handful of mud and, with a grin, let it fly.

It spattered all over Ella, who did not waste a second. *These are the things that cement a friendship.* Ella scooped up her own handful of mud and with a shriek threw it at the small girl. It hit Hope's neck and spattered up to her cheeks. The child giggled and threw another clod, hitting Ella on the back as she ducked. On and on went their mud fight—a release of pressure and anger and frustration—until finally, exhausted from laughing, Ella put her hands together to form a *T.* "Time-out," she gasped, smiling as she tried to wipe some of the dirt from her face.

Hope looked at her warily, but for the first time, there was a glint of happiness in her eyes. "I got you good with that last one."

"You did. I'll admit it," Ella said, smiling back. "But only after I nailed you on the rear end with *my* last one."

Hope smiled again and looked down. "Hey, look at this!" She knelt on the ground, looking into the riverbed where she had been grabbing ammunition.

Ella joined her and knelt beside the girl as she began to dig. "Not too much, Hope. We'll need to cover them back up."

"Come on. Just a little more. So we can see them better."

"Okay."

Ella and Hope looked down into a small new nest made of earth, filled with what looked like tiny baby mice, pink and blind in their suddenly opened home. "Aren't they cute?" Hope squealed.

"Yeah," Ella said with a grin, "if you like squirming rodents."

"They're not rodents! They're babies!" Hope cooed and laughed as the babies tumbled over one another in an effort to escape their invaders.

"We'd better cover them up, Hope, or they might get cold. Besides, we want their mother to come back to them, right?"

"Right."

"We'd better get out of here then. We've probably scared her so bad, she's halfway to the Rockies by now." Ella turned and offered the girl her hand. She tried not to smile too broadly as Hope accepted it and they made their way out from under the brambles.

"Ella?" Hope asked, as they walked in the rain toward the house.

"Yes?"

"How come my mama couldn't stay with me?"

"Oh, sweetheart." Ella stopped and knelt in front of her. "She dearly wanted to. Your dad's told me how it was the saddest thing for her that she wouldn't be around to watch you grow up."

Hope looked down at the ground, then glanced at Ella. "Do you think my mama would be mad if I liked you?"

"I don't think so. From what I've heard about your mother, she'd be very happy if we could be friends."

Hope bit her lower lip for a second, obviously deep in thought. "If you were to be my mother, would you go away too?"

Ella swallowed hard. This little girl had been through so much. But could she make such a promise? "If your dad and I ever get to that point, I promise you that I would try to stay with you for as long as possible."

"But she went to live with Jesus."

"That's right, honey."

"But you wouldn't, right?"

"I'd hope not, but you never know. Life is full of risks like that. When you love somebody, you're always risking that you might lose them. And that hurts. But if you never love anybody, then your life is pretty sad, don't you think?"

Hope nodded solemnly. She suddenly grinned. "Let's go tell Dad about our mud fight!"

Ella threw her head back and laughed. "Oh, I think he'll be able to guess, even though the rain has washed some of it off."

"Do you think he'll be mad?" Hope asked, looking up at Ella briefly as they started walking again.

"I don't think so, Hope. I think that he'll be delighted."

CHAPTER ELEVEN

*B*y the time they saw their guests to the door, Ella's sides hurt from laughing.

"She's a keeper," Dirk said in a stage whisper as he exited, looking back to wink at Ella.

"No kidding," Logan said, bending to give Ella a quick kiss on the cheek. "She fits right in."

"You're just saying that because I'm crashing on your couch," Ella said with a smile. "You know, hospitality and all."

"No, he's not," said Logan's wife, Reyne. She paused by Ella's side, and Ella felt as if she'd known Reyne forever. It was one of those rare, instant friendships that just started off right. Ella smiled at her and held her hand for a moment, hoping that Reyne could sense the care she felt for her already.

"We are so glad to meet you," Rachel said, stopping beside the two women. "Dinner was excellent. I'm sorry you're leaving tomorrow. I'd like to come again."

Ella smiled with her, embarrassed now by Matthew's friends' lavish praise and attention. She was amazed at their seemingly genuine acceptance of her right from the start. "You all have been so nice. You've helped make my visit truly wonderful."

"Well, we hope you can come again soon," Rachel said, casting a meaningful glance over her shoulder at Matt. "You know there are several positions at the county hospital."

Ella's grin grew as she nodded. "Matt's told me."

"All right, all right," Matt broke in finally. "All of you out. I want some time alone with this woman before she leaves me." He put his arm around her as the party left the porch and hurried down the steps to their cars, dodging puddles and mud as they went. And suddenly, Ella felt as if she were home. It was as if the Double M was her ranch, Matt was her husband, and Hope her child. Matt's friends were hers. Even Chad and Wellington were dogs she could get to love. She could see it all, feel it all. And it was wonderful. Oh, how she didn't want to leave!

"I can't believe it hasn't stopped raining! I wanted so much for you to see the whole valley."

"That's okay, Matthew," she said softly, smiling as his other arm went around her. "I'm already impressed. When I actually see the mountains, I'm sure I'll be in awe."

Matt turned her around to face him and after quickly scanning the room to make sure they had their privacy, kissed her softly. She hugged him fiercely, her arms just reaching around his huge torso. "I'm going to miss this place, Matt. I'm going to miss you."

He leaned back to study her face, and she met his gaze. It was as if they were silently communicating, and Ella loved every second of it. How long had she begged God for a man like this? How long had she cried out for a relationship with depth and desire? Tears sprang to her eyes as she thought about leaving him the next day. It was like a physical tearing inside. How could they part?

"What's wrong?" he asked in concern, lifting her chin when she dropped her eyes.

"Nothing," she said brightly, forcing a small smile.

"Ella—"

She shook her head. "Really. I'm fine. Just sad about leaving tomorrow."

"I know how you feel," he said, his face underscoring the pain in his voice. "Come with me, Ella." He took her hand and led her again to the front door and out to the porch swing. They sat down, and Matt cleared his throat. He looked so earnest it made Ella tear up all over again.

"Ella…I, uh, I know how important your work is to you. How you feel called to it. I love that about you. But what Rachel said…what I said to you earlier… Have you had a chance to think more about a job up here?"

"I have."

Drawing strength from her expression, Matt practically jumped off the swing and knelt in front of her. He took her hand, paused, looked down as if praying, and then looked back into her eyes. "Ella O'Donnell, I never thought I'd love again, but here I am, just crazy about you. Would you consider staying, for more than a job? For us? Ella, will you do me the honor of marrying me?"

EPILOGUE

*E*lla smiled as the school bus stopped at the end of the road and Hope's small body hopped off it. Ella had gotten home just in time to welcome home her stepdaughter. Hope loved first grade, mostly because of learning to read and write. She ran up the lane, and Ella sighed, trying to remember what it was like to have so much energy you wanted to run everywhere you went. She stroked her growing belly, which was straining her white maternity uniform's waistline, as Hope drew nearer. "Guess you're taking the extra juice out of me, eh, little one?" She directed her words toward her belly with a smile. "Ah, well, that's all right. I think you're worth it."

Ella opened the door and swung the screen door wide. "Welcome home, pumpkin."

"*Mom,*" Hope whined. "I told you not to call me that."

"I thought it was just around other kids."

"No, all the time."

"Oh, okay," Ella said seriously. "How was school?" She helped Hope off with her backpack and jacket, glad that she and the child had become such close friends. When Hope had first called her Mom a month ago, she'd had to leave the room to weep. It still brought her heart to her throat when the girl used the term.

"Oh, yeah, I made you something," Hope said, going back to her backpack and unzipping the pocket. She brought out two brightly colored, construction-paper cards and handed one to Ella.

Ella eased into a chair to look at it. "Honey, it's beautiful. Did you make it yourself?"

The girl nodded earnestly, lifting her eyebrows.

"What a good job you did! *'Happy Mother's Day,'*" she read aloud. "*'You're a good mom, Ella. Thank you for coming to live with us. Love, Hope.'*"

Ella swallowed hard. Was it the hormones, or were things always incredibly gut-wrenching around here? "Thank you, Hope. This is the greatest Mother's Day ever."

"It's your first Mother's Day," Matt said, coming into the kitchen. He looked over Hope's card and gathered the girl into his arms for a big kiss. "Next year, you'll have to teach your baby sister how to make a card. She's going to look up to you for that kind of thing."

Hope nodded gravely, thinking about the responsibility of being a sibling, and Ella spotted the other card in her hand.

"What's your other card, sweetie?"

"Oh," Hope said, looking a bit embarrassed. "It's for Mama. I mean my real mom."

"Oh," Ella said, hesitating for less than a second. "I know what we should do with that. Come with me. We're going for a ride." She reached up to peck her husband on the cheek, and Hope followed along behind her.

Matt came out onto the porch as Ella and Hope pulled up in the Subaru. Hope scampered out first and reached back to pull out a huge bouquet of white balloons. He shook his head, wondering what they were up to.

"Balloons?" he called.

Ella shut the door and nodded with a smile.

"Yeah, Dad," Hope answered him as they climbed the steps. "They're Mama's Mother's Day gift," she said.

"Beth's gift," Ella said, as she panted up the stairs. "Let's go do it now, Hope."

"Okay. I'll go get the card."

"Punch a hole in the corner of it!"

"Okay!"

Ella turned to him and spoke softly. "She came home with that card for Beth. I felt like we needed to do something special. So we're going to airmail it to heaven."

Matt laughed and pulled his wife to him for a hug and kiss. "You're something special, you know it?"

"I do. Don't you forget it."

Matt leaned down to her tummy and talked to the baby. "You hear that, baby girl? Your mom's terrific! You're one lucky girl."

"Her dad's not bad, either," Ella said.

"That's what I hear."

Hope arrived, card in hand, and the trio walked out into the yard. Chad and Wellington ran around them, glad for the company, while Ella tied the card to the bunch of balloons. Then she asked Matt to say a few words. As he searched for words, she separated two of the balloons so she and Matt could each hold one. Hope had the honor of holding the rest.

When they were all standing in a tight circle, Matt finally found his voice. "We choose this moment to remember what Beth was to us and always will be." He reached for Ella's hand, squeezed it, and then looked up in the sky. "Beth, honey, if you can hear me, we wanted to thank you for your time with us and let you know that we're moving on, never forgetting who you were to us. You were a great mom. So's Ella. I think you'd like my new bride. I think you would've been friends." He looked as if he wanted to go on but was too choked up to do so.

Ella spoke next. "I'm not here to take your place, Beth, but to add something to your family's lives in different ways. Thank you for making a home, husband, and child that I feel so good about adopting."

"Do you want to say something, honey?" Matt looked at Hope, tears streaming down his face.

"No. I just told her I love her in the card."

"She'll love getting it," Ella said. "Ready to send it?"

"Ready!"

Matt lifted the child, encircling her with his big arms. Together they and Ella raised their heads to the sky and watched as their balloons and a bright blue card raced upward, swirling and dancing around one another.

"Happy Mother's Day, Beth," Matt whispered, still looking up.

"Happy Mother's Day, Beth," Ella echoed.

"Happy Mother's Day, Mama," Hope said.

"Happy Mother's Day, sweetheart," Matt said to Ella, kissing her cheek.

"Yeah, Happy Mother's Day, Mom," Hope said, reaching out to hug her.

"Come on, Hope," Matt said, pulling her back to him and nuzzling his daughter's neck. "Let's go cook your new mom dinner. I think she deserves special treatment today, don't you?"

"Yeah!"

They turned to race back to the house, but Ella paused to walk just a bit behind them. She wanted always to remember this moment. For she felt truly beloved as a wife, mom, and mother-to-be. And there wasn't a house in the world that would feel more like her childhood vision of a castle than this place.

AUTHOR'S NOTE

Please respect the fine creation God has made in you. The American Cancer Society recommends that every woman get a baseline mammogram by age forty, and possibly earlier. Please ask your primary-care physician to help you decide when to receive your first mammogram.

After your initial exam, continue to seek mammograms every one to two years, as recommended by a doctor familiar with your family health history. Breast cancer is a highly treatable disease, but early detection is imperative.

For more information, call:

Susan G. Komen Breast Cancer Foundation 1-800-IM-AWARE or the Y-ME National Breast Cancer Hotline at 1-800-221-2141.

Dear Friends:

Thank you for the many letters and notes you have sent me! It was the continuing clamoring to hear more about Rachel and Dirk and the Elk Horn Valley *(Refuge)* that made me return for *Firestorm*. Writing can be a lonely business at times, and your notes of encouragement come to me as gentle hugs from unmet friends.

This has been a crazy year. Our daughters—Olivia, who will be six years old at press time, and Emma, who will be three—keep us hopping! And I just resigned from my beloved editing job, deciding to concentrate more on my faith and family and my fiction. Life, it seems, is a series of transitions. I just get comfortable in one spot, and then God decides it's time for me to learn new things. For a security hound, this comes as a hard lesson. I like to surround myself with the familiar and comfortable, rather than branching out and risking again. Yet when I do, I always am glad for that push out of the nest. This, I found, became Reyne's journey of discovery too.

Isn't that what crisis and troubles bring you? I find that in confronting my fears I lean most heavily on Christ. From that I draw incredible comfort and strength, and I seem to discover over and over yet another level of relationship with Jesus.

The firestorms of life are a gift in a way. And I celebrate that the God who helps us through is always present in my life, as he is in yours.

Every blessing,

Lisa Tawn Bergren

Write to me via my Web site!
www.LisaTawnBergren.com
or the old-fashioned way:
c/o WaterBrook Press
2375 Telstar Drive, Suite 160
Colorado Springs, CO 80920

TREASURE (Book 4) • Ever since she roomed with Bryn Bailey *(Pathways)* at Harvard, nautical archaeologist Dr. Christina Alvarez has been obsessed with finding her ancestor's sunken treasure ship. Only one man—Caribbean treasure hunter Mitch Crawford—can help her, and he refuses to do so. But Christina's fight to win Mitch over may lead them both to a treasure more valuable than either of them ever dreamed.

CHOSEN (Book 5) • As supervisor of the Solomon's Stables dig in Jerusalem, archaeologist Alexana Roarke—grad-school friend of Christina Alvarez *(Treasure)*—knows she is in significant danger. Yet she will let nothing impede her excavation, not even the concern of handsome, world-renowned news correspondent Ridge McIntyre. Her stubbornness, however, could cost Alexana her life—and a future with the man she loves.

FIRESTORM (Book 6) • As a forest firefighting crew boss, Montanan Reyne Oldre—friend to Rachel Tanner and Beth Morgan *(Refuge)*—once led a team of courageous firefighters into a blaze that ended in tragedy. Now that the flames of love have begun to flicker between her and smokejumper Logan McCabe, Reyne must face the fears from her past and battle the raging firestorm that burns in her soul.